What people are saying about
When Shadows Grow Tall

Showing a confident grasp of character and stunning worldbuilding, Maressa Voss' debut fantasy novel, *When Shadows Grow Tall*, shows us not only a society beset by evil, but gathers the company who must fight for truth and thus vanquish it. It's both a tender coming of age and a stirring call to arms, with a wonderfully deft weaving of magic and nature. Highly recommended.
Julie E. Czerneda, author of DAW Books's the *Night's Edge* series

Unlikely heroes abound in Voss' fantasy novel of magic ... Readers will be swept into an unusual landscape that's engagingly similar to our own in some ways; in this world, nature has been stripped of its resources and corruption has silenced dissent, though it's not too late for compassion to prevail. As the story, which features vivid descriptions and intricate history, weaves in elements of mystery, readers will wonder whom the heroes can trust; along the way, they'll enjoy scenes of fast-paced action and dangerous magic ... the work contains great beauty and a sense of hope, and readers will likely be excited for a sequel. A fun adventure that will keep readers engaged.
Kirkus Reviews

T0007315

When Shadows Grow Tall

A Novel

When Shadows Grow Tall

A Novel

Maressa Voss

**ROUNDFIRE
BOOKS**

London, UK
Washington, DC, USA

CollectiveInk

First published by Roundfire Books, 2024
Roundfire Books is an imprint of Collective Ink Ltd.,
Unit 11, Shepperton House, 89 Shepperton Road, London, N1 3DF
office@collectiveinkbooks.com
www.collectiveinkbooks.com
www.roundfire-books.com

For distributor details and how to order please visit the 'Ordering' section on our website.

Text copyright: Maressa Voss 2023

ISBN: 978 1 80341 517 8
978 1 80341 577 2 (ebook)
Library of Congress Control Number: 2023937336

A CIP catalogue record for this book is available from the British Library.

Design: Lapiz Digital Services

UK: Printed and bound by CPI Group (UK) Ltd, Croydon, CR0 4YY
US: Printed and bound by Thomson-Shore, 7300 West Joy Road, Dexter, MI 48130

We operate a distinctive and ethical publishing philosophy in all areas of our business, from our global network of authors to production and worldwide distribution.

For James, my compass rose.

Map of the Grasp

ASP

ISLES

TANSITUR

AECIR

SALICIN

KYTHERA

RAITA

THORTI

LAZARE

GULCH PASS

ELLEN

ULTHING

TALIS

AVERNIAN
GAP

UINS
OF
ERLIDAN

MORTALIS

WAXBILLBAY

MEORACHADH

N
W E
S

Prologue

It was the daylilies he was after. Their orange blooms reminded him of fireworks, all bright and blazing. Only the lilies were quiet and lasted much longer than those bursts of flame that lit the night sky on Mother's Day. Also, he could hold the flowers in his hands and see them up close, which he definitely could not do with fireworks, seeing as they'd blow him all to bits.

"Not the canna lilies, mind," rang the memory of his mam's voice, clear as a morning bell. "Those are no more edible than the shoes on your feet. And don't even so much as think about touching the wolfsbane. Do you hear me, Everard? Everard?"

Everard blinked. A grin bloomed across his face as his fingers brushed the purple hooded flowers of the wolfsbane growing along the stream's edge. It was the same purple as when the sun sets behind a storm. Wolfsbane would only kill him if he ate it; anyone with half a wit knew that.

But that was his mam, always worried he would cartwheel off a cliff or maybe trip on nothing and fall headfirst down the well.

Everard crouched low at the stream, a little thing flowing just enough that the edges hadn't gone all soupy green, but not so much that there wasn't an appreciable number of pollywogs, awaiting their froggy fate.

As it was, these ones had only the stubbiest bits of tail left and were using their tiny new arms and legs to glide along the muddy bottom. Five days more, Everard would wager, and they would spring forth from the pool. Then, they could go wherever they pleased. Everard swirled the water with a cupped hand, sending the pollywogs scattering.

It was nearing midday, the balancing point between yesterday and tomorrow. And tomorrow bore a promise. Tomorrow was

1

his Name Day. His tenth, but he could only rightly remember back to his fifth. His mam had made cream fritters with currants that year, and his mouth still watered to think of the steaming hot cakes, the burst of tartness on his tongue with each crimson berry.

Everard rose and stretched his arms towards the sky beyond the canopy, feeling excited and a little proud. He was just like the pollywogs, he thought, confined to live in a place that was altogether too small. Each Name Day brought him one year closer to freedom, one year nearer to adventure. When he was grown, he could go wherever he liked. He had heard of mountains so tall they disappeared into the clouds and the sea...The sea was a stream with no edges, with no end. Horizons, colorful and vast, stretched forth in Everard's mind, and he shivered. There would come a day.

He spotted them, growing there in a patch of sunlight, broken through the trees. He took up his satchel, leapt over the stream and bounded towards the bright spot. When he reached it, he knelt in the loam and saw that this patch of lilies was one of many. He smiled a little, knowing how pleased his mam would be when he came home with a satchel full.

One by one, he dug up the plants, taking care not to snap off any part of their spindly roots that his mam would boil with port and use to treat an ague or bruise the orange petals that would thicken his Name Day stew.

He snapped off one unopened bud from its stalk and popped it in his mouth. It gave a satisfying crunch and tasted like nothing so much as a radish with honey drizzled over it. No feast, but it was food, and not too bad tasting for all that it was just a flower.

As he worked, he sang beneath his breath.

That old pauper Pete
Had naught to eat

And so he boiled his saddle
Bereft of a seat
He used his two feet
And marched right up to some cattle

The sharp crack of a snapping branch rang out from behind. Everard paused and wheeled around, but there was nobody there.

So he resumed, imagining that he was Raud the Bard, who traveled to every inn and tavern of the Grasp, gathering stories and songs as he went, eating the finest pies for supper each night.

From patch to patch, he moved, his voice rising over the subtle din of the forest. With each verse, his voice grew bolder and louder until he sang with such might that he thought he had found the tippy top of his lungs, that place that everyone was always going on about.

"And so he boiled his – "

"Saddle!" A voice from behind cut through the air, sudden and sharp.

Startled, Everard dropped his satchel, his heart beating fierce. He whirled around.

A man stood there, mere paces away, his grin revealing a pair of missing teeth. There was a gleam in his eye that made Everard tremble. He was dressed like a peacekeeper, only his cloak and shield and sword were not the usual gleaming white but red, like a blood-soaked penny.

Everard's eyes darted this way and that. More men were materializing from behind the trees. He gulped.

"H-hello, sirs. What brings you to this corner o' the wood?"

The man who'd finished his verse leered.

"Why, we came to find you. I should think that much was obvious, boy-o," he said, gesturing to the men behind him. His was the only face twisted into a terrible grin.

"Can't think what you'd want me for," Everard managed, fear seizing him, making him tremble. He knew exactly why they'd come for him. But how had they known? He had been so careful.

"It's a wretched fate, I know," the man said. He snapped his fingers, and a small flame appeared between his forefinger and thumb.

He's like me, Everard thought, wild hope flickering through him that sputtered and died. Like dogs, the men crept closer, hemming him in. Everard whirled, but there were two more behind him.

He did the only thing he could. He jumped.

He shot through the canopy without looking up, showering twigs and leaves upon the men below. He felt himself begin to fall back down again and scrabbled desperately for a branch to grab hold of, missing several before his hand closed around one sturdy limb jutting out from the tree's middle.

"Neat trick, that," the man drawled from below. "Wager the master would appreciate your spirit. But, orders are orders, boy-o, and you've got to go."

Everard's hands were slipping, slick as they were with sweat. His right fingers lost their grip, and his arm fell limp to his side. His legs dangled, flailing like mad. He tried to jump again, but nothing happened. A foothold, he needed a foothold.

"Don't make me smoke you out. It's got to be by blood. I don't make the rules. Come on down; I'll make it quick."

Everard kicked out, aiming for a branch just beneath him. He landed, wobbled, and jumped again, shooting for an oak behind the men, this one huge with massive twisting branches. He flew through the air, reached, missed, and fell to the ground, his legs folding beneath him with a terrible snap.

Pain blazed through him from the bottom up. Everard rolled onto his belly and tried desperately to drag himself away. A pair of red-booted feet blocked his passage and he looked up.

The man with the fire fingers reached down and yanked Everard upright.

"Brave little boy-o," he said.

Then, there was movement, cruel and swift – the gleam of a sword blade, singing through the air. Everard grew very hot and then, very cold, and then, he felt nothing much at all.

His eyes fell on his satchel, brimming with day lilies – orange draining from the petals, green leeching from the stems – until all was white.

***

Color poured back into the world, and the height of day fell to dusk. The gentle humming that marked the transition from memory to present moment faded, and Lovelace came back into the heaviness of his body.

He withdrew his shaking fingers from the boy's forehead, willing his gaze to linger overlong on his face. It was smooth and clean as new-made cloth, and his eyes – nut brown and round as coins – were open to the sky. Lovelace smoothed the tangle of black hair and gently pressed the lids to close. He was dressed in a thin muslin shirt and pants, undyed and threadbare. Poor then, but not so poverty-stricken that he had been starving. Thin, but only in the way that young boys are when their exuberance outmatches even their appetites. Lovelace rose and leaned his head against the oak's rough trunk and closed his eyes to stem the revulsion rising sharply in his gut.

"Well?" came the voice of Gunnar from behind.

"He..." Lovelace began, his voice breaking. "He was brave to the last."

"The men in red again?"

Lovelace nodded, cleared his throat and spat, taking care to do so far from their quarry and the massive oak beneath which lay his remains. The boy sat propped between the thick tangle of roots, his thin arms and legs splayed grotesquely as if he were made to play jester to the wood. A great wound had gutted him from navel to neck, spilling his innards onto the ground between the crooked ruin of his legs. By the look of him, he had not been long dead; flesh flies hovered over the bloody cavity but had not yet delivered their descendants: those maggots that would feast upon the raw life offered there.

We missed him by a few bells. The thought made Lovelace sick. Had he and Gunnar left earlier, the boy might be with them, alive and gibbering about pollywogs and the flowers he would need to deliver to his mam before he left home for good. How he always knew he was special, always knew he was destined for more than a life selling foraged goods to the apothecaries of Ardeleur.

"It was the same as the last," Lovelace said gruffly, taking several paces back from the boy and the tree to gather his thoughts. He bent low to squat beside Gunnar, his fingers moving idly over the serrated edges of oak leaves and fallen acorns.

"More taunts than talk, the bastards," Lovelace said, his face upturned towards the sky. It welled with dusk like a bruise. "Still no word as to why, though a master was mentioned. And the gaffer had fire at his fingertips, though he was no dactyli I know."

Gunnar grunted, and Lovelace cast a sideways glance at his companion. What was he thinking? Was his stomach also twisted, with sadness and with shame? The question, much like its subject, was destined to dwell in the realm of the unknown. Gunnar never told.

"We need to make haste for the Meorachadh," Gunnar said, lissome form rising from his crouch. His eyes were mercurial, the color of quicksilver. They were locked on the boy's face with an unplaceable intensity. "This boy was nascent, a dactyli born. Alev did this. Manoc must know."

Lovelace knew that he was right. There wasn't time enough to bury him, not when there might be others in danger of the same fate.

Gunnar broke his gaze and turned abruptly, his stride brisk as he moved back in the direction of the horses.

Lovelace sighed, taking one last look at the oak. It was a giant, its broad trunk suggesting an age far greater than he or Gunnar could ever hope to live. It held the boy in the tangled embrace of its roots, grown humped and massive in their search for fodder beyond their foundation.

Kneeling, he crossed both his forearms and pressed them slowly to his chest in the dactyli formal salute. He bowed his head and inclined his body toward the blood-soaked earth, pressing his forehead there.

"Take him back, make him new," he said quietly.

His rise to stand was slow, as if he had lived one hundred years, though he could only claim a quarter of that number. He wound his way around the tree's great trunk. Gunnar was standing there, inscrutable and staring at a knot of wolfsbane growing up and out of the mud. Their purple blooms were dark with dusk.

Lovelace took up the blade at this waist and carefully unearthed three plants from root to stem. With a scrap of woven flax from the pouch at his hip, he wrapped them tidily, wiping the knife clean against the leg of his pants. He returned both blade and parcel to his pouch and took one leaping step across the stream, away from the oak, and the boy's new-made remains.

"I could kill four dozen men with this much wolfsbane," Lovelace said absently as Gunnar fell into step beside him.

"I don't know why you bother with such trifles," Gunnar said. "Poison is a weapon for cowards."

"Poison is a weapon, Gunn," Lovelace said. "Besides, it's better for the balance of things to match the essence of the killing to the man...or woman, for that matter," he grumbled, brushing aside the budding whorl of a bracken fern.

Gunnar's silence was telling enough. He disapproved, nothing new about that.

Lovelace didn't know why he'd bothered, either. But he wasn't going to tell Gunnar that. Finding the boy had left him with a tumult of feelings; vengeful was one of them. But there was no direction for the emotion, no recipient at hand upon which to bestow it, so he'd picked some flowers instead.

They walked the remainder of the distance to the horses, no words passing between them. Gunnar was already atop his gelding before Lovelace had untied the knot of his lead. His thick fingers fumbled with the reins, deep in thought as he was.

Once undone, he placed one foot in a stirrup and paused, looking up at Gunnar beseechingly. In his heart, anger and despair battled for precedence, two beasts with talons and teeth that threatened to tear him apart. Could Gunnar speak to no shared feeling, no inner anguish on account of the utter incurability of their shared circumstance?

His horse whickered softly and turned to nudge Lovelace with the velvet of her nose.

Onward, he thought. It was the only way.

"Back home then," he said with a nod. Gunnar inclined his head. His eyes, bright and cold as a distant star, locked with Lovelace's for only a moment before he turned his horse south, back the way they had come.

Chapter One

Kylene didn't notice the silent stream of golden wax creeping toward her stack of parchment until it was too late.

"Son of a Motherless..." She snatched at the stack and found the right corner already held fast to the rough surface of her desk. The remnant nub of a taper candle guttered, gasped, and gave out.

"...Goat," she breathed, her fingers prodding the sticky wax. She'd just have to wait for it to dry; no sense making a bigger mess moving around warm wax. Once dried, she would pare the parchment from the desk, and then each piece from another with a good, sharp knife. Easy.

She sat back in her chair. It's not as if the papers mattered, anyhow. They were just notes. Observations. Ideas. The scribblings of a sixteen-year-old girl. They mattered *to her*, of course. It was only that, in all likelihood, she'd never show them to anyone.

She probably *couldn't* show them to anyone, even if she wanted to. Kylene wasn't entirely certain what Osbert and his administration, the Fingers, thought of maidens conducting chemical experiments in their cellars, but she was pretty sure they wouldn't like it, if only as a matter of principle. For all she knew, her actions, innocent as they were, might even be expressly forbidden. It was practically impossible to keep up with all the bylaws; her father always quipped that the list, once unfurled, must stretch the entire length of the Grasp, if not twice over.

She drummed her fingers on the desk, feeling every bit the miscreant, sitting in the near-dark of the tiny root cellar beneath the house. Forbidden things were dangerous things, and the thought that the Fingers might find her, Kylene, to be a danger, well…It was one of the more amusing thoughts she'd had all day.

She reached for the timekeeper, which hung around her neck, now the only source of light in the cellar, and gazed down at its glassed surface, aglow with powder-blue light. Where there ought to have been twelve numbers around the edges of its oval face, eight tiny moons, intricately carved, were inlaid instead. Her father had gotten it for her at the grand markets of Lazare when she was five. The egg-shaped piece was set to mirror the passage of the moon across the sky, and right now, it was waxing, two days to full.

Kylene inhaled deeply, the familiar smells of the cellar rushing in to greet her like old friends. The rich rot of soil that had not seen the sun in an age. Cold stone, the sharp bite of strung allium, and the sweet and sour tang of pressed apples, slow-effervescing into jack. Also illegal, she noted with a smirk. Brewing anything stronger than a meek cider or a weak ale was forbidden, and she knew that for certain. "It's okay to break the rules when you're not hurting anyone…" She whispered her father's words and then the ones that had always stuck in her mind like burrs; "…and when the bounty outweighs the peril."

Overhead, she heard a rough scrape as someone pulled out a kitchen chair, a creak as they sat down upon it and then a rumble of laughter, rolling and deep. Her father, come to supper. Kylene stood up from her workbench, the wooden surface's many splinters and stains now secrets kept by the dark. She took up her satchel and carefully tucked away the bits and pieces of material she'd been working with that day into the crate below the desk. The finished draughts – three small corked glass bottles in sum – she scooped up. Stepping to her simples cabinet perched atop the apple rack, she deposited them safely inside.

Stepping back in the near-dark, Kylene turned to leave.

The saxesilt, she thought, pausing. She'd nearly forgotten.

She surveyed the shadows of the low-ceilinged chamber; on the lefthand wall, the apple rack – mostly empty now – and the sack of salt from the Godwit sea beside it. Jumbled crates with what was left of last autumn's harvest. To her right, shelves stacked eight high, the top two reserved for wheels of her mother's saxesilt cheese, bolted shut behind tight doors to keep the smell from infusing everything in the cellar with its unmistakable odor. She unfastened the doors to the topmost shelf where the finished cheeses were kept and was met with the fierce and immediate fragrance of the saxesilt; like axle grease and melon left too long in the sun. Tucking one of the rough-stippled wheels into the front pocket of her overalls, she crouched low. Beneath the cheeses on the lower shelves were a dizzying array of jars; marrow and ginger jam, mirthberry jelly and pickled fiddlehead ferns being the most recent contributions to the revolving stock of goods in which her mother took such pride. And...

As she leaned forward, the soft glow of her timepiece illumined what was kept hidden among the honey pots. A rounded clay jar, the same shape and size as that of its neighbors, half full of salt licorice. Her father brought back a demi-barrel from Lazare each spring and her mother hid jars around the house, lest every piece get gobbled up before summer even had chance to begin. She reached inside, seized two pieces clung together and carefully replaced the lid. She spun on her heel and bounced toward the stairs, salt licorice tucked snug in either cheek.

Seven steps up the stairs and her hand was overhead pressing on the thin wooden door, pitched at an angle against the backside of the house.

Kylene emerged from the underland. It was late summer and the sun had yet to scrape the horizon, its warm rays slanted in a honey sky. Squinting, she shut and bolted the door, and made her way through the garden tucked in the crook between the two wings of the house. Past trellised yellow squash and colossal wire cages, sagging beneath the weight of hundreds of tomatoes like so many summer jewels. A sweet, smoky scent rose – the last of the season's baneberries, warmed by the sun – their thin translucent skins revealing an interior like the opalescent insides of a seashell.

On the steps leading up to the kitchen, she stooped low and stepped stockinged feet out of her boots and onto the porch, warm wood worn by the tread of many feet. She swung open the door, stepped lightly over the threshold and was greeted by a scene as familiar to her as her own shadow. Her mother was beside the fireplace, a small leather-bound book in one hand, a ladle in the other. She was stirring the contents of an iron cauldron set above the hearth, her nut-brown hair pulled back from her face. Her pearl-gray eyes moved over the page she was reading like a needletail swift hunting dragonflies. Fragrant steam curled from the cauldron – onions, lovage, fresh cracked pepper, the tang of summer wine.

"Kylene, sweet!" She looked up, smiled and offered up the ladle. "Lovely of you to grace us with your presence this evening. I've used your wee morels in the stew, come, have a taste."

Kylene stepped toward the fireplace and dipped the ladle into the pot. The stew's surface shimmered with pooled fat, and her stomach responded to the sight with a brazen grumble. The morels Kylene had gathered the day prior floated on the surface of the golden broth like strange blooms in a bog. It was odd, Kylene had thought, to find morels so early in the year, but then again, the Mavros Forest was full of surprises.

"It's delicious, mother. But you already know that," she said, returning the ladle.

Her mother's grin widened, deepening the fine lines etched around her eyes. "Never does hurt to have your bell tinkled now and again, does it?"

"Whose bell are we tinklin'?" Kylene's father's voice, in imitation of the soft lilt of her mother's northern accent, boomed as he strode into the kitchen.

Rooms always felt smaller with him in them, though not in a way that was cramped or uncomfortable; there was just nothing trifling or subtle about him.

Her mother whipped around to face him, brandishing the ladle like a club. Drawn up to full height, her head barely reached his shoulders. "Sit yourself down, Aldus Gemison, if you know what's good for you. You've already eaten half my loaf and I've half a mind to send you to bed without supper." Indeed, great handfuls were torn from the rounded end of the speckled brown loaf resting on the kitchen table. The slab of butter beside it bore similar evidence of assault.

Her father bowed his head, the image of a penitent schoolboy: eyes wide, brows knit together in innocence. He took his place at the head of the table just as Kylene's sister, Petra, sailed into the room. She sat down dreamily, lost in a thought so absorbing that she nearly squashed Quibble, the cat who left their mother's side only to hunt, rut, relieve herself and, at least twice a year, give birth to a litter of kittens whose colors were never like her own thistledown coat. Quibble let out a yowl of displeasure and retreated to the windowsill behind Petra's chair where she crouched, circumspect, her amber eyes fixed on Petra's golden head with appreciable dislike.

Petra's gray eyes twinkled like spun silver as she focused them on Kylene. They traveled over her messy hair, the stains on her overalls and a small smirk formed at whatever private thought she was enjoying over Kylene's appearance. Her cheeks were rosy today, though that was likely due in part to the mulberry juice she habitually applied to lip and cheek. Their mother forbade them from visiting the apothecaries, and so without access to kohl and rouge and lily root, Petra was left to her own devices. *She's nothing if not resourceful,* Kylene thought grudgingly. Resourcefulness and an enduring desire to visit the apothecary without an escort were perhaps the only two things that she and Petra shared.

"What're we having for supper, Mumma?" Her question had a singsong quality that belied the fact she'd turned fifteen last spring.

Kylene rather thought the simmering medley of wine, mushrooms, butter and herbs telling enough and rolled her eyes at her sister over the table.

"Summer Wine and Herbs Stew, sweet," their mother said as she set an empty bowl before her. "Along with some mushrooms your sister found and...ah yes, the saxesilt. Thank you, Kylene," she said as Kylene withdrew the cheese wheel from her overalls and placed it in the center of the table beside the semi-savaged loaf. The rind of the cheese was a dull brown and covered in rough protrusions like the heads of stuck pins. It looked like nothing so much as a burl sawn from a walnut tree.

"And then, of course," her mother continued while making a decisive cut into the stiff rind of the cheese, revealing its creamy, blue-veined interior, "we have some brewer's bread, though you may find yourself hard-pressed for anything more than a mouthful since your father's had done with it."

Her father held both of his hands outstretched, palms facing upwards in what appeared to be supplication to the divine goddess Andara Gemison. Kylene giggled. If her father was praying to anyone, it may as well have been their mother. Nearly every person from Mossbridge to Locharn knew that Aldus Gemison found his faith in letters and numbers, not the Mother, her Daughters or any of her tiresome Sons of enterprise and industry.

"Ahem," her father cleared his throat, "soon as your mother rests her pretty feet we will begin with appreciation and insight."

Her mother raised one eyebrow, wiped her hands on the dishcloth hanging at her waist and seated herself at the other end of the table, nearest the fire. Kylene thought she looked tired today. There were lilac smudges beneath both of her eyes, like the press of faint thumbprints.

With a nod, her mother took Kylene and Petra's hands, and their father did the same. Outside, a lone carriage rattled over cobbles in an otherwise silent street. At any other hour, even here, on the outskirts of Mossbridge proper, the sounds of daily life – children shouting, anvils ringing from the smiths' guild next door, the neat clatter of horses' hooves – were a chorus that rose and fell throughout the day. But suppertime was stillness. Nearly all of Mossbridge ate at six bells sharp, since Assembly was held at eight.

No one missed Assembly. All of Mossbridge had seen with their own eyes what had happened to Fabrice, three years ago, when he'd refused to attend. *Actions have consequences,* Kylene thought with a tremor. She had been thirteen, and the wail of grief from Beata, Fabrice's wife, reverberated in Kylene's ears afresh. Her cry had echoed from the town square down each street stretching radial from it, and half of Mossbridge had come running to find Fabrice on the pillory. "May as well be the Gray Ages again," her mother had said, shaking her head sadly as they all looked on. Kylene hadn't understood, then, what was so terrible. The Pit, that prison kept on the outskirts of Omnia, seemed a far worse consequence.

It was her father who explained to her that the pillory may as well have been a death sentence, not just for Fabrice, but for Beata and their two small children as well. Beata spent the year feeding Fabrice with a spoon, all the while straining to maintain the running of the family's mill. At year's end, Fabrice was still alive, and Beata was near-broken. Even with the aid of other Mossbridgians, she still came up short when the Fingers came calling for contributions; the annual taxes for a household of four were too great for one woman to bear. By the time Fabrice was released, the family's estate had been seized, the operations of their mill taken over by a new family, all of whom wore Osbert's crest of balanced scales pinned to their lapels with an air of supreme smugness.

Kylene never found out what happened to Beata and Fabrice. They were expelled from Mossbridge, sent down the Middling Road with naught but the shoes on their feet and one knapsack of provisions between the four of them. Her mother had...

"Ahem," her father cleared his throat again. "Sincere apologies, Kylene. Are we interrupting some particularly exquisite thought of yours?"

Kylene's eyes snapped back into focus, where she found her mother and father staring at her. Petra rolled her eyes. "Weirdling," she mouthed at Kylene.

"I'm sorry, father," Kylene said grittily, fixing Petra with a stony stare.

He raised a single eyebrow, amusement faint upon his features. He bowed his head and closed his eyes. Petra and her mother followed suit. Before Kylene closed hers, she noticed that Petra's lids were subtly lined with what appeared to be charcoal.

"We give thanks for the bond of these hands, and for the bounty of this table. We are gathered here this evening to nourish body and mind. We must be hale in both, for without strength of mind and soundness of body, we cannot be the best sister, brother, mother, father and...friend, we can be." He had taken out "citizen" and replaced it with "friend" when they'd pilloried Fabrice.

"And now that appreciation has seasoned this meal, we may sup and share."

Thus concluded his sermon. They dropped hands and her mother reached over to ladle steaming stew into each of their bowls while Petra worked a saw-toothed knife on the mutilated loaf. She cut off the end with handfuls torn from it and placed the misshapen piece with impish pleasure on her father's plate.

"And what can you tell us about your learning for the day, sweet?" Her mother turned to Petra, who was delicately lathering her even bread slice with a uniform layer of soft, golden butter. Petra set down her slice, cocked her head to one side and squinted meaningfully upwards, as if she might find her answer amid the cobwebs in the rafters.

"I suppose I learned," she said at last, delight apparent, "that when boys are beastly to you, it means they actually like you."

Their mother smiled over the table at their father.

"Ahem." He cleared his throat loudly and ruddy spots appeared on both cheeks. "Evidence?"

Petra straightened, ready to give it. "Five days ago, Tommy Trice pulled all the ribbons out of Bernelia Stubbin's hair. One day later, I saw them kissing in the alley behind the cobbler's shop. Last week, Tommy Trice stole Delia Fornay's charcoal for her drawings. Nine days ago, they were sighted heading into the Mavros hand in hand. Yesterday, Tommy Trice tried to trip *me* while I was at market..."

"I hardly see how the singular behavior of this Tommy Trice amounts to an insight," her father said, his cheeks now scarlet. "Sounds like a lumpsucker to me," he said under his breath, prompting Kylene to smile broadly at her sister.

"Could it be that Tommy Trice likes *all* the girls?" their mother prompted, a certain measure of glee in her voice.

"You didn't let me finish," Petra said, pouting. "Today, I caught him staring up at my window looking most wistful. He tossed a note tied to a rock up into my room, nearly broke my mirror." Petra paused in reflection, appearing to be deeply concerned about this near miss. "Anyway, I told him to go find somewhere else to exist."

"Petra!"

"What? I told him to do it *kindly*. Any boy caught dead with Delia Fornay had better think twice before tossing rocks in *my* window," she said hotly. "I've got loads of evidence, Father, not just from Tommy Trice. There was the time Fynn Anglesy tied my braids in two while we were in Letters. It wasn't two bells later that he was waiting for me outside of Universals, asking if I'd like to go round for tea later. Of course, I did; it was Fynn Anglesy! And afterwards, we walked down to Fletching Pond, and we..."

"That's enough, Petra. Thank you for your insight," their father said hastily, his choked look dissolved into one of dismay. Their mother, meanwhile, had taken to gazing thoughtfully into the depths of her stew, amusement tugging at the corners of her mouth.

"It might be time for you to begin self-study, like Kylene," he said judiciously as he chewed. "I had no idea the Brickmore school was so...distracting."

Their mother raised her head at his words and examined a small wedge of saxesilt between her fingertips. "As I recall, Aldus Gemison, you yourself were quite horrid to me in our days at Brickmore. One would think any well-raised boy would act kindly to the new girl in town, shy and scairt as I was. If I remember correctly you tried to push me down a well..." She winked at Petra, whose face took on an even more beamish glow at the revelation that their father was not all rhetoric and reason and may very well have been, at one time, a real boy.

"Kylene?" her father turned to her beseechingly, red returned in force to his ordinarily olive complexion. "Shy and scairt," he muttered, shaking his head. "About as shy and scairt as a red fox was this one."

"Ahem," her mother cleared her throat and looked pointedly at him, one delicate eyebrow raised.

His eyes drifted up to the rafters and he inhaled mightily. "Your observations and subsequent insight are sound, thank you, Petra." He nodded at her before turning again to Kylene. "'Lene?"

Kylene had been watching the proceedings with pleasure; Petra always followed the prompt to the letter, even if her insights weren't exactly pioneering.

"I learned," she said, "that mulberries steeped hot with a decoction of iron not only create a double-strength dye, but also allow the finished preparation to adhere more strongly to your chosen medium. Though I wouldn't recommend lips, lest they turn to ash with repeated use." Kylene gazed levelly at Petra, who returned her stare with a look of mild indifference.

"A woman without paint is like food without salt, Kylene," Petra simpered.

"Where'd you learn that one, Pet? There's a saying that's sure to go down in the annals of history. Surprised you didn't share that kernel of wisdom for this evening's insight."

"It's not my fault no boys like you."

"That's ENOUGH." Their father's hand slammed down on the table, the force of it causing the bowls of stew to rattle precariously. "Evidence?" His voice was strained, the parallel lines between his brows drawn deep. Deeper, perhaps, than Kylene had ever seen them.

Kylene gave a toss of her head; she wouldn't let her painted prat of a sister unnerve her. "Decoction of iron steeped for four bells with a mulberry mash. Applied to flax, hemp, beechwood and...Fox fur."

Her father's face brightened as he spooned a morel into his mouth.

"How is it you managed the fox?"

"Helped McBane cure sheep gut for sutures. He gave me some scraps as a thanks."

McBane was Mossbridge's longest-practicing physic and the possessor of a reputation far from sterling. Kylene thought him brilliant, if not a little moonstruck.

Her father pressed the tips of his fingers together and nodded slowly in a manner suggesting approval.

"I look forward to hearing more of your observations in textiles, but I would be speaking falsely if I said I wasn't surprised by the subject, given your repeated refusal to join your mother and sister at the tailor's."

Kylene bowed her head, a faint flush creeping up her neck as her mother began her own insight. Kylene half-listened, hot guilt puddling in her belly for having omitted the truth about the real purpose of her iron decoction. She'd been making a mulberry and iron syrup, on McBane's recommendation, to treat the fatigue brought on by winter months. She was, in fact, working on a number of remedies that were meant to fortify the body during the days of hard frost.

It was just that most of them couldn't be found in the widely respected Malstrum's Book of Maladies, And How to Address Them. Malstrum had been a physic 120 years ago and while he was no quack, his compendium was only 400 pages long. Something inside of Kylene told her there was much, much more to medicine than 400 pages could hold. It was a conviction she and McBane shared.

She *had* been stirring the mixture with a beechwood stick and it *did* come out in the most shocking shade of purple. And had she not splashed her overalls – her *hemp* overalls – by accident? She looked down at her knees, where streaks of vivid purple showed like angry weals. So, her insight hadn't been a complete lie.

There was a reason, of course, for the half-truth. Three weeks ago, she'd been toying with the small amount of saltpeter she'd made, on the careful instructions of McBane. It *had* taken her a year to make and she'd been terribly curious to see whether she'd done it correctly. She'd just finished grinding the charcoal and a little sulfur and was mixing the three together when her candle sputtered and sparked and caught on the powder. The explosion was minuscule – she had only been handling a pinhead's worth – but Kylene had come up to supper with no eyebrows. The look on her mother's face had been one that she'd never seen before and Kylene thought her eyes might actually pop out of her head when she further explained, brow and lashless, *how* she'd gotten the saltpeter.

It wasn't something she planned to repeat and had, since then, resolved to keep her more intrepid experiments to herself, at least for a little while.

After her mother and father shared their insights, supper dissolved into the familiar lilt of clattering spoons and talk of summer's end, projects on the press and Mossbridge gossip. By Kylene's measure, both her parents' insights lacked inspiration, an unusual thing. Her mother claimed to have learned that the flavor of garlic was most fulsome when added at the very end of cooking and her father, that he slept better this time of year with the window cracked in just such a way.

She considered these bog-standard observations while she lathered butter onto a piece of bread; insights were foundational and both of their parents always went to great lengths to demonstrate the angularity of learning a thing. She was swirling the bread in her stew, watching the butter break ranks and begin to melt when a single loud knock sounded at the door.

Quick as fire scorches a feather, her father leapt out of his chair and sprang to the door. He peered behind the sun-faded curtains and paused, the expression on his face caught between curiosity and disquiet. Finally, he gripped the handle and swung the door open. The vanishing light of day flooded the kitchen in patches, a large figure obstructing its total possession of the room. A man stood on the porch, a beret held anxiously between thick twitching fingers. Kylene could scarcely see his face, backlit as it was by the sun, but she imagined, by the language of his shadow, that it was not a cheerful one.

"Chet." Her father nodded, the easy warmth that was his nature nowhere to be found.

"If'n you please, Mr Gemison. May I come inside?" The shadow called Chet looked behind one shoulder, then the other. Her father inclined his head and moved aside, the motion of his hand saying what his words did not. The man called Chet stepped into the kitchen and her father closed the door behind him. Once inside, Chet looked once more over both shoulders, despite the very solid presence of windows, a wall and the door behind him.

"You're making me nervous, man. You've come and interrupted me and my family at supper. Speak your piece now, don't dither."

Kylene could see now that this Chet was not much older than she was. His jaw, broad as it was, was patchily covered with what was meant to be a beard, beneath which lay a considerable quantity of red spots. His jaw went slack as his eyes roved anxiously from her father to her mother, then Petra, Kylene and back to her father again.

"Gob it up, man." Her father's voice was grim and something cold settled in Kylene's chest and began, slowly, to swell.

"I'm sorry, Mr Gemison. They know. About you and Wilfredi and the Constable and all the folks that have been meetin' 'gainst sanctions." Chet's voice ran like a downhill mountain stream, fast and dribbling. "They're planning on taking you in at this evenin's' Assembly, making an example of you. I don't know how." His voice broke, and he let out a strangled sort of howl. "I'm sorry, so sorry. There was nothin' I could do, nothin' I could do."

The kitchen was silent save for the repeated whisper of apology from Chet, who was now rocking from heel to toe, beret spinning like mad in his hands. The cold swelling in Kylene's chest burst, and then, there was nothing, save for a sullen ache in her skull between her brows. She turned to her mother, who always wore her composure like a plate of armor, polished to a fine sheen. It had been torn asunder, revealing a fear so ripe

Kylene was sure she could smell it. The sweet tang of red-hot iron, the bite of cold cut steel.

"What's happening?" she mouthed. Her mother merely stared, her eyes pools of grief, silver and deep.

Slowly, her mother moved toward her father. Petra, who had been watching with her rosebud mouth held open in a tiny O, began to sob quietly. Kylene watched as her mother placed her hand on the small of her father's back and stared up at him. He closed his eyes and kissed the top of her head with a certain tenderness that was far too finite, much too calm. It made Kylene want to scream.

Her father straightened and turned toward Chet. "You'd best be going now, you've risked much in coming here, and I thank you."

Chet bowed three times as he backed away toward the door, his face run over with misery. Turning, he threw the door open and ran. They watched him until the door closed with a thud and a click that rang through the hushed kitchen for what seemed a very long time.

Her parents stared at the space where Chet had stood, arms locked around each other so tightly there could be no space found between them. The dregs of supper's stew began to burn and the smell made Kylene want to be sick. It made her want to cry. It made her want to hit her father and ask him what was happening that had made her mother look the way that she did, like death itself had come knocking on their door.

Nodding to one other, her parents turned to face her and Petra.

"There's much and more that you should know," their father said, his words slow and thick with sorrow. "That you have every right to know. That you will know in due time."

"What does that *mean*, Father!?" Petra wailed. Her delicate hands were wound into fists and she held them tightly to her temples, as if she was working to keep her head in one piece.

"Your father is in danger," their mother said briskly. "He will need to leave town. Tonight. Before Assembly. Now. You remember Fabrice?"

Petra bobbed her head. Kylene sat still as stone, staring at her father, this man who now seemed a perfect stranger.

"Your father's offenses are much, much greater than were those of old Fabrice. We haven't the time to explain. He will need every inch of road he can get before Assembly begins and the Fingers are made aware of his leaving. Petra, I need you to go upstairs and fetch the wee satchel beneath our bed. Kylene, potatoes from the cellar, salt, whatever else you can find."

When neither of the girls moved, Andara's plate of mail seemed to knit itself anew so that it gleamed once again, whole and untarnished. Her eyes were fierce, whatever grief had been there banished. "*Now,*" she hissed.

Kylene shot from her chair and burst through the door, slamming it closed behind her. Her breath came in stunted bellows and she bent low, hands clasped on knees. Her head spun. *Father was a bellringer, part of the resistance.* The revelation came clear and sure as daybreak. *So stupid! How could I not have known!?* Kylene knew there were secret meetings, those who clung fiercely to the time before The Reckoning. They conspired in the night, dreaming of a day when that time might return again. But everyone knew those men and women were always discovered, sent away to the Pit, never to be seen again.

She knew how her father felt about Osbert, had heard him decry his evils, the crimes committed by his Fingers against all men and women. How could she not have known?

Kylene pushed herself off her knees and forced her breath to settle. There was hardly any time. The last color of day was slow-draining from the garden. Night would fall soon, and if he stayed, he would be taken.

Taking the path to the cellar door at a run, she came to a stumbling halt before it, threw it open and hurled herself down the stairs, nearly falling headlong into her desk. She steadied herself on the chair, trembling fingers reaching for match and candle. She lit it clumsily, jamming its base into a sconce and scanned the space. Her mind ran in a dozen different directions, and only half of them were helpful. Crossing over to where the crates were stacked, she tucked six small potatoes into the pocket on her chest then raced back to the desk, where she snatched up a leather pouch from the drawer. She upended the contents of the pouch onto the surface of the desk and dried milkweed pods caromed in every direction. Seizing the emptied pouch, she dashed to the salt sack, filled it to the brim with coarse gray granules, then drew the string tight, tossing it in along with the potatoes.

Kylene drew a deep breath into her lungs, her hands clutching either side of her neck as she stared at her simples cupboard resting atop the apple rack. Yarrow, *definitely*. Poppy salve? She hesitated. Her mother would kill her if she knew. She swept up the small clay jar and a miniature vial of oregano oil too, stowing these in her side pockets. Her eyes fell to the freshly corked vials of the iron and mulberry decoction. A prickle of tears blurred her vision and she blinked to sweep them aside. Without further thought, she seized one of them, turned to pinch out the candle with her free hand and hobbled toward the stairs, the clay pot and vials clinking precariously in her overburdened pockets.

The garden was wreathed in shades of purple and gray and the kitchen door was open. It was near-dark, and the light from inside spilled yellow onto the porch. Her father had Petra's chin in a gentle grip and he was speaking to her softly. Her mother stood close beside them, his traveling cloak clutched in her hands.

"Be good for your mother. And consider schooling with Kylene; you're more alike than the two of you would ever admit."

Petra nodded, tears streaming down her face, carefully applied cosmetics so muddled she looked as though she'd been in a street brawl and suffered a terrific loss.

"How will you take to the roads without your scroll, Father?" Petra asked, her voice quavering.

"I won't be taking the Middling Road, Pet. Besides, a scroll is no use to me now." The horrified look on her sister's face was a mirror of Kylene's thought; if he wasn't taking the Middling Road, it'd be the High or the Bottom. No one took the High or the Bottom, save thieves and poachers and peacekeepers and who knew what else.

Kylene decanted the potatoes and salt from her pouch into the satchel sitting upright by the door. Seizing it, she straightened and met her father's eye. *Will this be the last time I ever see him?* She couldn't bear the thought and so she pushed it aside and shoved the satchel into her father's arms.

"For pain," she told him, withdrawing the poppy salve from her pocket and placing it in the satchel. "For wounds. Apply before it festers," she said, inserting the oregano oil. "To staunch bleeding." Her father raised his eyebrow at the jar of dried yarrow flowers. "Chew them a few times and apply them like a poultice."

He nodded gravely, his eyes never leaving her face. "And, for...for strength of mind...and body," she choked back tears as she placed the last, her mulberry tonic, into his hands.

Her father set down the satchel and wrapped her in a hug so tight Kylene felt she might burst. Warmth radiated from his rough-stubbled cheek onto the top of her head and against her ear, his heart beat like a drum. "Curiosity and courage," he whispered. "You must never stop asking questions, my darling. If you don't go about asking questions, no one has to worry about the answers they're giving you."

Kylene nodded mutely and he let her go. He clapped a heavy hand on her shoulder before turning to face her mother, who placed the thick-woven cloak over his shoulders, her movements mournful, deliberate. Their eyes locked for one long moment, more words passing between their gaze than could be said aloud, and then she folded into his arms. In his embrace, she nearly buckled. She stayed for only a moment and quivered like a loosed bowstring as she withdrew herself from his arms. Wordlessly, he picked up his satchel and stepped from the light of the porch into the gathering dusk.

Kylene watched as he strode unswerving through the garden, toward the wooden gate which led through fields of golden wheat and ended at the edges of the Mavros Forest. Through it, he slipped and then, he was gone.

He didn't look back.

Chapter Two

An onshore wind sent spray from crashing surf onto a beach strewn with rocks that rose from the sand like jagged knives. The wind howled as it battered the cliffside, whose vertical face was slick with sea spray, rising tall and dark above the water's edge. It whistled where it found passage in caves beaten hollow by the sea.

The air was ripe with brine and wet stone and something foul, the rotting corpse of a gull, perhaps, or some similarly ill-fated sea creature who had had the misfortune of washing up on this cruel stretch of coastline, where no man would dare to make landing unless he was very desperate or very foolish.

Tiny bubbles rose forth from the sand like so many unseeing eyes and Lovelace considered the subterranean presence of sand crabs, tunneled down in burrows deep as shallow graves. Surely their lives were more peaceable than his own; bore down, feed, move with the tide. The near-inevitable fate of being snatched by some seabird might even be preferable, the way things seemed to be headed.

Another gust of sea spittle struck him full in the face, stinging his eyes and coating his beard with still more salt but he did not flinch. Much as he was disinclined toward the sea, this beach below the Meorachadh was the only place where he could be alone with his thoughts. It didn't matter that their halls were more empty now than they had been in 1,000 years; the stone that shaped its walls and passageways could still see him, could still hear him. And while that stone could not divine his thoughts, or speak to issue forth judgment, Lovelace could not help but feel the weight of its knowing, of those dactyli who had come before him, who had walked those same passageways pursuing the same fruitless cause as he.

He stabbed at a bubble, bursting it before it had chance to swell. His dactyli forebears had not seen their pursuit as worthless. They'd been fed on the same fodder as Lovelace, and grown large on their steady grazing of the noble and righteous path of truth. But things had been different, then.

Those dactyli had gone on their rangings just as he, gathering sgeuls from every crevice and every crag and in earlier times, from beyond even the furthest reaches of the Grasp. They had brought these hard-won sgeuls back to the Meorachadh so that the scribes might distill them, for rangers were nothing so much as hunters, gatherers of threads that only scribes could weave into tapestries of truth. These greater narratives they called sgeulachds, and they were stored and kept and once yearly, shared with those who would wish to know what certainties the dactyli could give them after another year of careful collection and curation. They were meant to be tangible, living things, these sgeulachds, illuminating patterns and cycles that could be kept in perpetuity, relied upon as the firmament upon which still further truths could be built, tall and straight as columns. Cuimhne Amas – truth absolute, the most noble of all pursuits.

For all the good it's done us, Lovelace thought gloomily as he wrung his salt-soaked beard.

He had been on 267 rangings, Gunnar by his side for all save the first. Together they had coaxed tales of treachery from trees, obtained old wives' tales from weather-beaten stone. They had taken accounts of great deeds and terrible deeds and everything in between from children and maidens, farmers and city folk. Gone were the acquisitions of natural phenomenon, the workings of the Mother, of the natural world. The dactyli masters presumed to know all there was of earth and its turnings, and had, for the last three hundred years, curved their wrinkled necks to mankind and his machinations.

But the minds of men and women were as twisted and gnarled as the singular branches of a juniper tree, yearning for the sky. And so their sgeulachds grew more and more strange, ever-reaching, ever-branching, ever-growing toward plateaus of certitude in an endless expanse. In time, their library grew bright with truths that battled one another, burgeoned with patterns that bore imperfect weaves. And the people, for whom the order sought to give succor with the depth and breadth of their knowing, slowly began to turn elsewhere for their solace, elsewhere for their schemes. And the dactyli had wilted like flowers gone overlong without the warmth of the sun, left to do as they had always done in their cold crypt by the sea.

***

Lovelace and Gunnar had returned to the Meorachadh the night prior at twelfth bell, the night around them black as cold fire, their cloaks soaked through with mist and hard riding. Lovelace wanted nothing more than a tall draught and a long sleep but duty prevailed, and Manoc would not wait.

The Meorachadh was silent, its thick walls staving off all source of sound from the world outside. They made their way to the high tower, where they knew Manoc would be, poring over some sgeulachd he'd pulled from the stacks, or else pouring himself into the creation of another. They moved through the Meorachadh's twisting halls, the air as still as winter frost. They saw no one, heard no one. Even the Great Hall was empty, the chill creeping from the darkened corners of the hall gripped like the cold hand of a corpse as they passed through.

At last they reached the stairwell winding and up, where the masters kept their quarters, where rangers and scribes and tyros alike were forbidden unless expressly called upon. Their climb was slow, their every footstep an echo of their failed errand,

and every failed errand before this one. He and Gunnar had not delivered good news to Manoc in a very, very long time.

They stood before the heavy oak door and knocked once. A voice, web-thin, issued from within and bid them enter.

Manoc sat at his desk, a great hulking thing that had been carved from ebony wood. Behind the black gleaming angularity of it, the old master looked small and rather tattered, his hunched form backlit by the soft red glow of a fire that burned low at his back.

Manoc, as ever, was ponderous in thought. The thin, crinkled folds of his cheeks and the deep grooves in his forehead were illuminated by a tablet of verdanite upon which his right hand rested. His eyelids, near-translucent in the light, fluttered faintly as he brought his left hand to pinch the bridge of his knife-edge nose.

He did not acknowledge their entrance. His whole focus was channeled inward, on whatever distillation he'd seen fit to work on at that Motherless hour when most creatures slept and those that did not were up to no good. The verdanite tablet resting beneath his hand grew brighter as they stood there, waiting, in the doorway.

They watched the crystalline surface of it emit a light that grew whiter, brighter and colder as it absorbed the dactyli master's drawn conclusions. What he might be distilling, Lovelace could not begin to guess. None of the rangers had brought back anything of import for at least a year, their efforts having been solely focused on acquiring the boys who would be tyros who might, after careful training and a final test, become dactyli. Boys who, for the last six years, had all been found dead.

Except Jules, Lovelace thought and his stomach twisted as he conjured an image of the one boy they'd managed to secure and save from certain death. Sweet Jules, the only tyro in the Meorachadh, an eager child with ears as big as butterfly wings and a head that barely reached Lovelace's navel. So ungrudging, so decent…so ignorant of the life he'd wasted coming here.

They waited, weariness washing over Lovelace in unyielding waves that broke over him like white caps, the steady drip of wet cloaks on worn floorboards the only marker of time's passage. They watched the verdanite grow brighter and brighter, green slow-suffusing the white of it, like plants blood slow-dripping into a chalice of milk. By the time Manoc looked up from his desk, the gemstone glowed green as new growth, saturated with the strength of his judgments; *a sgeulachd replete with worldly knowing,* Lovelace thought, the axiom a bitter kernel he found difficult to swallow.

"Tell me," Manoc murmured, his voice worn bare by age and circumstance and the hour of night. He fixed Lovelace with a sharp stare, his pale hawkish eyes challenging, willing Lovelace to have another shout at him, as he had the last time they'd delivered news that was none of it good.

Lovelace opened his mouth to speak but before he could, Gunnar bent low to kneel.

In the staid tones that were his constant, he began to describe how their assignment to secure yet another nascent dactyli had failed. How the boy had gone missing from his home, his mother despondent, her face blanched white with grief. How they'd followed his imprint from the town tavern to the edge of the woods of Ardeleur before Manoc raised a weary hand, stopping him.

"Was it *him?*" Manoc asked with a weighty significance that banished Lovelace's fatigue and ushered in anger, fresh and hot as bubbling oil.

"Of course it was *him,*" Lovelace broke in. "The boy was fresh-butchered as a lamb, trussed up the same as the rest of them, innards turned inside out." Lovelace stared Manoc down, his hands balled into loose fists by his sides. Manoc returned his gaze with an indifference that made Lovelace want to seize him by the collar and shake him; shake the inanity out of him, or else some reason into him.

The old man raised his eyebrows in a way that meant to ask whether Lovelace was quite done. As it happened, he wasn't.

"He couldn't have been more than nine," Lovelace growled. "What's the point of all these rangings? How many more boys need to die, how many more of our own need to disappear before we try and stop him? What in the name of the Mother's own two gracious hands are we waiting for?" His voice broke and something cracked inside of him. Perhaps it was the thin shell that had grown to encase the despair born within him, the day they'd found the first boy six years ago. The day Lovelace had learned that Alev was not gone from the world. An exiled dactyli was supposed to be as good as dead. Not so, with Alev.

What the man's intentions were, Lovelace was reluctant to contemplate. The simple facts – that he had raised a militia, outfitted them and was using them methodically to dispatch nascent dactyli – were enough to make him feel sick.

Gunnar cleared his throat delicately as though he might interject, though silent he remained. The rasping sound did, however, bring Lovelace back from the edge, and he summoned his luth to steady himself. A sensation like that of cool silk dropped down from the crown of his head, covering him over with a veil of self-possession. He unclenched his fists and the blood that boiled through his veins cooled until it was once again the warmth of a man to whom impulse was unknown.

Manoc's gaze remained fixed on Lovelace. It was remote, as impersonal as a mask made to adorn the anointed dead. Light eluded the master's fingers, which were pressed flat on the tablet of verdanite as if he meant for them to anchor him there. The tablet bathed the master's drooping features in a ghastly green glow, making him appear somehow less human.

"Action is useless without strategy, particularly against the likes of one such as Alev," he said finally, as simply as if he were informing Lovelace that yeast was needed to leaven bread. He opened a small drawer in his desk and placed the verdanite carefully inside without further comment, the unnatural green light of it extinguishing as he drew the drawer shut. When he looked up again, displeasure – grave and entirely familiar – was etched on the lines of his shadowed face.

"Why do you insist upon forcing me to remind you of the most basic of truths, Lovelace?"

Lovelace's fingers curled, tightening into iron fists.

"The time has passed for distillations and council meetings, *Manoc*. The *truth* is that Alev must be stopped," he said.

"And how do you propose we do that?" Manoc asked quietly, menace sharpening the edges of his every word. "Alev, his band of miscreants, what they are doing to nascent dactyli; it is a foreign stratagem, an as yet unseen course of nature, and as is thusly appropriate, we, the council, have not yet decided upon the right stratagem with which to counter. I implore you to hold your tongue and your..." the old dactyli pursed his wrinkled lips in disrelish, as if Lovelace had poured him a particularly sour vintage that had gone too long uncorked, "...zealousness while we confer upon the best approach. You can rest assured that we desire to see Alev put to justice every bit as much as you do and if you *think* that I do not see how much there is at stake as *yourself*, then I will be forced to assume you no longer have a mind that is sound enough to continue the eminent work of our order." He turned to the embers of the dying fire, his face never yielding anything beyond distaste.

"Now," he said levelly, taking up a poker to stab at the rubble of glowing coals with an impotence that was uncomfortable to watch. "What details can you yield from the boy's end?" He held out his other hand, spindly palm facing upward.

"We didn't collect a sgeul," Lovelace said brusquely, willing Manoc to ask why they'd neglected to perform the foremost of their duties: to collect an account of the event as it occurred in nature. Their own rendering could only provide an echo of the incident, a distorted moving image that would be seen by Manoc as baseless, worth as much as a sack of flour writhing with weevils. He and Gunnar were, after all, flesh and blood. As such, they would always create memories that were centered around themselves.

Lovelace hadn't taken a sgeul because the killing was the same as every other one before it. What was the use in gathering information when the only difference in detail was the name of the boy and the life he might've led? Twenty-nine times they had seen it – men in burnished armor, red and oiled to a shine. They were hardened men, men with eyes that flashed with glee or grim satisfaction as they carried out their assignment. Never once had Lovelace seen remorse or even hesitation, which led him to believe that Alev was selecting a particular type of man and promising something greater than mere gold.

And while they'd never seen Alev, never heard his name spoken aloud in any of the butchery they'd seen thus far, Lovelace knew in his heart that it was him. It had to be. How else were the men in red always, *always*, one step ahead?

Lovelace looked sidelong at Gunnar and realized that he hadn't taken the *sgeul* either. Curious. Gunnar was always the more meticulous one.

There was a hollow silence in the tower room, dispersed only by the occasional pop of low flame as it liberated the final traces of water and sap from spent wood.

"Then we are done here," Manoc said, his eyes never leaving the embers.

***

It wasn't that Lovelace regretted the loss of an ordinary life. He had, after all, gone willingly with those dactyli rangers whose knock had sounded on his door fourteen years ago, which was more than could be said for every whelp who was born with wind in their veins or earth on their fingertips. It was more common for boys to be peeled from their mothers' arms while their fathers looked on, the weight of coin in their pockets a small comfort, the belief that their boy had been *chosen,* a greater consolation still.

His mind drifted. Away from the cold wet sand beneath him, away from the bitter wind, away from this bootless errand of a life. He soared over Glendor. Lovely, quiet Glendor, with its fragrant wildflower winds, honeybees floating in the fields. That gentle basin between the rolling hills of Ardeleur to the east and the Hambrian plains to the west. Stands of gnarled oak, tidy plots ripe for planting. He veered sharply toward his mother, her petal-soft hands, her flour-dusted fingers, her voice like chimes, played by a gentle wind.

She'd let him go. It was what he'd wanted and she'd let him go and his heart broke anew to remember her face, wet with tears and splintered by a special sort of sorrow. It was the same look worn by the woman two days ago, whose own son had been killed for nothing more than the seed of power that lay within him.

For these last fourteen years, Lovelace had pursued pieces of truth, meant to be fitted together with their equals to make something larger, grander, more complete. *Cuimhne Amas*; the most high, truth beyond dispute, beyond the desires of women and men.

Lovelace shook himself of saltwater and rose slow from the sand, his insides hollow as a dried gourd. The sea pitched, gray and white like wings where the wind lifted it, and he turned to face the cliff, feeling that for all the apparent truths he'd gathered, he had very little conviction to show for it.

Chapter Three

The Great Hall of the Meorachadh was not like other great halls, at least not like those described in the stories or the songs. There were no windows to let in any shape of light or sweep of air. It might be stifling for lack of ventilation were it not cold as a tomb; there was no fireplace of any size, and what braziers did line the walls gave off a sullen sort of light that served the sole purpose of signifying that council was assembled.

There were no long tables for feasting, banners with regalia or tapestries woven with stories of bravery or piety or deeds of miracle. In fact, there was nothing at all in the Great Hall save a table shaped like a slivered moon and thirty-three rows of benches, all hewn from basalt, the same stone laid for the ceiling and the roof and the floors.

And there was the orb.

It was the orb that truly lit the Great Hall, not the hundred flickering braziers. Set on its dais at the front of the chamber, it bathed the long room in verglas blue, its preternatural light falling on the council's attendants like the kiss of a weak-sunned winter's morning.

There were three seated at the moon table. Three, where there ought to have been seven. They spoke in low tones, and as Lovelace approached from the back of the hall, they ceased their quiet chatter and turned in unison to fix him with stares of varied disapproval. Gottfried, the second eldest of the masters, was seated in the center.

Gottfried had a face that resembled an especially foul-tempered ostrich and a frame to match. *Overweening prick,* Lovelace thought, avoiding the man's beady gaze. He was looking at Lovelace as if he were a particularly loathsome locust he might like to crush in his beak.

Lovelace stopped short at the second bench closest to the masters, empty, save for Gunnar. Radigan and Lester, despite having a quarter of Lovelace's total rangings under their belts, were seated on the first bench alongside the two scribes, Tommaso and Bastian. The three younger scribes – Martin, Dalibor and Osman – were seated on the third and the *tyro*, Jules, was alone on the fourth.

Lovelace crossed his arms to his chest and inclined his head toward the three men across from him. Masters Manoc, Gottfried and Hugh; *each one more decrepit than the last,* he thought.

The three men acknowledged him in turn, and Lovelace took his seat on the bench beside Gunnar.

"As ever, Lovelace, we appreciate your mighty presence at these trivial things we call council meetings," Hugh said with a wheezing sigh.

"The pleasure is mine, to be sure," Lovelace said. He swept aside a lock of hair, plastered on a dry smile, and winked. The eldest master blinked once, not amused.

"Now that we have..." Hugh said, watery gaze sweeping over the four sparsely occupied rows before him, "...complete attendance, we may begin."

He broke into a violent coughing fit. They all waited as his wet lungs rattled wearily, each cough more punishing than the last. Just as Lovelace was about to nudge Gunnar to see whether he could force some air into the old man's lungs, the master managed to produce a kerchief from within the sleeve of his robe. He hacked into it several times and finally recovered himself with a single wet clearing of his throat.

"Ahem," he began again. "Last evening, Gunnar and Lovelace returned from an assignment to investigate a flare that we interpreted two weeks ago," he said, his voice thick and yawning. Even in frailty, Hugh spoke with an accent of propriety that did not come from any one pocket of land in particular, but from a long life of feeling superior to the world around him.

"Though they were swift in their mission when they arrived at Ardeleur they discovered that the boy had gone missing from his home one night prior."

Of course, everybody in attendance knew this already, but decorum overruled, and Hugh went on. "They trailed the boy's imprint to the eastern border of the woods of Ardeleur, where they then entered the forest and ultimately discovered his remains. All evidence points to his demise as being the unfortunate consequence of apprehension on behalf of the erstwhile dactyli Alev, the deed itself having been performed by his underlings."

Lovelace felt Gunnar tense beside him and looked down. His knuckles were white, his hands balled into tight fists where they rested on either leg.

"This is the fourth nascent dactyli that has been purloined from us in the last year alone..."

"They're not goods to trade at port," Lovelace fumed under his breath.

"As such," Hugh's voice rose, glaring at Lovelace, "it is increasingly paramount that we direct our attentions toward the source of the white flare, which has appeared again and this time, more strongly than ever we have observed it, in the mountains of Droch Fhortan."

Behind Lovelace the tyro, Jules, whimpered at the mention of the Grasp's mountain range. Lovelace shifted in his seat. In all his years of ranging, he had never set foot in the mountains himself.

"The council has spent considerable time in the Tasglann, evaluating every pertinent sgeulachd in our possession. We will stay the course. We must seek and obtain this white flare and redouble our efforts in securing each flare thereafter. As to the matter of Alev, we will not pursue him. Now more than ever we must preserve and rebuild the lifeblood of this order. We will not waste a single drop scouring the land for one errant dactyli."

The verdict hung low in the air as the ten remaining members of the order absorbed its implications. Lovelace sat, stupefied, feeling as one does in a dream when time is slowed and thought muddied.

Radigan and Lester twisted around in their seats to look at him and Gunnar and gauge their reaction to the news. Relief and apprehension battled for precedence on Radigan's smooth, unlined face, and a smile was beginning to spread across Lester's. *I could hit him, cocksure little lickspittle.* The cage of Lovelace's chest rattled as an ireful beast awoke within him.

"So you've all had a rifle through the archives? That's grand, that. And what did the peerless and perfect wisdom of our forebears tell you, that Alev is just another lusty advisor to a maladjusted king and his hunger for power will be his undoing in due time? I could've guessed you'd assign him some insipid trope."

Lovelace reared on Gottfried. "Gottfried, you trained Alev yourself; no one knows him better than you. The man has no interest in playing court mage. Osbert and his Fingers are naught but kindling for whatever inferno he has planned."

What Lovelace didn't say was that behind Alev, Gottfried had to be the most sinister son of a bitch Lovelace had ever met. The man's enormous wide-set eyes bored into Lovelace, his thin mouth drawn into a long frown.

"Alev is no greater than any dactyli present at this council!" Hugh said, bringing a palm to slam rather feebly upon the moon table. Lovelace felt the very air around him crisp, felt his skin tighten until it was dry as old parchment. It was true that Hugh's body was frail, but it was not the body that commanded a dactyli's luth; it was the mind. Hugh, presiding dactyli master of water, had siphoned a not insubstantial quantity of it from the air and the very bodies of those present at council, a none-too-subtle reprimand.

Manoc, who had been staring fixedly at the Great Hall's back wall, arched his eyebrows in faint surprise. Gottfried's black eyes, still locked on Lovelace, gleamed with approval.

"Alev ceased to be dactyli long ago," Gunnar said quietly, his gaze fixated on the orb. Lovelace glanced sidelong at Gunnar and then at the orb, its glassy surface swirling with colorless fog. As he watched, a muted burst of red winked softly before dissolving into milky wisps.

"His shadow grows tall," Gunnar continued. "It stretches across the Grasp like a sickness. You can see it in the faces of the people and taste it in the air. But then, you would know this if you ever left the confines of these walls." He took his eyes from the orb and bowed his head in mock deference to the three old men seated before him.

"Alev is a snake who only need be lured from his den," Gottfried spat. "The so-called sickness of which you speak is the result of Osbert's reform and the tireless machine he has created, not the handiwork of one fire-coalesced dactyli who, I grant you, has always exhibited a degree of aptitude for our craft that neither you nor your dimwitted partner could ever hope to possess..."

Hugh raised a wizened hand, quieting him.

"We will not intervene," he said. "The council has convened. Alev's hubris will grow, and with it, his carelessness. He will come to us and when he does, the ten dactyli here will show him the error of his ways. Until that day comes, we will concentrate on the acquisition of nascent dactyli and the requisite training that will rebuild our ranks."

"Alev is a predator the likes of which we have not seen, whose ilk cannot be found in the Tasglann's entire collection of sgeulachds," Gunnar said, his words soft, distant as a premonition.

"Hubris indeed!" Lovelace roared. "And suppose we four are on the road? Suppose we are picked off, one by one or two after the other? Suppose he allies himself with Osbert and together they come with his red guard and an army of mercs and wash this Mother-forsaken place into the sea? Do you really think we can hold against the 10,000 troops he is claimed to have at his disposal?"

Within him, the beast in Lovelace's chest crouched low, awaiting a counter. Before him, the benches buzzed with murmured exchanges between Radigan and Lester, Tommaso and Bastian, Martin, Dalibor and Osman. Beside him, Gunnar nodded, and Lovelace realized he was standing. His fists were clenched, his chest heaving, but he refused to use his luth to compose himself. He did not want to feel that inhuman calm, that infernal equanimity that was at the core of all the dactyli order had strived for and accomplished. This apathy, this detached observation, had kept their order from a thousand years and more of conflict. It had allowed them to amass an impossibly vast library of living knowledge, untainted by ego, untouched by inequity. And here they were, collapsing beneath the weight of it, so accustomed to inaction that they could not even recognize that the hour of their own destruction was upon them.

"1300 years," Manoc said. His voice was grave and surprisingly resonant, like a bell struck in the dead of night. "That is how long the Meorachadh has stood longer by half than any dynasty in the known world. It is true that Alev has proven a considerable..." he reached for the right rendering, aware that his choice of word could bear out all manner of consequence. "...complication. Indeed, each of his acts: the detection, the hunting and subsequent disposal of nascent dactyli pose questions beyond our ability to answer. Still, it remains: to seek him out would be a wise man's folly; we will stay the path."

"1300 years," he said, his voice softening into something closer to melancholy. "And longer still have we dactyli sought truth; in ardor, backs bent low, saddle-worn, run ragged by the road. Longer still have we assembled it, minds working through the black of night, stripping away the personal, the impressionistic. We have born out true histories, veracities beyond the whims of men and women. Cuimhne Amas. It is our birthright. It is our burden. Meorachadh or no, the dactyli will persist, and we must do everything within our power to see our work carried out by those born to it."

Gottfried and Hugh were nodding vigorously. "Here, here!" Radigan said while Lester clapped loudly. The scribes were quiet. They had taken the oath. They were, all of them, nothing but grains of sand that moved only by the will of the tide.

"There won't be any dactyli left to pass on your precious traditions," Lovelace growled.

"*Our* traditions, Lovelace. I am pleased we are all in agreement," Hugh said, inclining his head toward Manoc. "Now, to the matter of the white flare. We have established that last evening's transmission came again from the mountains of Droch Fhortan. The flare was stronger than any I have seen in my ninety-two years. Gunnar, Lovelace, much as your impudence fills me with shame, you are our highest-ranking rangers. You will make for Mortalis. Tonight. There, you will assemble an escort, who will assist you in finding and securing the bearer of the flare."

"An escort? From Mortalis?" Lovelace almost laughed. Mortalis was not the sort of place where one went looking for heroes.

"Yes, Lovelace, an escort. There are, no doubt, still men there who would honor the Covenant of Clasped Hands. You have spoken volumes of the danger you face while on the road, have you not? Let it be shown that we have heard you. What better way to bolster your security than allying yourself with honorable men of vim and vigor? You are to gather as many as you see fit, discretely, of course, and ride for Droch Fhortan at daybreak. Radigan, Lester, you will ready yourselves for the next dispatch. As soon as we..."

"An escort will slow our progress," Gunnar said.

"You only think that because you have an injurious relationship with your own mortality," Hugh spat. "It is abundantly clear that we cannot afford to lose you or Lovelace, much as your total lack of regard makes me regret allowing either of you to coalesce."

"I cannot think that the men of Mortalis are fit fighters," Gunnar continued, even-toned. "Their people are much changed since the Covenant of Clasped Hands was forged and their township founded."

"A load of tap-shackled fops is what they are," Lovelace muttered.

"I am sure you can find at least one man equal to the task of fulfilling his forebears' oath," Hugh waved a hand dismissively. "Now. You have your instructions; I suggest you prepare for the ranging you've been given. Council is concluded."

He rose from his seat, crossed his arms to his chest and inclined his head. Gathering his robes around him, he turned to make his slow, shuffling way to the high tower. Gottfried rose next, his round middle swerving precariously as he turned to follow. Manoc remained seated.

Thunder rumbled through the hall. Had there been windows, a burst of lightning would have set the hall alight moments later. It would be a nasty ride to Mortalis.

Radigan and Lester were off, Lester declaiming about some firewall he'd developed. Lovelace turned to watch their retreating backs. "...hot enough that no creature can pass through. Goes up like *Whoooooosh,*" he gesticulated wildly with his arms. "We'll give him the old what for, eh, Rad? We'll see who's the better at battle magics."

Lovelace snorted. If Lester did have chance to come across Alev, he'd be a cinder in seconds.

One by one, the scribes filed out. Who knew what they did these days. Without new-gathered sgeuls, there was no work for them. Lovelace supposed they must be in the Tasglann day and night, poring over sgeulachds, searching for precedents at the behest of the masters, precedents that Lovelace was certain didn't exist.

Young Jules slid off the bench behind him and walked up to the orb, where he perched himself on the stool set behind it. His legs did not quite reach the floor and stuck out from underneath his gray homespun, dangling like the knotted cherry stems. The tyros had always shared the task of orb-watching – among other such menial work best described as scullery drudgery.

By all accounts, Jules had shown an early affinity for water. *Not that he has any time for training these days,* Lovelace thought as he watched the boy stare at the orb, the tip of his pink tongue peeking out the side of his mouth.

"Come," Manoc said, regarding Lovelace and Gunnar with a slight tilt of his head. "There is something I wish to show you in the Tasglann." He rose and walked stiffly toward the back entrance, head bowed in quiet thought.

Lovelace looked to Gunnar, who shrugged as the stone floor shivered beneath their feet, another thunderclap shaking the slabbed surface.

"Wise man's folly," Lovelace said, shaking his head. "More's the pity, when fools may not speak wisely about what wise men do foolishly."

Rising, Gunnar arched his eyebrows in faint surprise and frowned.

"Heard it in a sgeulachd once – arts section. Can't remember the name of it or the bloke who wrote it," Lovelace said as he pushed himself off the bench and rose to stand beside Gunnar. "But I liked it, so I remembered it. I always thought it described our circumstances."

Gunnar made a noncommittal grunt as he started toward the Tasglann.

"We're the fools, you see…" Lovelace said, moving with him.

"I understood as much."

***

They walked side-by-side, the narrow hallway lit with braziers identical to those in the Great Hall, their dull yellow light making small doors visible now and again – storerooms, mostly, and living quarters for scribes. As far as Lovelace knew, they'd not been used in fifty years.

They reached the end, where the stairwell that led up the north tower to the masters' chambers rose darkly before them. But that was not where Manoc had gone.

The iron door that guarded the Tasglann was cracked open to their left. A shard of brilliant green light fell from the opening, the radiance of it a stark contrast to the shades of black and gray that were the Meorachadh's hallmark.

"Nice of him to leave it open for us," Lovelace said, referring to the stone seal which had been slit to allow for the door to open. It was basic earth magic and easily done by either of them, but still, it did seem to indicate a certain goodwill that scantily lifted the strings of Lovelace's heart. Beside him, Gunnar gave a grunt that, in this circumstance, indicated skepticism.

They let themselves in. Light fell upon them, irradiating their faces and limbs with a spectral green glow. The first time he'd seen the Tasglann, he'd nearly fainted from the shock of how strange a place it was: hundreds of shelves towering from floor to ceiling, tens of thousands of glowing verdanite slabs upon them.

Starting down the center aisle, they passed "Agriculture," then "Alchemy," "Arts," "Animal Husbandry." Few topics had escaped the collection and curation of dactyli scribes over the last millennia.

The organization of the chamber was rigorous. Each aisle was marked for category, and each row within it detailed with subsections. They were likely ordered alphabetically as well; Lovelace had never bothered to check. He did know that every verdanite tablet was labeled in a ridiculous shorthand that only the scribes could understand. He noted, as he passed, the inscription on the small placard of the one closest to the center aisle in the section marked

Philosophy:

Duty. Mor. Vir. Rsn. Rnwy HC, byst, qnt. loss, paradox.

And below that, in even smaller script:

Eth. Psy.

The postscript connected a sgeulachd to others within the collection. "No truth stands alone" was one of the many aphorisms a young tyro heard during their early instruction.

They found Manoc toward the back of the aisle marked "Capstones." He was halfway up a wheeled ladder, leaning forward to inspect a placard at close range. Verdanite glowed from the leather pouch slung over his shoulder, the light escaping from the drawstring closure like a beacon.

It was an unusual aisle in which to find him. Capstones were a tyro's final examination before they were allowed to attempt coalescence. They required an original distillation demonstrating the candidate's ability to distill myriad sgeul into one definitive sgeulachd. Lovelace had known that he would be a ranger and so his chosen subject matter hadn't exactly rent the earth in two from the force of its brilliance. The work of a scribe had never called to him; too much pondering, too much sitting, more pondering, and still more sitting...

Lovelace stopped short before a small rectangular verdanite tablet with the notation, "Bedevere, Lovelace – Brewcraft and assoc. meditations."

He smiled. For his capstone, he'd chosen something close to home. Something that would stand as a tribute to the barley fields of Glendor and the good folk who grew it. Something that didn't have a whiff of despair or tragedy about it: those themes that were to scribes like honey wine for those with a thirst.

On the ladder above them, Manoc took hold of a large verdanite tablet roughly the size of an apple. He held the stone at a distance and regarded it with some disquiet as if the thing might explode. Placing it with care into his sling pouch, he swiftly descended the ladder in a way that disguised his age. For all that his shoulders were humped and his gait stiff, the man still moved like a wild hare.

He descended the final steps and moved past Lovelace and Gunnar without a word. Not so very unusual behavior; Manoc was only one for talk if the talk was necessary. If he had something to say – presumably he did – he didn't want to say it here. Once, Lovelace had wondered whether this was simply a personality trait of those dactyli coalesced with wind.

Lovelace turned to Gunnar and shrugged. They turned back toward the center aisle and moved to keep up with the old master. When they were out of the stacks and returned to the atrium, they found him by the hearth; his back turned, his hands clasped before him.

"I will not waste my time or yours showing you these three sgeulachd now. I suggest you engross yourselves with them on the road," he said without turning.

Lovelace glanced at Gunnar, who appeared unmoved by this strange declaration. Sgeulachds never left the Tasglann.

"I can only guess at the potential significance of the first two concerning the white flare. They are both from 'Origins.'" He paused and turned. There was an expectant look upon his features, as if perhaps he was waiting for one of them to call him a cracked kettle. Lovelace opened his mouth, but only in a small expression of shock. What was that that he detected in the old master's voice? It seemed to him he heard the tiniest undercurrent of excitement.

Manoc reached for the sling pouch at his back.

"The third tablet is the capstone that Alev distilled, eleven years ago."

Lovelace was sure of it now. There was the foreign whisper of thrill to Manoc's words, the tenor not unlike that of a much younger person on the precipice of doing something very daring indeed. Lovelace glanced sidelong at Gunnar, who was peering at Manoc with a sharpness that suggested he too was attuned to this startling sea change.

"I am not so foolish to think that a simple council mandate will dissolve your adamancy about what ought to be done about him. You are right to fear him," he said, his eyes ablaze, his words like heavy stones lifted off Lovelace's shoulders.

"I thought it might be useful to have a capsular look at this archived bit of his mind, as he was *then:* on the precipice of becoming who he is today, whatever that may be..." he trailed off as he reached into the pouch. He withdrew the largest of the verdanite and handed it to Gunnar, who turned it over in his hands and examined the backside.

"There are runes etched here," Gunnar said, squinting at etchings barely visible by the stone's brightness.

"Indeed," Manoc said. "Interesting, is it not?" He withdrew the stone's placard from the pocket of his robes and handed it to Lovelace, who read aloud.

"Eldorm, Alev – Aggregation and Awakening of Elemental Power."

"At the time, we found his capstone to be impressive, if not a bit ambitious, for one so young. Grandiose, though hardly practical, or so we thought. You might find it useful," Manoc said.

"I just have one question," Lovelace said, searching Manoc's face. It occurred to Lovelace how old Manoc must be and how tired he appeared. The skin of his face was paper thin. Cast as he was in green by the light of the Tasglann, he was gaunt as Dearil – that seventh son of the Mother, the issuer of death – made flesh.

"Ask it," Manoc said as he handed the pouch to Gunnar.

"Do you agree with Hugh and Gottfried?"

There was a wobble to Lovelace's question – a pleading note within his words that he did not intend – that reeked of desperation. Shame burned, hot and acrid, in his belly, but he had to know: might Manoc think differently? Or was he just another old man too calcified in body and mind to see that there might be another way?

The master's gaze upon him was heavy. "I agree that it would be folly to seek Alev," he said with great care.

"Fuck your semantics. Do you agree he poses no existential threat? Do you…"

"Clearly Alev is an existential threat," Manoc's voice cracked like a whip and grew so large that Lovelace shrank back. "Twelve rangers missing, presumed dead. Twenty-one nascent dactyli put to the slaughter, torn from our grasp like so many blades of grass."

"Then why not sway the council?" Lovelace reared up. "Hugh is a willow that bends to the strongest wind. You'd've outnumbered Gottfried. You could've…done something. Anything."

Manoc stiffened and brought himself up to his full height, a head shy of either man that stood before him. A wind, hollow and whistling, came up to spiral around them. The edges of Lovelace's cloak snapped around his ankles, and cold ashes were sent to scatter from the hearth.

"The worlds of men will rise and fall and I will not interfere. As leaf to wind, reef to tide, iron to forge and mount to quake, I will remain impartial. I am the keeper and the scrivener. Cuimhne Amas, I solely seek, Cuimhne Amas, I humbly protect."

Lovelace remained expressionless, listening to those vaunted words. He shoved his tongue into his cheek to stem the flood of comments welling within him, the chiefest of which revolved around the inefficient use of metaphor.

He had spoken those words, had meant them too. What boy of twelve didn't want to take an oath that joined him to a thousands-year-old order with promises of supernatural powers and sacred purpose? What boy of twelve can understand the implications of speaking such simple words, words that would forever tie his hands behind his back?

The air around them settled and Lovelace was left with a grim sense of foreboding. He supposed they could rebuild their ranks *if* they managed to find the boy who bore the white flare, and *if*, as the masters presupposed, he did indeed possess a power...beyond.

And the Grasp would suffer. For while he could not fathom the bounds of Alev's design, there was no doubt in Lovelace's mind that it was not some singular revenge he was enacting to get back at the order. How many men and women would live in the shadow of his malice? It was beyond reckoning.

But the people would rise from the ashes of whatever devastation Alev wrought; they always did. *And we will not interfere,* Lovelace thought, embittered. Never mind how much good they could do with the cumulative weight of knowledge which occupied the Tasglann, untainted by the morass of mortal design. *We will remain impartial.*

The only comforting thought that he could summon, bitter morsel though it was: Alev was systemically purging the Grasp of all potential protege. At the very least, the black dream of a dactyli army with him at the helm could be put to bed.

Manoc cleared his throat. "I will not deny that these are trying times," he said softly. "Nor will I deny that Alev is a source of terrible dread, not just to dactyli, but to all within the

Grasp. Perhaps, even beyond..." he said, raising bony fingers to tug at an earlobe as he considered his next words.

"It is important, in times such as these, to recall one of the foremost tenets of our creed: the annals of history are filled with men as terrible as Alev and trying times like those upon us. Our lives are but a sliver of the great wheel of time which ever turns."

Lovelace regarded Manoc squarely. "Charming," he said. "I love a little black despondence before a ranging, particularly one upon which you think the whole fate of the order hinges. We've a job to do, aye? So let's be on with it."

Manoc bowed his head, and Gunnar turned to stride toward the cabinet to their right. He threw open its heavy oak doors, revealing a single slender pile of verdanite, shining clear as crystal and rising to the height of a man. He paused and turned aside, the same question in his eyes that was already falling from Lovelace's lips: "Why is the raw store so low?"

"Ah," Manoc said, with the nonchalance of one pointing out animal-shaped clouds in the sky. "The gem guild sent a missive saying they can no longer transact with us. One of Osbert's latest decrees."

Lovelace frowned, moving closer to the cabinet. Gunnar took up three small pieces and Lovelace grabbed another, his mind working.

He examined the stone in his palm. It was a wondrous thing, with straight lines and sharp-squared edges, so transparent he could see the blood pact scar that ran from thumb to pinky across his palm with perfect clarity.

Except there were two scars where there ought to have been one. Birefringence, it was called, a property causing light to split into two beams when it passed through the stone. Some clever dactyli hundreds of years ago had figured out the same principle worked for preserving both sgeulachd and the myriad sgeul that went into the making of it; the finished work and its references. Verdanite could only be found deep in the mountains of Skole, the furthest northern settlement in the Grasp, and had been highly prized ever since.

Lovelace's frown deepened. "What of the mining guild?"

"I'm afraid they are similarly prohibited."

"More decrees every day," Lovelace said gruffly, pocketing the tablet. "Ready?" he asked Gunnar.

Manoc crossed his arms to his chest in farewell, and Lovelace couldn't help but notice how very small his blue-veined arms were beneath the billows of his robes.

"Remember your teachings," he said. "People are not skilled in seeing things beyond the immediate, but we are. Do not forget the sustenance upon which fear feeds." His words sent a prickle down Lovelace's spine, for they were spoken with a gravity befitting not a ranging but a final farewell, a portent for which the outlook was grim.

As Lovelace spun on his heel to depart, he caught a glimpse of Manoc turning back toward the hearth; his figure stooped, caught between green light and shadow as he stared into a cold and empty grate.

Chapter Four

Robins warbled overhead, and Kylene dug in the dirt with a fervor. The sun sank low in the Mavros Forest, bathing the wood in a golden light and taking with it her hopes of uncovering anything significant in the dirt beneath her fingertips.

She had been digging a mote around a gnarled yew tree, its trunk wider than she was tall.

She worked tirelessly, her instrument of choice a rusted hand trowel, the worn wooden handle of which had left splinters deep in her hand.

With each jab and every scoop, she recited the verses that had brought her to this place, determined to find the secrets that they held and where her father might have gone.

An oak does stand
So tall and proud
Blue spruce is evergreen

The pitch of pine
Is fine and strong
Elder endures between

A yew will keep
Your secrets all
So whisper what you know

'Tween life and death
It dwells betwixt
In light and in shadow

This was the fourth yew tree she'd delved around, her weary shoulders aching as she worked to excavate its base. The slender muscles of her forearms twitched with fatigue. She was stripped down to her shift, the thin fabric of it clinging to her like a second skin.

The night had been a restless one, and her thoughts were thick as cold stew and muddled with uncertainty. All day, she had grappled with how to feel, what to think. Memories sprang forth from her mind like weeds: her father speaking softly with strangers at the kitchen table, books stacked high on his study desk, letters sent under cover of darkness, fragments of phrases.

Were any townsfolk to happen upon Kylene at that moment, they would surely consider her quite mad, covered in dirt as she was, toiling in the earth, her scant dress a scandal.

But there was no help for it; her father was gone, and she was spinning like a weathervane in a winter storm.

By the time Kylene had come down for breakfast, her mother had left, gone to tend to the printshop and the many tasks that lay ahead. There would be favors to call in, tasks to pass on. It would take every ounce of her cunning if she were to meet the demands of the Fingers when they came calling for contributions in two months' time.

When Fabrice was relegated to the pillory, the once plump and rosy-cheeked eldest child of he and Beata was transformed into a gray slip of a thing with a lope in her gait, the result of an accident at the mill. The once brawny and jovial Beata became a mere shadow of her former self by the time Fabrice was released, as if she herself had been ground down by the family's granite millstones.

It was a water-operated mill that ran from their three-story home beside the Farrow River, and it was Fabrice who knew the workings of the gears, the intricacies of water rushing through the sluice. No amount of aid or determination could make amends for his loss.

Kylene knew it was only a matter of time before her mother would need her in the bindery.

As it was, this morning had been hers and hers alone, and she intended to make the most of it.

It was the echo of his yew verses that had brought her here. They were somehow more intact than the other half-formed yarns unraveling in her mind. Again and again, they surfaced, like buoys in a storm: Her father reciting the lines over the roar of the press. Idly repeating its verses over a summer picnic along the Farrow River. Making Kylene and Petra say the words back to him during suckling pig dinner for equinox last spring.

They felt important. She didn't know why or how; she just knew, somehow, that they mattered. So she had ventured into the heart of the Mavros Forest to delve among the towering yew trees.

Her raw and reddened hands wrapped tightly around her trowel as she fell back into the familiar rhythm of digging in the dirt.

A yew will keep
Your secrets all
So whisper what you know

Surely he's left me some clue, she thought as she hit a root, hard and unyielding. The shock of it reverberated up her arm.

Kylene couldn't shake the feeling that there was more to the story of her father than what her mother had revealed last night. He was a bellringer, she had told Petra and Kylene. But not just any old rebel, the likes of which only hint at treachery after a few pints in the pub, or nod knowingly upon overhearing a sympathetic point of view.

No, he was a leader of the movement and had been since the day Osbert came into power six years ago. Worse still, the family's printshop had been churning out pamphlets that denounced Osbert's regime, mixed in among the sanctioned work. And Mossbridge held Assembly, which meant the Fingers maintained an office in town, which meant that her father might actually be mad to carry out such activities, fraught as they were.

Kylene was well aware of the consequences of sedition. The infamous snake pit was displayed on signs affixed to walls throughout town, its imagery vivid and grotesque.

Kylene almost laughed at the irony of it. The poster she had torn down from the side of the theater that morning, as she hastened toward the Mavros Forest, had been printed by her father.

Posters of the pit had been a fixture around town for as long as Kylene could remember, but she'd never really given them much thought. They weren't heretics. Her family's press was one of Osbert's most productive. They had taken on some of his biggest and most ambitious projects.

She set down the trowel. Wiping a forearm across her sweat-drenched brow, she took the crumpled poster out of the pocket of her cloak and scrutinized its contents. A drawing, rich in detail, showed a man at the bottom of a deep pit. Surrounding him were hundreds of snakes, spitting, biting and striking at his scraggly flesh. The man's mouth was rent open in what could only be interpreted as terror.

"We do not abide snakes in the garden," it read atop the illustration and beneath it, "Death to serpents."

A shudder ran through Kylene. Sedition was a capital offense in the Grasp, and capital punishment was the pit.

A sharp wind peeled through the Mavros Forest, rattling the leaves overhead and she shredded the poster into hundreds of tiny pieces, casting them into the wind. Anger, hot and slick, surged in her breast as she watched them dance, frenzied.

Her mother said she didn't know where he was going, didn't know who betrayed him, didn't know whether they'd ever see him again. They needed to be strong, she said. For him. For each other.

He should've told us more, then at least we could be together.

The thought was a dagger thrust into the very center of her heart.

***

She dug past twilight. Until her hands were cracked and bleeding, until her back screamed in protest and yet, she discovered no secrets in all of her digging. Exhausted, she surveyed her work in the violet-blue dark of new night and felt a twinge of shame at the destruction she'd wrought, the work she'd done for nothing. Shallow trenches surrounded six of the yews in the grove, her work like some pitiful attempt at a siege against the keeps of their enormous fluted trunks.

Earlier in the day, she had whispered to one of the yews she sat beneath now, reciting lines from his poem, feeling foolish even as she spoke. She had confessed to the tree her lie about the mulberry tonic at last night's insight.

Their last insight. And here she was, talking to trees. She knew they wouldn't talk back. And even if they might, her father wasn't the sort to prance about the Mavros Forest, telling trees his darkest secrets so that they might one day relay them to his daughter in turn.

Her father was practical. *She*, was practical. If he'd done anything with a yew tree, it would be to use it as a marker, the place of burial for important materials or else...

Realization shot through her like crackling fire.

His study. She leapt from her seat beneath the yew and whirled, staring at the coiled-rope folds of its trunk. Understanding burned through her. *Of course.*

There it was. As a key slow-turns the oiled gears of its rightful hole, her father's poem clicked into focus, unlocking the truth of it in her mind.

In his study there lived a box. It was the finest box Kylene had ever seen, wrought as it was from the amber-red heartwood of a young yew, with carved peacocks and songbirds and creeping vines along its sides. It was kept on the highest shelf, alone and apart from the countless artifacts that crowded the others. And though her father was a man who loved his trinkets, the box was held apart, with no other bauble or book beside it.

She seized the trowel with her raw and bloodied hands and let her gaze travel up the yew's trunk and into its spreading canopy. Its thick limbs were bowed low with the weight of years but were not yet so heavy that they touched the earth and began to walk, spider-like, taking root beyond its trunk. *Little wonder the yew is thought to hold both life and death in its limbs,* she thought, surprised to find small reverence creeping in.

Gathering her shift, she moved as if in a dream, outstretching her hand to place a palm in something like supplication against the trunk. A moment passed, then two, and she withdrew, shaking herself of her useless reverence. With what deity was she hoping to commune?

No one in her family kept the faith. She didn't even know who was the patron son of trees, or if indeed it was a son who presided over such things. She supposed it could have been the Mother herself, who tended to and nurtured all things living, or one of her nameless Daughters. The act was a diversion that made her feel like she'd betrayed her father, who was always critical of the faith. The Mother, her Sons and Daughters: the patron deities who presided over all aspects of mortal life. "No father to speak of, and they couldn't even be bothered to give the daughters names?" He would often say. "That's not the world I live in."

She shoved all further thought aside and turned to run through the forest. The only secrets the yew had for her were in that box, waiting for her in her father's study.

She leapt over rotting logs, and snagged her shift on brambles as she flew toward home. Fatigue weighed down her legs, her skull felt as though it might split in two and her hands were scoured raw, but she paid it no mind. She had unraveled her father's riddle and now, answers – glorious and sweet – would be hers.

Chapter Five

The lights of Mortalis lay below, glimmering up from the valley like a mirror for the stars swallowed whole by the black storm above.

The one-bell ride had felt like five. *A bad omen,* Lovelace thought, water cascading down his riding cloak in rivulets. Despite the cloak's double weave, a cold, wet patch was spreading at the small of his back, and his pant legs were damp enough to need a good wringing. The horses tossed their heads restively as Lovelace and Gunnar reared up side-by-side on the edge of the ridge, the gelid wind whipping their wet manes in lashes crueler than what was ever dispensed by either man's hand.

"What do you say, Gunn? How about you give us a wee break? It's right painful, this wind," Lovelace said, the gale threatening to drown his words.

Gunnar frowned, though in truth, the expression was impossible to see, given the curtains of slanted rain and the secreting away of the moon by storm. It was more that Lovelace expected him to frown, so he imagined that he could see the expression very well, even masked as it was by shadow and storm. Despite the dark, Lovelace *could* see that Gunnar somehow managed to look more composed than Lovelace felt. There was no single thing about the outline of his bearing that suggested he might be cold or uncomfortable, not a hunch of the shoulders nor shiver of limb. Lovelace sat up straighter in his saddle and pushed the heavy, sopping drapery of his curls away from his eyes.

"Well?" Lovelace asked, rubbing numb hands together under his cloak.

"I am not a court magician who moves the wind for a jape," Gunnar said with a growl.

"Surely not!" Lovelace said. "No one could so much as look at you and acquire such a notion. A tiny respite would be nice, don't you think? Just a bit of a break as we negotiate this Mother-forsaken drop down the ridge. I'd do it myself, but I have the weakest bond with wind of all the elements. It is far too..." He paused, flicking his wrists and fluttering fingers, "...mercurial. Give me tactility. Give me stone, give me soil, give me wood, and I'll build you an entire village before you can so much as swallow a single pint but wind..." he gave an exaggerated shudder to mask what was a shiver, "...just not enough substance for me."

"You have mentioned," Gunnar said, his speech pricked through with nettles. He began to toe his horse down the steep notch descending to Mortalis below.

"Nothing lost for trying," Lovelace grumbled, leading his horse to follow down the pack mule path. They'd be warm and dry soon enough. While there was a definite dearth in Mortalis – most notably in the arenas of virtue and morality – the place certainly didn't lack for creature comforts.

Mortalis was known the Grasp over for three things: loose laws, talented women and an ale called muskhane. *Bog water,* Lovelace grimaced as Gunnar disappeared from view. Wheat-based and distilled with the potent leaves of the Motark tree, the brew was prized by a particular type of tippler for its simultaneously sedative and stimulatory properties, an alluring combination, to be sure. Lovelace was certain it was illegal, but such a distinction had never stopped the good people of Mortalis from anything before. Being forbidden only added to muskane's mystique.

The only time Lovelace drank it, he woke up on a barn roof, stripped of his purse, his pants and his dignity. He was left with a foul taste in his mouth that lingered for a week. Certain things didn't belong in ale.

His horse misstepped, and Lovelace tensed, his heart skipping a beat. This wasn't their first time using the Corlian Ridge, but previous encounters didn't necessarily enhance the experience. The other, more traveled, route, which conveniently entered Mortalis from down a gentle slope through tidy fields of wheat and stands of boxelder, would've been preferable. But, it also would've added a bell to their journey; bells were something they could not afford.

Better to take the back way, Lovelace thought drily, recalling his own words. They just had to zig and zag their horses down a granite cliffside, in driving rain and lashing wind, with no moon. His horse lost its footing again, this time pitching him forward, nearly tossing him arse over teakettle into the rump of Gunnar's horse.

Mules don't get enough credit, Lovelace thought. They'd negotiated the ridge once on pack mules and while the animals were not particularly graceful, they were as deft on their hooves as sailors on a gangplank.

They were about halfway down when Gunnar's horse tripped, took a knee and slammed Gunnar into the rock face on their left. He grunted as his shoulder connected with solid granite. It was a fortunate twist of fate that they were on a zag, not a zig; otherwise, they might've lost the horse altogether. *Gunnar no doubt would've recovered himself in some infernally graceful fashion,* Lovelace thought as he watched the shadowy outline of the man bend low and murmur some inaudible assurance into the spooked horse's ear. In moments they were off again.

As he started his horse down again, Lovelace was left to wonder whether the ridgeline had been maintained at all since its construction. No sooner did he have the thought than the path began to narrow, tapering dramatically until it was as slim as the broadside of a sword. A sickening sensation swooped low in his gut. *Not likely, then.* Dark as it was, he could not see where the path opened up again.

Willing himself not to look down, he dropped the reins and closed his eyes.

One, two, three, four. He counted steps and small mercies; the wind was northerly, and the rock face shielded them from the sweep of its icy fingers. At thirty-two steps, he wiped fresh sweat from his brow and opened his eyes to find that he was through; the path was now as wide as a broadsword was long, a distinct improvement.

He squinted to assess what degree of peril remained. One more zig and two more zags. *Thank the Mother below.* He had not come this far in life only to let a cliffside bring about his demise, no matter how sheer.

Finally, the path opened up such that two horses might fit side-by-side, and Lovelace vowed, silently, to never take the Corlian Ridge again, whatever the weather.

The rain ceased its driving and began to fall, feather-light. Clouds, gray and thin, marched north, commanded by a clearing wind so fierce it was as if their horses had been rigged with sails. "Another omen," Lovelace muttered, the chill wind on the back of his neck like icy daggers. Whether good or bad remained to be seen.

"Couldn't have let up just a bell sooner, then?" Lovelace said to no one in particular, his head upturned toward the sky. He strained his eyes and could make out the unmistakable outline of the Capering Colt, its orange lantern twitching in the distance. Paces ahead of him, Gunnar was urging his horse to a canter and Lovelace sped up to meet him.

He pulled up alongside Gunnar and felt a small sense of purpose swell within him. Maybe Manoc was right. Perhaps they would find allies here. Perhaps allies were just what the order needed. The town's lights glimmered in the distance, steadily growing larger as they drew near. Gunnar's gaze remained fixed on the road ahead, his expression inscrutable. Lovelace cleared his throat.

"I think we ought to shore up our story."

Gunnar remained silent, but Lovelace could sense his companion's attention, the weight of his gaze an unspoken reply. To be doubly sure, Lovelace cleared his throat again, this time with intention.

"What do you think about adding a bit of pomp? Really sell the whole ancient covenant thing. 'We call upon the honorable men of Mortalis to sally their pact,'" Lovelace said, making small circular motions with his right hand. "Some such honor this, glory unending that, should do the trick. Do you want to do it or shall I? It should be rather exhilarating for the townspeople, don't you think? Imagine! Hundreds of years after Kito and the general's pact, two young dactyli come a-riding in..." A familiar thrill rippled through him. It was a feeling that was always brought on by a ranging. *A good omen, then.*

"I'm sure they will find it very exhilarating," Gunnar said with a sideways glance. "I hardly think the town square will be ripe for a call to arms at this hour of night."

Lovelace waited for him to complete his thought.

"I'm not convinced we should announce ourselves at all. You know what it's like right now. Best to keep quiet, put our ears to the ground and have a word with Hovart, see if we can't round up a few good men on the underhand."

"Right," Lovelace said. Of course he was. "So we sit down in the Colt, slip in real indistinct-like. Sidle up to Hovart and get the lay of the land, the murmurings of the people, and then..."

"Why don't we just start with a pint," Gunnar said. It wasn't a question.

"Right, a pint," Lovelace said as they pulled their horses up to the small stable that ran along the backside of the Capering Colt.

From the shadows, a boy emerged. He looked Lovelace and Gunnar up and down with shining eyes and then moved on to appraising their mounts.

"Welcome to the Capering Colt, m'lords. Can I take your horses? Give 'em a rub down fine as any they've ever had, I will. Must be chilled all through with this wind." The words fell from his mouth in a stream. There was an eagerness to them that suggested he'd decided the men were worth something.

Lovelace smiled. Had their horses been bony or their cloaks threadbare, the boy would've likely melted back into the shadows. They must look fine indeed to deserve such a welcome. That, or Mortalis had fallen on hard times of late.

Lovelace hopped off his horse, patting her neck as he gathered the reins. He handed them to the boy, an idea worming its way through his mind, working to fruition. He put on a slight frown and evaluated his fingernails in a way that he hoped suggested a well-bred blend of boredom and vanity. They were cut brutally short and not oiled, but the boy didn't know that.

"The horses will take your best feed and fresh spring water. Ensure it isn't brackish. Nadine here will throw a fit if her bucket is sour," he said as loftily as possible. He pawed through his purse and plucked out a thin copper penny. He fingered it idly and cast a sidelong look at the boy before drawing a silver tun from the purse's clinking depths.

"The penny for the horses and the tun," he said slowly, looking directly at the boy for the first time. He was thin as a willow. "If you can round up three of the most able-bodied men of honor in Mortalis. Tell us your name."

"Pif, m'lord," the boy squeaked with enthusiasm.

"Pif. That sounds more like a function of the body than a proper name for a lad. Have you heard of the Covenant, young Master Pif?"

Pif nodded eagerly, his round eyes alight. "'Course, m'lord. Grew up listening to the tale of the general and all. Don't know a soul who don't know it," he said seriously.

"Good," Lovelace said as Gunnar dismounted from his horse. He could feel Gunnar's disapproval radiating from him as he came to stand in silence behind Lovelace. But the charade seemed to be getting the proper response from the boy, and he was nearly through anyway.

"I am called Lovelace, Lovelace Bedevere. And this is Gunnar Algar, and we..." he said with pronounced dignity, pressing a hand to his chest, "...are dactyli." He paused to gauge Pif's reaction to this news, which, as he correctly suspected, was one of eyes-wide, mouth-open awe.

"We have come to sally our pact with the men of Mortalis and require a small contingent to accompany us on our quest. These men must needs be of great virtue and prowess, for they will accompany us to Droch Fhortan, where we will perform epic deeds and allow temsik to unfold."

The boy called Pif gave the appearance of thinking very hard. He stuck out the tiny tip of his tongue from behind closed lips, squinted his eyes and scratched the center of his forehead with a pinky finger. Whether it was because he didn't know what virtue or prowess was or because he didn't know any men with such distinction was as yet unclear. Pif ran his eyes along the length of Lovelace, then Gunnar, then he fixed his gaze upon the silver tum, which gleamed a dull orange in the lantern light.

"Aye, m'lords," Pif said, bobbing his head. "I know of such men. We Mortalis folk are prepared as ever for the summons. Shall I bring them here for you to measure the make of 'em?"

"Yes, young Pif," Lovelace said, his voice nearly breaking as he wondered briefly what would possess a woman to name her boy such a thing. "That will do nicely. We will be below for another two bells. See that they arrive before we retire to our rooms. We will be off with the dawn on the morrow."

Pif needed no further encouragement. He bobbed his head again and just as he was about to dash off into the dark of the street, Gunnar cleared his throat. Pif took one look at him and inferred his meaning: Horses first. *Smart lad.* He took the reins of both their mounts and, with soft clicks of his tongue, ushered them into the dark stable.

"You," Gunnar said, rounding on Lovelace, "are a knob."

Lovelace shrugged. "What's the harm?" he said, "We don't want to spend any more time than we have to hanging about this tin shack of a town. Children are crafty wee things with energy to spare. I'd wager my boots you were wily at his age."

Gunnar grunted in partial concession, and they moved toward the back door of what Lovelace considered the finest establishment Mortalis had to offer. Music, laughter and clinking glassware grew louder as they approached.

Mortalis was a town of middling size and therefore boasted enough watering holes for their types to bear distinction. The Colt, a sprawling two-story stone tavern, was among the more welcoming of places, attracting patrons of all stripes. Thus, when Lovelace swung open the door, a colorful array of patrons were scattered about in various modes of recreation.

The bustling tavern ensured that their arrival did not cause much of a stir. To their left, a group of men played a raucous game of Hart and Hound at a high table beside the thick-paned smoked-glass window. Somewhere toward the front, an unseen fiddler played 'Featherbed,' a lively tune that had several folks stepping along.

Gunnar and Lovelace made their way to the bar, past several small tables lined along the right-hand wall. Painted women in garish dress had installed themselves there, many of whom *did* notice their arrival and made this known by wagging fingers or fixing them with bold stares beneath heavy lashes. They strode past, pushing their way through a gaggle of beardless boys eyeing the women with a mixture of longing and fear until they finally managed to press themselves against the bar top.

Between a wistful-looking man stirring his ale with his thumb and a woman with streaks of flour in her unruly black hair, Gunnar and Lovelace found their place. A large boot of muskhane sat empty before the woman, and she was staring listlessly at the yellow foam at the bottom of her glass. The unmistakable smell of grass that had first been pissed upon and then cut still lingered.

Hovart was in full swing. He pulled a pint of dark beer with one hand and mixed something faintly green in delicate crystal glass stemware with his other. His silvered hair was pulled back into a sleek tail, and his eyes scanned the room like a man on a duck hunt.

"All right, Hovart?" Lovelace asked, his shout barely audible over the din of the place. There was much to be said about Mortalis and its profligacy. None of the same could be said about Hovart and his enterprise. The onyx bar top was always buffed to a shine, the floors never sticky, the food fresh, and the fights mostly justified.

Hovart gave him a brief nod and then moved toward the end of the bar to serve a nervous-looking couple their drinks ensconced in crystal. He strode back and reached over the bar top to deliver the thumb-stirrer a brisk backhand.

"Come off it, Ned. Whatever it is, it can't be all bad. I can't have you sitting here looking wetter than a bedsheet; it's bad for business."

Ned appeared momentarily stunned, his thumb raised mid-stir. His gaze shifted slowly to Gunnar on his right, his eyes wide and slightly unfocused, before returning to Hovart. He fumbled in his coat pockets for an inordinate length of time before coming up empty-handed.

"You can pay me tomorrow, lad," Hovart said grimly. The young man nodded glumly, slid off his seat and sidled into the crowd. Hovart shook his head.

"Whatever troubles young folk is a world away from me. None of 'em know what it means to struggle. Soft as lambswool and nowhere near as useful. Gunnar, Lovelace."

"Hovart," Gunnar inclined his head in greeting.

"You reminded me of my Da just then, Hovart," Lovelace grinned. "Minimizing the trouble with a well-meaning thwack was his special remedy."

"Different folk need different medicine," Hovart muttered as he drew two pints with two hands.

Lovelace opened his mouth to mention that Gunnar and himself were not so old and had troubles that Hovart might find respectable when Gunnar cleared his throat and cut straight to the heart of it.

"Strange as it may sound, we are here to issue a summons for the Covenant. Do you know any men who might be adequately prepared?" Gunnar said in a rough whisper.

Hovart fixed him with a stare, his blue eyes sharp and searching. Averting his gaze, he took up a rag and wiped his bar top in tight, uniform circles. Silence stretched out between them, like a wire held taut.

When there was no more bar to buff, he looked up.

"You'll take the house supper?" he asked, as if he had not heard Gunnar and his appeal to fulfill a hundreds-year-old contract.

"Aye," Lovelace said.

"Take a seat. I'll bring it to you," Hovart said briskly.

Lovelace cast a glance at Gunnar and shrugged. They took up their mugs of ale, raised them above their heads and wove their way toward a dimly lit table in one of the tavern's many corners.

Lovelace had only taken one blessed sip of his ale and was remarking on its stoutness when a staggering figure cut a path through the bustling crowd, headed directly toward them. His gait was uneven, his face splotched, and his eyes shot through with the red of a man whose life begins and ends with a bottle. He came to a jarring halt just short of their table, misjudged its location in space and sent a substantial quantity of ale and foam flying with the impact of his swollen belly. *A past and present drunk*, Lovelace thought as he wiped flecks of foam from his beard. *Lovely.* Still, he looked formidable enough. At least that much could be said.

"Have a seat, please. Has our young friend Pif sent you to see us?" Lovelace asked jovially as he recovered what remained of his drink. Swaying slightly, the man took a chair from the next table over and dragged it scraping across the floor. He set it before them and sat upon the thing with such force that it sounded as though a leg had splintered.

"I'm hearin' the time has come to f'fill my duty," the great man said. His voice was as deep as a well and dripping with drink.

Gunnar looked about as pleased as a peddler in a rainstorm. Not that the man sitting across from them could work out as much. Up close, Lovelace could see that his eyes were unfocused; they flitted from Lovelace to Gunnar and everywhere in between like a woozy butterfly.

Lovelace was tempting fate by entertaining the man, but it wasn't as though there were legions of suitors eager to woo them.

"Got a name, fella?"

"Marcus." He had a full bottom lip that hung heavy, parting his lips and revealing a scraggly bottom row of teeth stained a light shade of green, marking him as a long-time lover of muskhane.

"Have you any skill in arms, Marcus?" Gunnar asked in a tone of voice so withering that even Marcus himself could not help but notice. The man's bloodshot eyes narrowed, briefly crossed and he brought forth a massive fist. For a moment, Lovelace thought he might wind up and bring it crashing into either of their jaws. Instead, Marcus stopped and rolled up his sleeve to show them a crudely carved tattoo of a serpent draped about the hackles of a wolf.

It was the crest of Mortalis, the symbology derived from the original pact made so long ago. The wolf was meant to represent the Mortalii and the snake, dactyli. As far as Lovelace knew, it was not a sigil that the dactyli had ever approved.

"I'm a descendant direct from the general, 'course I fight. Been trainin' since I was a spit."

Lovelace had no doubt he could fight, if he could stand up straight. "*You* are General Marcus Haver's progeny?" he asked, trying his absolute best to keep the disbelief from dripping down his every word.

"The one," Marcus said, settling back into his chair and looking mightily chuffed.

"Enjoy the grog do you, Marcus?"

He heaved his great shoulder in a shrug, "No more'n the next man."

Lovelace and Gunnar locked eyes. If the next man did happen to enjoy a drink any more than Marcus, he would most assuredly be dead.

Lovelace sniffed, drank the rest of his ale in one and set down his mug with decision.

"Right. Thank you kindly for your interest, Marcus, but the journey ahead of us will be quite dangerous, and, well, I'm just not sure you're up to snuff."

He'd said it lightly, but he knew what would happen next. One very large, muskhane-soaked man with a head swollen by tales of glory denied the call his forefathers waited for generations to hear.

It was too bad; the wolves of Mortalis had regressed to dogs to the point where even a hound would be affronted by the analogy. Men who had once perhaps been virtuous and brave had been slowly squandered over centuries of increasing idleness and excess, and Marcus here was the very paragon of decay. Not that he could understand as much.

On cue, Marcus kicked out the chair beneath him, brought himself to his full height and reared back, making to swing at Lovelace. Instead, he lunged forward and fell over like a metronome. His great frame crashed into the table, splitting it in two and sending their mugs of ale arcing into the air. Gunnar had smoothly stood up as Marcus had gone down and was patting a damp spot on his cloak with immense distaste. Knowing that Marcus would fall, Lovelace had also avoided the fracas.

The fiddler screeched to a halt. There was a collective gasp and a hush as folks peered at their previously unassuming corner. For the briefest of moments, the Colt was utterly still.

"Nothing to see here, folks; Marcus here has simply gotten lost on his way to bed," Lovelace said cheerfully. A few snickers rippled through the crowd.

Lovelace removed his luth from Marcus's firmly rooted shoes, now affixed to the wooden boards of the floor. It wasn't difficult to will the worn cork of the shoes' bottoms to sprout limbs and hook into the floorboards.

The fiddler drew one long, tentative note and then took up a much slower ballad and the chatter resumed with an awkward upswing that didn't quite match the previous tenor. Several patrons looked on, waiting to see what would happen next. Lovelace looked to Gunnar, who gestured openly, and Lovelace knelt beside the fallen log of a man.

"Look here, friend," Lovelace said, pitching his voice low. "We appreciate your willingness but we won't need your support and don't have time for trouble. If you grew up on the stories, then you know what we can do, and you have some idea of what I just did. Now I suggest you pick yourself up and leave here before I can think of something more clever to do with you."

Marcus grunted as he struggled upright, no easy feat considering he weighed about fifteen stone and was drunker than a boar in an apple orchard. Still, he persevered and managed to bring himself to his knees and, finally, his feet. He fixed Lovelace with one long, bloody look before turning and shoving his way through the crowd, the stink of his bare feet signaling his passage nearly as effectively as his girth.

Gunnar smiled, a phenomenon that never failed to surprise and delight. It somehow aged him, but not in a number of years. Instead, it served to remind Lovelace that Gunnar was indeed human and had in fact spent a defined quantity of years negotiating time and space just as any other.

"A fitting exit, Lovelace. Very inventive," he said.

Lovelace returned his grin. "Sometimes the spirit guides the luth in just such a way," he said and then, in a more sober tone, "If he had brains, he'd be dangerous. Were you planning any defense at all, or were you just intending to let him clobber me?"

Gunnar waved a hand dismissively, "You seemed to have a firm grasp on the situation. We needn't have met the man at all if you'd kept to the plan."

Lovelace recovered their empty mugs and raised them at a nearby serving girl, who curtsied primly, swept them out of his hands and sashayed out of sight. "On the contrary, my friend," Lovelace said as he knelt to detach Marcus's shoes from the floor. "Marcus confirmed what we already knew: the men and women of Mortalis are no more equipped to aid us in arms than a cat is to cuddle. We've just expedited our decision-making process."

A couple of serving boys came to haul away the split ends of the broken table as Lovelace tucked the shoes into the darkened corner behind his chair where they wouldn't be found until morning. Best to have their presence kept mum. The folk of Mortalis, unlike most of the rest of the Grasp, still saw the dactyli as sages of a sort and would be asking for all manner of charms and guidance if they knew there were two in their midst.

Hovart appeared with a small wooden bench laden with a cream-colored soup, a plate full of seeded crackers and a wedge of crumbling cheese.

"I see you've met Marcus," Hovart said, pulling up a small stool.

"And what a pleasure it was," Lovelace said. He reached for a cracker and dipped it into the soup. "We'll pay you for your table, or at the very least fix it before we go, whatever suits you. I apologize for the fuss."

Hovart waved a hand indifferently. "A fix'll do fine." He ran a large hand over his stubbled jaw and cast his eyes upwards as though consulting with a phantom advisor who might help him choose his next words. "I've given your request some thought, and I've got to level with you, boys. You'll find strength in Mortalis, wits in Mortalis, bravery in Mortalis, but all three in a single being is a rare thing." Hovart lowered his eyes gradually, fixing his fierce gaze on Gunnar, then Lovelace. Lovelace was struck by how very blue they were; like the heat of a flame not yet turned white.

"There are two who might suit, but I cannot, in good conscience, recommend them to your keeping. One is Ailwin, a young lad who works for me. Fine mind, braw. Dependable. Perhaps to a fault. But he's young, and he has his mother to care for," Hovart said, nodding his head toward a tall lad with a shock of brown curls moving about the tables, gathering glasses and chatting with patrons.

A strange look came over Hovart's features, and it took Lovelace a moment to realize it was embarrassment. "The other might be equal to the task were it not for his advancing age. As it stands, I fear he would only slow you down," he said. He looked down at his hands – the knobbed veins, the stiffness of his fingers – and turned them over slowly, a faint expression of loathing etched upon his features.

"That's alright, Hovart," Lovelace said gently, "We had orders direct from the council to make the request. Had to be done, but we are of the personal opinion that an escort is unlikely to improve matters. We'll make the journey alone and be no worse off. There is something you can help us with, however. We could do with a little provisioning. Thanks to Osbert and his trade restrictions, we're light on supplies at the Meorachadh."

Hovart nodded, relieved to be diverted. "That I can do. What are you thinking?"

Lovelace nodded at Gunnar, who began to list their needs.

"Salt fish, or any meat to last," Gunnar said. "Willow bark, as much as you can give. Ink, perhaps some scraps of parchment. And sea fireflies, if you have them. We nearly killed ourselves going down the Corlian Ridge without light."

Lovelace's eyes widened with disbelief. *Ink and parchment? What's next? Soon we'll be reduced to mere sedge farmers, with nothing but an empty hall full of memories.*

"Aye," Hovart nodded, calculating. "Room Two, it's turned down. I'll have Ailwin bring the particulars up for you soon as I can pull a little string. The fireflies will take some work, mind."

He rose to leave. Admiration and regret surged within Lovelace as he watched him walk to the bar, back straight and movements sure. So much remained unknown about the man, so much Lovelace would love to ask. What was the name for that sense of loss, that feeling of longing for something never truly known? It was an ache of a particular sort that Lovelace knew well.

"Hovart..." Lovelace called.

The silvered man turned, blue eyes ablaze.

"We'd have you in a heartbeat if you thought yourself able."

At that, Hovart grinned and inclined his head, then slid quietly back behind the bar.

***

Lovelace and Gunnar ate and drank in silence as they waited for the remaining two champions of Mortalis, as chosen by young Pif. They watched as the Capering Colt grew more boisterous, more colorful; it was, after all, the best entertainment they'd had in a moon.

The second man arrived just as they were finishing their second ale. He wore a richly embroidered navy cloak and a sordid smile that boasted more gold teeth than white. When they rejected him promptly, his smile grew wider, insincere as a thief's promise.

His name was Draven, and as he walked away, Lovelace felt a little sick to his stomach. Smiles like those were like the ghost of a knife in the back. He resolved to take extra precautions when they tucked in for the night.

"Regular old gombeen, that one," Lovelace shuddered as he watched the man slide into a seat at a table with equally unsavory-looking companions. "I wouldn't trust that man as far as I could...What's that saying again?"

"Throw him," Gunnar said. "An utterly useless phrase. I meant to ask: What's temsik?"

He was making his way through his third ale, and his gray eyes were shot through with threads of silver, a sure sign he was deep in either thought or drink. Hovart, bless him, stocked strong ale and while selective of its recipients, always ensured Lovelace and Gunnar received the right draught. Both of them were feeling the effects of it now, powerful as an undertow.

"Hmm?" Lovelace asked, shaking himself slightly. "Oh. Heard it in a sgeulachd in the Theology section of the Tasglann. Means fate. It's not from the Grasp; Dimunish, I think the faith is called."

Gunnar nodded and took another long swallow of ale. Lovelace was about to probe Gunnar for what he knew about sgeuls that had been gathered from beyond the Grasp's borders when Pif came bounding up to their table like a hare shot out of the brush.

"M'lords," Pif said, bowing and breathless. Excitement shone from his thin face and he shifted from foot to foot, unable to keep still.

"Have you met Draven and Marcus then?" he asked, eager as a rosebud in the morning dew.

"Aye," Lovelace said levelly, meeting the boy's eye. "We have."

"I'm suppose'n you'll want to know who the third is then," Pif said in a sly way that made Lovelace smile and suspect that he and Gunnar had been misled.

"We would, though even if he's as good as Draven and Marcus put together, I'm afraid he'd still be lacking," Lovelace said. He crossed his arms and leaned back in his chair. The boy was a canny wee thing.

Pif's face fell a bit, but Lovelace's words did not deter him from unraveling the yarn of his scheme. Reminiscent of a rooster fluffing his feathers, he shook himself and gave a jocular bow: cloak tucked behind his back, left leg straight as a pin, right knee bent low. Where had a grubby little stable boy learned such a proper bow? The smile on Lovelace's face grew larger; it couldn't be helped. Out of the corner of his eye he saw that Gunnar, while not precisely smiling, had a gleam in his eye.

"Pifalion Oxalis, at your service, m'lords. I can pick locks and take right proper care of horses. Decent enough with a shiv and the finest man with a slingshot you ever did see, or ever will," he added as he produced a well-polished elm wood slingshot from beneath his cloak. Pif paused and looked Lovelace and Gunnar up and down, searching for clues as to how they might be receiving his proposal. Lovelace kept his face carefully composed so as not to give the boy any inkling of feeling. So Pif continued, his words faster and higher pitched than before.

"I can cook a mean pot 'o wurstling stew and mend most types of clothing. I've never lost a fight or even been given a beating, on account of me being quick as a wink, or so says my mum. I don't eat much, and I'll do whatever you say so long as you let me come on your quest," Pif concluded, breathless, color rising in his cheeks. He took a huge gulp of air and waited for a reply, eyes roving and hopeful.

At this hour of night, the Colt was loud, the well-lubricated sound of revelry bubbling up unrestrained from every corner. But no noise in the place matched the shared uproar of laughter let loose by Lovelace and Gunnar. Lovelace pounded the bench with a balled fist, and Gunnar threw his sleek head back, his shoulders heaving.

Hundreds of years of proposed partnership and the most honest man on offer was an eleven-year-old stableboy named Pifalion. Pif for short. It was too much. For a single, suspended moment, all the weight of their state of affairs tumbled off them in waves of mirth, so thick and steady they were caught in it like flies in slow-rolling pitch.

Pif stood, still frozen in genuflection, his thin arms flung back behind him. He wore a look of utter bewilderment. For all his previous cunning, he appeared to be entirely unequipped for how to respond or what to make of the laughter that bordered delirium, risen so quickly at his expense.

Lovelace ebbed a bit, wiping the tears from his cheeks and flinging them from his beard with both hands. All sense of propriety, false or otherwise, vanished as he addressed Pif with as much sobriety as he could muster.

"Pif," he started. "Did you mean to send us the best Mortalis has on offer, or did you only mean to highlight your own valor by showing us the very worst?"

Pif's throat bobbed up and down. "Oh no, m'lords, Mister Marcus is very strong and a hundred times the son of General Marcus himself. Mister Draven is..." Pif shivered, "...very able, m'lords, very able. As for myself.." He wrung his hands as he thought hard on what to say. "...I merely thought to round out the bunch with my bevy of services."

The boy was remarkably smooth of tongue, that much was certain. Lovelace wondered how much trouble it would fetch him, if it hadn't already, in a town such as Mortalis. It was a thought that made him feel suddenly and strangely protective of the lad, a useless feeling, given that they'd in no way be able to offer the boy anything remotely resembling protection.

"Young Master Pif," Lovelace said, with all the kindness he felt in his heart, "we would be honored to add such a capable... person as yourself to our ranks." Pif beamed and straightened, his hands clasped eagerly before him.

"But Gunnar and I have decided against an entourage and, as such, must decline your generous offer, much as it pains me to say," he said, meaning it. Beside him, Gunnar nodded as he regarded the boy with a faint mixture of fascination and pity.

All the light went out of young Pif, snuffed out as suddenly as if he'd been a candle and Lovelace's words a wet forefinger and thumb.

Pif nodded mutely and dropped his gaze to his feet. "So you'll not be taking Draven or Marcus either, then?"

"Sons to dust, no. We'd sooner take you than either of those execrable excuses for men, if you'll excuse my lack of tact. No, we'll go it alone. But," he said, taking two silver tuns from his coin pouch, "your services have been excellent, and we thank you most kindly."

He reached forward and gently took Pif's hand, unfolded it and dropped both coins into his palm. "For your courage."

Pif nodded, the extra tun unnoticed in his outstretched hand. He stood up straight and bowed again. "It was an honor, m'lords," he said, with as much dignity as a broken boy's heart can muster and turned, vanishing into the crowd of the Colt as quietly as a moorland fox.

/

Chapter Six

They woke to a dawn that was fresh and crisp as a new apple, the storm of yesterday a distant dream. Lovelace and Gunnar rode through Mortalis in the quiet light of day's first rays, past the clean, shining glass of storefronts, over smooth-paved cobbles washed clean by the rain. Daybreak was not a time of high regard in Mortalis and thus, their passage through town toward the Middling Road was peaceful and full of promise.

Hovart was true to his word; when they rose that morning, a large muslin-wrapped parcel was on the desk and a note that said, 'May troubles neglect you and the Mother protect you.'

Hovart had made good on all of their requests, and then some, including also two sheathed, elegantly worked daggers made from a curious kind of an ash-gray metal that shone like oil in the sun. Where Hovart had come by two such fine pieces of weaponry was another question for another time.

As they turned away from town and onto the Middling Road, Lovelace felt the press of the hilt on his hip. The feeling of it was a comfort, and not because he felt better protected for the wearing of it. He was far more dangerous with a twig or a pebble to hand than a dagger, strange as the thought might seem to any other man. No, the dagger simply reminded him that he was not alone, and that there were still those in the Grasp that would stand with him, no matter the consequence.

The Middling Road was a dirt-packed thoroughfare as wide as two full-sized carts, in some places wide as three. It was newer than the High Road and the Bottom Road and considerably so, having been laid in the living memory of most, whereas the High and the Bottom were said to be as old as the Grasp itself. Dactyli knew this not to be true, of course, and that, in fact, the High Road had been the first road constructed 1700 years ago and added to again and again until it began the sprawling, whirling thoroughfare it was today. The Bottom was cut some 700 years later, once more and more folks began to populate the Grasp's southern portion.

It was pleasant, the Middling Road, with its clean-picked surface and bustling sense of possibility. Even in the morning light, it was abuzz with activity.

Gunnar and Lovelace rode easy so as not to draw attention to themselves, and by the time the sun had risen full in the sky, they'd already passed two peddlers, a band of troupers, several horse-drawn carriages, half a dozen carts with contents covered and a single rider on a particularly fine bay stallion. Despite Mortalis being tucked away in the grassy plains of the Grasp's southeast, it was still a well-traveled town. What the place lacked in moral and ethical fortitude it more than made up for in the way of goods and services, so Mortalis enjoyed a celebrity unknown to the other towns in the east. There were always folks coming and going to drink from its well. Since Osbert had come into power, the renown of the place had only grown.

As they journeyed on, the road began to twist and turn, its path becoming more serpentine as they left behind the plains of the south, with its shocks of yellow sneezeweed and purple fringe, for wooded glades and sloping hillscapes that grew steeper with each bell that passed. They were not far from the crossroads now, not far from where they would change their route and take the High Road. Seeing as how both the High and Bottom roads were prohibited from use, Lovelace was enjoying their last few moments before he would necessarily need to revert to the status of an outlaw. Not that he wasn't already an outlaw by the very nature of his being a dactyli, but ordinary passersby didn't know that. Out here on the road, Lovelace looked like any other man.

They rounded another curve in the road, surrounded on either side by a glade of dogwood trees toward the end of their bloom. Their mildly offensive scent was so diverting that

Lovelace barely noticed Gunnar pull up short before him. *To say rotten fish would be a kindness,* he thought as Gunnar made a short hissing sound through his teeth. Lovelace looked up. They were roughly one hundred paces from a band of peacekeepers, almost hidden from sight at the long end of the curve. Lovelace subtly reared his horse and sidestepped her toward the edge of the glade and away from the road, where Gunnar waited like a loaded spring.

There were six in all, recognizable by the white horse-hair plumes which sprouted from their polished steel helmets. Lovelace and Gunnar retreated deeper into the glade, though it seemed they were in no danger of being noticed. The peacekeepers' attention seemed wholly consumed by a clamor akin to a nursery with several dozen squalling babes. The hairs pricked up on the back of Lovelace's neck as they carefully led their horses away from the road.

He dismounted, handed his lead to Gunnar with a nod and crept closer, stopping short behind a boulder. Crouching there, he peered over its lichen-encrusted surface to find the peacekeepers' efforts focused on an elderly man. Beside him was an old handcart with high walls and peeling paint, turned on its side. The man was, justifiably, in hysterics. Twenty-odd squealing piglets ran amok as the cart driver scrabbled around in an attempt to recover them. He had scooped up two of the frantic things and tucked them under one arm and was reaching for a third when he was seized by two peacekeepers and forced to his knees.

"Your scroll," said one of the peacekeepers distantly, his hand outstretched. He was still horsed and had a casual demeanor, entirely unperturbed by the riot of piglets skittering underfoot. This close, Lovelace could see the finely wrought filigree around the winged edges of the man's helmet, glinting in the sun.

The cart driver gave no reply and instead made a grab for another nearby piglet who was happily bathing itself in the dust of the road. At this, the horsed peacekeeper nodded and the cart driver's captor slapped the man across the face, hard.

"Answer," his captor grunted. Shocked, the cart driver drew back, and a red spot bloomed on his unshaven cheek. The remaining two piglets that he had managed to tuck under either arm wriggled free.

"I have it here, sirs...I had it here, if you'll only give me a moment to find it somewhere in my things." His eyes darted frantically to and fro as, one by one, his hogs disappeared between the dogwood trees, curled tails vanishing beneath the carpets of sweet woodruff running rampant beneath their trunks.

One of the escaped piglets slowed to nose around at the base of a dogwood near Lovelace. A sudden urge to grab it seized him, to preserve it for the man's keeping; the piglets were, after all, likely the man's livelihood. He stared at its pink snout as it rooted around, avid and snuffling, and knew that he could not take hold of the little creature without alerting the peacekeepers to their presence.

A sick feeling was settling in Lovelace's stomach as he crept back toward Gunnar and the horses. *Poor chap*, he thought, nodding to Gunnar as he swung himself back onto his horse. They moved further into the glade until the sharpness of the piglets' squeals lost its edge, until the sounds of woodland enveloped them entirely. It was a light sound: airy and open, teeming with earnest birds' trills and whoops. The wood remained indifferent to the misdeeds transpiring within its borders. Not half a mile away, the harassment of a man continued, his mistreatment unremarked upon, for the wood had seen it all before, and would see it all again.

But the wood was aware. It remembered, remembered everything it saw. But not as men and women remember, whether fair or foul or fickle. It did not change the things it had seen for convenience or advancement of its own aims. And this archive, this recollection of events, did not become muddled or metamorphose over time. The memories lived, unspoiled, for as long as the thing that saw it remained whole. Large stones and tall trees were best, of course, as they were the most fixed, the most firmly rooted in the fabric of time and space. It was this crystallization of *things,* this keen sense of awareness, that the dactyli had discovered, and it was what underpinned their ceaseless quest for truth.

"Anything worthy of mention?" Gunnar asked, drawing Lovelace from his reverie.

Lovelace shrugged. "Looked like a scroll stop. You know the kind. The fellow's robes were tattered, and he was unkempt as anything, but those were his piglets, no question about it. They probably took one look at him and assumed he stole 'em, treating him like downright vermin with no probable cause."

"Cold iron," Gunnar grunted, his face a canvas for his unspoken disapproval.

"Keepers of the peace indeed. I'd like to serve a little roadside justice of our own to those little pricks," Lovelace said. He absently plucked a fallen dogwood bloom from his horse's mane. The round, wilted petals were the precise shade of the piglets.

"Roadside skirmishes are not the dactyli way," Gunnar said, sounding remarkably like Manoc. "I wonder how many more we will encounter before we reach the crossroads. Their presence thickens with each ranging. I like it not."

Lovelace grunted. "We'll see how much longer the dactyli *way* remains a path to follow if Alev has anything to do with it. What're the odds he's already had done with this white flare?"

Gunnar's eyes narrowed. "Cynicism is not your color, Lovelace."

Lovelace grinned; it was the closest thing to a joke Gunnar had told in recent memory. Still, his amusement was a shallow pool.

"I'm serious, Gunn. You ever think about life beyond the dactyli way? Think of what we could do for the people of the Grasp. Think what we could do to a pack of peacekeepers like that next time we run up on them giving an honest man trouble."

"You don't know whether he's honest," Gunnar said plainly as he took his horse right, back toward the road.

Lovelace's horse snorted, sensing the tension of its rider. "I don't know that he's not! How'd you like to live with everyone assuming you'd done something wrong, that your mere existence was enough to warrant suspicion? I tell you, it does something to a man to make him feel guilty just going about his business."

Underneath Lovelace's skin, anger simmered. Over the past eleven years, they'd gathered enough sgeuls to witness much of the injustice wrought by Osbert's rule, even if they were not his citizens. But were they not, in some way, subject to his tyranny? Osbert had, after all, slandered their order, decried dactyli as charlatans of the worst sort; serpents that befouled the garden – his garden, the filthy, insatiable, lying swine.

The low-hanging branch of an oak scraped against Lovelace's cheek, drawing blood. "Son of a Motherless sodding cretin," he cursed and pressed a hand to his cheek. He glanced ahead to Gunnar, who, straight-backed and silent, seemed to be having considerably less trouble in the general run of things. *Bloody man was born with half a heart,* he chafed, turning his horse to follow.

*****

They approached the crossroads with enough light in the sky to see the clearing before them waver with the dying heat of day. After bells of hard and hot riding, they brought their horses to a walk as they approached the meeting of the roads.

The Crossbones – known for its peculiar decor of bones marking the intersection of each road at its center – resembled a poorly crafted wheel. The Middling and High roads, along with several narrow byways no wider than a country lane, protruded from its center like mismatched spokes. Lovelace had traveled through the Crossbones countless times and had only ever seen animal bones adorning the thoroughfare; the knobby legs of a chicken or the curved ribs of a hog. As the Middling Road deposited them into the clearing, they walked past a set far too large to belong to any creature in the vicinity, propped up against a nearby oak. A sudden chill gripped Lovelace. Against a nearby oak stood a pair of long white bones that were unmistakably human, the smooth rounded top reminiscent of the handle of a walking cane.

Lovelace's features contorted into a practiced nonchalance, concealing any trace of surprise. He surveyed the wide clearing – hemmed in by gnarled oak trees and dotted with wagons and small makeshift camps – and noted a conspicuous lack of peacekeepers. Amid the sea of canvas and tarpaulin, one imposing bell tent stood tall, reaching half the height of the towering oak under which it had been erected. The presence of human bones notwithstanding, it was a familiar sight. Such scenes were common at crossroads throughout the Grasp, providing wayfarers with temporary refuge among the company of strangers.

Lovelace stole a glance at Gunnar and inwardly groaned. His companion's jaw was tightly clenched, his chin held high, and his eyes flashed silver as he scanned the Crossbones with the wary hostility of a man expecting an ambush. *And I'm supposed to be the one who can't keep my sentiments to myself,* Lovelace thought wryly. *So much for passing through unnoticed.* Neither of them was particularly subtle looking to begin with, but a person's expression and posture are the opening lines of a story. While Lovelace settled easily into "beleaguered traveler of little importance," Gunnar didn't derivate from "man with whom you absolutely do not wish to trifle."

As expected, Gunnar's presence in the clearing had an immediate effect. Like a pebble dropped into still water, the travelers' faces rippled with varying degrees of hostility, intrigue or fear. Lovelace sighed inwardly, resigning himself to the fact that they were unlikely to pass through unnoticed. He inclined his head to a group of peddlers gathered around a small campfire, passing a skin between them. They hardly spared him a glance, but their eyes were fixed on Gunnar with open apprehension, the skin momentarily forgotten and held aloft in the brown withered hand of the oldest of the three.

They moved past a hooded figure brushing down a weary-looking nag, a mother and her small children darning cloth out of the back of a tattered wagon and a trio of well-groomed young men whose appearance raised suspicion. On a large, tawny hide from a beast that Lovelace did not recognize, the men played Japes, their laughter clear, bright, and unspoiled by hardship.

When they passed the final camp and were almost through, a shout rang out from behind.

"Hoy, dactyli!"

They turned to behold a hollow-cheeked and pock-marked man whose tattered garments hung loosely on his emaciated frame. He stood with one fist clenched and raised halfway to his chest as if he meant to beat his breast but lacked the vigor to do so.

"False shepherds," he said in a dry, cracked voice. "Yarn spinners. I wish ye a death that's painful slow and just o'er the horizon, ye fruitless sons of whores." He spat and stiffened, standing as tall as his warped body would allow. His neck remained craned forward, his shoulders rounded and stooped, as if he had spent his life tethered to a yoke like a beast of burden.

Lovelace froze, his heart pounding in his chest. Though the man posed no real threat, the venom in his words struck

Lovelace like a lash. Gunnar's quicksilver gaze flashed in warning, communicating a message clear as a bell: not today.

Tension thickened in the air and a myriad of unhelpful impulses consumed Lovelace. A physical reprimand was out of the question. And what good would it do to tell the wretch off? Sadness flowed through him, sticky like sap, staining his insides with regret for how far the dactyli had fallen in the eyes of those they'd only ever sought to help.

Bluffing their way down the Middling Road was a useless endeavor now. Taking the High Road was a punishable offense, but who cared? All pretense had been shattered by the simple, scathing words of one embittered man.

Without a word between them, Gunnar veered sharply to the right, his intentions mirroring Lovelace's own. They urged their horses forward to a gallop and charged down the High Road, kicking up dust and leaving the hostile horde of Graspish people in their wake.

***

They rode until full dark, until the pale eye of the moon peered down at them through the canopy of overgrown forest that threatened to devour the High Road whole. The air had grown thick with thunder, and when the clouds gave way to crack beneath the weight of rain, Lovelace and Gunnar left the road and made camp in the protective crook of the exposed roots of an ancient cedar tree.

Tomorrow, they would ride hard for Droch Fhortan. And ride hard, they must. They could not afford a leisurely passage; who knew whose eyes had been watching at the Crossbones and what intentions lurked in their hearts?

Tonight, they would sleep beneath the cedar tree's boughs and endure the storm that gathered around them.

Only when a fire burned low between them, and they had filled their bellies with half a loaf of bread and an entire bottle of ale, did Lovelace finally turn to Gunnar.

"Gunnar, I've been thinking..." Lovelace started.

Gunnar raised his eyebrows warily, as if Lovelace had said something vaguely dangerous.

Lovelace let out a long-suffering sigh as he faced Gunnar. "I've asked before," he said, frustrated already by the lack of insight he was likely to receive.

"You're always stirring up silt with no answer in sight, and even then, only if you're in a generous mood." He remembered the last night he'd asked, in a tavern on the outskirts of Omnia, and how Gunnar had locked eyes with Lovelace, looking for all the world like he might, for once, give Lovelace an honest response. He instead took a long draught and told Lovelace his beard had ale foam in it.

Gunnar was reclined by the fire, poking at the smoldering branches with a stick. He pursed his lips and did not look up.

Gunnar hated personal inquiry, small talk, talking in general. But that didn't stop Lovelace from trying. Lovelace felt the same way about silence as Gunnar did about speaking, and he considered himself the keeper of a fair balance between the two of them. They were both stubborn men, and where Gunnar was iron-willed, Lovelace was persistent.

So, when he did not respond, Lovelace pressed him further, "Look, Gunn, I know that talking about anything deeper than a muddy puddle is not your highest joy but given the state of affairs, who knows how much longer we have?" Lovelace added a faint but pleading note to his question, hoping to appeal to Gunnar with the ephemerality of life and the mounting danger they found themselves in.

To his bewilderment, Gunnar nodded at him, "Go ahead then, say your piece."

Lovelace shifted his weight, leaning against the gnarled roots at his back. He drew in a deep breath, preparing to articulate his thoughts with care. "When we are not channeling our luth, when we are just..." he paused to find the proper wording, "...ordinary men – you know, chopping wood, drawing water from a stream. How then do you keep the sgeuls of the world from running around like mad in your head? How, after everything you've learned, you...and I, being what we are – how do you stop yourself from venturing out to try and save everyone?"

Gunnar's eyes darkened as he fixed Lovelace with an unyielding stare, a frown creasing his forehead.

"You're right. You have asked me this many times," he said, pausing as he pushed himself up to a seated position. "When's the last time you used an ax to chop wood?"

"It happens more than you might think," Lovelace said through his teeth.

"Furthermore," Gunnar said, brushing cedar needles from his elbow, "no one has had to restrain you from rushing in to save everyone. You could've come to the aid of that pig farmer, but you did not. Why? Because you know, as well as I do, for all your lofty notions, that it would have been a miscalculation. And you have learned, as I have, that we cannot afford to make miscalculations. Where would you even begin, knowing what you know? Where is the most important place to turn your efforts? Would it be famine? Disease? What of war? Political unrest? We have learned many things from our exposure to the world of truth, and the foremost of them is this: Wicked people will always do wicked things, and good folk will suffer. It is the nature of things."

It was more than Gunnar had said in one breath for an age. Lovelace opened his mouth to retort but instead mumbled, "I wouldn't exactly say it is the *foremost* of things..." He stopped himself from saying more. To that point, they would never agree, so he said nothing at all, lest he discourage his companion back into silence.

Gunnar was staring into the fire, chewing slowly on his heel of bread. Lovelace watched the flames hiss and pop, hoping that he might speak again.

"I suppose there is no time when I am just a man, that is, when I am without my luth," Gunnar said.

Lovelace stared at him in disbelief. "Is such a thing even possible? We weren't taught anything of the sort." In fact, there had been no teachings whatsoever around the mental or emotional aspects of being a dactyli. They had learned only instructions and discipline.

And power, a power that was beyond belief, but bridled always by purpose.

Gunnar's smile twisted into a grimace, and he still would not meet Lovelace's eyes. "I learned early on that I could not be what we are or know what we know and live," he spoke in a voice like brittle steel, "So I hardened my heart. I saw no other way."

Lovelace thought back to a younger, angrier Gunnar, who spoke even less than he did now.

"But you were always cool as marble," Lovelace commented. "Surely your heart was already hard."

"My heart was broken," Gunnar said roughly. "It was not hard."

Lovelace found himself leaning forward, so close to the fire that he could feel the heat of it crisping the hairs of his beard. He sat back and considered this revelation. He and Gunnar were like pups from the same litter, yet Gunnar's past, his regrets, his desires for the future remained hidden from Lovelace, as mysterious as the inky underbelly of the moon. He kept them locked away with his luth, but how?

Lovelace pondered his next words. He longed to pour out his troubles, let them mingle with Gunnar's, and perhaps find solace in their shared despair. But he knew better. To do so would only cause Gunnar to fortify his defenses until they were once more impenetrable.

"Will you tell me, then? How it is you can maintain your luth at a constant?"

Gunnar chewed on the last of his bread, brushed beads of rainwater from his cloak and took a respectable swallow from his bottle of ale. Lovelace waited.

"I suppose when I am not focusing it on a task, when I am 'chopping wood and drawing water from a stream,' as you say, it is still with me." He furrowed his brow in dissatisfaction and waved his hand aside as if to clear a fog.

"When channeling my luth, there is no separation between it and me. Every sgeul, every emotion, every thought is tightly bound by it. I am bound by it, like chainmail. We are one." He tightened his hand into a fist to emphasize his point.

Lovelace nodded, this part he knew full well, only he'd always visualized his own luth as more of a sturdy fabric with a tight weave.

"Well," Gunnar shrugged. "When I am not channeling, my luth covers me lightly, like a veil of smoke. Sgeuls are still there but I can only see their shapes, silhouetted and colorless."

"But you are still channeling, if your luth is still there," Lovelace said.

"Only sparingly," Gunnar said.

"It's a feat beyond reckoning," spoke Lovelace. "Nigh impossible."

To draw upon the luth, one must possess an unfathomable degree of concentration, a skill that took them both years to hone. Yet, such mastery came with a cost. Petty displays of power, like unlocking the stone door at the Meorachadh, were trivial on their own, but they accumulated quickly. A day spent performing such acts would render one listless, their head slumping into their soup come suppertime.

But grander feats of channeling were altogether different. The senses dulled, and sounds faded, colors went pale one by one. Someone could be engulfed in flames and still shiver with a chill in their marrow, uncertain if they still breathed. At a certain point, one simply...ran out. Lovelace had collapsed and lost consciousness precisely twice because of such channelings. He had needed weeks to mend.

Fabled were the dactyli who delved even deeper, who channeled their luth beyond senselessness. The extent of their ventures remained unspoken, for the tales were too ghastly to recount. Stories of men with eyes like pools of milk and pallid skin who neither spoke nor seemed to hear. They lived but only just, dependent upon others to feed, clothe and care for them.

"It's no wonder you sleep like a standing horse," Lovelace said, his voice tinged with awe.

Gunnar fixed him with a penetrating stare. "Are you finding your circumstances to be an improvement upon mine?"

Lovelace faltered, uncertain of how to answer. If what Gunnar said was true, it meant he'd spent years depleting his life force faster than he could replenish it, exerting a measure of control beyond what they'd been taught. Lovelace conjured an image of Gunnar as a hollow shell, his eyes vacant and lifeless.

He reached out for the bottle and took a gulp of the bitter brew to clear his throat and his mind of the image.

"How did your heart get broken?"

Gunnar's eyes blazed, their intensity almost blinding in the flickering light of the flame. His voice, when he spoke, was soft as a sunrise.

"She..." He began and stopped abruptly, his spine rigid.

One word, and Lovelace's jaw dropped. But he heard the same faint rustling noise that gave Gunnar pause and recovered himself, tuning his ears to the disturbance. It was growing louder, competing with the keening of the wind.

With a nod to Gunnar, Lovelace rose to his feet, centering himself and seeking out that place of silence in his mind. Thoughts hurtling like shooting stars settled to glitter, cold and clear, against a black velvet expanse.

Gunnar was standing beside the cedar tree, his eyes closed. The flapping edges of their cloaks ceased, and the drumming of the rain grew distant. The wind's agitation could still be heard, but it could not penetrate the cavity created by Gunnar's luth. In the time it took to butter bread, they had transformed themselves from hunted to hunter.

They moved quickly, smoothly and without speaking. Twenty paces, and they were nearly on top of their pursuers. In that space of time, Gunnar had summoned an orb of fireball lightning, a fiery mass the size of a pumpkin that glowed red, orange and yellow. It hovered dangerously at Gunnar's fingertips, hissing and spitting sparks that sizzled and sputtered on the damp forest floor. By the bound lightning's light, Lovelace could make out two shadowed figures grappling in the mud.

He closed his eyes and the ground beneath the two silhouettes collapsed under them with a great crack, trapping them in a hunter's snare. Lovelace leaned over to peer down into the pit and noticed that one of the two figures was quite small. *More's the pity,* he thought grimly. A woman, perhaps. Though any woman that had managed to find them on the High Road in this kind of storm was one of whom to be most wary.

Gunnar stepped forward toward the edge of the hole and willed the fireball to descend into the freshly sunken pit. The smell of faint decay, that strange, sweet signature of the underland rose as the fireball sank lower. When it came to a hairsbreadth from the heads of the now-stilled shadows, they peered down to behold their quarry.

The scraggly face of Pif, the stable boy and Ailwin, Hovart's barkeep, gazed up at them with eyes wide, the pair of them sodden to their shoes. Underneath the leaves and mud plastered to their faces, they both wore expressions of unfeigned amazement.

Gunnar's fireball vanished with a crack, leaving behind an afterimage that seared Lovelace's vision. He blinked several times to clear the phantom lightning and considered the best means of rescuing the boys. Somewhere beside him, Gunnar was muttering blackly.

His vision adjusted to the dark and he scanned the surroundings for a suitable tool – a rock, a thick tree branch, anything that would suffice. He wasn't keen on digging up more earth, so he settled on a cedar sapling whose roots dangled treacherously over the edge of the freshly sunken pit. Focusing his luth, he trained his gaze on its reedy excuse for a trunk and envisioned a ladder.

In the eye of his mind, he envisioned a ladder and conjured the wisdom of a winged cedar seed, with its earnest knowledge for how and when to sprout and grow. He envisioned a ladder, and imbued the sapling with the energy of springtime growth. He envisioned a ladder, and willed the tree to sprout rungs and rails, heard slithering and snapping as the roots of the cedar grew tenfold, thickening and reaching and curling until it reached all the way down to the bottom of the pit.

Lovelace inspected the gnarled aberration of the cedar's newly forged root system, reaching down the side of the pit's wall. It was a pithy thing, but it would suit. Briefly, he wondered what would happen to a sapling with such prodigious roots, then leaned over to call into the dark earth.

"Come out of there, quarter-wits. It's story-time for the pair of you."

The hesitant voice of Pif echoed up, "If it's all right with you, m'lord, I think I'd rather keep myself down here for a spell."

His words were followed by tentative scuffling; Ailwin was making his way up the ladder. Moments later, he pulled himself up and over the mouth edge of the pit. He stood there, silent and shamefaced, a flash of lightning revealing damp curls clinging to his forehead.

Gunnar turned back toward camp. The wind and rain returned in force as soon as he turned heel.

"Come on out, lad. If it's punishment you're afraid of, I won't hurt you," Lovelace called to Pif. Then, muttering, he added, "Though I can't say the same for Gunn."

He turned to Ailwin.

"Thought you'd have yourself a little adventure, eh? He's just a boy; what's your excuse?"

"Nothin' for me at home, sir," Ailwin said.

"You might be right about that," he said with a grudging nod as the top of Pif's head poked out from around the twisted tree. The boy's eyes shone from the mouth of the hole, like those of a mouse unwilling to abandon its hiding place.

"That'll do," Lovelace said, and he grabbed Pif by the scruff of his coat, hauling him out.

He marched the two of them back to camp, where Gunnar was polishing off the last of their ale. Lovelace sat them both beside the fire, broke what was left of his bread in two, and handed a piece to each boy.

"Answers, now. You first," he nodded at Ailwin, who held his piece of bread in cupped, quivering hands as if it might implode. Lovelace produced his spare cloak from his satchel, tossed it to Ailwin, and then looked to Gunnar. He didn't move. Lovelace rolled his eyes and tugged Gunnar's spare from his satchel. The woolen garments were woven with fine-waxed thread and were a vast improvement over the soggy, tattered jackets that barely shielded either boy from the rain.

With some reluctance, Ailwin stripped the sodden coat from his shoulders and examined the spare he'd been given, his eyes traveling over it in open fascination.

"But how is this not wet?"

"Beeswax thread finer than you could dream of," Lovelace said. "Speaking of dreams, I'd like to have a few before the dawn breaks, if you'd be so kind…"

Ailwin draped the woolen cloak around him and took a deep breath.

"I overheard the request you made of Hovart…"

"Ah," said Lovelace.

"…and I knew I was meant to go," he said. "I pledge myself to the dactyli brotherhood, as I'm sure my father would have done, and his father before him. I…" he leaned forward as if he might kneel, and Gunnar shoved him back down.

"Don't…" He growled.

The boy had the decency to look mildly abashed but managed to continue.

"I promised my mother that I would not fall the way of depravity, as so many do in Mortalis. She was convinced that the dactyli…she knew one once, or so she said. A good man, she thought. She was convinced that one day the brotherhood would have need, that one day they would come calling. And last night! There you were. Just like she always said. And I kept my honor, always, as she said I must," he finished out of breath, with a stolid earnestness that made Lovelace fight back a smile.

"And you thought it would be best to bring along an esquire?"

Pif, who was drowning in the spare cloak, glowered at Ailwin. He shook his head vehemently. "No, m'lord, we followed you separate, only just stumbled into each other a'fore you found us," he said.

"He bit me," Ailwin said with quiet disgust.

"So I'm to understand you both managed to track us, unseen, for the entirety of the day, unbeknownst to each other and unbeknownst to us?"

Pif's eyebrows shot skyward and he nodded eagerly. Ailwin shrugged.

"And just how did you manage that?" Gunnar asked, sinister-soft. Lovelace could see Ailwin pale by the light of the flickering fire. *Good, at least the boy can sense peril.*

Pif, on the other hand, did not seem to notice that Gunnar was both very displeased and very dangerous.

"I knew you'd have to make for the crossroads, at least..." he started with apparent self-satisfaction, "...and seeing as I couldn't time a ride precise-like when you left, me having no horse and not wanting to steal and all, I hitched a ride with Old Gerold. He always leaves when the moon is high, for his trade, see. Says the sun is bad for his eyeballs, makes him sneeze. Anyway, I hitched with him all the way to the crossroads and waited for you there. When you finally came in, all fine-like and proud at eventide, oooh such a great kerfuffle was caused after you made for the High Road. Mighty strong opinions flying about the clearing and some none too generous, you ought to know. I'd made my own camp to bide the time and I suppose I meant to flag you down once you'd got there but you were off like birds and no hope for me catching you so I ran and ran down the High Road 'til 'twas full dark with no sight of you, just hoof prints slow turning to mush with the rain and all. And then, Ailwin here rode past me on just about the oldest nag I ever did see. By the Mother's bones, he gave me such a fright. I called out to him, figured he must be following you as well. We walked along for a while, him refusing to let me go further, me insisting that of course I would be...it was my plan to begin with, I said, I've just as much right to be here as you do. Then he noticed your horse tracks going off into the thicket and turned and told me to stay with the nag, lest she spook in the storm. I followed him of course and well, now we're here."

He looked at the two of them, beamish and breathless, puffed up and proud like a tiny kingfisher who had just nabbed a fish twice its size.

Lovelace sat back, mildly stunned.

"Clever, really, waiting at the crossroads. A guess with good chance, but clever nonetheless," he muttered to himself.

"Clever?" Gunnar snarled. "Clever? Don't praise the boy. It was luck in insane quantities. You," he practically spat at Ailwin, "are twice his age and, therefore, twice the fool."

"Perhaps also twice as lucky," Lovelace said thoughtfully. "You'll have to excuse Gunnar, boys. He doesn't really know how to speak to children, doesn't really know how to..."

"I'm not a child!" said Pif and Ailwin as one.

"And what do you propose we do, Lovelace, with two boys greener than moss on the north side of a tree?"

"Well, we can't send them back. It's a miracle they made it this far," Lovelace said.

"Of course we can't send them back. If the folks at the crossroads were talking, as he says, at least one of them has told the nearest pack of peacekeepers about two dactyli going down the High Road with two boys on their heels."

"My coin's on the poxed man," Lovelace muttered.

"I'm not as green as you'd think," Ailwin protested.

"And I'm not lucky," Pif insisted, "Just savvy is all."

"That kind of attitude will get you killed, lad," Lovelace said sternly before turning to Gunnar.

"Come on, Gunn, you know as well as I do they can't go home by themselves; they'll get taken up by some peacekeepers quicker than you can make lightning strike. Mother help any other lone boys on the road that might dimly match their description. We'll keep them with us for the ranging, have them keep as quiet and out of the way as possible," he said, staring Pif down pointedly, "If we do our jobs right, like we always do, we'll detain the white flare, deliver these two to Mortalis safe as kittens, then home again, home again, jiggity jog. Thus will begin the great rebuilding of the brotherhood dactyli."

If Gunnar's eyes were capable of rolling, which Lovelace wasn't entirely sure they were, they would have at that moment. "They are an even greater danger to us than they are to themselves," Gunnar said, his arms crossed.

"No help for it, Gunn, we're duty-bound."

Cheerful as a pig in shit and twice as stubborn was what his Da had always said of Lovelace. As a way of living, it had generally worked well for him.

Gunnar propped up his satchel to use as a pillow and said nothing.

"Come on, Gunn, the irony. Taste it! The ancient pact is upheld for the first time since its inception – how many centuries ago, seven hundred? – by a pair of bright-eyed boys, one of whom could be carried away by a gust of wind, both of whom possess far bigger stones than you or I have got," Lovelace said with a laugh. He couldn't help it. What would Manoc say? No sooner did he conjure the image than he realized that he was perhaps the only dactyli left with a sense of humor.

And still, Gunnar said nothing.

"That was elegant, your fireball lightning. That's what that was, wasn't it? Can't say I've ever seen anyone do that," Lovelace said, half hoping to pour oil on troubled waters, half genuinely awed by Gunn's instinct.

To his satisfaction, Lovelace saw a slight easing of the tension in Gunnar's shoulders. *He's been routed, and he knows it.*

"It was easy enough with this storm," Gunnar said. "All I had to do was borrow and build." Without another word, he drew his cloak tightly around him, settled himself on his satchel and turned his back to the warmth of the fire.

It wasn't as though Lovelace found great joy in assuming the responsibility of two boys who were not only recklessly overzealous but also seemingly unaware of the very danger that came with their zeal. He shared Gunnar's apprehension, yet he set great store in the irony of the world. If these two green boys were indeed the ones to fulfill a hundreds-year-old pact, who was he to deny the exquisite beauty of such a twist of fate? *That* was temsik, if he remembered rightly. And it was true; they couldn't very well send them back the way they'd come.

Lovelace eyed the boys levelly.

"You'd better pray to whomsoever is your patron son or daughter that that nag is where you left her in the morning, unless you wish to ride two on a saddle with him tomorrow," he gestured toward Gunnar.

"I tied her up proper a'fore I followed Ailwin, m'lord. She should be alright" Pif replied.

"Assuming she didn't choke herself to death from fright with this storm..." Ailwin muttered.

Pif scowled at him and began to fashion a makeshift bed out of leaf litter. With a bow of his tiny head toward Lovelace, he nestled beneath his cloak and fell asleep in mere moments.

Lovelace watched the boy fall asleep with envy. When he did sleep, it was the sleep of a man half-dead, worn out by days of hard riding or stretching the limits of his luth.

And his dreams were always sgeuls, never visions of the promise of tomorrow or distant realms full of color and wonder. He relived only the past – sgeuls of his Ma and Da, his brothers and sisters. Sgeuls of boys he and Gunnar had found – would-be dactyli – like seeds in barren soil, never to take root and sprout.

Ailwin's concerned voice pulled him back to the present.

"Are you alright? Your eyes were turned to glass, staring into the fire like that. I've been saying the same thing to you over and over."

Lovelace looked at Ailwin and, for the first time, really saw him. His eyes were long of lash and brown and set in a face shaped by high cheekbones, his mouth hard-lined but not so severe as to be grim. He looked like he didn't smile much. *The boy's had his share of hardship,* Lovelace thought. There was a slow-burning hunger in those eyes, fierce with longing.

"I'm sorry, lad, go on and give me a good shake if you catch me like that again. What was it you said?"

Ailwin peered at him curiously from beneath those thick lashes. "I only meant to thank you, for taking me on. For not making me go home..."

"Don't thank me until it's over. You haven't even had the good sense to ask what it is you've gotten yourself into," Lovelace said. He poked and prodded at the oddments in his satchel to make it smooth enough for sleep.

Ailwin smiled thinly, "I hope not to disappoint you," he paused, hesitating, and awkwardly added, "I'm sure I will learn a great deal."

"I'm sure you will, lad," Lovelace said. "I'm sure you will."

Chapter Seven

Hammer blows on hot steel, that's how Kylene's heart felt as she tiptoed through the garden, the rhythm so full in her ears that she could scarcely hear anything else in the night.

She'd waited until her mother had gone to bed, until the splintered moon had risen and begun to fall again. Her mother would be worried and no doubt thought that Kylene had run off to search for her father. But Kylene knew *that* would be foolish. She had seen the peacekeepers lurking around town when she'd returned from the wood, and she knew why they were there. They were there for her father. But they wouldn't find him, and if she wasn't careful, they would catch her before she could decide what to do.

So she had waited, waited until the night was still and silent. Waited until she could reclaim the yew box in secret. When she'd emerged from the Mavros Forest to find six peacekeepers knocking on Mrs Halsey's candle shop next door, it was like a great invisible hand pressed against her chest, holding her back. She knew they weren't looking for her, and yet...

Kylene crouched low by the back porch and groped in the dark for one particular log among the timber stacked against the side of the house. The scarce moonlight did little to guide her, but she didn't need it. With a quick tug, she pulled out the log and retrieved a key from a hidden compartment beneath it. To the unobservant eye, the smooth ash log, stripped of its bark, was just one among many in the stack of rough-chopped oak. It was as obvious to her as an apple in a barrel of oranges. But then, people rarely do pay attention to details, or so her father had told her when he shared the secret key with her all those years ago. Kylene thought that he was right, mostly.

She slid the brass skeleton key into the lock and turned it with a quiet click. She let out her breath as the door swung open without protest.

The house was silent, save for Petra's snores drifting down through the floorboards and the faint crumbling of dying embers in the hearth. Kylene slipped off her boots and crept towards the stairs.

The first step groaned as it bore her weight, and Kylene silently cursed. With an experimental toe, she prodded the next to see if it too had an opinion about her midnight prowl.

It gave a small squeak, and she slowed, taking ages to find the quietest part of each step until she reached the landing. She froze, sweat beaded on her forehead, the gentle sawing of Petra's snores floating through the closed door on her left.

She took one light step towards the study, then another. With each, Kylene felt the weight of her actions pressing down upon her. The forbidding oak door – slightly ajar – creaked as she nudged her way through and into the room.

The study was shrouded in darkness, and the floor was so cold it seemed to seep into Kylene's bones. But her eyes were drawn to the desk, with its brass-clawed lion's feet and her father's leather-backed chair tucked tidily beneath it. Beyond the desk rose shelf after shelf, towering like sentinels. They were filled with books and artifacts, and a thrill of anticipation ran through her; she and Petra were only allowed into the study if invited. Thus, Kylene had been in her father's office not tens of thousands of times, as she had the kitchen or her bedroom, but dozens.

She walked toward the shelves as if in a trance, her hand sweeping lightly across the desk's whirled grain surface, and over a smooth, squat inkwell. And then she saw it, the yew box. Her heart leapt into her throat. Carved from the tree's heartwood, it glowed with a warmth that burned bright in the darkness.

Another step, and she was on her toes, reaching, her fingers gently running along the carvings on its side, more intricate than she remembered. She traced the outline of a plunging songbird, curling vines, the unfurling petals of a trumpet flower.

With trembling hands, Kylene removed the box from its place of rest. His secrets were in there; she was sure of it. But then, she heard a sound that made her heart beat its wings like a caged bird.

The creak of the study door. She whirled and saw him. He was walking toward her slowly, his eyes locked on her with purpose.

She tucked the box under her arm, took two bounding steps toward the window, bowed her head, and crashed through the thin glass headlong. Glass shards rained upon her as she landed on the tile roof in a heap. She scrabbled to her feet and peered down. Three figures were waiting in the pale moonlight. Men, all clad in armor, gleaming white. Peacekeepers. *Curses.*

They looked up at her in surprise, and she felt her mind grow calm, her senses sharpen.

She whirled and saw the man punch a grieved fist through the remnant shards of glass still clinging to the window frame.

"Stay right where you are, girl," he growled. "Nowhere to go. We need to speak to you about your father."

"In the dead of night?" She laughed, the sound of it strange, high-pitched and distant.

He grunted as he smashed through the last remaining shard and hoisted himself through the frame.

She scrambled on all fours to the other side of the roof. Below, just beyond the garden wall, was the family's horse, Sable, tied up and sleeping. *Strange Father didn't take her,* she thought as she slipped down the gutter pipe onto the horse's back. The mare whinnied softly as she slipped the knot holding her to the hitching post.

From above, the voice of her mother rang out through the night. "...come into my home in the middle of the night! We haven't seen hide nor hair of him, as we told you quite plainly already. Where're your papers? I demand to see your papers!"

Her mother's voice was steady, betraying no fear, and Kylene knew she would be alright. But Kylene felt an inexplicable urge to flee, driven by a certainty that whatever was in her father's box was important. That it held the key to the answers she was seeking. She would not let them have it. She whispered a command to Sable, urging the mare forward and away from the safety of home into the predawn dark.

The cobblestones flew beneath Sable's hooves as they raced through the streets of Mossbridge, the wind whipping her hair into a frenzy and bringing stinging tears to her eyes. The box, nestled snugly against her side, was a hard comfort, and a grim smile rose unbidden to her lips.

Mile after mile, she spurred Sable down the Middling Road. She passed the crossroads for Omnia, Taliis and Ardeleur, her eyes fixed on the horizon. Eastward she raced, fueled by an unshakable conviction that whatever lay ahead was worth the risk.

When the sun reached its zenith, she slowed her pace. She led Sable off the road and followed a trickling stream to its source: a sun-dappled spring presided over by a great beech tree and dozens of its slender descendants. The water was cool and inviting, and Kylene couldn't resist the urge to soak her feet in its clear blue depths. It was only then, as she slipped her bare feet into the waters of the spring, that she realized she'd left her boots on the back steps of the garden porch.

She wilted like a cut flower and lay back on a blanket of soft creeping spurge, her legs hanging limply off the pool's edge. The water swirled around her feet, washing the dust of the road from between her toes, and Kylene closed her eyes. Her father's yew box rested on her chest and she traced the engraving on the lid, a peacock with tail feathers splayed proud.

The tears came then, a flood of sorrow and confusion and frustration that she could no longer contain. They streamed down her dust-caked face, trickling down her temples, soaking her matted hair, falling until sleep claimed her, troubleless and deep.

***

The day was well worn and the light slanted when Kylene stirred. The shadows had grown large, their fingers stretching toward the growing dusk. She felt like a wet rag, wrung out and dirty; despite her weariness, the reality of her circumstance jolted her upright. There was no way around it. She was an outlaw now.

The Fingers would sketch her face on a poster next to her father's. They might even make her mother do the print job. Together, their likenesses would stare out all over Mossbridge, along with all the other bellringers and miscreants, seen by every person she's ever known. She had run from them, taken evidence, evaded capture. In a daze, she gathered bits of dried twigs and leaves to build a fire. She needed to rest, to gather her wits and her strength. But most of all, she needed to know what was in the yew box.

It occurred to her then that the yew box may have nothing of worth. Kylene paused in her gathering and felt cold tendrils coil like snakes in the pit of her stomach. She'd never seen her father take particular care of it. Had she made some desperate connection in the fever of her despair, one that had made her an exile from her own home? Could she have been that foolish?

The wind began to grow teeth, biting at Kylene's skin. She shivered, and her belly grumbled. Her night would be long and miserable without a fire and some food and so she pushed the thought from her mind with some force and continued to gather dried moss and bits of beech for kindling.

It was golden bell by the time Kylene was done, her favorite time of day. She took one long, sweeping look at the glade and in spite of everything, couldn't help but marvel at the beauty of it. The sun had yet to slip below the horizon, and everything in sight seemed to glow. The saw-toothed edges of beech leaves glimmered, and the spring pool sparkled like a cut sapphire. Even the soil, dark brown and moist, seemed flecked with golden sunlight.

Soon, she knew, everything she saw would give way to purples and grays and moody blues, and then only for a moment. The steady siphon of night would slow-sip all the color from the world, and in turn, give way to a different kind of magic. Her lips twisted into a pained smile. *Magic is for Mother-worshippers and lackeys of the Sons,* she remembered her father saying once. To him, the world was one great puzzle with limitless solutions, some known and others still veiled in mystery. "Why not call the mysterious bits magic?" she had asked him.

Things had gone pretty well for her first day as an outlaw. She hadn't been caught, and she had a fire to keep her warm and a stash of food to sustain her. At least that much could be said.

She'd found water chestnuts, whose fronds wavered on the water's surface, with their edible seeds that grew in the silt at the bottom of the pool. Armfuls of wild onion and sorrel. Lady's seal, its tender shoots and white knobby tubers that resembled tiny bones.

And finally, her greatest stroke of luck: an entire skirtful of unripe hazelnuts, each nut a perfect circle that peeked out shyly from beneath delicate green coverings like ruffled capes. It would take weeks for them to ripen, but it would be worth it.

As she surveyed her cache of foraged goods, a trickle of gratitude washed through her. The teachings of the Mavros

Forest and McBane had not failed her. She couldn't help but smile. At least for the next few days, she wouldn't go hungry.

It wasn't until it was full dark that Kylene finally managed to get a bit of dried moss to catch. She set the smoking bits to her stack of sticks and gently coaxed the thing to life with careful, bated breath. The air had grown cold and still, and the sounds of the wood at night – insects and small rustlings in the undergrowth – were made monstrous by the absence of the wind.

With the fire crackling and tubers roasting, Kylene set to work peeling the brown skin from her water chestnuts. When a small pile of cream-colored chestnuts gleamed before her, she bit into one tentatively. It was crisp and tasted of apples, only nutty, and Kylene was starving. Before she knew it, she had wolfed down every last one.

When she'd devoured each tuber and every last nut, she stared at the yew box in her lap. It was sturdily built, wide as two handspans, heavy as wrought iron. Kylene shook her head. *No.* It only felt that way because of what it had cost her.

Nerves gnawed at her insides as she traced each tail feather atop the box. "Stop that and just open the thing," she whispered, clicking the brass fastening on the lid. It swung open, revealing stacks of folded paper and a silver signet ring.

Exhaling, she snatched up the ring and examined it by the light of the fire. It was lightweight and finely made, but unlike her father's signet, which bore a feather quill, this one was engraved with a honeybee, its wings opened in sweeping flight.

She slipped it onto her pointer finger, surprised at how snugly it fit.

Kylene examined the stacks of paper. Most were thin and crisp, made from wood pulp like the kind her father sourced from Omnia for the press. A few pieces were ragged fiber stock with blearier ink. She examined one closely. Linen, probably.

And then there was the velum parchment, rich and creamy, with a broken wax seal bearing the tip of a creature's wing.

His secret correspondent, she thought. Anticipation simmered low in her belly as she selected this piece and began to read.

Mr Gemison,

Your missive has reached us with haste. Regretfully, we have not been able to locate the gentleman you mentioned, whom we shall call Mr Pontrefait. The master has not seen him since their time together at the place with a hundred names. He has some inklings regarding his whereabouts, yet none so certain that we may risk our current station.

We have read your text and find your theory astute and fitting. The master commends you on your findings. We will deliberate more on this during your next visit, so that we may advance our cause.

We shall occupy the eastern quarter in the next moon's turn and look forward to your visit.

Regards,
Quin

Kylene stared at the oblong looping script that twisted and turned across the parchment. A large tendriled K was stamped on the page's bottom right corner. She scratched her head and set the parchment aside, rifling through the remaining papers in the box. More letters, most from this Quin person, and several from a Mr Jacobin, whose letters were twice as cryptic. His were always written on stiff, pulped paper that was no doubt newly made when he set ink to page. Mr Jacobin mentioned many things that Kylene added to her mental treasury, but the phrases made little sense to her – men who could walk on smoke, dragons that whisper, the tyranny of Mons. It made little sense.

Beneath the stacks of folded papers, she found her father's notebook.

It was small and worn, with supple tan leather soft from use. Her father kept it close, tucked away in his back pocket. She had seen him scribbling in it often – seated on the wood-chopping stump in the garden or in the early morning stillness of the print shop before the place began its rhythmic stick and pummel song of ink on type, gears working, the smell of damp paper and fresh ink permeating the air.

She clutched the book to her chest and inhaled sharply, then hurried to feed a few more sticks to the flames. Then, inching as close as she dared to the modesty of its warmth, opened its feather-soft cover.

The first dozen pages were like spiderwebs. Words and phrases, symbols and notations were caught on the page like so many insects, ensnared there by the inspiration of a single moment. Arrows, circles and lines connected one to another and another and another. Kylene flipped through the pages faster and faster, her heart racing as she found that the web of ideas wove on and on.

The notebook was filled with frenzied text and sketches, as if the author had succumbed to madness. It reminded Kylene of her own journals back home in the cellar, a thought that brought a thin smile to her lips. The likeness also meant that the web probably wasn't chaos at all but a map with a pattern that only needed to be puzzled out.

Turning to the final few pages, she was surprised to discover a poem among the jumbled notes. *Rather odd addition*, she thought, as she began to read.

The tyranny of monopoly
Ridgelines too tall to cross
Abandon hope, creativity
Your goods, all worthless dross
The ugly crown that's wrought of gold
And singly worn in greed

When one is judge of life for all
The common folk do bleed
The last of these
The worst of three
Divinity a sport
Those sacred trees
Become diseased
Your faith they will distort
The binding of all three thought-forms
Send freedom to its grave
So stand up tall, the Mons need fall
Chin up, you must be brave

Kylene traced her fingers over the neat lines of her father's tidy, squared handwriting, struggling to reconcile the poetic words with the man she knew. She had a strong sense that he'd written the poem himself, even though she'd never, not once, known him to write poetry. In fact, the riddle about the yew was the closest thing to a poem she'd ever heard him recite. The idea that her father, pragmatic to a fault, would indulge in writing something so intentionally ambiguous – and in verse, no less – made laughter bubble up unbidden to her lips.

She reread the poem, her shoulders shaking with laughter that felt and sounded out of place.

So stand up tall, the Mons need fall

The Mons? She scratched her head. She'd read something about a people in the far east with that name. Somehow, she didn't think her father was referring to people.

She read the poem for a third time and noticed that there was only one word with 'mon' in – monopoly. It couldn't be that obvious.

A singular arrow led to the poem from the previous page, so Kylene flipped back and found the name Benedict Pontrefait scribbled and circled, along with a list of addresses so small Kylene had to squint to make them out.

Two of the addresses were listed in Omnia. The other five were in either Kythera or Ulthing, the two border countries to the Grasp's east, the only two places that touched the Grasp besides the swell of the sea. Kylene had never been, but she knew her father had several times for business. From Kythera, he always returned with delicious, spiced olives and the rarest of inks for the press – vivid purple made from a particular species of sea snail and red derived from the resin of dragon's blood trees. He always returned with shadows under his eyes and a smile on his face that was warm, if not a little worn, from long days on the road.

"What else were you doing there?" she whispered into the night.

She stared at the name Benedict Pontrefait, which had several arrows leading from it, upwards and downwards and backward another page. Backward, she decided, and flipped through two more pages full of dates, single words and quotations. The biggest of these were encircled and written in large, deliberate font. Dactyli and Omnia. *Odd,* Kylene thought. The two words were entirely at odds with one another.

Omnia was one of two large cities in the Grasp. It was also the place Osbert had chosen for his seat of supervision when he'd moved his company from Stonegate. *Supervise,* she remembered her father practically spitting. *The words this man uses. It's subjugate! Sub-ju-gate.* She shook the memory from her head.

Omnia had always felt to Kylene like a distant star, glittering and just out of reach. She had always wanted to go with her father, but he had held firm that no, not until she turned eighteen could she join him there on one of his trips. *Omnia's a ripe place,*

'Lene. Lots going on there. Your mother and I just want to make sure you've got your full wits about you before you go, is all.

She'd been asking to go since she was nine. Aside from having an enormous market that was said to be as big as her entire town, second only in size to the one in Lazare, Omnia was where the University was located, and the University was the only place where she could learn as much as her head could hold.

For Omnia and dactyli to appear in the same breath was odd for this reason. Omnia was culture, knowledge, possibility. The University was there. Inventors and craftsmen and artisans. And as much as she despised Osbert, the Fingers and his peacekeepers, he'd seen fit to station himself there.

No one seemed to know for sure *what* exactly dactyli were. At best, they were wise men, mystics with magical powers that they kept hidden from the rest of the world. At worst, they were crackpot fools or swindlers who sold fortunes for peasants' fruit.

Everyone knew about A'Tabhann, those three days of the year when they opened the doors of their dark and mysterious fortress to all the folk of the Grasp and beyond, welcoming all who came with queries of every shape and size. It was like the oracles in the old stories. Kylene had only been there once as a small child with her father and mother; staying in the nearby town of Mortalis when her father had ventured to the fortress. Her memories of the festival held in Mortalis in conjunction with the opening of A'Tabhann were happy ones. Her mother's red cheeks as her father whirled her around in the tavern of an inn. Petra, her feather-white curls orange and sticky with apricot juice. Races and games, men, women and children all playing, smiling, laughing.

She never did ask her father what his query had been. Now, she wished she had. And that A'Tabhann was the last in what Kylene had heard several folks say was a thousand-year tradition; Osbert had forbidden it six years ago, decrying the dactyli for impostors and worse in his manifesto, Pathway for the People.

Still, it was said that Osbert and his peacekeepers went nowhere near their strange fortress, so they were doubtless still around, doing whatever they did. It seemed obvious to Kylene what they did: they studied. But how, if they never left? Although many doubted their abilities, most seemed to think that their responses to queries over the centuries were wise and, in some instances, beyond mortal reasoning, at least if you listened to the most superstitious folk. But why all the rubbish about magical powers? If their knowledge was so great, why not open the doors of their learning to all, like the University in Omnia? It was all too strange by half and sounded more like a tale spun from the pages of a storybook rather than the logical reasoning Kylene relied upon.

A sharp crack rang through the air, and her heart leapt into her throat. She spun around, brandishing a burning branch. By the light of its meager flame, she could make out the outline of an enormous owl, perched in the low-hanging branches of a nearby beech.

The creature seemed oblivious to her presence, intent instead upon eviscerating what appeared to be a hapless field mouse. Its small bones were the source of the sound that brought her jarringly back to the present, reminding her that she was not, in fact, in her tiny cellar trying to find the answer to her latest question. She was on the run, in the woods, with no shoes and no clear path forward.

She sank back into the shallow depression at the base of the beech, a sense of unease settling over her like a heavy cloak. Taking a handful of roasted tuber roots from the embers, she placed them carefully in front of her to cool, her mind racing.

It would take her days to sort through everything in the box, and even then, would she know what the Mons were? Where her father might be? Where she ought to go next?

Her eyes glazed over as she flipped through addresses, names, pages and pages about mercantilism and printing and tyranny, more phrases that didn't make sense and then, like a beacon in the dark, a page with a strange word splashed across the top.

Kapnobatai.

Kylene was chewing a particularly tough root when she saw it and spat. The K was done in the same vining style as the stamp from the letter. Hungrily, she pored over her father's notations beneath the heavily inked word. They appeared, dated and shorthand, in what Kylene realized represented a log of separate visits. The first was dated two years ago, almost to the day.

Found after years of searching. Their home in the Mountains of Misfortune is seasonal, residing in the west end. I have only just begun to earn their trust, as they do not, by tradition, invite in outsiders unless they intend to join them.

And then, five months later, *Discussions of the press and what it means for the fight. They have many ideas. More to follow.*

And finally, *Met the master on last visit. A remarkable man. We are working on a pamphlet for dissemination. They have the mules. There has been...*

The text came to an abrupt halt. Perhaps she or her sister interrupted him when he'd been writing the last notation, or someone else at the print shop. The date was only three months ago. So he'd been looping the trip into his quarterly trips to Arandale...if he had been going to Arandale at all. There were seven visits in total, all within the last two years. How could he have kept such an enormous secret from her?

Feelings of betrayal swirled within her, and she swept them aside before they could settle, like a broom to dust. A small spark of excitement flickered within her as she scanned the notes again. This page held as much information as she could hope for. She knew where the Mountains of Misfortune were, or at least, where the mountain range was. How to find these Kapnobatai was another matter entirely, but at least she knew which way to point Sable, and that was a start.

Kylene hugged the notebook tightly to her chest, answering the question that had been running through her mind since she had fled. *Yes.* Retrieving the box had been worth it.

As she held the notebook close, she noticed that the spine was stiff, more rigid than a book of this make ought to be beneath its soft leather sheath. Kneading it experimentally, she found it moved freely and was not bound to the leather.

The light of her fire was too low to see by, so she looked with her fingers instead. She felt for an opening on either end of the spine and soon found it. With her little finger, she pulled the lip of the top of the spine's seamed edge aside, revealing a cavity within. Was it what she thought it was? She tilted the book upside down, and something fell out.

It was. It was a single movable type, the kind that her father used on his press. She snatched the smooth, slender piece of metal from the mess of dirt and leaves. It shone dimly in her grubby hand, its mixture of metals shone like a compact silver wand in the dying fire's light. She smiled. To her father, this was the closest thing to magic there was.

She flipped the spindle to see the letter and nearly dropped it when she saw it was a K. The letter was hand-carved and grooved, shaved and rasped and shaped, hardened and tempered. It was perfect, and she knew in her heart it was meant for her.

This is the key that unbolts every door, Kylene. It was what he always said to her when he set the type to print. When she was young, she would stare at him wide-eyed, believing him, imagining doors as tall as trees, doors with locks shaped like flowers, doors that only she could open with her secret combination of letters, words to which only she knew the meaning.

As she grew older, she would shake her head and laugh at her father's fervency. They were just letters in the alphabet; she'd learned the alphabet when she was four. How revolutionary could something as fundamental as speech be?

Words are power, Kylene. Words are magic. Never forget. With these letters, I can put all the words in the world together. However I like, or you like, or anyone with a mind to put thought to paper likes.

She had once asked what made the press so special, so different from any other way of communicating.

The difference, you ask! Shouting from the town square or writing a thing down is a day with no wind; a seed can't travel very far from the tree from which it came. Words on paper, printed one hundred times in the space of a day, are a gale force! Your idea will spread and sprout miles and miles from you. Far and wide your words will go, with so many seeds to scatter.

But it would never be as he said. Osbert commissioned all the presses. Set to print *his* laws, *his* stories, *his* letters and *his* words. Her father knew as much. It was why he did not shout with enthusiasm as he pulled the bar of the press, imprinting another page from yet another copy of Pathway for the People or Seven Miners or The Hungry Merchant or The Tall Book of Tales.

Kylene tenderly tucked the metal piece back into the book's spine. Maybe she was beginning to understand.

She lowered herself to the ground and curled inward beside the low-burning embers. She should feel more; she knew that much. Fear, perhaps? Uncertainty? She lacked so many things – her scroll, a map, and shoes, for a start. She also knew she'd turn to stone if she dwelled on these thoughts too long. She had to keep moving forward, no matter what lay in store.

So Kylene lay down her head and let the crackling embers of her dwindling fire lull her to sleep. As she drifted off, a map of the Grasp unfolded in her mind, mountains and valleys and townships blossoming like roadside weeds. She smiled to herself, remembering her father's words about her memory being like a butterfly net, capable of capturing all manner of beautiful, delicate things without harm.

The steady 'hoo' of the owl was the last thing Kylene heard as she slid into the realm of dreams, its slow, steady song mooring the heavy beat of her expectant heart.

Chapter Eight

Dawn broke as easy as an egg, spilling its bright rays onto the wet, bedraggled wood. By the time they broke camp and found Ailwin's nag, it had begun to steam the forest dry with its raw, honest heat. By a stroke of great fortune, Ailwin's nag was still tethered to the tree where he had left her. They found her unscathed, if not a bit disgruntled by the large number of flies buzzing around her ancient, flea-bitten head. Lovelace was marveling that the old girl hadn't strangled herself to death from fright when Gunnar discovered that the nag was, in fact, deaf and at least half blind.

For breakfast, they shared Ailwin's brevis bread. He broke off fist-sized pieces for himself, Gunnar and Lovelace and about a finger's-worth for Pif, who accepted the offering by thumbing his nose at Ailwin behind his back. They ate standing and in silence, the hard, compact bread barely edible. All around them, a warm westerly wind rustled the trees, shaking water from their heavy limbs.

It was self-evident to Lovelace that the only option was for Pif to ride with him. Privately, he had real concerns that Ailwin or Gunnar may very well kill him should he be saddled with either of them. The way the lad ran his mouth was so excessive that it bordered on the impressive. He was like an over-gorged river, meandering and moving a mile a minute, on and on and on.

And so it was, with Pif wedged behind Lovelace, Ailwin atop his nag and Gunnar bringing up the rear, that two dactyli and two Mortalii made their way up the High Road, allied in shared purpose as the Covenant had always promised.

By the afternoon, the four of them were soaked in sweat and beginning to chafe. They had gone most of the day at a trot which, to Gunnar's displeasure, was as fast as Ailwin's nag would go. Neither Ailwin nor Pif was at home in a saddle, just as Lovelace was not accustomed to sharing his, let alone with someone whose tongue flapped like a flag in the wind.

In the end, it was Lovelace who declared it quits, far earlier than was their custom. With a decisive, "That'll be all," he pulled his horse off the road, eager to be done for the day despite the early hour. No one offered protest.

They were still two days' ride from the fringe of Droch Fhortan, and the woods had given way to sparsely treed woodland, where dried feathergrass and blanched lupine wavered between granite boulders tall as houses covered in dusty gray-green lichen. The flatter, forested plains of the southern reaches of the Grasp had given way to textured hills, rambling oaks and the occasional stand of pine. There was a notable lack of places to hide.

They made camp in an elbow-shaped enclosure between two boulders taller than two men put together. Upon decamping, Lovelace dispatched Ailwin and Pif to find some roughage to accompany the salt fish that would be dinner. His motivations were manifold. First and foremost, he was curious about their foraging skills, particularly since both had boasted some ability. Pif's opinion of his own abilities lay firmly within the category of mastery while Ailwin had straightened and claimed to "know his carrots from his hogweed" with some measure of confidence. Less obviously, Lovelace was interested to know how the two fared in a shared pursuit and whether they might kill one another in the process.

Lastly, and most significantly, he was itching to examine at least one of the pieces of verdanite Manoc had given them. Since they left the Meorachadh, it had been one ceaseless step after another and Lovelace was no less hungry for answers now than he was then. It was high time they delved into one, and he preferred the boys weren't around for such a thing. Too many questions, and they were already too curious.

The sun was relentless, and Lovelace sat with his back to a boulder, sweating freely. His saddlebag lay open at his feet, its contents spilling out as he rummaged for the pouch of verdanite. Gunnar, meanwhile, was standing atop the smaller of the two rocks, having shuttled himself there by way of the wind. He was scanning the sloping horizon line, eyes sharp and squinting against the dazzling light of late day.

Lovelace rolled his eyes. Gunnar couldn't fly, per se, but he certainly wasn't as compelled by the earth's pull as most living things. Lovelace always maintained that being earth-coalesced was best, except when Gunnar would propel himself upward onto some ten-foot tall parapet with the same effort it took most to jump. Only then would Lovelace think being a wind dactyli might not be so bad.

His fingers were swollen with heat, making it difficult to find the soft leather of the pouch that held the verdanite. He let out a grunt, mild panic flooding him as he searched. It quickly ebbed away as his probing fingers found the pouch's drawstring. The heat of the day's ride had left him feeling somewhat tattered, and he needed nothing so much as a cool pool of water to wash off some of the dust of the day.

It was late summer, and the land looked as parched as he felt, most of its greenery given way to withered stalks of golden brown. Still, he pressed his fingers to the earth, feeling whether there might be a source of water with which he could create a small aquifer when Gunnar landed lightly in a crouch beside him.

"Let's see one," he said, nodding at the pouch in Lovelace's lap.

"Just a minute," Lovelace said peevishly then heaved a heavy sigh.

No water nearby, above or below ground, at least that he could sense. Were he water-coalesced, he could draw on finer sources. As it was...it would be warm ale or nothing.

Lovelace pulled his luth away from the earth's underbelly and upended the pouch onto the ground, the green glow of the three slabs sparkling preternaturally in the sun-bleached grass.

"Which one sings the sweetest, Gunn?"

Gunnar leaned forward and examined the stones. Wordlessly, he reached for the middle of the three, a near-perfect square roughly the size of a husked walnut. He inspected it closely, holding it to the light and scrutinizing it with one eye squinted as though he were a jeweler and the verdanite a priceless sapphire. Satisfied, he returned it to Lovelace.

"Together then?" Lovelace asked, the verdanite resting in the center of his outstretched, upturned palm.

Gunnar nodded, reaching for the stone once more. "Quickly," he said.

Lovelace took a deep inhale, and together they were away.

***

In an instant, the fragrant notes of parched grass and dried oak leaves faded, along with the birdsong and buzzing of insects that had clung lazily to the warm summer air. There was the gentle humming, the slow-draining of color and form from the world and then, silence.

Lovelace took a deep inhale. He supposed that these things didn't disappear so much as fade into an almost inaudible whisper, as if a very heavy door had closed on a chamber full of chatter.

There were different sounds now, different smells that took precedence.

He knew that Gunnar was beside him because he could feel the shape and power of his luth, though he could not, and would not, be able to see him.

Lovelace opened what Manoc would describe as his inner eye. His real eyes remained shut, lodged firmly within his skull affixed to his body, which was still sweating and sore, propped up against a boulder on a Mother-forsaken errand that continued to grow more problematic by the day.

Lovelace found himself in the Refractory, one of the primary classrooms in the Meorachadh for tyros, especially when fire was the element being worked. Instead of the typical basalt, the eight walls were made of slick obsidian, with a textured surface that shone like oil in the dim flicker of lamp light. Unlike most in the Meorachadh, the ceiling was low, a design that made it easier to contain and control energy. *A necessity when instructing fifteen-year-old boys to conjure flame with their fingertips,* Lovelace thought wryly.

As sgeuls do, this one's opening sequence began when the two heavy stone doors opened, revealing Manoc and Gottfried, both considerably straighter of back and smoother of face than when Lovelace saw them last, three days back.

A prickling sensation skittered down the back of his neck as Gottfried's beady eyes stared through him, though he knew Gottfried saw him not. In a sgeul, Lovelace and Gunnar were less than flies on a wall, lesser even than the meanest ghosts. They were mere voyagers to a moment preserved in crystal.

Alev followed behind the masters, tall and lean as a whipcord, and Lovelace recoiled.

Alev had always made him uneasy, even before he knew what he could do. Alev carried a tension about him, like a crossbow loaded and nocked, as if he might, at any time, let loose his charge.

Here he could not have been more than seventeen. His face was as still as death, his features chiseled from alabaster, betraying no hint of thought or feeling.

"Masters Gottfried, Manoc," Alev gave a small, stiff bow to the older men, who returned the gesture. Gottfried's bow was notably deeper than Manoc's, who eyed Alev with deep distrust.

Lovelace realized then that this must be the physical portion of his capstone, one of two exams that would make him a dactyli.

"I have walked through the fire, red, blue, white heart of flame," Alev proclaimed, his voice formal and proud, "And I have emerged, unbroken and unburnt."

Lovelace rolled his eyes. To his right, he felt a faint vibration, indicating that Gunnar was having a similar reaction. The formal declaration of elementary coalescence was customary at the beginning of the physical capstone. If he remembered correctly, Lovelace had stated, "I know earth and earth knows me." If he had to guess, Gunnar had probably said something like "Wind."

Alev stood with his head bowed in the center of the hexagonal chamber. Manoc nodded to Gottfried, whose voice echoed oddly off the low ceiling, "Would you like to begin as examiner or examinee?"

"Examinee," Alev said quietly, his dark eyes fixed somewhere distant. They smoldered like new-made coals.

Manoc lifted his hand, palm outstretched, and with a sweeping gesture, made as if to close an imaginary door.

From this movement, a small cyclone formed, swirling dust and debris until it grew into a towering force, tall as the ceiling and wide as two men. The twister barreled toward Alev, who idly flicked his wrist as if to swat a bothersome insect.

The fire from the nearest lamp shot out of its reservoir and leapt like a small fish into the center of the cyclone. The twisting vortex halted abruptly, the flame within it a seed that grew and grew until the whole of the cyclone was a whirling inferno, the air around it shimmering with heat.

With a snap of his fingers, Alev condensed the fiery mass into a blazing missile that flung itself at Manoc's gut and disappeared on impact. Manoc's knees buckled, but he didn't lose his footing. Lovelace smelt burnt cloth.

"Defense only, Alev," Manoc wheezed, clutching his abdomen. Lovelace grimaced. Manoc was the only master Alev didn't have wrapped around his finger. He'd likely been relishing that particular opportunity for some time.

"My apologies, Master," Alev said, his voice sharp. He didn't sound the least bit sorry.

As Gottfried stepped forward to conduct his investigation, Lovelace noticed a look of mild glee and something more – admiration, perhaps – flickering in the master's eyes. *Lick-arse,* Lovelace thought. Alev had always been Gottfried's little pet. Lovelace wondered if maybe this was what Manoc had intended to demonstrate: that Gottfried would ultimately betray them and ally himself with Alev, if he hadn't already.

Lovelace watched as Gottfried spat into his hand and dropped the spittle to the floor. *No,* Lovelace thought as he watched the spit augment and shape itself into thin coils of ice. Gottfried may possess a certain degree of malevolence, an excessive fascination with power, even, but he wasn't built like Alev. Alev had always scoffed at authority and viewed the order's single purpose as something of a joke. *Gottfried's given his life to the work. Alev always wanted more.*

Hugh nodded, and the ice rope lashed out as if flung by a practiced human hand. Alev stood motionless as the rope snapped around his neck and slowly began to constrict. He'd let the cord fall there deliberately; Lovelace knew he was quicker than that.

A slight grimace, or a twisted grin, crossed Alev's features, and he blinked once, long and slow like a lizard eyeing its prey. The coil of ice around his neck hissed and melted. For a moment, his face was shrouded in steam and hidden from view.

Alev held his arms outward, his palms facing up and stretched wide. He would appear almost supplicant were it not for the air of superiority etched upon his marble face.

"If I might transition to Examiner?" he asked.

Manoc and Gottfried locked eyes, silent understanding passing between them.

"Proceed," said Gottfried.

Alev took a step backward and bowed his head. Moments passed, each one stretching out like a bowstring drawn taut, until suddenly, a searing wall of fire erupted out of the air, completely concealing Alev behind a thick panel of roaring flames. Lovelace watched in awe and horror as Gottfried and Manoc backed slowly toward the wall at their backs.

The flames swelled, their scorching heat and size rising by degrees. Somewhere behind them lurked Alev. Lovelace crept along the wall to be beside Manoc, who had flattened himself against the smooth obsidian. He was grateful the elder master had selected the sgeul from the walls rather than his own memory, sparing them the blistering heat he endured. Lovelace could see it was near-blistering by the sweat rolling down Manoc's face, the shimmer in the air around them. As it was, Lovelace could only experience the heat as the obsidian did, hot but not a threat to his physical being.

Manoc and Gottfried, with all their elemental knowledge and experience, wore expressions of muted terror as the firewall closed in on them. A sickly sweet odor rose in the fast-thinning air, a smell that Lovelace could not place, but which made his stomach turn fiercely.

The flames were perilously close to the wall when they ceased their rapid expansion and began to recede, leaving just enough distance for a two arms-length of space between. Lovelace inched along the glassy obsidian, trying to glimpse Alev. As the sgeul was from the obsidian's perspective, he could only skirt around the perimeter, catching only chaos of flame as he circled the room. Alev was nowhere to be found.

Abruptly, the flames ceased their upward riot and spiraled with alarming velocity into a thick, horizontal column. Lovelace watched in sheer horror as it spun faster and faster. His inner eye, were it a physical thing, would be as wide as a saucer.

Lovelace glanced along the wall at Manoc and Gottfried, whose faces reflected a mixture of awe and fear as they stared into the whirling cylinder's center. The shape of Alev was materializing there, a long, dark shadow immobilized in the center of the flame like the slivered pupil of a cat.

Transfixed, Lovelace watched as the shadow moved toward Manoc and Gottfried. The flames continued to leap and swirl in concentric circles and then, Alev's hand appeared.

The rest of him followed, his naked form stepping out from the fire, entirely unscathed. He wore a look of indifference on his face, as if he had not just emerged from the eye of a blistering inferno unblemished. He stood before the cylinder of flame, still spinning behind him in a truly dazzling display of power and control. Alev stared at Manoc and Gottfried boldly, his expression changed to one of unmistakable defiance.

Both men stared back at Alev, Gottfried with an expression of slack-jawed awe and Manoc, a wariness that ran bone deep.

"That was something, Alev," Manoc said levelly.

"Something!" Gottfried practically squeaked. "That was the most marvelous display of power you or I have ever seen, Manoc, with our own two eyes or in sgeul." He turned to Alev. "You must tell us how you've done it, dear boy, and more critically still, how you've managed to remain unburnt." His beady eyes shone with greed; the fact that he'd nearly been killed by one of his favorite students seemed, somehow, to elude him.

"In time, Master Gottfried, in time," Alev said, with a tone one might use to chide a persistent child.

Gottfried clapped his hands and turned to Manoc, who was still eyeing Alev with profound mistrust. "We will need to discuss with Hugh and Basil, but I think we can safely count him as ascended, can we not, Manoc? Fully fledged! My word, my word. What a display…"

Manoc was silent. The look of Alev, stark naked, his skin unblemished as the day he was born, made Lovelace's non-corporeal skin crawl.

"It is my wish to be called Alev the Unburnt," he said quietly. Only then did Manoc break his stare to let out a harsh bark of laughter. "Dactyli do not have epithets, Alev," he said.

"But I will," Alev said, his eyes burning with defiance.

Manoc's brow furrowed more deeply and he opened his mouth to respond. Instead of his usual gruff timber, a shrill voice issued from his lips, "M'lord, M'lord, M'lord," it said, like the trill of morning bird song.

Lovelace sighed inwardly. The boys, returned from their assignment.

With some reluctance, Lovelace allowed his luth to recede into passivity. The Refractory dissolved, its obsidian walls, the forms of Manoc, Gottfried and Alev all blown away like dust in the wind.

In their place, the outlines of Ailwin and Pif took color and shape. They stood before him and Gunnar, still propped against the boulder and engaged with the sgeul. Lovelace pinched his shin, and Gunnar came to, blinking furiously against the harsh light of the setting sun.

Both boys looked to be several shades of spooked, as if they'd just stumbled upon a pair of men possessed by some underland demon. To be fair, they *had* discovered he and Gunnar leaned up against the wall like marionettes with strings cut, eyes closed and more than likely twitching.

Pif held fistfuls of sorrel and Ailwin was wreathed in bilberry branches. Before Lovelace could offer any words of praise on their finds or attempt to ease the awkwardness of their intrusion, Gunnar made a clicking sound with his tongue, the same noise he used to shoo away the horses.

"Don't just stand there looking daft," he said. "Get the fire started. Pull out the salt fish. Make yourselves useful."

Ailwin dropped to one knee and relieved himself of the berries draped about his shoulders. With brisk efficiency, he began to pull one berry after another from the bramble, all the while keeping his eyes fixed straight ahead. Pif, on the other hand, stood there slack-jawed until Lovelace gave him a nudge on his shoulder.

"Kindling, lad," Lovelace said, his nudge sufficient to rouse the young boy from his stupor. He nodded mutely and scampered off like a wild hare.

"A proper treat, that," Lovelace said as he watched the boy disappear into the dry creek bed. "Didn't know the boy was capable of being rendered speechless."

Gunnar's tone was sharp. "How far did you get before you disengaged?"

"To the point where Alev got all menacingly prophetic. Didn't hear how Manoc responded, the boy cut in."

"Nothing much after that," Gunnar said, his nostrils flared. "Manoc didn't feed into his little palaver. He just concluded the capstone and told him to expect the council's decision by midmorning the next day."

Lovelace frowned, delving deep into the recesses of his memory. "The day he was conferred, he disappeared the next night, didn't he?" Lovelace had been all of fourteen.

Gunnar nodded, his jaw clenched, prompting Lovelace to continue.

"I didn't think much of it at the time; I was just glad to see him gone. I slept much better at night, knowing he wasn't three doors down. I was always looking over my shoulder after that fire in the stables. Bastard almost killed me for having a bit of fun."

Indeed, the masters had concluded that an oil lamp had spilled near the manure pile where Lovelace had been mucking stables. Lovelace, having only one week prior transmuted Alev's porridge into mud at breakfast, causing the older boy to choke, had come to a different conclusion.

"I remember," Gunnar said.

"What I can't work out is why they didn't do something when he nearly killed them in the midst of his capstone. Spineless swine. Why did they even confer him?"

"Useless to not confer him," Gunnar said. "Like as not, they thought they could temper him. Fools..." he shook his head in disgust.

Lovelace grunted in agreement, stroking his beard. "Vainglorious, thinking they could turn him into a tool. A knife in the back is what they got instead. No one said much of anything when he left, as I recall. He's not the first dactyli to go rogue, after all. What was that one's name, the water dactyli Manoc holds that fearsome ill will toward?"

"Badi," Gunnar said. There was a sharp crack, and Lovelace whipped around to see Ailwin, ears pricked, two ends of a bramble broken off in either hand.

"Right, Badi," Lovelace said, eyeing the boy curiously. Ailwin resumed his task but wore a troubled look and appeared to be doing his best to avoid making eye contact with Lovelace.

"In any case," Lovelace said, turning back to Gunnar. "I reckon Manoc gave us that sgeul to show us what we're dealing with. I suppose it had a rather stirring effect, though not one that left me inspired to meet the man in a duel. That was proper diabolical, what he did in the Refractory."

As he spoke, a weight settled in his stomach. What they'd seen was unnerving, beyond what Lovelace dreamed was possible for their kind. Dactyli always displayed varying degrees of talent for elemental work. He and Gunnar were leagues more competent than Lester and Radigan, the gormless fools. But Lovelace had never seen anyone do what Alev had done in that sgeul.

Gunnar frowned, the deep-set lines etched around his mouth thrown into stony relief by the sun's dying rays.

"There's something that doesn't fit..." he started.

"M'lords!" came the breathless voice of Pif as he tumbled into camp. In one outstretched hand, he held a dead squirrel by its bushy tail. In the other, a slingshot. It was a wicked-looking instrument that was burnished to a shine and cunningly carved from a single piece of ebony wood. How the boy came to be the owner of such a weapon was a question, to be sure. How he came to be so handy with it was another. By the looks of it, the squirrel had been hit squarely between the eyes by an object no larger than a thimble, resulting in a quick, clean death.

"Pif," Lovelace said, inclining his head to the bright-eyed boy, who had already pulled a remarkably sharp, slender knife from his pouch and was beginning to skin the squirrel with astonishing precision. Ailwin froze in his attempt to start a fire with his flint and steel and stared at Pif, bewilderment and envy vying for precedence on his features. Even Gunnar was eyeing the boy with mild amusement as he slashed and tugged at the animal's skin in all the right places, so that it pulled away from the pearly purple-pink flesh with ease.

"Hot food caught fresh stoutens the heart, m'lords," Pif said matter-of-factly as he made a tidy cut into the squirrel's abdominal cavity and expertly removed its entrails.

"Indeed," Lovelace said. He pried his eyes away from Pif and fixed them on Gunnar, who, bereft of anything to do on account of their underlings, had taken to picking dirt from beneath his nails with the tip of his field knife.

"Save the other two for later, then?"

"Aye, time enough," Gunnar said without lifting his head.

It was something of a relief to Lovelace that Gunnar too lacked the fortitude for another of Manoc's sgeuls. If he allowed himself to stop and think of what Alev was now capable, the greater powers he might have unlocked in the years since, with nothing to govern him, no one to bridle him, Lovelace might be inclined to stay right where he was, live out his days as a woodland hermit, trade his tricks for beer and bread from passersby, maybe take up carpentry.

But he refused to speculate on what Alev might want, and he shoved the thought of the dead boys and Alev's power from his mind. In spite of the warm and mild night descending upon them, a shudder traveled through him at the image of Alev stepping clean through flames.

***

When the sun dipped below the horizon, Lovelace, Gunnar, Pif and Ailwin gathered around the fire to share a companionable meal of bilberry and sorrel-stuffed squirrel. Despite all preconceived notions, it was delicious and did indeed seem to stouten even Gunnar, who by meal's end gruffly praised Pif's cooking. "Very good," he'd said as he licked his fingers clean. Those two words set a smile on Pif's face bigger and brighter than the waxing moon that rose, slowly and surely, overhead.

The boys regaled them with tales of their upbringing in Mortalis, and Ailwin recounted stories of the eccentric clientele who patronized the Capering Colt. They spoke of horses, and hunting, and the sea, how neither of them had ever seen it, despite it being only a day's ride away. Lovelace and Gunnar mostly listened. Whether it was because the boys had learned something during that long day's ride or were simply glad to be heard, neither of them pressed Lovelace or Gunnar about who they were or what they were about, which was either very wise or very foolish, given their present involvement.

Lovelace couldn't decide which.

They turned in early, just in time for a cool east wind to make them all glad of the fire at their backs. Lovelace was reminded, not for the first time, of the duality of a thing. Fire can kill, just as it can feed.

Tucked in beneath his cloak, belly full and eyes bleary, he watched the leaves of an oak tree overhead gently waver and thanked Pif and Ailwin for the meal, meaning every word. To allow either boy along on this quest was folly, but to his surprise, he found he was grateful for their company, even still.

As he closed his eyes, the sleepy voice of Pif came drifting across the fire, "'Twas a pleasure to cook for m'lords, sure and true. We'll see if'n I can't manage to catch us a badger on the morrow. I saw some tracks. I've a lovely recipe for spit-roast badger that'd be a proper treat after another hard day's ride, m'lord, a proper treat."

Chapter Nine

It had been two days. Two days of riding with fair weather and good foraging and sleeping beneath stars clear-seen. It had gone so well that Kylene was beginning to wonder whether she was made for life on the road.

She looked down at the pair of leather boots wrapped snugly around her feet, got from a trade she'd made with a passing peddler. For the price of her father's yew box, less its contents, she had gained not only boots, but one thick woolen blanket, a satchel with several clever pockets and a small knife that she'd decided to name Clover. The trade had gone splendidly, leaving her feeling rather skilled in the art of bartering despite having never done it before. She wasn't sure what the yew box was worth, but had devised a story about it being carved from a yew that marked the burial place of Strobius the Annealed, patron son of craftsmen.

She was nearly at the crossroads, or at least, she ought to be, if the directions given to her by the peddler were correct, a prospect which had her beaming with anticipation. The crossroads was where all manner of folk gathered, or so she was told. People from Lazare or Omnia or perhaps even from beyond the Grasp's borders. Surely there would be someone there who knew something about the Kapnobatai. And if there was no one to give her a clue as to where she might find them, well, she'd just set up camp and wait until someone came through who did.

But as afternoon gave way to dusk and she rounded a bend in the road which widened into a circular clearing, Kylene felt dread spread like ice through her limbs.

This could only be the crossroads; six paths converging, caravans and campfires and travelers settling in for the night, just as she had imagined. But something was wrong.

She looked around and became startlingly aware of many eyes upon her. Not a single pair of them belonged to a woman. Her heart quickened. Worse still, there was no look of warmth or welcome about them. They were eyes that leered, eyes filled with wariness, eyes that blazed with madness.

She'd been fortunate, all this way up the Middling Road. She could see that now. *Stupid,* she thought. That she could consider herself safe from harm because she could negotiate with peddlers and tell wild grapes from moonseed, and sweet almonds from bitter.

Still, she held her head high and walked Sable straight through the clearing, certain now that her plan to set up camp was not a good one. She would just make herself inconspicuous, keep going down the road, maybe then...

"Hey sweetheart," a man called to her from the back of a threadbare caravan. Her blood ran cold.

"Plenty o' room for you in our caravan, if'n you need somewhere to rest those pretty bones o' yours."

With enormous effort, she kept her eyes forward, fixed on the other side of the clearing. She was halfway across. Two roads, one straight ahead, the other veering right, loomed before her. Both were wide enough that they must be the High and the Middling roads. But which should she take?

Her thoughts were interrupted as Sable reared back, her forelegs lifting off the ground. Kylene made a mad grab at the horn of her saddle, just in time to avoid being thrown from her seat.

"Well blow me down. Here I am, darlin', what're your other two wishes?"

Kylene stared down at the cause of Sable's fright. A man – terribly filthy, with silver for teeth – stood before her. He reached for Sable's reins, the afternoon sun flashing off the metal of his smile.

Her instincts took over. She dug her heels into Sable's flanks and catapulted forward at a breakneck pace, nearly knocking the man off his feet.

"...was only thinkin' you and your pony might like some help beddin' down for the night," he called after her.

She spurred Sable on through the clearing and around the curve in the road until she was sure they had shaken off any would-be pursuers. She slowed to a canter, her heart still pounding like hooves on hard dirt.

Without the crossroads, how would she know where next to go? A shudder rolled through her as she thought of what might have transpired, had she made camp there.

Dense trees and creeping vines narrowed the path, and it dawned on her that she'd taken the High Road. No sooner did she have the thought than she became aware of a faint sound, barely audible over the sounds of the wood. She listened closer, her heart skipping a beat when she realized what it was. The sound grew louder, unmistakable – the clatter of hooves, a rider in pursuit.

She tried to urge Sable forward, but the little mare hesitated and balked as the rider closed in on them. In a split second, the stranger had pulled his horse around to block her forward passage, leaving Kylene face-to-face with a man not much older than herself.

The fabric of his black velvet cloak shimmered and he wore a high-handed sort of smile. Kylene had seen the kind before; it came from a lifetime of having your way, no matter the price.

A gold pin held back the sweep of his cloak's fabric, finely wrought in the shape of a badger. *Mining family then*, her mind working furiously as panic churned in her gut. Mossbridge was far from the mines that dotted the northern and western portions of the Grasp, but she knew a sycophant when she saw one. It wasn't a requirement to wear the pin; her father never wore his, a garish gold lump meant to look like an owl.

The man's smile widened as his eyes swept brazenly over her face and down to her newly shod feet. Warmth rose in her cheeks, and she fought to maintain composure.

"My name is Vicente Arando, miss," he said, pressing his hand to his heart, "and I am at your service." He inclined his head toward her, but his eyes – dark and glittering with curiosity – never left hers.

"Kylene," she said as she angled Sable to cut around Vicente, only to have him sidestep his enormous gelding and block her way again.

"Kylene," Vicente repeated thoughtfully, tasting the name on his tongue. "A lovely name, if you do not mind me saying so. Tell me, Kylene, where are you going?"

She stiffened. As it happened, she *did* mind him saying so.

"If you are at my service, as you say, then surely you will let me pass and continue on my way. My business requires my timeliness as well as my discretion."

Vicente gave a throaty chuckle, amusement writ large on his features.

"It has been some time since a woman comported herself to me with such mystery, and with such eloquence, and never one so young. Come, let me walk with you, at least. A woman alone on the High Road, a woman alone on the road at all! It would be unthinkably ungentlemanly of me to allow you to continue without an escort."

She could refuse his offer and risk the consequences, or she could allow him to play whatever game he was playing in the hopes that she could lure him into a false sense of leisure, whereby she could make her escape.

Vicente's smile widened as he watched her make these calculations. *His teeth are far too white,* she thought distantly.

She didn't relish the thought of denying someone like Vicente on sight, not without good reason. She swallowed the bubble of apprehension that was welling up inside her. Perhaps he knew something of the Kapnobatai, something that she could use to her advantage. Perhaps this encounter might serve to turn the tide.

Kylene gave him a placid smile. "A companion would be welcome until I reach my next way station," she said.

Vicente's smile froze, his head cocked slightly as though he was surprised by her response. But the moment was brief, and he sidestepped his horse again, allowing Kylene to pass.

"Let us traverse the dark and dreadful High Road then, and hope that we do not run afoul of bandits. Or worse," he said, giving her a practiced wink as he urged his gelding onward.

Kylene rather thought that Vicente was the worst thing that could befoul her on the High Road, but she kept that to herself. Instead, she mulled over ways to use him to her advantage.

Perhaps if she could get him talking...Most men loved to talk about themselves; she had little doubt that Vicente was no exception.

She straightened in her saddle. "What brings a son of the miner's guild to the heart of the Grasp? I thought our best reservoirs were in the north and western corridors."

Vicente waved his hand, unconcerned. "I came down to the Mortalis on behalf of my father. We received a survey from the Fingers about a potential valarum mine in the rock face of the valley there."

Valarum. The word carried weight. It was used in lamps and, when combined with copper, projected light at a great distance, a distance far greater than oil lamps. Her father had one in his study and it bathed the whole room in a cold silver glow.

"And how were your findings?"

He shrugged. "That remains to be seen. I hardly do the prospecting myself. I come for the negotiations, a job I am quite good at. And then, I'm left to my own fancies."

He turned to her, curiosity made plain on his face.

"You are a remarkably well-spoken girl. How is it that someone with such a fine manner of speech finds themselves alone, on a road forbidden by the Minister without express permission, dressed like they've been pulling weeds in the garden? You *are* a curious thing."

Panic rose in her chest and Kylene realized she had made a mistake. Ought she have played dumb? She'd never encountered a situation where being clever hadn't been at least a little bit helpful. She kept her eyes fixed on the road ahead, not daring to meet his gaze.

"Don't bother with a lie. I'll know it the second it leaves your lips," Vicente's honeyed tone was like a blade at Kylene's throat. Her skin prickled, and sweat – cold and fine-webbed – broke out along her brow.

Kylene forced a shy smile and pitched her voice higher, thinking of Petra.

"It's just that nobody's ever called me well-spoken before."

Vicente shook his head. "No, no, no. I've met children who are better actors than you. Put away your dimwitted act, it is distasteful and it doesn't suit you," he said.

She was silent and stole a sidelong glance at him, taking in the burnished silver that buckled his harness, the stiff leather of his tightly stitched saddlebag. He smelled of vetiver – too much of it – and was a handsome man, but there was something about the hard-set edge of his jaw, the wire-tight smile he wore, that made him distant and cold. *Very well then,* she decided. *Should he seek a battle of wits, then he'll not be disappointed on my account.*

"Surely you recognize a jest when you see one," she said, adopting his scolding tone. "A question for a question. What do you want to know?"

The corner of his mouth curled into a smile that did nothing to warm his features.

"You are fun," he said appreciatively. "I accept your challenge, and I will even let you go first."

"Honest answers?"

"Honest answers."

The setting sun filtered through the dense canopy of the High Road, and a wind, cold enough to sting the skin of her cheeks, blew through the trees. She would need to act quickly.

"Why are you following me?" she asked, facing him with a look that she hoped was half as imperious as his own.

"My dear," he said, practically purring, "you cannot be so tactless as that, where is the excitement in being so utterly blunt?" He made a tsk sound and muttered, "For all her cleverness she has zero manners."

He turned to meet her gaze with a black gleam in his eyes that nearly unseated her. *Like pools of ink,* she thought. Vicente, she realized with a sudden chill, was teetering on the edge of madness.

"Observe. Oh, Vicente," he said, his voice pitched high, "pray tell, how does one acquire such a chiseled visage as yours?" His left hand held the reins aloft and slack, a mirror image of her.

She stared at him blankly.

"Go on, ask me," he snarled, and Kylene reared back.

"H-how is it that you are so handsome?" she stammered, unable to say his name.

He smiled again, that same terrifying grin that might have been beautiful were it not so monstrous.

"You flatter me with such a question," he said, transferring the reins to his right hand. "How keenly observant you are! The answer to your question is a simple one: I get it from my mother. She is the most beautiful woman, with hair like black silk and unsurpassed elegance from her neck down to her dainty feet. You would not believe her beauty if you saw it, I assure you."

Kylene's eyes widened. Behind them , the slow-setting sun flickered.

He turned to her, and she fought to wrangle the fear that was surely splayed across her features.

"My turn," he said, "What are you running from?"

"I-I thought we were starting with families, being coy..."

"We are starting with whatever I want us to start with," he hissed, practically spitting at her. "I will ask you again. What are you running from?"

Kylene paled, "The peacekeepers," she whispered.

Vicente clapped, his delight palpable.

"I knew you were interesting," he crowed. "Your turn."

Kylene tensed, unsure of what to say.

"Tell me about where you are from."

He furrowed his brow thoughtfully. The road was growing darker around her, and with it, her hopes of escaping from this madman.

"My family originally comes from Prasad. Beautiful, peerless Prasad. We have a small estate on the northernmost tip of the peninsula, where peacocks roam, and starlings sing, our own private stairwell down to a beach with the most perfect green sand, fine as...well, fine as the finest sand. And the bluest water you've ever seen," he paused, wistful.

Amazement crept around the edges of her fear. She'd never seen someone express themselves so...irregularly. He moved between moods like a hummingbird between flowers.

"But that was years ago. We only return there now in the winter months, when it is fearsomely cold everywhere else and the night lilies are in bloom. Mother loves the night lilies," he said, his look distant, elsewhere.

"But that was years ago," he said, repeating himself. Then, as a dog might shoo a fly, he shook his head and straightened in the saddle.

"Now we live in Omnia," he said matter-of-factly. "I have my own flat that is three stories tall and suits my every need. Well, most needs. It was sad to leave Prasad, of course, but now we are closer to the heart of things. It is better for business."

Kylene remained silent, half terrified to speak, half curious about what would happen if she left space for him to unravel.

"I like living in Omnia," he continued. "Everything new happens there first. But even new can grow boring. I find it necessary to escape as often as I can, lest I slip into fatuity. One cannot live exclusively in the city, else they will forget the largeness of the world."

It was the most sensible thing he'd said, and only belatedly did Kylene realize it was a fragmented quote from Eldemere, one of her father's favorite writers.

They rounded another curve in the road and, for a moment, rode together in silence, their horses kicking up pine needles and trampling the trailing vines of wineberry brambles that crept, red and sticky, onto the path.

It was the landscape that had awoken something within him, Kylene decided, something wild and untamed. They were in a liminal space, out here on the High Road, neither fully within the bounds of civilization nor entirely outside of it. The further away from others they traveled, the more Vicente's nature revealed itself. Any fascination Kylene might have had with his mercuriality was replaced by a dread so total it was a wonder that she could still breathe.

"Go on," he urged, breaking the still. "I know the question you want to ask: why would a mining family choose to leave the very land that sustains them?"

The gnarled trunks of the surrounding pine trees loomed over them like skeletal sentries, their branches reaching out to snatch at the sky. Kylene needed this game to end. Needed to be far, far away before Vicente decided to stop playing nice.

"Why did your family leave Prasad?"

His smile gleamed like a knife in the gathering gloom. "Why, The Reckoning, of course. Father always knows upon which side his bread is buttered. When Osbert made his move, we allied with him immediately. I recall the moment well, standing in the drawing room. Father didn't tarry for a moment. He merely stared at the fire, threw on another log, gave it a good hard poke and then sent his man Moritz to secure a hundred of the finest mercenaries from Ulthing as a show of tribute, of strength."

His smile widened. "Many of the men we bought for him are now among the top-ranking officials of the peacekeepers. We paid dearly for The Reckoning, of course. All enterprising folk did. But, it didn't take long for our family to learn how to thrive in this new world and so, here we are." He let out a deep, exaggerated sigh, "Some folk are simply born to triumph, to rise above the rabble. It is the way of things."

He turned to face her, his body twisting with lightning speed. Kylene startled, and Sable nearly tripped. Within her chest, her heart was hammering.

"Why are you running from the peacekeepers, Kylene?"

Kylene had every reason to believe that any falsehoods she presented to Vicente would cause him to lose whatever sense of courtesy he offered her. So she resolved to tell the truth, at least, a shade of it.

"They were trying to take something of mine. I could not let that happen, so I ran."

Vicente's face twisted into feigned indignation.

"Those scoundrels! How dare they?" He leaned in, his eyes shining. "Do you have this thing now?"

"I thought we were only allowed to ask one question at a time," she shot back, regretting her carelessness at once. To her relief, he appeared to enjoy her rebuke.

"Well played, clever girl. Go on then, your turn."

"What do you know of the Mountains of Misfortune?" She asked, her words tumbling out in a rush "...And the people who live there?"

His expression soured, and he sighed deeply, as though he found the question terribly dull.

"They are called the Mountains of Misfortune for a reason. Anyone foolish enough to enter them invites misfortune upon themselves," he rolled his eyes and then paused, glancing at her sidelong as if weighing the merits of sharing more.

"Perhaps the most intriguing thing that can be said about the Mountains are the people who supposedly live in caves to the North, or perhaps it is the South. I do not know. They are said to shun the ways of a sophisticated society. I have even heard it told once that they eat nothing except honeybees with stingers removed."

Kylene's heart leapt. The Kapnobatai. It must be them.

"But surely your family has prospected there or at least taken a survey of the mountain range and encountered some of the people who live there?" she said, holding her breath. She knew she was treading dangerous water by expressing interest, by pressing him further, but she would be nowhere if she could not find the Kapnobatai.

He turned his horse abruptly, mistrust sparking in his eyes. The movement almost threw her from her seat.

"And what business have you in the Mountains of Misfortune, mm? I've answered your question, now answer mine. Who. Are. You?" He licked his lips. Up close, Kylene could see they were dry and peeling in places, like a lizard shedding its skin.

"I've told you, my name is Kylene, I'm…" she reached for how to define herself.

She was…a girl. Just a girl. She didn't know who she was, apart from a daughter, a sister, an unwarranted apprentice to a mad physic. How did anyone define themselves?

"I'm a bellringer," she said at last, raising her chin in defiance.

Vicente's smile was broad, a wicked curve from ear to ear.

"I knew you were deliciously depraved. Come, night is falling. Let us make camp before it does. I hear a stream not far off. We will wash our hands and feet, and I will try to convince you to come over to the good side. It is not too late, you know," he gave her another smile and trotted forward, failing to notice that Kylene had reared Sable to a standstill several paces behind him.

She was done playing along like a good girl with less sense than a whetstone. Vicente would no longer sharpen the knife of his scheme upon her.

"I am not wicked, and I *am* on the good side. You and Osbert and everyone who follow him speak of freedom and fairness, and yet you carve up the earth like it all belongs to you," her chest heaved, and her words reverberated down the road. Half of them were her father's, and as she gave them voice, she realized she understood them now more than she ever had.

Vicente stopped without warning, and Kylene could see the bladed edge of his shoulders stiffen, sharp in silhouette against the sun's last rays of harsh splendor.

She thought of setting Sable to a gallop, back the way they had come, back to the crossroads, where there would surely be some safety in numbers.

He turned his gelding slowly. There was no exuberance in his face now, no feigned joy. Only a grim mask of spite.

His voice was low, slow, deathly quiet.

"Do you know what I can do to you?"

Sable pawed at the ground nervously, and she felt the animal quiver between her legs, wanting to take flight. All Kylene needed was the right moment to make her escape.

"What're you going to do? Strap me to your horse and bring me in? I'd like to see you try."

He stared at her, and she stared back. Then, with the ferocity of a wild beast, he sprang forward, closing the gap between their two horses. He was lunging, reaching for her. There was no time to react. He wrenched her face close to his, nearly pulling her off of Sable, a fistful of her hair crushed tightly in his velvet-gloved hand. Up close, he smelled strongly of peppermint, his black eyes limned with the barest hint of teal.

"What makes you think a dirty little slip of a bellringer like you deserves that length of my time? I will have done with you before the moon has risen, or sooner."

He tore Kylene from Sable and threw her to the ground. Sable reared, her hooves stamping down to the left of Kylene's head, only just missing her. The horse took off at a mad gallop, the clatter of her hooves fast-growing distant as she disappeared down the road.

Shapes and colors whirled in Kylene's blurred vision, the blackened form of Vicente the focal point around which all else swirled. He dismounted leisurely, and she heard him sigh as he peeled off one riding glove, then another, tossing them into his saddlebag carelessly, as though he'd just finished a very long day's ride.

He moved toward her with predatory grace, and she scuttled backward on hands and feet like some hapless crab.

In two swift strides, he seized her roughly by the shoulders, hauled her up, and dragged her off the road and into the thicket. Kylene's head throbbed and her vision swam as she struggled to fight back, her limbs heavy, her ears ringing. Finally, he released her and she dropped to the ground like a stone.

He knelt beside her, brushing a loose strand of hair from her face with chilling tenderness.

"I would've rathered your full cooperation, dear one. I suppose I could give you another chance, mm?" He ran his fingers gently through her hair, traced the line of her clavicle from her shoulder to her neck.

A scream stuck in her throat. She wanted to run, but her body was rooted to the forest floor. And so, silent and still, she waited.

The mingled smell of peppermint and mulch filled her nostrils, and she wanted to be sick. *But that would be a mistake,* said a small voice in her head. She forced down the bile rising in her throat.

"You are *such* a clever girl, but even the cleverest have much to learn. Do you know what I think? We were fated to meet one another, so I might teach you some things. We will start with your adorable allegiance to the losing side," he said in a dreamy voice, moving ever closer to her.

His face was so close to hers that she could feel his warm breath on her neck. Slowly, she began to advance her right hand toward the knife strapped to her upper thigh, still hidden beneath the thin cloth of her shift.

She had strapped it on only yesterday, moments after the peddler and she parted ways. She had felt ridiculous putting it there. At the same time, doing so had also made her feel invincible. It was not a knife for killing. It was a knife made for paring mushrooms from rotting wood, for coaxing roots from hard-packed soil.

He was doing something, preparing himself. She hardly knew what. Her focus was centered on her right hand, idle but poised, lingering on the hilt of her silver knife. Nothing else existed save her hand and her blade, and the place where she would bury it: the soft part of his neck, just above the collarbone.

He murmured something, honeysuckle-sweet, and she realized he was making to tie her hands behind her back.

That wouldn't do.

She tore the blade from its makeshift holster and plunged the length of it into his throat, the steel biting through his flesh with surprising ease. With strength she did not know she possessed, she wrenched the knife free in one savage movement, and Vicente fell, gasping.

Kylene scrabbled away, the rough earth tearing at her hands and knees. With trembling limbs, she hauled herself to her knees then, her feet, swaying dangerously, knife poised and at the ready.

Blood spurted from his neck like a fresh-broke well, more geyser than stream. From where he had fallen, he struggled to his knees and reached for her, his hands slow-dripping with his own crimson blood. Kylene hadn't known that blood had a smell. It was horseshoes and head nails and her mother's kettle, hanging in the hearth.

He lurched toward her with arms outstretched, and she staggered backward, barely evading his grasp. He fell forward onto his shoulder, his mouth opening and closing like a fish on dry land. Kylene watched with detached fascination, transfixed by the spectacle of death drawn so near.

She forced herself to tear away her gaze and turned, taking one dragging step, then another, and a third before collapsing into a heap. The world around her dissolved into a crimson-black nothingness. The last thing she remembered, before all the light went out, was McBane, and how he'd explained to her that the throat was the fastest and surest way to kill a man.

Chapter Ten

On their fourth day as a troupe, the oaks gave way to mountain laurel, alpine currant, juniper and cypress. The air grew thick with mist that rose up from the ground and clung heavy to their cloaks as they wound their way further up the High Road, closer to Droch Fhortan.

It was a queer thing indeed that they had not encountered other wayfarers. Such an occurrence was rare, even for the High Road. Despite its restriction, there was always the odd peddler trying to get to the next town with haste or away from one in which a trade had gone sour. And brigands, trouped or otherwise, were not an uncommon sight, using the road as a sort of retreat in between schemes.

Ivan's Law ensured no one ever bothered their fellow travelers on the High Road, mostly. It was an unwritten understanding among those who traversed it that one's affairs were their own, no matter how unsavory. All who used it acted in a spirit of rebellion against Osbert and thus were more alike than not. The Law took its name from a freebooter infamous for cutting throats. The rumor was that he held his blade against a cobbler on the run and uttered the now-famous words, "Keep your throat for blasphemin' the old goat." The cobbler must've kept his word, else the tale wouldn't have spread about the Grasp like wildfire.

It was passing strange to have seen no peacekeepers, who still patrolled the High and the Bottom Road just as they did any other square mile of the Grasp. Their absence made Lovelace expressly uneasy. He would've expected an outfit or two, or fresh tracks, at the very least, indicating recent passage.

As they ascended up and out of the valley, they caught sight of the first of Droch Fhortan's tallest peaks. Its smooth, rounded top was capped with snow, resembling nothing so much as a thimble atop the thick thumb of a giant.

Last night, while the boys were out scrounging up fodder for supper, Lovelace and Gunnar examined the second tablet of verdanite thrust upon them by Manoc. A sense of betrayal still simmered in Lovelace; the slab was nothing but a retread of an old sgeulachd they'd long since committed to memory. What was Manoc playing at?

The sgeuls installed within the verdanite were a mosaic of tales, originating from the time of the Meorachadh's construction, and the battle that almost transpired between the dactyli and the king's troops assigned to exterminate them. Andromere, as it was called then, did not encompass the land east of Droch Fhortan and was governed by a warlord king named Ferromir. Few knew these details, now.

Kito, the presiding dactyli master, and his brethren used their formidable abilities to rent open the earth in a near-perfect circle around their stronghold before the battle began. The king's troops, awestruck and unnerved by such magic, were cut off in their advance by the chasm.

General LeMarc, the highly decorated commanding officer, lay down his arms, renounced his fealty to Ferromir and pledged himself to the order on the spot. One by one, his soldiers did likewise. After witnessing the earth being rent in two by the sheer will of man, General LeMarc and his troops were convinced that there was something on earth worth fighting for that bore greater distinction than King Ferromir and his insatiable whims.

The dactyli – confident as they were in their ability to protect themselves and desiring, as they did, to continue their work without interference – tried to release General LeMarc and his men from their oaths. In the end, General LeMarc and his troops refused to abandon their newfound purpose. Thus, the township of Mortalis was founded, and the Covenant of Clasped Hands forged, no matter how trifling such an alliance might be for the likes of the dactyli.

It was a story that all dactyli were shown as tyros, still in the process of understanding their purpose, what they were, and who they would become. Lovelace had always thought of it as nothing more than an origin story, a cozy tale meant to share over cups. Now, he was left puzzling over its significance and how it could possibly be of use.

The closer they got to the mountains, the larger the question of what to do with the boys loomed. To keep them safe, they must be kept close. And with the unknown dangers that lay ahead, preparation was critical.

And so it was, for the first time in an age, that a dactyli would attempt to explain their ways to an ordinary person. Lovelace had volunteered. In some small way, he relished the opportunity and imagined feeling lighter after sharing what had been so long forbidden. A burden shared was a burden halved, after all.

"Gather up some kindling for the fire, boys, and keep your ears pricked. I've an important thing or two to share about the road ahead," Lovelace said, perching himself crossed-legged on a slab of cold granite. *Nervy as a turkey before a roast,* he remarked as he pressed trembling fingers flat on either thigh.

They were within spitting distance of the pass and had found a suitable spot to rest for the evening. Since Lovelace had taken on the task of educating the boys, Gunnar would do the surveying. After tying up the horses, he disappeared into the mist-shrouded cypress.

Lovelace cleared his throat. "Now I suppose the both of you have some idea of what Gunnar and I do, seeing as it's obvious we don't sit around and tell fortunes all year long," he said, clearing his throat again – this time more forcibly – as he watched them set about the task of fire building.

"I can stab at a guess, m'lord," Pif said, his voice a vibrant trill that echoed oddly among the towering cypress and tumbledown traces of mountain that cropped up here and there like sleeping giants.

"You go all about the land gathering wisdom to bring back to the Meorachadh for safekeeping," he said, excitement causing each word to quaver. For four days Pif had been peppering them with questions that had largely gone unanswered.

Lovelace grunted in surprise, "And where, pray tell, did you hear that, lad?"

Pif shrugged and stooped low to pick up a wispy piece of beard lichen, fallen from a nearby tree.

"S'pose it just makes sense. S'far's I know most folk don't even know dactyli have ranger types, so when you told me that's what you were, and me knowing – of course – that once upon a time there was A'Tabhann – though it was a'fore my time – where'n you lot used to give out wisdom like sweets...I put one and one together."

A broad smile spread across Lovelace's face and he glanced at Ailwin. Sure enough, he was digging the pit for the fire with an expression on his face that would've curdled milk.

"Don't bother with the old man's beard, lad," Lovelace told Pif. "Too much moisture in it. Even if you manage to catch it, it'll make the fire squeal like a stuck pig."

Pif scrutinized the lichen, sniffed it, tasted it, and then dropped it with a nod. He began to scurry from juniper to juniper, collecting dried needles and tucking them under his arm, ears pricked for whatever came out of Lovelace's mouth next.

"You've got about the short of it. Gunn and I are rangers. The ones that used to mete out wisdom at A'Tabhann are the masters. A master was once a ranger or a scribe, which is the other type of dactyli you can become." He scratched his head and paused. "Though, to be fair, it's rare for a ranger to be made into a master, seeing as it's the scribes who are the most intimate with the organization of the Tasglann. Anyhow, so there's scribes and rangers, then masters..."

"What's the Tasglann?" asked Pif.

"It's our library of sorts, where all the work of our order is maintained."

"So you have a great collection of chronicles, then?" asked Ailwin.

"Well...In a sense. But it's not quite like your libraries. For starts, there are no books..."

"How do you have a library with no books?!" Pif said, dropping an armful of juniper needles into the center of Ailwin's pit with fresh indignation.

"We use a different sort of system."

"What sort of system, then?" Pif said. He shook his head as if Lovelace might be delusional and whispered, "...A library without books, the idea!" They both stared at him, skepticism written plainly across their features.

Lovelace hesitated. How to explain that the dactyli had discovered a way to house memories within the crystalline structure of a stone? How then to describe that not just one memory is stored, but many, and not just the many, but also one – carefully constructed by a scribe – comprising, melding, orienting all of them, the sum of which they called a sgeulachd. Truth made crystal.

How then to tell them that some of those memories weren't even those of a human, but events chronicled from the vantage point of a well-positioned redwood tree or a firmly lodged boulder? He shook his head, wishing for inspiration that did not belong to him.

"I can't explain what sort of system now," he said shortly, patience taking flight with the swiftness of a starling. "Now, where was I? There are rangers, scribes...masters. There. So, we rangers exist to perform two duties. One, to gather wisdom, as you say, and two, to root out and find nascent dactyli..."

"Young dactyli!" shouted Pif.

"Yes, Pif, young boys like you who have the potential to be dactyli. And that is why we are here today. We've been sent on a ranging to secure a boy who has the potential to be dactyli, possibly the greatest yet that we have seen..."

Lovelace's words hung heavy in the air. "Like you," he had said, and at once, Ailwin's brown eyes and Pif's muddy green caught flame from the spark of his ill-chosen words. For once, Ailwin beat Pif to the blade.

"How do you choose?" he said, the question quiet but heavy-laden, full of hope and yearning.

"You either have the potential or you don't, lad," Lovelace said, gentle as he dared. "And it's not something that can be taught to just anybody. It is a gift you are born with, a rare and precious thing. We have an instrument at the Meorachadh that was created using magic lost to us today, by one of the first of our kind, a dactyli named Oi..." he said. The image of Alev amid a great whirl of flame sprang up in his mind. *Lost and mayhap found,* he thought darkly.

"It's a great orb about the size of..." He scanned their campsite for a likely boulder and found one directly behind Ailwin, roughly the size of an archery target. "...that rock there."

Ailwin nodded solemnly, not even bothering to turn around. He fixed his face into a look of concentration as he began to splinter pieces of dried cypress with his blade, an ancient-looking piece of iron that he kept remarkably sharp.

"But how do you know for sure that it can't be taught, that you have to be born with it?" Pif asked, not so easily deterred.

"Well..." Lovelace started. *How indeed?*

"It's just the way it's always been. Dactyli aren't made. I mean, we're all taught once we get to the Meorachadh; how to control our powers, how to exercise them. But there's never been a taught dactyli who didn't display a tendency first..."

"How do you know for sure? Have y'ever tried?" Pif demanded. "Show me. Show me how to do something. Dig a hole. Light the fire."

Lovelace sighed. "It's not that simple, lad. You're asking the impossible."

He sympathized for them both, really, he did. Several days on the road with him and Gunnar, displaying even simple magic as they had, was bound to entice a young boy. Still, this wasn't a time for play or a show of soft feelings; there was real and present danger that they must be made to understand. So he took a deep breath and tried again. "Right. So, as I mentioned, we have the orb. And every so often, the orb will show flares. Bursts of colored light, that's how nascent dactyli show up, and we know roughly where to search. It's a model of the Grasp, you see, and a bit beyond, but not so far as the lands beyond the sea."

"What's beyond the Grasp?!"

"There's land beyond the sea?"

"Enough," Lovelace had to keep himself from shouting. "Nascent dactyli show up as a flare, a burst of energy, if you like, which is what, in essence, our powers do with the elements: concentrate and manipulate energy." His words came tumbling out, pouring from him like so many ants from a hill.

"There are two things about this circumstance that make this different than our typical rangings."

He didn't want to frighten them, but it needed to be said.

"One, the flare is white. Now, usually, a dactyli shows a special affinity for one of the four main elements that make up this world: earth, fire, wind, water. I am an earth dactyli, Gunnar is wind."

"What makes an earth dactyli an earth dactyli an' a wind dactyli wind an' so on?"

Lovelace inhaled sharply. He could feel the familiar stirrings of his outbred temper, hot within his chest. He exhaled slowly, letting the air out in a hiss before he began again.

"I can't answer any more questions now, lads; we'll be here all night and a day and another night besides." *If not longer.* The years had dulled the extraordinary nature of his life, but this conversation was an unpleasant reminder that he and his craft were far from ordinary.

"Anyhow, an earth dactyli would appear in the orb as green, water, blue and so on..."

"What about fire? Is that red?" Pif's mouth formed into a tiny O and he immediately clapped two small hands over his mouth.

"Yes..." Lovelace said, gritting his teeth, the unwelcome image of Alev stepping through flame arising again.

"White is an anomaly," he said, forcing the memory aside. "Nowhere in the entire Tasglann is there mention or instance of a white flare. The masters have developed the theory that a white flare is the manifestation of one capable of wielding all the elements, an ability not seen since Oi himself, the one who created the orb and founded the order."

Ailwin nodded as if everything Lovelace had said made perfect sense. He'd finished digging the fireplace and was beginning to stack his splintered pieces of cypress onto the hearth while Pif continued to pile small logs and juniper needles to kindle the flame.

Somewhere distant, the faint sound of footfall as Gunnar continued his survey, out of sight, undoubtedly laughing silently as Lovelace floundered to explain the gravity of their circumstance. But there was no time for self-doubt. He still hadn't conveyed the actual danger pervading the whole thing.

"The white flare aside, this ranging is an outstanding circumstance because for the last seven years, our kind has been hunted. There was one dactyli who left our order thirteen years ago. He is the hunter. He disappeared for a time, doing Mother knows what, but he resurfaced seven years ago. Moreover, he is rooting out and dispatching nascent dactyli before we can secure them. And the accursed thing is, he's succeeding."

"Dispatching?" asked Pif.

"Killing them," said Ailwin quietly.

Both boys stared at him with a mixture of pity and wonder.

"That's…that's a lot. An awful lot for two such men to bear, m'lord," Pif said.

"Right. Well, now you know what we're up against," Lovelace said gruffly, unwilling to take pity from a stripling of a boy, no matter how well deserved. "Stand aside now, lads."

They stood back without a word, and he turned from them, crouching before the fire to worry away at tinder and flint.

"If you don't mind, sir," Ailwin said tentatively. "How has he been succeeding? Surely the power of all is no match for a solitary fugitive."

"There are two answers to that, lad," Lovelace said between flint strikes. "One, is institutional corrosion. The second. Is as yet unknown to us."

The fire caught with a great, sucking *whoosh*.

"This man, Alev is his name, was a passing clever dactyli when he was at the Meorachadh. Could be that in the absence of rule and reason, he's developed skills beyond what is known. Gone rogue," he said, trailing.

"More-uh-chath," Ailwin said. "So that's what the fortress is called where you live, where A'Tabhann once was held?"

"Aye, that is where both Gunnar and I have lived for most of our lives. Myself since I was no more than Pif's age and Gunnar, I think he was sixteen."

"We thought the name was sacred-like," Pif said, wide-eyed and clutching his sling. "Heard it called the Fortress at the End of the World, Dactyli Drey…"

"We see a lot of types coming through the Colt," Ailwin said suddenly, staring at the flames crackling in the pit. "And I can't say as other folks in the Grasp see you as kindly as most of us in Mortalis do. There are many who would call you false prophets, or worse."

"The order is on its deathbed," Gunnar said as he strode into the clearing.

Both boys straightened visibly as Gunnar crouched and splayed his fingers before the fire to warm them.

"It is in an era of decay," Gunnar continued, staring into the flame. "If we have learned nothing from a thousand years of sgeul-gathering and sgeulachd-making, it is that things grow, things die, things are reborn. Nothing is obliged to stay the same. The order is no different. It is inbred conceit that prevents the masters from seeing it themselves."

Lovelace gaped. It was a damnably forthright thing to say and not in any way keeping with Gunnar's usual brand of wool.

Of course, Gunnar was right. Their eyes met across the flame, and Lovelace was struck by what he saw in them. There was an animation, a liveliness about them that Lovelace had seen but rarely.

"What do you say then, Gunn? Have you found us a trail?"

"Aye," said Gunnar. He leaned back against a fallen log and began methodically to remove the dirt from beneath his fingernails.

"Has he been this way then, the white flare?" Lovelace asked.

"She has," Gunnar said.

Lovelace blinked. "Come again? What do you mean by she?"

Ailwin and Pif stared, eyes equally wide with curiosity. The fire had grown and stood nearly as tall as Pif. It was crackling, ravenous, the sound of its hunger a riot overlaid upon the stark silence that marked the day surrendering to night.

Gunnar looked up at Lovelace, the light of the fire flickering bright in his eyes.

"I meant what I said. She has."

Chapter Eleven

Kylene awoke to night, indifferent and dark.

She startled, remembering. A sharp intake of breath. A pounding in her skull. Her heart was in her throat. From left to right, she moved her head, slow as a slug over leaf mold. The moonless sky above, black, covered over in gray clouds like shrouds; she could scarcely see the world around her. Slowly, it came into focus, and when it did, she saw the dark mound.

Vicente lay in a heap, a shadow in the night. *Strange, how tidy.* The clean contours of his shadow were in stark contrast to the reality of his bloody end. Nausea rose up within her in a roiling wave and she retched, violently, onto the pine needles beneath her.

Guts purged, she staggered to her feet and trudged, step by heavy step, back to the High Road. Her passage was dragging, stumbling, swerving, her feet snagging on twisted roots.

At last, she found that bend of road where he had torn her from Sable just as a thin sliver of moonshine began to show meekly through the clouds.

Amid trampled vines, she dropped to her knees, searching for a remnant of her father's letters, his notebook, a scrap of paper...anything that might serve as a symbol to show her that all was not lost.

Nothing. There was nothing left. The saddlebag and everything inside of it were with Sable, wherever she had ridden off.

With a further turn of her stomach, she became aware that she'd forgotten her knife. It was her only possession now, save for the torn and dirty fabric she wore that was once a dress. She peered down at her feet. At least she still had her boots.

Forcing one foot in front of the other, she retraced her wobbling passage back to the dark place where she had killed him.

Killed him. She'd done it on purpose. It seemed impossible. Glimmering there, beside his head, lay the knife. It shone like a jewel in the leaf litter, stopping her short. Another wave of sickness racked her body. She gasped, heaved and it was done. Swallowing the great lump in her throat, she squeezed her eyes tight, took one deep breath and moved forward to retrieve it.

She picked up the thing hastily and lurched, nearly stumbling onto Vicente's lifeless body. Recovering herself, she bent low to wipe the blood, sticky and black, onto the hood of his outspread cloak.

She rose and stood. Too quickly, far too fast. Her head spun, and her feet grew roots. The night was clear around her, yet it lurched in her vision, keeling like a sea in a storm.

Her gaze fell upon him, and she steadied herself, desperately trying to shove aside the revulsion that pulsed through her. *Take heed, Kylene, take heed.*

His boots were fine – a rich orange leather, oiled to a shine, and newly soled. His pants, too, with stitches so tight it seemed as though they hadn't been stitched at all. And his cloak. The black velvet of it had shimmered, obsidian-bright, when he moved this way or that.

A shudder ran through her. *No.* She wouldn't carry a thing he'd worn, couldn't bear the thought or feel of shared cloth on her skin, no matter how lustrous. Leaving him where he lay, she forced herself away.

His horse was there, where he'd left him. *Strange*, she'd been there only moments ago and had not noticed the great black beast.

The gelding whickered at her, regarding her with eyes large and liquid, like tar gone running. But they were not unkind, those eyes, not cruel as his master's had been.

An animal, she decided, *does not belong to a man.* She outstretched her hand and let it settle upon the animal's muzzle. Without thought, she unbuckled his saddle, her hands moving clumsily, numb from being so still in the cold.

Finally, he was free of it. She shoved the burden off of him, and it landed on the ground with a thud. The horse trembled as she gripped his mane in both hands and swung herself up and onto his sleek back.

With a press of her heel, she nudged him onward through the night.

***

Beneath crusted lashes, she opened her eyes to tendrils of mist curling around trees. Somewhere behind the birdsong that filled her ears, the fine-pitched sound of a whistle burst through the veil of morning.

Atop the still-moving body of Vicente's horse, bent at the waist with her face pressed against the ridge line of his mane, she rose sharply.

Acid churned in her stomach, and fear crept down her arms, covering her in goose prickle. Someone was whistling 'The Bonny Dunes of Locharn,' and they weren't far from here.

She felt ragged, torn in several different directions. The urge to scream, to run, to be sick and to cry all clamored for precedence, overwhelming and desperate. Before any of these could come to pass, a peddler rounded the corner, his falsetto finale ringing gaily from between two front teeth.

The man froze at the sight of Kylene, and she at him. From top to bottom, he took her in, from the fineness of her horse to the tattered drapes of her dress. Without a word, he took up the tune again, softer this time, as he worked a bottle loose from a knotted rope haversack draped around his mule's neck.

It took Kylene a moment to realize it was the same peddler she'd treated with not two days back, *or was it three? And what had his name been?* Her memories were fragmented, sharp as splintered wood.

She shook her head, trying to clear it, to grasp onto something solid. It beat like a drum, with pain, with fear, and a sudden animal urge shot through her, demanding she turn tail and disappear into the brush.

And then she saw Sable.

The horse tied loosely behind the pack mule regarded her solemnly, as if she, too, remembered their parting conditions. The saddlebag still hung suspended on either side of her ribcage.

Kylene could not flee. Not yet, at least.

"Here you go, missy, here you go," the peddler said, offering her a bottle.

She stared at him.

"Water, miss, it's only water," he said, shaking the bottle to emphasize his claim.

She snatched it from his hands and gulped down its contents. It tasted like chalk, but it washed away the bile from her tongue.

As she slopped and spilled half of the water down her front, she looked down and saw that she was caked with mud and blood.

"I see the road's been fearsome unkind to you, miss, and I'm that sorry to see it. Took your horse not a bell back; she was proper spooked. Fed her some barley, and set her to water. She ought t'be alright." He eyed Kylene nervously. "I might offer the same to you; a mouthful o' food and drink. It might not set you to rights as quick as your horse here, but I'd wager it'd be a step in the right direction."

Kylene shrugged stiffly and said nothing. *Respond,* she commanded. But her mind was working fearfully slow. It felt dull, like a blade whose edge has grown tired from the repetition of blunt force.

"I-I'll thank you kindly to return my horse and all of the things you may have found on her," she said, forcing her eyes up to look at...*Gingham, his name is Gingham,* she thought muddily. She then remembered she was speaking.

"*All* of the things, assuming you still have them?"

He nodded slowly and raised a single hand in gentle treaty.

"Of course, miss, and might I ask, without seeming presumptuous like, if'n you have need of two horses, wherever it is you might be going?"

Her gaze shifted downward. The dirt beneath her boots was the precise shade of brown as her mother's saxesilt cheese.

Her entire being seemed to be in revolt. Her limbs were obstinate, her speech halting. A mutinous rebellion was being launched against the intact part of her mind that was reasonably sure he meant her no harm.

With a grimace, she slid off the back of her towering mount. Her body was battered, aching and stiff, as if she'd been put through a meat grinder while she slept dreamless in the saddle.

Kylene stood stationary in the middle of the road. The morning air was cool and fanned her feverish brow. She clutched Vicente's horse by the reins and forced her gaze to meet Gingham's.

He took a small step forward, both hands raised.

Her instincts gave an almighty shriek. She threw the reins at Gingham and sprinted toward Sable. The mare whinnied in surprise as Kylene clambered onto her back, hunching low over her neck and resting her head on the soft place between her ears.

Realization struck her with sudden, chilling clarity. Her mind had been cleaved in two – one half, the rational, sensible part of her, and the other, an animal that roared and raged and threatened to consume her. Her body, for the most part, was obeying the animal.

She needed her sensible half to assert its dominance, to bridle the wild and regain control.

With great effort, she focused on his eyes – a watery blue like thin-stretched sky – but she could not maintain the gaze.

"Take the horse," she said, her voice rasping like a hinge that needs oiling.

She plunged her hand into Sable's pack, searching for the packet of letters and her father's notebook. Her fingers brushed them, wrapped tightly with twine and seemingly undisturbed.

The peddler bowed his head. "I thank you kindly, missy. What can I give you that might be equal to this fine animal? It wouldna sit right with me if I didn't give you something in exchange."

Kylene paid him no heed, her fingers fumbling with the rope that tethered Sable to the mule.

Gingham rummaged around in one of the heavy-laden packs atop his mule. From the depths of one, he produced a hard biscuit wrapped in wax paper and took one step closer, offering it to her.

With cautious steps, he approached Sable's saddlebag and deposited the biscuit inside. Kylene sat frozen, hardly daring to draw breath as he drew near.

"Where will you go?" he asked, retreating with equal care.

Her gaze traveled down to the space between Sable's ears. It was soft and brown with sparse white hairs which fluttered in the morning breeze.

She knew she should answer. That Gingham may very well possess something – information or item – which could be of immense value to her. That he had shown no intention of doing her harm.

But the best she could manage was the meanest of replies.

"The Mountains of Misfortune," she said, pulling the words from deep within her. They still sounded grating, foreign. Had she been screaming last night, to have altered her voice so?

"Know of them?"

Gingham shifted nervously.

"Aye, miss, I do. But what business could you possibly have there, less'n of course you're headed for either Gavilene or Arcellen?"

"I'm looking for the Kapnobatai," she said, her two halves warring within her.

The pity in Gingham's eyes evaporated, replaced by a deep curiosity tinged with a bit of wariness. He squinted and cocked his head, reassessing her. Then, he looked up and down the road as if he expected to discover someone dropping eaves.

"Aye," he said, his voice dropped to a hoarse whisper. He returned his gaze to her, appearing powerfully torn on how best to respond.

"They'll be in the eastern portion of the mountains, concluding their summer work and gathering the last of the mandrake roots and sun cabbages before they move west for the winter," he said, clearing his throat. "I tell you this because yon horse is worth most of what I've got in both my packs. The information I'm prepared to give you might be worth more, mind. Aren't many who know where'n the Kapnobatai are at any given time. They'll be on the western portion come middle 'o fall, but since we're only in the last days of summer's end, I imagine you'll find them there still, on the east side, that is."

He leaned forward and crooked his finger, bidding her to come closer. Kylene shifted in the saddle, her leaden bones having none of it.

"Take the High Road near as far as Arcellen. A bell or so before you get there, there'll be a fork in the road and a shabby sign saying Damp Gulch Pass, one o' the two passes you see. You'll know it by the tumbledown ruin of a temple behind it, was dedicated to one o' the Sons. Not sure which. It's that fork you'll want to take, else you'll end in Arcellen met with a bunch o' suspicious, short-minded mountain folk. You'll be a quarter o' the way up Damp Gulch Pass – which won't be easy t'go up, mind – before you'll see a redwood with its heart cleaved straight from it." He inhaled sharply, taking a deep breath. "There's a stream that runs straight 'neath it, comes from the top o' Droch Fhortan, east to west. Follow it east. If you look real close like, you'll see it's a path that's there beside the stream but it's trodden so light and with such mindful feet most folk would ne'er know the difference. Start at dawn from the split redwood, to mind your time."

"What did you call them?" Kylene asked sharply. She had grabbed onto his every word, the shape and the sound of them, committing them to memory. In some small way, the act had anchored her, kept her from drifting away in the sea of wild thought and feeling.

"Droch Fhortan – the Mountains of Misfortune – though few know it by that name these days. Thought you might, though, seeing as how it's the Kapnobatai you're seekin' out, and hardly anybody knows about them." He paused and gave her a remarkably fluid bow. "'Ceptin' o' course the most discerning of us tradesfolk, and then o' course the persons the Kapnobatai seek to treat with."

"And after I head east along the stream at dawn, as you say..."

"Ah. Then, you will follow the stream until the sun is high in the sky." He scratched his head, which was topped with a woolly knitted cap. "Yes, at this time o' year, that'd be about right. Follow the stream 'til the sun is high. And then, you wait."

"Wait for what, exactly?" she asked, tendrils of suspicion coiling loosely around her chest. More and more, this sounded like some quest of legend. She needed facts, not far-fetched vagaries and directions that seemed best placed in bard song.

"For a scout to come and find you," he said, suggesting that much was obvious. "I believe they send out two a day. One in the morn, one in the afternoon. They're proper busy, are

Kapnobatai. Timely, though." He pulled the thick cap off his head and scratched his balding pate with an uneasy hand.

Kylene's eyes drilled into Gingham, trying to find the truth within his words. His answers *seemed* to come from experience, and she had trusted him upon their first meeting two days ago...*or was it three?*

She had thought him an honest sort of fellow then. Someone who considered the art of trade as something of a code to which he was compelled to adhere. And now? She should be wary of everyone, especially one who earned their daily bread through commerce. What did the peddler have to gain by helping her?

"And I'm to believe that if I follow your instructions exactly, I will find the Kapnobatai and keep myself away from harm?"

He laughed. It had a slippery quality, like a fish trying to wriggle from her grasp.

"Missy, you're dreaming if you think you're out o' harm's way, slip of a thing that you are, out here on the High Road all alone, askin' stray peddlers for information that elsewhere might get you killed. No, you're not out o' harm's way. But if you keep to my instructions, aye, you'll find yourself with the Kapnobatai, and they'll take you in too, fine folk they are. Don't talk much, but they're fine folk."

"How many days' time?"

"Three, if you're quick about it, only sleep when the sun does and..." He winked at her, "...Stay out o' harm's way, as you say."

She nodded her thanks.

"Think nothin' of it," he said, noting the gesture. "Say," he continued, peering at her curiously. "Are you sure you wouldn't rather come with me, miss? I'm heading for Mortalis. There're folks there who'll see you home, or else join you on your journey, for a price. I could see you have the necessary coin to ensure you're proper taken care of."

But Kylene was already digging her heels into Sable's flanks. She had what she needed, nothing more and nothing less.

"You've been kind and fair," she called out, looking back only to ensure he did not follow. "You have my thanks."

As she rode, the chilly air bit into her ears and brought tears, hot and stinging, to her eyes. She spurred Sable onwards. The unknown road stretched out before her in a blur and all Kylene could do was pin her hopes on the cryptic words of a stranger, and pray they would not lead her astray.

Chapter Twelve

The Damp Gulch Pass lived up to its sodden name. For two long days, they combed the treacherous terrain from the break of dawn to the dying embers of twilight, soaked to the bone and chilled to the marrow, to no avail. In spite of their efforts, the girl remained elusive.

But they were not entirely empty-handed. They had learned some things while tramping up and down the pass. Through paper birch and red pine forest, they tracked her imprint, her passage meandering and feather-light.

She was a wild thing, that much they could glean from the traces she left behind. Somewhere between Pif and Ailwin in age, her hair was dark and hung down to her waist in a great mass of unruly curls. She was fine-boned but not small. And she moved through the landscape with easy, feline grace, suggesting that she had made these mountains her home for many years if not all of her life.

They had witnessed her power, seen her dowse out water from deep within the earth and bid moss to weave itself into thick blankets. They had also seen her split whole trees with a single glance and, just this morning, coax to life a flame with nothing more than a whispered exhale.

As they pieced together the splinters of her life from the trunks of birch and pine, they concluded that she did not stay in one place for long.

Lovelace did a great deal of explaining the intricacies of terracommunication to the boys. Ailwin at least seemed to grasp the concept, raising fewer queries than Pif, who couldn't quite wrap his head around the fact that stone and wood had eyes and ears, that the earth could experience and record events as they did.

"I can't understand it!" Pif said on the third day of their search. They'd risen with the sun and were following a scant trail found by Gunnar the night before. It was early still. Blue mist hung low overhead and the birds were beginning their morning song.

Pif had taken to resting the palm of his hand on boulders and trees, as he had seen Lovelace and Gunnar do. He would stick the tiniest bit of his tongue out of the side of his mouth and squeeze his eyes shut, giving his face the grooved appearance of a peach pit. His attempts to terracommunicate had begun with a cocksure confidence that quickly devolved into bitter frustration as he failed again and again.

"I told you, lad, it's not so simple as just closing your eyes and stilling your mind. You've got to have the disposition for it," Lovelace said, as he had, time and time again.

Pif remained unconvinced.

The boy was sure that he could learn anything he put his mind to, so long as the instructions were sound. Most recently, he had formed the opinion that his inability to grasp the art of terracommunication did not stem from his inadequacy but from Lovelace's ineptitude as a teacher.

Pif's constant badgering for more information grated on Lovelace's nerves, and he found himself giving the boy small bits of advice to keep him quiet. The strategy hadn't had the desired effect.

Gunnar wouldn't stand for this, he thought as he watched Pif remove his hand from the unfurling tendril of a fern, huffing. *He'd cuff the lad on the head, give him one of those looks, and that'd be the end.* As it was, the boy was pushing *him* around like a peddler's cart.

"All kinds of memories pop up when I quiet my mind, like wee mushrooms, but all of them are mine."

Lovelace winced at the boy's strident words, which rang out through the mist like a struck bell.

He removed his hand from the trunk of a red cedar, where he had managed to extricate nothing save the endless passage of deer and robin song.

"Keep your voice down, lad," he said, looking down to see Pif staring at him, eyebrows raised expectantly. Why couldn't he just crush the boy's dreams and be done with it?

Lovelace gave a heavy sigh. "You can't trust short-lived plants like ferns; you need something that's been around for a spell longer than a season," he said, picking up his satchel to move deeper into the forest.

"But wouldn't a younger plant be better? If'n she's been here this season. Less memories to sift through, don't you think?"

The question made Lovelace pause. It was an obvious observation, yet one he had never considered. He grunted in faint surprise, reaching for a nearby fern erupting from the trunk of a slender young hemlock. Running his fingers over the soft, tiny hairs of its underleaf, he wondered whether a fern *would* suit.

"I was taught that trees are best. They have a substantial lifespan and are patient observers. Ferns, on the other hand, are short-lived and prone to drama. And they have an insatiable thirst. Alters their point of focus," he explained, trailing off. Pif stared at him, clearly expecting a more substantial response.

Lovelace took a deep breath and continued to walk uphill through the mist. "You can access a tree's mother's memories as well if you really want to, but they'll be pale and fragmented. Like patchwork. A tree's own memories are fresh as sap, springy like green wood, if you'll forgive the figures of speech. Take this hemlock, for instance," he slapped the dull green-gray bark of a trunk that was twice as broad as those surrounding it – the mother tree.

"If I wished to access its memory of a girl, I would simply empty my mind and ask it to show me. Now, you'd need to be more specific if we were in a town or some such place where there's all manner of girls passing by at any given bell. In this case, it's not likely that many girls will pass this way, so it'll be a less difficult sgeul to find. Visualization, plain and simple. Of course, you can go processionally through time if you wish, starting at the beginning and working your way backward, skipping where needed. That's painfully tedious, though. Better to have an idea before you ask," he paused, taking a ragged inhale. That was it, more or less, and if that wasn't enough for young Master Pif...

"Still, a fern makes sense, given what we're out here lookin' for..." Pif muttered as he dropped down behind a fallen log to place a hand delicately on its mossy side, the tip of his tongue poked out in concentration.

"I suppose," Lovelace cleared his throat loudly, "that a fern *might* suit, given the circumstances," he said, shifting his hand from the trunk of the hemlock and placing it furtively on the fern growing from a crack in the bark. He'd become so accustomed to terracommunicating with trees the notion that the rest of the world was equally outspoken had fled his purview.

"As for stone, well, it's possible to tap into, but it's never the preferred medium," Lovelace continued in a hushed tone. "They've been around for so long their memories are passing mad, all jumbled and muddled. It's hard to get a clear picture unless you're powerfully focused or highly skilled."

His voice dropped to a murmur as he channeled his luth into making contact with the fern, who immediately divulged the events of the last month in a cheerful, endless stream. It was peaceful, rhythmic: the awakening of an alpine forest from late winter onward – painted lady butterflies and woolly beetles, mountain goats with shaggy white coats, the occasional herd of elk.

Somewhere distant, he could hear the faint echo of a scream. It was no memory. He opened his eyes to find Pif crouched low by his side, his hand on his sling.

The scream had punctured the present, quiet velvet of morning. The peaceful feeling that had come over him as he'd watched the forest come alive via fern turned sour. Heart thumping, he took off in the direction Gunnar and Ailwin had gone, hurtling over fallen logs and zigzagging through the trees. Pif followed behind him without a sound.

The scream belonged to Ailwin. Judging by the sound of it, he wasn't far off. Lovelace took off at a run for where he'd heard it echo: the mountain's sharp brink. Ailwin and Gunnar had meant to examine the cave systems that dotted the mountainside, connected like latticework.

Abruptly, the forest opened up to an expanse of sky, with a bottomless drop to a canopy shrouded in clouds. The height was dizzying, and Lovelace instinctively threw out an arm to stop Pif as he came skidding to a halt, hot on his heels.

"Follow behind, not too close now," he said to Pif as he began to move down the jagged face using hands and feet, onto a ledge like a shelf wrapped down and around the mountainside. They moved quickly, hugging their bodies against the rock as they edged toward the wide opening of the first cave.

Its mouth gaped open, a cavernous maw as wide as three horses nose-to-tail. Lovelace and Pif peered around its edge.

There, at the back of the cave, was Ailwin.

Kneeling and unaware of their presence, he had a wound on his thigh that trickled blood. Five men clad in red-burnished mail bore down on him in a semi-circle.

Gunnar was nowhere to be seen.

Lovelace's heart pounded in his chest as he and Pif edged away from the cave mouth.

His mind raced through every possible action plan, dismissing each idea as soon as it had risen. He knew what was needed.

"Stay back, do you hear?"

Pif gave him an affirmative nod, but there was something about the shine of his eyes that Lovelace didn't like. The boy was far too at ease in the presence of danger. None too gently, Lovelace grabbed his wrist. It was so slight that the tip of his thumb wrapped all the way around and touched the opposing knuckle of his middle finger. He fixed Pif with a fierce stare.

"I mean it, Pif. If ever there was a time not to match a sling to a sword, make that five of them, it's a cliff face with no cover," he whispered hoarsely. "I don't care how good of a shot you are. You'll stay here as you're told, and if I'm taken, make like a hare and find Gunnar."

Pif nodded again. He lowered his sling but did not return it to his sack.

Lovelace steadied himself and stepped forward into the mouth of the cave, fully visible to the men encircling Ailwin. A look of faint surprise registered on Ailwin's face, quickly replaced by grim determination.

The men were closing in, their taunting words lost to Lovelace's ears.

With a deep breath, he took another step forward and spread his arms wide.

This could go one of two ways.

"Hoy!" Lovelace's cry echoed off the cave walls threefold. It was enough to turn the heads of three of the men. The other two remained fixed on Ailwin.

Not amateurs, then, Lovelace thought as he channeled his luth and lunged forward, bringing down a curtain of granite rubble. The sudden barrage scattered their ranks, giving Lovelace the opportunity to tuck and roll into the corner of the cave, securing a high-ground position.

But one of the men had only been knocked off balance by the rubble and immediately charged toward Lovelace. Lovelace raised his arm, and from the granite floor of the cave, a stone spire rose and impaled the man through the middle.

Lovelace sighed. He hated killing.

He took up a loose rock, pulverized it to dust in his hand and threw it into the face of his next attacker. The man hacked, staggered, and in his blind stumble, attempted to launch himself at Lovelace. He sidestepped the clumsy swing of the man's sword with ease, slid a shiv from his belt and brought the butt down hard on the base of the man's skull.

"Weapons are still good for some things," he muttered, preparing himself for the next.

Lovelace barely had time to react before the third man was on him. He didn't have time to ready his luth for a counter-attack. The man raised his sword.

He fell like a stone, felled by magic that did not belong to Lovelace. He stepped over the downed man, noting the coin-sized wound at his temple. His eyes flicked to the mouth of the cave opening, where Pif stood reloading his sling.

The fourth man came at him. He didn't have time to think and raised his arm to bring up another stone spire. It rose abruptly, narrowly missing the man but diverting him enough that Lovelace briefly wondered where-in-the-name-of-all-four-elements Gunnar was. He threw both arms down, and a spiraling stalactite erupted from the ceiling into the man's path. He bounced off the glittering stone face-first and dropped like a rag doll.

Lovelace wasted no time. He closed on the felled attacker and shoved his boot against the man's throat. He looked to the back of the cave, where the last remaining man held a blade to Ailwin's throat. It was wickedly slender, and the man pressed hard enough that a rivulet of blood dribbled thinly to the floor.

"What'll it be then?" Lovelace asked, grinding his boot more firmly into the downed man's neck. Beneath his boot, he squirmed and grunted like a stuck pig. Pif slid into position at Lovelace's side, sling poised and aimed at the man holding the knife.

"We're on the job, mate. Same as you. Tell your little boy soldier to lower his weapon, and we'll be on our merry way. We don't want any trouble," the man's voice boomed, his scarred face twisting into a grin that exposed a row of broken teeth.

A twisting, textured scar ran up the side of his cheek, over his eye and into his hairline. It wasn't the mark of a blade, but of flame.

Lovelace nodded at Pif, who glowered at the man and reluctantly lowered his sling.

The man's smile faded as he looked Lovelace up and down with something bordering revulsion. "Can't think a man such as yourself has much need for a lad like this," he said, indicating Ailwin with a nod. "He hasn't got enough potential for you, does he? Leave him to us. We'll see he's proper taken care of."

Lovelace met the man's eyes with a level gaze.

"Ailwin can decide for himself," he said, his voice low.

"Free country and all that. Alright then, lad, what'll it be? Come with me, join our band of brothers, give your life some real meaning. Or," his expression softened to one of mock pity, "continue wandering the countryside with this sorry bugger and his little friend until we come to make a proper end of you."

Ailwin locked eyes with Lovelace, lifting his chin as much as the man's grip would allow. He worked his throat and spat at the man's feet. Blood dribbled down his neck as the knife cut deeper.

"I'd sooner die," he gasped.

Stupid boy, Lovelace thought.

The man's jagged smile widened. "Suit yourself," he sneered, closing his eyes. A small flame flickered to life between Ailwin's feet. It was a feeble thing, but Lovelace noticed that the man appeared to be...feeding it. Indeed, it had already doubled in size and was beginning to lick the edges of Ailwin's cloak.

Lovelace couldn't make sense of it; the man was no dactyli. The conjured flame was weak and unoriginal, and it appeared to be taking an immense effort for the man to maintain.

He still held Ailwin, knife to throat, and was unfazed by the growing closeness of the fire, whereas the pain on Ailwin's face was made plain.

Lovelace's panic grew with the blaze – too many variables, too much unknown.

But then, a sudden gust of wind swept the man off his feet and flung him against the cave wall.

"Bloody finally," Lovelace muttered as Gunnar stepped into the cave. He raised his hand, commanding the air itself. The flame twisted and turned into a whirlwind that spun up and out of the cave mouth.

Gunnar raised his hand and gripped the air before him. From where he lay crumpled on the floor, the man with the burned face clutched his throat and writhed.

Gunnar strode to tower above the man as he struggled.

"You are done here," he said, dropping his hand, "Begone."

The man wheezed as fresh air filled his lungs. With a bitter laugh, the man rose to his feet, his mutilated face twisted into a sneer.

"Today, you win, dactyli. Enjoy it. We'll be back. We'll be back when you least expect it." The man straightened and brought himself up to his full height, just shy of Gunnar.

"Your precious Meorachadh will be ashes and dust, ground into nothingness by the Unburnt himself," he said, tracing two fingers over his ruined cheek.

"No piece of it shall remain standing, no stone unscathed. And you, dactyli, will be left with nothing but a memory of what once was. It is our time."

The mad glint in the man's eye was as bright as the fire he'd conjured.

"Begone," Gunnar said again, his voice hard as iron. Lovelace eased his foot from the man's throat beneath his boot and watched him scramble to his feet. The burned man gave him a nod and they took off running.

They bolted out of the cave, not stopping to consider the ledge before them. They leaped, as one, into the unseen depths below. Lovelace, Gunnar and Pif ran to the edge and watched as the men fell, red cloaks flapping, arms outstretched in supplication. Then, they were gone, disappearing into the swirling mist.

The hair on Lovelace's neck stood on edge. Did they aim to fly or to die? Had they harnessed the power of the wind to escape, or was their plunge suicide chosen in the face of failure? Neither boded well.

They stood transfixed and watched the slow-moving mist below, stunned by what they witnessed.

A low groan from within the cave shook them from their trance.

Ailwin.

His legs and feet were badly burnt, his shoes a ruin of charred leather. The wound on his thigh was not lethal, but deep enough, he had lost considerable blood and was flitting in and out of consciousness.

"Will he live?" Pif whispered, his eyes flickering from Ailwin to the man impaled on the spire and back again.

"Aye lad, he'll live. But he'll need a proper healer and rest." Lovelace mentally cataloged the herbs in his pack and those they'd seen in the area. It would be up to him to heal Ailwin, and he didn't like the look of those burns. He cursed himself for not acting sooner, the stench of seared flesh curling in his nostrils.

He shoved his remorse to the dark recesses of his mind and moved toward the man felled by his stone spire.

Burned Ones, he thought, willing the rock dust at his feet to reform into solid stone and snake its way up the man's ankles and wrists. *Was Alev building an army? Teaching them the dactyli trade?* It seemed so unlike Alev, but the evidence was nigh on unmistakable. Only one further question remained: how?

He left the man bound where he lay. Lovelace didn't expect to get any information from him; if comrades wanted to return for him, let them. But not before they set him to question.

He joined Gunnar, who was gazing out into the abyss with a fierce expression.

"As good a place as any to hole up while we get him healed," Lovelace said. "The boy can watch over him while we continue the search."

"Yes," he said, turning to face the cave. His eyes fell on the unconscious man, and his lip curled in distaste.

"Do you really think he's destroyed the Meorachadh?" Lovelace asked.

"I think it is possible."

"Burned Ones, he called them. And Alev, the Unburnt. How has he been building an army right beneath our nose?"

"I don't know," Gunnar said. "But an army he appears to have, and a zealous one at that. I didn't like the look in that one's eye."

"Me neither," Lovelace said. "And that fire. He conjured it."

Gunnar pursed his lips, cleared his throat and nodded slightly.

Lovelace continued, "Do you think Alev's teaching them, somehow? It wasn't a powerful fire, mind, but the ability was there, plain as day."

Gunnar's jaw was clenched, deliberating. He turned to the man impaled upon the spire and inspected him with a critical eye.

"Nasty bit of work, Lovelace, would you..." he said with an inviting motion of his hand.

"Aye," Lovelace said, transforming the stone into dust. The body of the man fell into a crumpled heap, rock dust mingling with black blood. Gunnar ushered in a gust of wind and swept the broken body out of the cave and over the ledge.

Outside, the sun broke through the curtain of mist. It filled the cave with a weak yellow light, the contrast a small comfort to the cold damp.

The light shone onto the back of the cave wall, illuminating Ailwin, who brought up two hands to shield his eyes. A narrow opening in the cave wall beside him caught Lovelace's eye, and he moved forward to investigate. As he drew near, the boy dropped his hands, his gaze fixed on the cave's opening, mouth wide in surprise.

A slight noise interrupted the silence; the sound of a person clearing their throat.

As if guided by the same hand, their heads turned to the disturbance.

A girl stood before them like a premonition, seemingly materialized out of the air. She radiated a dazzling golden white, backlit as she was by the sun.

Lovelace gaped. The silence – of the cave, the empty air beyond its mouth, of the forest still further – was as loud as anything.

"Are you looking for me?"

Chapter Thirteen

Time became unmoored. The white flare; it was her. It had to be.

She stood poised, a creature of the forest. Her head held high, her limbs tense; ready to run at the slightest rustling.

And then, in the same timid rasp, she asked again.

"Are you looking for me?"

"Yes," Pif and Lovelace intoned as one. Pif's mouth hung open; his brown eyes were wide and brimming with fascination.

Lovelace studied her and could see now that she was not so young as he'd supposed but a woman nearly grown. If he had to guess, she was likely closer to Ailwin in age than Pif.

She had the shape of one who spends their days moving over rough terrain. Her arms were lean and muscular, indicating she climbed trees or rock faces often and with ease. And while she was by no stretch of the imagination clean, she wasn't precisely dirty either, hinting at a more civilized past.

Lovelace could not find the words. All the conjecture and speculation about the white flare had been for naught. He and Gunnar, the masters, every dactyli left in the Meorachadh, every dactyli before them, for that matter – all of them, utterly wrong.

"Hello," Gunnar said, breaking the silence. "Yes, we have been looking for you."

He paused. His manner was gentle, slow, the same he used for spooked horses.

"Is this where you live?"

The girl pawed the ground nervously then gave a timid nod.

"Some of the time," she said, the words spilling from her like a secret.

"You must be hungry!" Pif burst out. He had been examining her wiry frame openly and drawn what was likely, to him, an obvious conclusion.

She shook her head, panic flitting across her features, and she took a step backward.

Pif withdrew a piece of salt fish from Lovelace's pack, brandishing it at her as if she were an animal he might lure with bait. Lovelace raised his arm to silence Pif, and the look of panic she wore gave way to one of deep misgiving, her eyes roving back and forth between each of their faces, shining with calculation.

"Is he hurt?" she asked, nodding toward Ailwin. He was conscious, but only just, and it was difficult to tell whether the look on his face was utter bewilderment or delirium. *Poor lad likely thinks her some apparition from beyond the veil,* Lovelace thought.

"He is," Gunnar said.

"Can I look at him?" she asked, her eyes only briefly grazing Gunnar's before returning to Ailwin.

He nodded, making a motion with his hands to suggest that she was welcome.

She advanced toward Ailwin with silent footsteps and knelt beside him. With great tenderness, she moved her fingers a hairsbreadth above the wound on his leg, tracing its outline slowly. She crouched low, sniffing it twice before her eyes moved over his shins and his feet with an absorption that treaded fascination and fretfulness.

"His feet are the worst," she declared, her gaze fixed on Ailwin's wound.

"If you mean to leave," she continued, her words still fast and tumbling, "it will be terribly difficult for him to walk. Perhaps impossible. He ought not to move for a week, at least."

Lovelace was sure now that she had not grown up wild. Though her voice was rough and unused, her speech was articulate. Even as she struggled to assemble her thoughts, her eyes betrayed a calculating intelligence.

The girl's gaze drifted off as if she was peering into a far-away world, one only she could see. They all waited. A steady trickle of water droplets echoed loudly from a drip line in the ceiling.

"I have some things that might help him. Stay here," the girl commanded, her voice firm and resolute.

Yes, ma'am, Lovelace thought as he and Gunnar nodded. Pif still held the salt fish, mouth agape.

Without another word, the girl rose from the floor and tiptoed behind Ailwin toward the narrow opening in the cave wall. She slipped inside and vanished from sight.

Pif shook himself like a wet squirrel.

"What're we..." he started. Lovelace cut him off with a sharp shake of his head.

"You'll frighten her," he whispered roughly.

Pif gave an obedient nod.

"If you're keen on being useful," Lovelace continued, nodding toward his pack. "Set a proper table, why don't you?"

Pif hesitated. "What about..." he said, nodding toward the stone-shackled man in the cave's center.

"Gunnar and I will take care of him."

Pif bobbed his head and dove into Lovelace's pack.

Gunnar turned away and gazed into the abyss beyond, where a lone falcon circled in the endless azure sky.

Moments ticked by that stretched into an eternity of uncertainty. Lovelace's mind began to conjure the possibility of escape; a secret back passageway, a hidden route through the stone. After all, what reason had they given her to trust them?

Just when doubt began to tip into fear, she emerged from the cleft in the wall. Clutched in one fist was a pounding stone, and across her shoulders, garlands of herbs, tied and dried and draped like a mantle.

Without regard for their stares, she walked to the other corner of the cave, where she knelt before a natural depression in the rock and unshouldered the herbs. A hushed silence fell over the cave as she pinched off pieces and parts of the plants one by one and dropped them into the depression. She ground the plant mixture with a practiced hand and a quiet reverence. When she finished, she withdrew again into her inner cavern.

Lovelace couldn't resist the pull of curiosity and scurried over to the place where she'd ground her herbs. Poppy, thyme and pieces of a bright orange flower he didn't recognize were a wet, pulpy mass in the depression. He didn't know the orange flower, but nodded his approval at the thyme and poppy.

"Ahem," she cleared her throat behind him.

He whirled, heat rushing to his cheeks.

"I don't mean to poison him if that's what you're seeing about," she said, a hint of acid in her words.

"I see that," Lovelace said, the heat of his embarrassment still lingering.

"You know something of medicine, then?" she asked.

"Some," he said. "We have some willow bark to hand if you'd like to use that. What you have here is interesting. What's the orange?"

She shot him a look that suggested she found him exceedingly thick.

"Holligold," she said, producing a jar of golden honey from behind her back. She mixed this sparingly into the herb mash until it became a paste, which she lathered onto several pieces of torn clean cloth with a deft hand. Strip by strip, she bandaged his burned feet and legs and the cut on his thigh so carefully that Ailwin did not wake. By the time she finished, the creased lines of pain that had marred his brow were made smooth.

"Willow bark would be most welcome. I don't think the wounds will fester. They were clean enough," she said, rising up. "But I'd like to see how he fairs in the morning."

They were all staring, eyes wide in wonder.

"We can eat now," she announced, raising her eyebrows at the makeshift table set by Pif, a large stone around which he'd set several stones meant for sitting.

Pif sprang into action, "Yes, m'lady," he said. "Here we've got salt herring, fresh caught from the..." he paused and looked to Lovelace, a question on his face.

"Idean. The Idean Sea," Lovelace said, concealing a smile.

"Aye, Idean," Pif said, unfazed. "And fresh-baked bread, though we've been many days on the road, it's not so fresh as it once was. M'lord Lovelace here made it hisself and it is mighty fine for all that it is a bit hard now." He took a bite of the loaf to exhibit that it was still entirely edible.

"Lovelace is an unusual name," she said, looking directly at him for the first time.

"My mother gave it to me," Lovelace said dumbly. Her eyes – brown and large and luminous as a doe – were boring into his with an unnerving intensity.

Gunnar moved to sit beside Pif, and Lovelace did likewise. Together they formed a loose circle around the large stone, which Pif had laid with the fish, bread and the last knob of cheese from the Meorachadh's larder.

She bit her bottom lip and then, without a word, withdrew again into her quarters.

Pif shot him a puzzled look and Lovelace shrugged. This time, she returned quickly with something dried and green folded in her hand. She darted forward, placed it beside the cheese and then sat, folding her limbs neatly beneath her. It was green onions she'd brought, Lovelace saw as he leaned forward for a piece of salt fish.

The smallest of smiles curled onto her lips as she took a tiny bite. She moved the morsel around her mouth as if she wished to siphon the very essence from the fish before.

"It is very good," she said. "Thank you."

As they ate, the group enjoyed a stilted silence, what words were spoken chosen with care. Bite by bite, the cord-taut tension that marked those first moments lessened, if only a little bit.

It was Pif who did most of the talking, Pif who, above all, seemed determined to win her over. Throughout his long-winded joke about a prince with three heads and his faithful dragon, Caval, she listened with grave intensity in between bites of cheese and fish. Upon conclusion of the joke, her eyes were dancing in merriment, and she let out a warbling sound that Lovelace supposed was a laugh.

***

As midday approached, they finished their meal. The cave had warmed to a soporific level. Fat flies hung lazily in the air, lured by the odors of feeding and fighting. Lovelace had managed to revive Ailwin long enough for him to take some water, some willow bark and a little food before dozing off on a makeshift bed fashioned from all of their cloaks. He was fast asleep now, his hands folded over his chest which rose and fell – Lovelace was pleased to note – with rhythmic ease.

"You stay here, lad," said Lovelace to Pif. "Gunnar and I are going to have a walkabout, make sure there aren't any more of those men about. Protect Ailwin," he said. He watched the girl slip quietly into the cleft in the wall and prayed she'd be there when they returned. He had a feeling it wouldn't be easy to find her again.

"Protect the girl," he added under his breath, the unspoken *Don't let her escape* plain on his features.

Pif nodded solemnly and touched his hand to the sling at his waist.

"Good lad," Lovelace said, giving the boy's bony shoulder a squeeze.

"I don't imagine you want to squander your luth by ferrying him out of here. Would you lend me a hand?" Lovelace asked Gunnar. He nodded and reached down to grab the unconscious man beneath the armpits. Lovelace took him by the feet and nearly choked; the man had an odor that would make a tanner retch. With a heave, the two of them hoisted him between them and made their way outside.

The man moaned, stirring slightly, but remained unconscious as he and Gunnar emerged to the deafening hush of the open air before them. After a morning spent confined in the dim damp of the cave, the vertiginous drop over the cliff edge was dizzying. Lovelace averted his gaze, looking instead into the face of the man they bore between them. He was tall and slight, younger than Lovelace had anticipated. As he peered closer, he noticed a welt on his face, livid and red. It was a brand, the shape of a V turned onto its side seared into his cheek, just below the bone.

They traced the narrow path leading back to the woods and moved in silence, the weight of the man between them slowing their progress. When they reached a meager stream some distance away, they dropped him unceremoniously to the forest floor and paused to refresh themselves with the cold, clear water. Soon, the man regained his senses and glared at them with unfocused, spiteful eyes.

"It appears your comrades have left you in a rather perilous state," Lovelace said.

The man craned his neck to survey his stone-shackled wrists and ankles, then turned his head and spat, only narrowly missing Gunnar's feet.

The man wasn't long for this world if this was how he would accord himself. On the list of things that raised Gunnar's hackles, spitting as a form of insult was right up there with putting a horse away unbrushed and offering coin for his private thoughts.

On cue, Gunnar hauled the man up by the collar, pulling him close.

"Do it again," he growled.

The man paled but, to his credit, didn't back down. He began to work up another gob, and Gunnar threw him back down, shaking his head in disgust. He stretched out his hand in the air before him, and the man clutched at his throat with his bound hands, his face purpling like a bruise.

"Where is Alev?"

He gasped as Gunnar released his hold.

"Wouldn't you like to know," he said, panting hard. He had a clipped accent that sounded like he came from the east. Lazare, or further.

"We would, actually," Lovelace said, bending low to whisper in the man's ear. "He will kill you, you know. You really shouldn't have tried to spit on him. He hates that."

Gunnar squeezed again. This time, he didn't stop until the man's eyes bulged.

"A'right, a'right," the man wheezed as air flooded his starved lungs, and Lovelace could see it in his eyes: desperation and defeat, the slightest glint of hope that mercy would be his.

Without warning, a sound like a whip cracked in the air. Lovelace wheeled, hands raised, luth at the ready.

The air around them quivered and a voice, deep and disembodied, spoke.

IMMOLATO.

The man burst into flame. The smell of fat searing and hair burning was immediate, as was the terrible, gut-wrenching scream. It was cut short as quickly as it began, consumed by the hiss and crackle of rising flame.

Gunnar was crouched low and poised to spring. Lovelace spun behind a tree and scoured the area, his heart pounding.

But there was no one in the woods around them.

Lovelace looked over to the crackling flame that had only moments ago been their captor. The tinder of his person burned – faster, higher, hotter – than anything he had ever seen.

Gunnar strode into the woods, vanishing from sight for a moment before returning with a shake of his head. The source of that bone-chilling voice was nowhere to be found.

"Let's be away," Lovelace said. They retraced their steps back toward the cave, any sense of surety set afire by the might of a single word.

"Alev," said Lovelace, his eyes flickering nervously over every boulder and tree.

"Mm," Gunnar replied, his voice low and gruff.

"But that's..."

"Impossible," Gunnar said, quickening his pace. "And yet, he is not here. We would know if he was."

"Which means..."

"Yes," Gunnar said, lengthening his stride.

Lovelace's mind was a tempest. Their captive had been bound by some sort of sorcery. They had to act, and quickly. But how? The implications of what they had just witnessed were beyond anything they had anticipated, beyond anything they were prepared to confront, beyond the limits of what they believed possible.

"Gunn, wait."

Gunnar stopped, his broad shoulders heaving with exertion.

"What're we going to do about the girl?" Lovelace asked, catching him up.

A small muscle twitched in Gunnar's jaw.

"Protect her, I suppose, though I doubt there is much we can do that she could not see to herself," he said.

Lovelace nodded. "We can't take her back to the Meorachadh. The road is paved with peacekeepers, and now, these Burned Ones. And Alev is setting people on fire, from what...*beyond*? I don't like it, Gunnar. I don't like it one bit."

Gunnar's eyes met his. They were troubled; their normal silver-gray misted over like a storm gathering on the horizon line. The moment their eyes locked, Lovelace's pulse quickened, and his palms grew slick with sweat. Each breath was shallow, labored, difficult to draw, and his heartbeat pounded in his ears, the thump of it wet and sticky.

He inhaled deeply, let the air out slowly through pursed lips. He focused on his surroundings, on sensations – the warm air pressing lightly on his skin, the gentle babble of the nearby stream. Blackberries, growing on the other side, their prickled boughs bowing low toward the water's surface, plump purple berries shining in the sun. He knelt to pick one, all the while working to keep his thoughts, and the feelings that accompanied them, from enlarging beyond control.

Finally, Gunnar spoke. "I agree."

"You what...?" Lovelace said, looking up from across the stream.

"I don't like it either," Gunnar said.

Laughter, unrestrained and inexplicable, erupted from Lovelace, shaking his body from head to toe. He laughed until tears rolled down his cheeks, until his belly ached, until Gunnar took him by both shoulders and shook him back to the world.

Lovelace wiped his eyes and shrugged.

"What're we going to do about these young ones?"

Gunnar heaved a sigh, turning away from Lovelace to grip the low-hanging limbs of a young magnolia tree with both hands. "What do you think?"

"They'll have to stay with us. Ailwin and Pif know too much, and they have been seen. They are at risk so long as Alev is abroad."

"I agree," Gunnar said shortly, surprising Lovelace.

"And the girl..." Lovelace broke off. What would they do with the girl? She had uprooted everything they knew about magic. Her mere existence shattered the illusion that magic was a man's trade, and along with Alev's Burned Ones, that it was an inborn skill. What does one *do* with a person who heralded such change?

"We protect her, whatever the cost," Gunnar finished for him, and Lovelace knew he was right.

As they approached the granite backside of the cave, Gunnar offered to take the first watch. Considerations darted around Lovelace's head, like so many minnows in a pond. He hadn't realized they'd nearly returned to the cave until he remembered something important.

"The last verdanite tablet," he said, reaching into his pocket.

Gunnar's shoulders tensed, and a look of great foreboding flitted across his face that mirrored Lovelace's own feelings.

Since that fateful night in the Tasglann, when Manoc had given them the three tablets, Lovelace believed the stones might hold the answers or some guidance to aid them in their quest. The first tablet had been instructive, to say the least, but had done little to imbue them with anything close to confidence. And the second – the origin story of Mortalis – General LeMarc's surrender and the subsequent Covenant of Clasped Hands felt more like a history lesson than a meaningful clue. That left the third tablet, and Lovelace had pinned an unreasonable hope onto its contents; that somewhere within it lay a key. So long as they did not engage with the tablet, that hope could remain alive.

"Here, then?" he asked, withdrawing the verdanite.

Gunnar nodded. Folding his legs beneath him, he sank to the ground. Lovelace joined him, placing the stone between them. The smallest of the three, there was no single chip or scratch marring its surface. Its edges were sharp and corners cut with perfect angularity. For a moment, they sat in quiet reverence. As the high noon light shone down upon the stone, it glowed all the more brightly, scattering emerald light among the cedar leaves and coloring them with a faint, greenish glow.

Their hands outstretched in slow motion. When Lovelace's finger met the stone's peerless surface, he closed his eyes, exhaled and let go.

The familiar loss of shape and form, the gentle humming – the transit from reality to memory – was a well-worn path in Lovelace's mind. This time, he found himself in a dark forest, darker by half than the one where his body remained.

The canopy of trees overhead was so tall and thick he could scarcely tell whether it was day or night. The smell of wet stone and rich soil was ripe in the air.

To his left, Lovelace saw the trunk of an enormous tree waver, its surface purl like a ripple in a pond. Gunnar was here.

Lovelace moved slowly, absorbing every element of the sgeul in as much detail as possible. He had never seen a forest like this. The trees were taller, their trunks thicker than any he had ever seen. Here was a forest that had not been touched and shaped by man's hand.

Lush green leaves like crushed velvet climbed up trees and over rocks in such proliferation that he scarcely noticed a person, seated there upon the ground.

Startled, Lovelace jumped. Given his bodiless state, it was really more of a jarring vibration. Of course, the figure did not notice but remained – cross-legged, straight-backed and still – their back leaned against the base of an enormous granite boulder that had been cleaved in two.

As Lovelace peered around, he noticed that the split rock was the largest of many that formed a circle. They were so covered in lichen, moss and leaf litter that he had not noticed them before.

The figure was slight and wore a cloak of mottled gray, a great hood cast over their head so that their face was hidden from sight.

And then, in a voice that seemed older than the forest itself, the figure began to speak.

"When the sands of time have consumed all that is known to man, we will remain. We, who grasp the hand of time and compel it to retain its true form. When the ravages of history have been wrought by conquerors and their treacherous revisions, we will remember. We will seek always truth, a word that means so much to so many and so little to so few."

As the figure continued to speak, a cold notion gripped Lovelace. He knew, beyond a shadow of a doubt, that he was in the presence of Oi, the creator of their order and the inventor of the orb.

"There will come a time when we will be undone. Destruction is as inevitable as death. But nothing is ever lost; it is only made new."

The figure's voice rose, prophetic tones echoing through the ancient forest.

"Hold dear those that seek truth, but beware of those who find it."

As suddenly as it began, the sgeul faded, and Lovelace tumbled back into the present, where the shock of sunlight streaming through the trees momentarily left him blind. Across from him, Gunnar was still seated, his eyes dancing with amusement and fixed on a point above and beyond Lovelace's head.

Lovelace turned and startled, his heart leaping in his chest. The girl stood behind him, grave as world's end.

"For the love of the...How did you...?"

"Many ways in and out," she said with a shrug.

"So you saw it all, the fight in the cave. Did you just see...?"

She nodded, her eyes fixed on the verdanite. "The red men have been searching for me for two-and-a-quarter moons. I was in my cavern when your boy appeared. He found the opening and was about to climb inside when he was beset upon."

So she had seen their magic, had seen Lovelace impale a man, and Gunnar force the air from the lungs of another.

Lovelace nodded slowly, "We don't mean you any harm."

Her eyes pored into his, as if she might root out whether what Lovelace said was true by looking deeply enough. An odd ripple went down his spine. Was she reading his mind?

He was holding his breath, he found, awaiting her appraisal. Finally, she dropped her gaze and nodded once. Whatever she had seen in him had been enough.

"I know what you are," she said. "Why are you here?"

There were too many answers to that question, but before Lovelace could reply, Gunnar spoke.

"If you know what we are, then you know you are one of us. That is why we are here."

She shook her head defiantly. "Women are not dactyli. Besides, I was not born like this. Whatever I am, it is different from you."

Gunnar spoke again, "It would appear that in that regard, we were mistaken. And it is common for your...abilities to lie dormant until awakened."

"Aye," Lovelace chimed in. "It bursts out of you when you least expect it, when you're young. It was said seeds would sprout in my fists when I was just a babe, for example."

The girl nodded thoughtfully, her eyes cast downwards. If Lovelace had to guess, she too had these anecdotes and was thinking back on them now.

"We'd best return to the cave," she said, fingering the shape of what looked like an overlarge locket beneath the rough fabric of her shirt. "More of them will come. I would sooner be prepared, or gone from this place."

Chapter Fourteen

With each passing day, the wild part of Kylene's mind receded, like the ebbing of a tide from a rocky shore. The slightest rustle in the forest no longer made her heart race, and she was less afraid of shadows that lurked in the trees. As she and Sable continued down the road, searching for the sign that read Damp Gulch Pass, she immersed herself in the countless puzzles her father had left in his notebook and in so doing, kept the savage memory of Vicente at bay.

Still, sleep eluded her. When she did drift off, the same terror plagued her night after night. In her dreams, a cloaked figure astride a monstrous black stallion would charge after her, yellow teeth gnashing and eyes burning crimson. She would run, but the figure and his horse would bear down on her until she awoke, limbs trembling and covered in a cold sweat.

It was not until the third day that she saw a handful of folks the nearer she drew to Arcellen. Farmers, by the looks of them, with their sun-tanned faces and mule-drawn carts either empty or filled to the brim with sun cabbages, the spiraling pale green heads of broccoflower.

Not one of them offered her greeting, instead looking her up and down with eyes clouded over by suspicion, every bit as untrusting as Gingham said they would be. She must have looked most disreputable, in her tattered dress with the dirt of seven days begriming her skin. She put her head down and kept moving, her heart racing until they were long past.

Gingham was true to his word. It was on the fourth day that she arrived at a faded and peeling wooden sign. 'Damp Gulch Pass,' it read. Behind it, the moss-eaten vestiges of what once might have been a small stone structure hinted at a disused temple. To which Son it had been dedicated was now a mystery.

Beneath the old sign was another printed in fresh red ink with the official seal of the Fingers – a tight-gripped fist holding a set of balanced scales – it read: 'Expressly Forbidden by Fingerling Decree.'

After nights of poring through her father's notes and days mulling over their consequence, she was beginning to understand the nature of things in the Grasp. The prohibition of the mountains could only mean one of two things: either the Fingers wanted exclusive access to certain resources, or they were involved in activities they wanted kept hidden from the public eye. Her father had documented various regions throughout the Grasp, some speculated and others confirmed by agents like him, where activities like mining and hunting were taking place for the benefit of the Fingers and to the detriment of those who once depended on them for their livelihoods.

As she turned onto the pass, a foreboding thrill ran through Kylene's body. It was a fleeting sensation, for the wet and unkempt passage proved to be every bit as difficult as Gingham warned. At every turn, the wind howled and threatened to throw her off Sable, who grew less and less eager to continue the further they pressed on.

On the morning of the fifth day, Kylene found herself at the tree without a heart. She was hungry, saddle-worn and weary in every way, worn so thin she nearly rode right by despite its prodigious size.

Just as Gingham said, there was a stream cutting straight across the path, which she followed with some difficulty as thick-growing brambles threatened to choke the thin ribbon of water from either side.

Kylene doubted she would reach the right place by the time the sun was high. *Wherever that is,* she thought, her stomach rumbling once again. Still, Gingham's instructions had been unerring in their description thus far. So when the sun reached its zenith, she dismounted Sable, left the horse to nibble at the blackberries ripening on the vine and waited.

She considered passing the time by further scrutinizing the contents of her father's notebook, but her head felt raw and dull, her mind unable to focus on the strange messages and symbols. When she tried to focus on the text, she felt much like a bumblebee, flitting from word to word, unable to settle on any one notion worth exploring.

So instead, she lay beside the stream and allowed the world around her to fade into the background.

Time passed, and with it, a creeping surety that the stream had a melody.

It was like nothing she had heard before; a symphony of whispers, cries, yearning. She tilted her head, trying to make out the words she was certain hid beneath the burbling notes.

"What is the stream saying?" asked a voice from behind.

Kylene jolted upright, the animal part of her roaring to life within her chest. Her hand went to the blade at her thigh.

Before her stood a man. Taller than her, but only just. His hair was straight and brown, and he wore plain robes of woven yellow, the color of fresh-churned butter.

His hands were clasped behind his back. Her tired heart thudded as she clutched Clover. *Friend or foe, friend or foe, friend or foe?*

The man offered her a slight smile, and Kylene forcibly shoved her mind in the direction of sense. She had come here willingly. There was meant to be a person, and that person would take her to the Kapnobatai. The Kapnobatai had answers.

She withdrew her hand from the blade, though the act made her feel much like a plucked chicken.

"Hello," she said, bobbing her head. "I seek the Kapnobatai. I was told this was where I might make myself and my interests known to them."

"Indeed, you are correct," the man said, his eyes twinkling. "This is where seekers come." He paused, observing her. "You need not fear. The Kapnobatai are a non-violent people. We do not while away our time bringing harm to others. We have found that there are more important things in life."

He smiled again. It scarcely touched his lips but shone from his eyes like lamplight.

She bobbed her head again, unsure of how to proceed. His formality made her acutely aware of her unkempt appearance, and she swallowed the small lump of shame that had formed in her throat. She took up a daisy, and began to shred its white petals with trembling fingers.

"You'll follow me, if you please," the man said. "It is customary for us to blindfold those who seek our company, so as to maintain a small sense of privacy," he added, with a note in his voice she couldn't place. "But something tells me that today, that won't be necessary. If you'll please..."

Offering no further explanation, he turned and strode briskly through the forest, his pace brisk and light of foot. Kylene watched him go, his retreating back growing smaller and becoming increasingly obstructed by trees.

She blinked once, threw the daisy's yellow heart to the ground, took up her pack and, grabbing Sable's lead, followed him through the dense thicket.

***

It was a winding path through rugged terrain, to the place where the Kapnobatai kept their summer home. And while the distance was short, the way was anything but straightforward. The turns and twists, the ups and downs, had left Kylene disoriented and lost in the labyrinth of the wilderness. It didn't matter that she wasn't blindfolded; the path was a jumbled mess of directions that would have been impossible to recall. Yet, her guide did not break his stride once, nor did he turn back to see whether Kylene followed.

It was after a hairpin bend, climbing out of a small gorge and around a towering hemlock, that the thicket opened up, and Kylene beheld a sight that left her breathless. The mountainous terrain, which had enveloped her since she began her ascent up the Damp Gulch Pass, gave way to a meadow. And there, scattered like so many tiny fortresses, were bee boxes – hundreds of them, as far as the eye could see.

The air was alive with the gentle hum of a thousand winged creatures. They drifted lazily above a sea of blossoms – bee balm, sage, phlox and countless others whose names Kylene did not know. She was brought to stillness by the wonder of it, the line of Sable's lead slack in her hand. Only when the horse gave an almighty snort, a bee having landed on her snout, did she realize her guide was skirting around the edge of the field, already halfway across it.

She followed his path, identifying the various herbs and flowers along the way – hyssop, holligold, thyme, lavender. The fields were not just fodder for the bees; they were for medicine making, she was sure of it. The flowers had a chaotic orderliness that must have been shaped by human hands.

Upon reaching the end of the field, the man had disappeared. No matter. She was here. They weren't far now. Excitement swelled in her chest as she tethered Sable to a nearby cedar and stepped into a lightly treed glade, where she was met with the quiet bustle of a village. Men, women and a few children – all dressed in yellow robes the color of freshly churned butter – moved about the glade. Their work centered around what appeared to be a herb and honey processing operation ambitious in scale. Nearby, a cluster of women sat chatting as they bundled bright lavender boughs into bunches. As she walked, she passed two people with fine cloth masking their faces as they headed out into the field.

The village was comprised of intricately designed buildings, some cleverly slung in trees with ladders reaching high to their thick-beamed floors. Most of them were on the ground, though, and all were constructed with the same meticulously planed timber.

Cedar, she thought, taking an almighty inhale. The smell of the wood mingled with that of the flowers, of honey, of grass warmed by the late afternoon sun. Had she, perhaps, fallen asleep by the stream? If this was all a dream, it was the most pleasant one she'd had in ages.

Her guide awaited her outside a cabin unlike any Kylene had ever seen. The structure lacked proper doors or adjoining walls, inviting the warm summer air to drift effortlessly through its open space. Intricately worked cedar columns adorned with curling vines encircled the perimeter. From its pointed top, a sturdy roof sloped at a sharp angle, beneath which delicate latticework windows allowed light to filter freely.

With a gesture, her guide beckoned her inside. She stooped low to enter beneath the angled roof, and straightened to find herself in a sparsely furnished room. The floor of it was hard-packed dirt, and a long table marked its center, around which sat a dozen individuals, both men and women. All eyes were turned to her with open curiosity written across their features, and Kylene's heart hammered. Her gaze fell upon the table's center, upon which sat blue glass jugs, wooden cups, quills, pots of ink and scrolls, more scrolls than could be counted. Some of them were heavy with ink, covered edge to edge, while others remained pristine, empty and inviting of ideas. *Paper is precious 'Lene, never let a single inch of it go to waste.* Her mind raced with the possibilities: This was the place.

"Cael," said a woman with short-cropped black hair, seated furthest from the door's entrance. "Would you please introduce our guest?"

Her guide – Cael – made an informal bow and gave the woman an apologetic smile.

"Eliza, it would be my honor. Regretfully, I have not, as yet, learned the young lady's name. Given the state in which I found her, it seemed prudent to bring her to safety, at which time she could decide whether she might share her name and her story with us, or not."

The woman – Eliza – nodded, her sharp features conveying approval of Cael's decision. "Thank you, Cael." She turned her gaze to Kylene.

"Hello..." she paused, inviting Kylene to the table with a sweep of a slender hand.

Kylene hesitated. She would move, but her feet had grown roots. Cael gripped her elbow gently, urging her forward. His touch sent hot streaks down her arm to the tips of her fingers. She wanted to tear her arm from his grip. Instead, she moved forward, her steps heavy, trudging, twelve pairs of eyes a weight upon her. What on earth had befallen her, they wondered, to make her look and act this way? Cael pulled out a chair, and she perched tentatively on its edge.

"We welcome you to our summer home..." Eliza said, raising an eyebrow.

"Kylene."

"Kylene," Eliza said, a small smile playing at the corners of her lips. "I will admit to being very curious about the circumstances that have brought you to our doorstep. As you have come to discover, our doorstep is as far-reaching as anyone could hope to find."

Kylene sensed further invitation in Eliza's words, but there was something else there too, something darker. Was it an accusation?

Fear chilled her to the bone. What if she'd made a terrible mistake in coming here? What if these people could not be trusted? She swallowed hard, torn between the urge to protect herself and lie, and the desire to reveal everything. Would she ever be of one mind again?

For a moment, she sat in silence, her mouth opening and closing with indecision. Then, she closed her eyes, inhaled deeply and let the truth spill forth from her lips, like blood from a wound.

She told Eliza everything. From her father's yew poem to her flight from his study, her days on the Middling Road and Gingham and the black gelding she had stolen from a dead man, a man she herself had killed.

At first, her words were stumbling, stuttering with starts and stops. But then, something shifted within her. Her words grew teeth. They smoldered and seethed. They came hissing from her, spitting, roiling off her tongue. By the time she was done, she was all burnt up inside, empty, a charred, blackened space where once there had been flame.

The sun slanted low through the latticed roof, casting distorted shadows across the broad table and painting strange patterns on the faces of the silent council, with Eliza at its head.

"It is a remarkable story," she said at last.

"I thank you for telling it. It is with some regret that I share that I have little to offer you, at least in the way of news about your father. We have not heard from Dirk for three months, and I fear the worst. There are others like your father, bellringers who have grown bold of late, bold enough to attract attention. They are being hunted down and snuffed out like candles, their flames pinched by the forefinger and thumb of the Fingers."

Kylene bowed her head. There it was. A faint surprise flickered through her for the nothingness she felt inside.

"Osbert..." she said, her voice flat and hoarse.

"I would not be so quick to lay blame on Osbert."

Kylene's head spun. It was always Osbert. He was the fist, the one who controlled the Fingers, the one who bled the world of color. How could he not be to blame?

Eliza turned to a man on her left, who gave her a prompt nod. She repeated the gesture with each person around the table, all of them nodding in agreement, with the exception of one white-haired man. He neither nodded nor shook his head but made a single sharp chopping motion with his hand, his gaze fixed sharply on Kylene. With a small shrug, he returned to a notebook laid open before him, where he resumed writing in a dense, cramped hand.

Eliza rose from the table, commanding attention without effort.

"Cael will show you where you can sleep, bath, eat, put your things. You must be tired."

Kylene dipped her head in acknowledgment. Her head was crammed so full of questions they seemed stuck. Not a single one would issue forth from her mouth.

"My horse, Sable..." she managed to utter as Eliza moved toward the door.

"We have a stable," Eliza said. She stopped and turned, peering at Kylene from the room's wide entrance. The yellow robes she wore were knee-length, and Kylene couldn't help but notice that her feet and shins were crisscrossed with fine scars like spiders webs, silver against the tan of her skin. She gave Kylene one long sweeping look and turned, gliding out the door.

The remaining men and women began to talk among themselves. Some followed Eliza, while others stayed seated. Kylene remained frozen in her chair, trying to ignore the sidelong glances aimed her way.

Cael bounded up from a darkened corner, where he had silently watched the proceedings. He offered Kylene his arm and she stared at it.

But Cael was unperturbed.

"Come along then, if you please," he said, shooing Kylene out the door. Kylene trundled out into the open air, her gait awkward and bow-legged after several days in the saddle. Cael, on the other hand, bounced ahead of her, his buoyant stride taken on tiptoe. As they walked, Cael pointed out the buildings meant for filtering honey and drying herbs. And then there were the kitchens, open to the air with several large cook pots, hundreds of glass jars and vials, stone crocks and one great oven with a roaring fire in its hearth. All of the buildings were erected around an enormous ash trunk stripped of its bark and limbs, with strung flowers fanning out from its length, wavering in the gentle morning breeze.

Kylene had been staring over her shoulder at the pole as Cael rounded a corner and stopped unexpectedly. She nearly ran into him.

Here, a small way from the center, the trees were larger and more densely clustered, so thick that, at first, they diverted her attention from the hundreds of swinging beds strung between low-hanging branches. All of them were empty and swaying gently, much like the flowers on the pole.

"We have quarters indoors as well, Miss Kylene, but most of us are partial to the night air at this time of year."

Night air, the words echoed in her head. She felt like she was floating, swept along by some unseen current in this strange place. The low hum of cicadas or something like them filled the air, and the warm scent of cedar and nectar of flowers wafted around her.

"Thank you," was all she could manage to say.

Cael pointed to a dirt path that rose up and around a large boulder, disappearing from sight. "There are springs up that way, a little bit of a walk. They are sulfurous pools for bathing, not drinking. Drinking water is from the spring..." He pointed to another path to the right, leading downhill through the column of trees. "There. You'll have bathed in sulfur springs before?"

She shook her head.

"Ah," he said, a look of fondness coming over his features. "I cannot help but think you will be most delighted. Might I recommend you wait till after dinner, lest you fall asleep without first getting a bite to eat."

At the mention of food, Kylene's stomach grumbled, and Cael grinned. This time, it was with his teeth as well as his eyes. "Good," he said, clapping his hands together. "It has been an age since we had a proper guest. Dinner will be served from the roundhouse. You saw it next to where you met Eliza and the rest. It will be quieter than usual, with so many of us out and about, on the roads. It is the season for commerce, after all."

With those words, he started back down the path, leaving Kylene where she stood.

Commerce doesn't sleep for seasons, Kylene thought distantly, thinking of her father. It was something he might have said.

Was that it? The Kapnobatai did not know where he was or might be. And there had been no suggestion of aid, unless she counted their hospitality. All of this had been for nothing; her journey, Vicente, boiled down to inconsequence.

She cursed herself, hot shame bubbling up inside of her. Why had she not asked about the nature of her father's relationship with them? Were the Kapnobatai bellringers, and if so, might they connect her with others who might know more about her father and where he might be?

Lost in her thoughts, Kylene walked between the trees, letting her hand run along the fabric of the hammocks. They were made from heavy muslin and reminded her of the sails of ships she'd seen drawn in the pages of storybooks.

She came to one of the hammocks at the far end, strung higher than the rest and placed her hand lightly on the heavy fabric.

How might it feel to lie suspended? She climbed the broken limbs of the tree and allowed herself to tumble into its folds.

Enveloped in the hammock, she rocked back and forth, wondering briefly how one was meant to emerge from such a bed without the use of wings. She thought of chrysalises and moths and creatures who hang, suspended, to rest, and before the sun had begun to touch the surface of the horizon, Kylene fell into a sleep both dreamless and deep.

***

There was one caterpillar in particular, fat and green, inching its way toward her along a vine. Kylene stared at its suckered feet, the way they gripped the vine like sticky little fists. When it reached her, the caterpillar stopped as if she had been its destination. It raised its head and, in its eyeless way, regarded her in a manner that made Kylene feel like she was being spoken to, as if the caterpillar had something of great import to tell her.

The caterpillar continued to weave its head in the air, coming closer and closer toward her. She leaned forward, intent upon hearing what it had to say.

And then, it poked her – poked her with its fat, soft head right in between her eyes – and then she woke to find a child, a boy, his sticky finger pressed against her forehead and his bright brown eyes staring at her intently.

"Time for ups, miss!" The boy said. He couldn't be more than five.

Kylene came to with startling clarity. It was early and her eyes were crusted over with sleep. A thin blanket covered her and her limbs ached, suggesting she hadn't moved a muscle while she slept. Hunger gnawed at her belly.

"Breakfast?" She croaked hopefully, looking up at the child who had woken her. He regarded her with a critical eye.

"Course. Can't start the day without proper food in the belly," said the child, his soft-edged consonants confirming his age, though they belied the intelligence in his eyes.

Kylene attempted to extricate herself from the hammock, unsure how to do so without falling onto the ground.

"Feet first," the child said, seeing her struggle. She swung her feet over the edge and, gripping the heavy fabric with both arms, rolled her lower half over the edge until her feet grazed the earth. She released her grip and fell backward, landing on her backside.

The child stifled a giggle, and Kylene quickly picked herself up, straightening her torn and dirty dress. A hot flush crept up her chest and into her cheeks.

"This way," he said, beckoning her to follow. She trailed behind, noticing as she passed other hammocks that everyone else in the glade had risen. Had she slept through the entire night and the dawn?

They turned the corner, and the smell of woodsmoke greeted them. Fires burned bright and hot beneath cook pots in the kitchen, and a woman ladled something that smelled of cloves and cream into bowls for the small line before her.

Folks ate at three long tables sheltered by a low-slung roof. The wood was like nothing Kylene had seen before, creamy brown with dramatic dark streaks running from edge to edge. The air hummed with the quiet animation of conversation and birdsong – light, trilling, hopeful.

Kylene paused, struck by the otherworldly strangeness of it all. But hunger pushed her forward, propelling her toward the roundhouse where food was being served. She kept her head straight and her eyes downcast, so that she might not draw attention to herself, outsider that she was.

The child was waiting for her, holding out a steaming bowl of porridge. Kylene took it gratefully and was surprised when he grabbed her by the hand. It was soft and warm and earnest, and Kylene let him lead her to an enormous countertop, where there were dozens of jars with all manner of provisions – nuts of every kind, candied roots, dried fruits and amber crystals that sparkled in the early morning light. Kylene bent low to inspect them.

"Toppings, miss," the boy said, pulling out a stool so that he could reach the array. He grabbed a jar of candied violets and, in a demonstrative fashion, placed a few on top of his own porridge. "That's honey crystals there. My favorite, after the violets, course."

Kylene had never eaten her porridge sweet. She always took it plain, the way her father ate his. Her mother would allow them a pat of butter and some salt fish every now and again, but only as a special treat.

The woman who had been ladling the porridge sensed her hesitation and tottered over to Kylene with her own steaming bowl.

"Hard to decide, isn't it? It's honey crystals, ginger root and hazelnut for me. Keeps the gut in check, with just a bit of sweet to put a sparkle in your day." She winked, reaching for the jar of dried ginger root.

Kylene quickly spooned the same onto her own bowl and walked out past the ash pole and toward the tables. She was startled to spot Cael waving her over with a grin. He was seated with a woman with long blonde hair and a man with nut-brown skin. She could not help but notice the man's forearms – they were some of the largest she had ever seen, thickly corded with muscle.

"Good morning, Miss Kylene," Cael said, greeting her as she sat down. "I trust you slept well?"

Kylene nodded, settling in at the table.

"This is Sabina," he said, gesturing to the blonde woman, who nodded in greeting. "And Asa," pointing to the man. His face split into a wide smile, and Kylene felt heat rise in her cheeks.

"A pleasure," she said, taking up a spoonful of the porridge and sliding it cautiously into her mouth.

"Oh!" The oats were creamy, the ginger spiced, the hazelnuts crunchy. And the honey crystals. She could taste every flower in that field; bee balm and chamomile, rosemary and lavender. She groaned slightly, and Sabina, Asa and Cael laughed.

"I like your porridge approach," Sabina said, hiding her laughter behind a spoonful of her own blueberry and apple-laced blend.

As they ate, Asa, Sabina and Cael spoke of the coming day. Kylene only listened, intent on her meal.

Sabina was sharp-tongued and quipped about how waspish the bees were at this time of year. Asa, quick to laughter, was a builder of things. He spoke at length about a project nearing completion in the western quarter of the summer grounds. By the sound of it, it was something that was a cross between a bridge and a waterwheel.

Cael hardly spoke of himself but made many gestures and noises as the other two talked. When asked what the day would bring for him, he merely shrugged and smiled, saying, "Another day a minstrel on the path."

A distant chime sounded, and Sabina swirled her finger around the rim of her bowl, savoring the last remnants of berry-stained porridge and Asa rose to stand. He was very tall, as tall as her father, at least.

"It was a pleasure to meet you, Kylene," he said, staring down at her and smiling, his gaze steady and warm. Horrifyingly, heat crept into her cheeks once more. She gave him a quick nod and buried her face in the remnants of her porridge.

Cael was the last to rise.

"I'm happy to see you so well this morning," he said to her, bowing his head. When he brought his eyes up, they met with hers. In them was a faint sadness that had not been there before.

"Thank you for all of your kindness," she said. "It has been..." she looked for words and found there were none.

Cael leaned down and placed his hand on top of hers. "I cannot imagine," he said. "Eliza has requested your presence in the meeting chamber. I believe she will share some things with you that, if nothing else, will provide you with some comfort, if not direction, in your journey."

A spoonful of porridge stuck in her throat.

"When?" she asked, forcing a swallow.

"Just as soon as you've eaten and feel yourself able," Cael said, turning to go.

Kylene stared after his retreating back, lost for how to communicate the comfort she felt in his presence, the warmth of his simple kindness at a time when all else was foreign and foreboding.

"Cael!"

He turned, his eyebrows high, the corners of his mouth upturned.

"Thank you," was still all she could manage to say. This time, though, there was something in her words, something that transformed his small smile into a broad, beaming thing. He tipped his hat toward her and turned, bouncing on his toes as he went.

***

It was late morning when she ducked beneath the lintel of the meeting chamber's door. She found only Eliza and the white-haired man – *the only one who did not nod* – waiting for her. Relief washed over her; she'd expected the whole council.

Taking her time with the porridge had helped. She'd waited until every last person had gone, until only a handful of people were left in the village center, all confined to the kitchen. It had given her time to prepare herself. She would be unyielding. She would stand before the lot of them and demand answers.

Now, with Eliza and the man's eyes upon her, she felt small beneath their gaze.

The man gestured toward a chair seated directly across from him and Eliza. Kylene drifted over and lowered herself into it, its wooden legs scraping across the dirt floor.

"Thank you for coming," Eliza said. "Before I share what I know about Dirk Gemison, Rufus would like to ask you some questions."

"I am at your disposal," she said, trying to sound more confident than she felt. She could not hold the man's gaze long. His eyes, she found, were black as midnight, a night sky without stars. She would swear that yesterday they were blue.

"What is your name?" Rufus barked, his question lashing out at her like a whip.

"Kylene. Kylene Gemison," she stammered, taken aback by his abruptness and trying to ignore the tremble in her voice.

"Look at me when you speak," he snapped.

She hesitated, took a deep breath, drew herself up and met his gaze. His eyes pored into hers and somewhere in the back of her mind an animal instinct sparked and sputtered. *He can smell your fear; show him you're not afraid.*

"Why are you here?"

Kylene raised her chin defiantly. She had spent days in the saddle, on the run. Torn and blistered the skin of her hands, foraged her own food. She had stolen a horse. She had killed a man. She had not come this far to be pushed around by anybody, let alone this strange old man.

"To learn anything I can about the whereabouts of my father and the secrets with which he was so engaged."

"How did you learn about us?"

"Correspondences found in my father's office, and notations in his private journal, which he left to me."

"How did you find us?"

"The same. His notebook, clues there..." She hesitated, unsure of whether she might bring reproach upon Gingham for his having shared their location. "And...a peddler I met on the road. Gingham was his name."

Rufus' eyes burned into hers, the black of them smoldering like coals. For a moment, she felt he was reading her thoughts, probing her mind for whether her statements were true or false.

The black in his eyes turned to ash, and he inclined his head sideways toward Eliza with a small nod. When he returned his gaze upon Kylene, it was once more the perfect blue of a robin's egg, the ash of them blown away by a clearing wind.

"Thank you," he said, with sincerity and something closer to respect.

"You're welcome...?" she said, her heartbeat slowing as the tension drained from the room. She couldn't help but feel like she'd passed some test and looked to Eliza, whose own penetrative gaze was hardly a comfort.

"Yesterday I told you truthfully that I did not know your father's fate, but there is much more that concerns Dirk Gemison and the greater task at hand to which he was so dedicated. If you have a mind to hear of such things."

When Eliza spoke, it was with a measured certainty that brooked no challenge, and Kylene understood then and there that if the Kapnobatai had a leader, surely it was this woman.

"I would make one request of you," she said. "If indeed you profess to have a mind to hear of such things, it must be not as the daughter of Dirk Gemison, but as a daughter of integrity and inquiry."

While Kylene wasn't entirely sure what Eliza meant to convey, she believed she could agree to that much. Certainly, she liked to ask questions. But could she claim integrity, having done what she did?

She gave her acquiescence with a solemn nod.

"Very well," Eliza said. "I invite you to ask any questions that might arise but request that you reserve them until I have finished sharing everything I have to say. So..." She pressed the tapered points of her fingers together and brought them to her lips, briefly resembling a young girl lost in thought.

"I met Dirk Gemison nine years ago, only two years after Osbert completed his installment of the Fingers and perhaps six months after one of his men had directly approached your father. This was when they informed him that he would no longer print histories, poems or novels but would instead be tasked with upholding the integrity of the voice of the Fingers. Of course, print-keeps all over the Grasp were being asked to do the very same. Those that refused met a quiet but bitter end."

Kylene was only five years old, but the memory was crystal in her mind. Her father, sitting at the dinner table, his massive fists clenched before him, voice low with anger, simmering on the edict that had been issued.

She saw now how that moment had come to bear on his entire life. To him, it was an utter abomination to be so coerced in what type he set to text.

"Your father came to me with the first pamphlets he was asked to print. He was deeply dismayed. They spoke of sacrifice for the sake of the common person. These ideas weren't bad on their face, and he was initially conflicted. Osbert's decrees were designed to appear as if they brought equality throughout the land. But something was not right; he felt it in his bones, so he came to us."

Eliza took a deep breath through her nose and reached for a mug at the center of the table. She took a long draught, pausing to consider its contents. The white-haired man did the same. Kylene noticed a third one that must be for her. She reached for it and took a tiny sip. It smelled of honeysuckle and was cool as it slid down her throat.

"Your father, like so many others in the Grasp, agreed to the yoke of Osbert and his Fingers. It seemed an improvement for the organization of things, given that the land was still reeling from the rule of the Weasel King some fifty years prior and the bedlam that ensued when his monarchy fell. It was before your time, but you may have heard of the looting, the killings. It was not chaos, as the Fingers would have you believe, but it was a dangerous time for many people. Many would say that the Grasp is a far more dangerous place now than ever it was in that time of perceived lawlessness. Your father is one of them, as am I."

Kylene's heartstrings lifted a little to hear Eliza speak of her father in the present. She leaned forward in her seat and pressed both hands into the table, working hard to sift through every detail of what Eliza had to say.

The Weasel King. There was a history book her father kept in the secret door in the cellar, where all of his forbidden books lived. It detailed the fall of the king and each king that came before him, of which she recalled there were many Umfreys, Humfreys and Dumfreys. Most of these men were poor, insignificant rulers, more interested in hunting and feasting and women than ruling a kingdom. But the Weasel King was different. He brought the people of the Grasp to task in a way his predecessors never had, and he did it with unspeakable cruelty. They called him Weasel because he'd been found in a hole beneath the floorboards of his castle's cellar after the common folk and nobility alike had razed it to the ground.

Kylene looked up and found that Eliza was waiting for her to resume her attention, her thin dark eyebrows arched high.

"The Grasp was in a sort of fugue state. It was relatively easy for Osbert to claim it and make people think that surrendering small parts of their freedom would grant them safety, security. I will admit his strokes were most masterful, the way he masqueraded bondage for freedom. But the price they pay is too great, and in the end, a toll far worse than the risk of banditry. And I fear this is only the beginning."

Eliza's slender hands wrapped around her mug. She brought it to her lips, sipping delicately and staring into its contents. When she looked up again, her eyes hooked into Kylene's. Outside, the clear, descending call of a shrike sliced through the air, piercing the stillness and sending a shiver to run cold fingers down Kylene's spine.

"Your father, he was the first to seek us out. He had a hunger for information, and a thirst for aid. The Kapnobatai have dwelled in these mountains long before Osbert, longer even than the Weasel King and his ilk. We are watchers who bear witness to the ebb and flow of power in these lands, though others in the Grasp enjoy more celebrity and claim the same title by another name. For many years, we have lived among you in quiet, our presence known only to those brave or desperate enough to find us."

Symbols, lines of text, expressions and poems that Kylene had read in her father's notebook swirled before her, a muddled patchwork that she struggled to piece together. It was a marvel, to think that an entire tribe of people had lived tucked away in these mountains for so long, unbeknownst to the rest of the world.

"There was an age," Eliza continued. "Forgotten by most and known to a few as the Terrors. By our records, it spanned two-hundred-and-thirty-five years, a dark and savage era of bloodshed and misery. During this time, the first of us fled to the mountains, seeking refuge from the war that consumed the land. But the world was different then, Kylene. It was vast and unyielding, full of wonders and terrors you can scarcely imagine. But these are tales for another time."

"No!" Kylene burst out, unable to contain herself. She'd heard stories – folk tales – of red riders and ghost ships, distant fires in the night, on the ground, and in the sky. Hunger gnawed at her. "I want to know everything."

She was leaning forward in her seat as far as the table would allow. Her hands were clenched along the edge of it, gripping the wood like claws.

Eliza smiled, not in pity or cruelty but in pleasure. She gave Rufus a nudge, and he grunted, his blue eyes sparking like a sword upon a grindstone.

"You are Dirk's daughter through and through," she said. "And more than that, a seeker of truth, a daughter of integrity. I sense that you crave not merely knowledge, but understanding."

Rufus shut his eyes with a snap and began to mutter under his breath. His words, more babble than speech, grew in speed and Kylene recoiled. Eliza placed her hand gently on the man's arm, though her gaze never left Kylene.

"Not now, Rufus. In time…" she said, and the man's eyes popped open, the black of them returned, endless pools in which Kylene felt she might drown. She averted his gaze, discomfited by his strangeness. The animal part of her tugged at the muscles of her legs; she pressed her feet flat against the earth to still the twitching urge to run.

Eliza cocked her head, considering her. "You may know everything that we have to give, so long as that knowledge is the choice that is right for you."

Kylene's eyes darted back and forth between Eliza and Rufus, whose black stare was still fixed on her.

"We do not know where your father has gone," Eliza continued, "but Rufus and I have some ideas. Rather than sending you on a bootless errand for which you are, to be quite candid, wildly unequipped, we have a proposition for you."

The tips of Kylene's fingers went white and numb as she gripped the table's edge with renewed force. She forced them to soften and brought them to lie flat on the table.

"I'm listening," she said, her voice barely above a whisper.

Eliza leaned forward, the intensity of her gaze a fixed point in the mad swirl of Kylene's thoughts. "We propose that you remain here."

Kylene opened her mouth to protest, and Eliza held up a single finger, silencing her.

"We propose that you remain here, for a time. We are weeks away from closing the doors of our summer home, at which time we will move west, settle into the caverns and shift into our winter rhythm. In the summer, we are a hive. As bees, we buzz about, gathering, building, growing. But the winter is when our true work begins."

Kylene's breath caught in her throat.

Eliza's eyes glinted in the slanted sunlight streaming through the windows.

"In our winter quarters, we have a vast library, enshrined in the caverns, with chronicles that go back eleven hundred years. It was this knowledge that your father sought, and it is this knowledge that we offer to you now, should you choose to stay."

Kylene's head spun. Eleven hundred years. The oldest history her father had possessed was a four-hundred-and-fifty-year-old illuminated manuscript, and he had treasured it above all else. With the press having only recently been invented and the turmoil that had gripped the Grasp from one monarchy to the next, much of true history had been lost to the sweep of time. The opportunity to access that much knowledge would have been beyond dreaming for her father.

"We will offer to send three emissaries," Eliza said, her voice slow and measured, her every word selected with care. "One to each place with a high probability of your father having sought refuge there. We will send those emissaries today if you choose to stay."

The weight of her words settled on Kylene's shoulders, dragging her down into a sea that swirled with unseen depths.

She looked down at her hands and twisted her fingers into knots.

"These emissaries will have no hope of returning in time for our relocation to the caverns," Eliza said. "Their travels will take them too far to return before the first winter storm, after which time the caverns will be inaccessible. Because of this, we would ask that you stay with us for the remainder of our time here in the summer grounds. Help us with the harvest. Regain your strength. And in winter, you will have the opportunity to reflect and to learn; more than you could ever imagine possible."

"And after winter?" Kylene asked, her voice a ragged whisper.

"After the spring thaw, the emissaries will return. With luck, one of them will return with relevant information as to the whereabouts of your father, if not with your father himself."

Rufus continued to scrutinize Kylene's face, searching for any hint of doubt or hesitation. Kylene swallowed hard, and stared back, refusing to break his gaze.

"Where will you send your emissaries?" she asked, tipping her chin a little higher.

Eliza nodded, unsurprised by Kylene's inquiry.

"Rufus and I deliberated on this matter late into the evening. You must understand that Rufus, your father and I spent years building a nexus that now calls itself, collectively, the bellringers. Many might claim to belong to our organization, but only a handful are privy to its inner workings. Your father may have sought refuge with one of these individuals within the nexus rather than returning to us."

"And who are these individuals?" Kylene pressed, and again, Eliza nodded.

"A Mr Pontrefait, located in Omnia, a man by the name of Badi, who has for many years been settled in Atria, and Thaddeus Almatian, who lives in the border city of Lazare."

The hair on Kylene's arms stood straight up. *Mr Pontrefait...* *Omnia.* She could reach Omnia by the next new moon. The University was there, surely her father would have gone to where he could do the most to advance the cause, and with the number of times Mr Pontrefait was mentioned in his notes...

Images fluttered through her mind, each a gold-limned leaf blown by some unseen wind. Her cellar, damp earth and beeswax candles. The print shop, fresh ink and the great creak of the press, her father's hands, setting the type. The Mavros Forest, the sweet smell of decomposition, wet leaves and worm-riddled clay. McBane's infirmary, tansy and rue, and his secret room beneath the floorboards where he conducted his experiments, with Kylene at his side, experiments that neither the Fingers nor her parents would ever have approved.

All gone. She knew it in her heart, though she hadn't spoken, let alone thought of, this truth until now. And with that knowing, the weight of decision settled within her like a stone sinking to the bottom of a pond. Her eyes were moist and she blinked several times to refocus them so that she might meet Eliza's gaze.

"I will stay with you," Kylene said, her voice stronger now. "If you'll answer one more question."

Eliza remained motionless, her eyes sparking like flint-struck stone, inviting, accepting.

"Why help me?"

Eliza did not hesitate.

"For the same reason that we helped your father," she said simply.

"But why do all these things? Why help us when you don't even live among us? It's not your battle to fight."

Eliza's smile was a sad one. "Once, we lived among you. And we have not forgotten what it feels like to bear the yoke of a life lived in fear. We would not leave our kith and kin in such a way."

Kylene nodded, and her heart stirred with hope, a newfound purpose emerging. Eliza's words rang true, dispelling any lingering doubts, and despite everything, Kylene found she trusted this woman, as her father surely had when first he came across her. As their gazes locked, a silent understanding passed between them; she and her people would help Kylene follow in her father's footsteps, wherever they may lead.

***

Kylene emerged from the meeting chamber; the child who had woken her that morning was there, waiting for her. He swung his short legs up and off of the stump on which he sat and introduced himself as Hendry. He spent the better part of the day leading her around the grounds, his small, warm hand wrapped in hers and imparting upon her the functions of the encampment's many structures and activities of late summer. When the sun began to set, Hendry bid her farewell, and Kylene, heeding Cael's words, made her way toward the sulfur pools.

As she trudged up the pine needle-strewn path, Kylene could no longer ignore the ache of her limbs, an insistence that trod the line between exhaustion and agony, sharp and screaming. It was the kind of pain that reminded her of her journey thus far, and the trials yet to come, and she welcomed it with grim satisfaction. The red-orange dirt beneath her boots glowed in the sun's fading light.

She reached the top of the hillock, placing her hand on the large boulder there and peering shyly around its edge, catching a glimpse of the sulfur springs below.

She counted thirteen pools before her, some still and smooth as glass, others alive, seething and steaming. They ranged in size from an arm span to that of a large pond too wide to throw a stone across. Gigantic granite boulders, overrun by bright green moss, marked boundaries and borders. Enormous ferns erupted from each crevice, fronds gently beckoning.

She made her way down, taking care to avert her eyes from the handful of people enjoying the pools. The smell of brimstone was strong, and her nose wrinkled as she skirted around the first pool, where a man and woman sat with arms wrapped around each other in a lover's embrace, their foreheads touching as they murmured to one another. The second pool was smaller than the first, no bigger than a handcart and empty, and the third might have been considered a pond. In it, three young girls swam like frogs from one end to the other. With a mild sense of alarm, she realized that she could see the pale moons of their backsides, answering one of her questions, at least.

The fourth pool was empty. This one was still and small and shaped like an egg, with a high-backed stone seat extending out of the water that beckoned her to sit. She looked around sheepishly, gathering her shift's dirty, ragged hems in bunched fists.

No one watched her. No one seemed to care that a stranger meant to disrobe in their midst.

She wriggled out of the ruined fabric and dipped a toe into the water. It was warm – almost hot – and silken to the touch. In one smooth step, she slid into the water like a beaver, like a muskrat, like a girl with seven days of dust on her skin.

The water shimmered and purled like cobalt ink, so rich a color it scarcely seemed real. Deeper, she waded, digging her toes into the pebbles at the pool's bottom. She moved slowly, deliberately, and when the water was up to her neck, she submerged her head, holding her breath for as long as she dared. She heard hissing, felt the heat of vents beneath the surface, and she broke through to the air, gasping, the feel of it on her face a cold kiss.

She arced her arms through the water's velvet resistance and reached the stone seat. Her hands found its slick bottom, and she slid up onto it. Resting her head against the stone, the heat of the water eased the tension from her muscles, soothed the meanest of her pains. She closed her eyes, wet lashes heavy on wet cheeks, and thought of her father. If he had seen fit to give up their family for the sake of freedom, she hoped it was worth it.

Chapter Fifteen

"What I can't figure out," Lovelace said, his voice echoing off the cave's damp walls, "is that whole bit at the end. 'Beware of those who find it.' Assuming that was Oi...the whole damn order was built on the idea that truth ought to be sought, so why be wary?"

It was a question aimed at Gunnar, who was sitting with his back against a sunlit portion of the cave wall and cleaning his nails with a pointed piece of bark. He did not look up. Ailwin, however, was more than happy to share his perspective.

"Perhaps Oi was prophecizing the coming of Alev," he called from his dark corner, where he was tying together sprigs of dried herbs. He'd asked the girl how he could thank her for her healing and she'd disappeared into her inner cavern, only to return moments later with armfuls of dried plants. Ailwin had, happily, been tying prim bows for the better part of the morning, his bandaged legs stretched out before him. "Like, truth is a metaphor for him, and we ought to be wary of him."

Lovelace shook his head. "It still doesn't make sense. Our prerogative is to root out hidden truths, or else truths that parade around, wearing many masks. I'm not overdrawing it when I say it is our sole purpose as an order."

"There's your problem," Ailwin said, quick on the counter. "Clearly you lot are too narrow-minded. Maybe Alev has found a truth that is truer than true, truthier than any dactyli has ever before found, and that's how he's so powerful. Would the prophecy not be true then?"

He wore a crooked little smirk that did little to soothe Lovelace's mounting agitation.

"There's no such thing as truer than true; there's either true, or not true," Lovelace said as he paced the length of the cave like some restless ghost.

"That's not true," Ailwin said, setting down his posy. His smirk shifted to a sympathetic smile. "There are all sorts of things in between true or not true. There are half-truths, white lies, black lies, red lies, gray lies...Truth comes in all sorts of shades."

Lovelace gave a huff and continued to pace. Out of the corner of his eye, he could see the upturned corner of Gunnar's mouth as he bent over his left hand with the bark. *Once again, old stone-tongue is of no use,* he thought. Why had this become a battle of wits? Why did it feel like he was losing? He summoned the right counter to set the boy to rights.

"Cuimhne Amas, boy, objective truth. Call all your other truths how you want, they're like butter or sugar or rhubarb after a boil. Pieces of the pie. We take those bits and bake the blasted thing. It's why we gather memories from both humans and the earth; stones and trees have no stake in human interest or care for right and wrong. You need all of them, human and earth memories, to have Cuimhne Amas."

"I just don't think perfect is a thing that can be had. Least of all, where truth is concerned."

The reply from Ailwin was simple, yet it caught Lovelace like a glancing blow. For a moment, he was struck silent, not by the profundity of Ailwin's words but by the inflexibility of his own. Once, he had been a lad who asked a cartload of impertinent questions, and here he was shouting down Ailwin with the same tired notion as the masters; that youth disqualifies a worthy mind.

"What in the bleeding earth is a red lie, anyways?" he asked, hoping to change the subject and wash the foul taste of his words from his mouth.

Ailwin shrugged. "Red lies are meant for malice. My Mam always said my father was a liar painted red."

Their routine of the last two days – eating, patrolling, theorizing and sleeping – had gone stale. And yet, in the cramped monotony, Ailwin had grown increasingly sound in both body and mind. His physical condition was significantly improved, attended as he was by the painstaking attentions of the girl. With one hand leaned against the back of the cave mouth, he rose to put pressure on the more burned of his two feet, testing its ability to bear weight.

"Anyway. It's got to mean generally. Prophecies are always meant to be taken generally," he said, wincing as he took one full step forward. "Everyone knows that."

Lovelace watched as Ailwin's eyes flickered toward the girl, who was contorting her body into a strange shape. It was a thing she did each morning. Her arms were behind her back, her hands clasped, and she was folded at the waist. Lovelace couldn't tell whether she was listening or not; he rarely could.

"How do you figure?" he asked, intrigued by this newfound bravado of Ailwin's. It was not hard to guess at its source.

"Take the prophecies of Magda the Meek, one of the most fabled prophetesses there ever was, even born in Mortalis, as it happens," he said as he leaned back against the cave wall with a casual cross of his arms. "Was a bard by the name of Lochinver, wrote a song of her some years after she passed. Went about gathering as much as he could about each and every prophecy she'd laid, and how they hatched. Anyhow, I remembered as how I'd heard his song the first time. 'Twas at the Colt. He twanged his lute and laid out one prophecy after the other, with that slow-picking way of his. By the end of it, with all of old Magda's predictions and their outcomes laid bare, it was plain to me as the nose on my face. Wasn't some magic power of seeing the future that old Magda possessed, but a way of reading people like, and understanding the turnings of the world, the patterns beneath the mire of it all."

Over in his corner of the cave, Gunnar gave a quiet grunt of approval. It was a keen observation, especially as it pertained to those self-proclaimed sages in the world of men. But it wasn't enough, couldn't be enough. Oi wasn't some half-penny prophetess with a knack for reading faces.

Oi had built the orb. Had given the dactyli their name and set them to task. Did Lovelace not possess in the blood that coursed through his own veins some power that was beyond the ken of common folk? As supernatural as any prophecy come to bear the fruit of truth? There had to be a hidden meaning in Oi's prophecy that was eluding him.

He said as much to Ailwin, who gave a smug chortle that made Lovelace want to cuff him over the ear. He didn't, of course, even if the boy was being an insufferable little prig. The lad *had* sustained a traumatic injury on their behalf.

"Perhaps," Ailwin said, "though it's like as not you'll discover the true shape of it when the story's reached its natural end."

Lovelace gave a grunt and rose.

Why could the path forward not be straight? Gunnar and he were just two rangers with a prophecy, saddled with a peculiar girl and two lost boys. They were good at following orders, good at swift determination, but the grand scheme eluded them. The task of stepping back to see the broader panorama and crafting a precise plan of action was beyond their grasp.

He excused himself under the pretext of searching for Pif, who had been gone overlong in search of some game. Frustrated by all the riddles, he grunted his intentions to Gunnar and shouldered his satchel with thoughts of dwindling provisions and a notable lack of ale.

He emerged from the cave, squinting against the bright sunlight that seemed to hammer into his skull. He placed his hand on the rough, sun-baked surface of rock that formed the cave's outer wall and closed his eyes. Through the tactile connection with the stone, he recalled the events of that morning, watching as they played out in rapid motion behind his closed eyelids. He sifted through the humdrum scenes of sky and the sounds of their distant murmurs until he found what he was looking for – Pif, turning right as he emerged from the cave.

Lovelace inched along the slimmer edge of the ridge to the right of the cave, following it until he was off the mountain face and once more among hemlock and cedar trees. Placing his hand on a nearby cedar, he learned that Pif had gone northeast. He set off, wiping sticky sap from his hand onto his pant leg, moving slowly as he picked his way through the undergrowth and the thorny brambles of his thoughts.

The last two days had brought little resolution. They could not return to the Meorachadh just as surely as they could not deliver the boys to Mortalis. Even if the man with the burned face had lied and the Meorachadh still stood, the road there would be fraught with danger.

The more he thought about everything that had transpired over the last several days, the more obvious it became that Alev had not simply vanished, only to reappear and exact some singular revenge.

He had built an army. Worse, a zealous force of acolytes who seemed to think him some kind of godhead. And why shouldn't they? Somehow, Alev had imbued them with some lighter shade of fire magic, convincing them of his divine authority.

Lovelace reached the next branch of Pif's path and leaned forward to place his palm on the broad trunk of another cedar. He stopped, his hand hovering over the rough grooves of its surface.

Something was wrong. There was a smell in the air, a shock of charred fabric and burnt leaves tainting what had been crisp and cedar-laced. He slammed his hand down onto the trunk.

The boy, he thought, alarm washing through him as waves. *Show me the boy.* He let out his breath. There was Pif, turning left, creeping north, sling half-raised, in pursuit of some prey or other.

Still, the smell. It stuck in his nostrils, sickening him, laying waste to any lingering notions of safety.

He tore up the mountainside, stopping every so often only to ensure he was still on the boy's crooked-as-a-hare trail.

His lungs burned. Beads of sweat ran down his forehead, stinging his eyes and spilling into the tangle of his beard. Surely he should have caught up to the boy by now; how long had he been searching?

He stopped short before a colossal cedar and cupped his hands around his mouth, bellowing into the still forest air.

"Pif!"

His call echoed down the mountainside, bouncing between trees and rocky outcrops, tumbling on and on until it faded away to silence, somewhere far below. But there was no answer, only the persistent songs of birds and the eternal stirring of the forest.

How far was the boy willing to go for a bit of squirrel flesh?

He gasped for breath. His chest was tight, and his lungs felt as if they might rip at the seams. Had he only imagined the smell of burning things? He bent at the waist, recovering himself, the ragged sound of his breath overloud in his ears. With one hand on his knee, he leaned forward to touch two fingers to the cedar.

A shock went through him, sudden and sharp.

Burning leaves, the smell no longer a faint imprint but an indelible taint. The air was tinged with the palest shade of red, like when wildfires burn so bright they blot out the sun.

But there was no wildfire here. There was only Alev. Pif was nowhere to be seen. Lovelace watched, transfixed in horror. Alev was staring right at him, so close to him that Lovelace could see the whites of his eyes, so real it seemed he could reach out and touch him. Indeed, there was a sharpness to his form that was aberrant, as if the cedar had remembered him… differently than most subjects.

Impossible, Lovelace thought, willing his eyes to stay locked with Alev's unseeing gaze. *The earth is without favor, without fear.*

"Hello, Lovelace," said the none-too-distant memory of Alev. "I assume you're the one that has come to search for the boy. You always were the imprudent one. Besides, Gunnar was never one to stick out his neck for another."

The purr of Alev's voice – like a cat before a bowl of cream – made Lovelace's stomach curl.

"The boy reminds you of yourself, does he not?" Alev's lips flattened into a grimace, his version of a smile. "A pity for him."

"As you might surmise," he continued, his black eyes boring into the precise place where Lovelace stood. "I didn't come here to reminisce about what a noxious weed you are; I came here to parlay. You have something I want, and I have something you want. Thank you for finding her for me. It seems my men were inadequate to the task, but you rangers do know your business, don't you?"

"Here are my terms: The boy for the girl. At the bottom of the eastern pass, there is a clearing with a stone circle. You have one day."

A column of flames went up, encircling Alev and shrouding him from view. The column towered and roared, swirling as high as the canopy was tall. It was extinguished almost as quickly as it appeared, and Alev with it. The only indication that he had once stood there was a small circle of scorched earth, the outline of which smoldered and smoked.

The sgeul ended so abruptly Lovelace felt he had been spat out. He blinked. The forest was precisely as it had been in the sgeul, save for the bloody tint of the air and the unnatural heat, like standing before an open oven. He looked down, and he felt like he'd been gut-punched. There it was, the burnt patch of earth he'd neglected to notice before. What else had he missed?

He took several steps beyond the burn mark and began to pace, using a bit of his luth to quell his rising panic.

He had two options: He could go after Alev now. He couldn't be far and would never expect Lovelace to do such a pea-brained thing. And as neat a trick as his up-in-smoke departure was, Lovelace doubted that he had gone far – dactyli magic had limits. It *has to have limits,* he thought, realizing he was clinging desperately to the notion.

Lovelace *was* the second most competent ranger in the Meorachadh. The thought brought a black smile to his face. And what a distinction *that* was, more competent than Radigan and Lester, who he was pretty sure needed signposts to find their way out of an open field.

No, Lovelace was no match for Alev alone, even before the bastard had gone and acquired all of his corrupt fire magic. Were they made to fight like cocks in a ring, it would be Lovelace who would go down squawking, eyes gauged, bloody throat streaming.

His other option was to do exactly as Alev said: be at the foot of the eastern pass, on time, girl in tow, like a good little boy.

Either way, it felt like a trap. And what were his plans for the girl, anyhow? Lovelace couldn't shake the feeling that something darker than even death was at play.

A heavy sigh escaped his lips. He hated that he had not been born with a little more magic, or at the very least, a little more courage to know what was right. But he was short on both, so he turned and ran back the way he had come, stumbling down the hill as he went, feeling every bit as frightened, as uncertain as he had the day he'd been taken so many years ago when he knew not what life had in store, only that it would never be the same again.

***

Lovelace stopped short at the mouth of the cave, stooping low to recapture his breath. His sides were stitched, and his lungs felt like they'd been scraped with sandpaper. He could feel the eyes of Ailwin and Gunnar on him, watching him hack and heave.

Gunnar approached him slowly and placed a hand on his back. Lovelace looked up, surprised by the gesture. Gunn's face was inscrutable as ever, a faint quirk of his left eyebrow the only hint that he might be concerned.

"Alev," Lovelace managed to choke out.

Gunnar inhaled sharply, his nostrils flattened.

"The boy, he's taken the boy. Followed his trail. Showed up out of nowhere, up in smoke. Knows we're here."

Gunnar nodded once, his eyes flashing with calculation.

Lovelace straightened, the burning in his chest giving way to a tight grip like great hands squeezing. Shame, perhaps, for being so daft as to have let the boy go off on his own.

The girl emerged from her cavern, a ghostly trace of grave concern impressed upon her face.

"It was a sgeul. He wants the girl in exchange for the boy," he said, shooting her what he hoped was a look of meaningful apology.

He turned back to Gunnar.

"Told us to meet him at the foot of the eastern pass in a day," he said.

Gunnar's face betrayed no thought, his eyes fixed somewhere distant in the blue abyss of sky beyond.

"The girl is more valuable than the boy," he said absently. It was as much a question as a statement.

"Surely we'll not treat with that bastard!?" Ailwin shouted, hobbling over to stand before Lovelace, indignation and panic fighting for precedence on his fair face.

At the back of the cave, the girl stood, her slender hands wrapped around her waist, her eyes wide as a deer's, caught in the sudden glare of a hunter's torch. Their gazes all converged upon her.

The air around her quivered faintly, but it was not fear that radiated, Lovelace saw. It was energy. Her skin shone with a soft, white light so subtle that most would not recognize the magic in it. And her eyes. They grew wider; in them a fierce certainty shone like pearls beneath the sun.

"We must retrieve him," she said.

The glow vanished. She knelt beside her small stack of herbs and began to gather them up, like she meant to pack and be gone forthwith.

"We can't just trade her!" Ailwin said, looking pleadingly from her to Gunnar to Lovelace and back again, his eyes locked on the girl's back with an implacable intensity.

"No, lad, we can't just trade her," Lovelace said softly, looking to Gunnar.

A hush enveloped them, and within its folds, Lovelace sensed that he and Gunnar were of one mind.

"Us, then?" he said. "Shall we say hello to our old friend?"

Gunnar was staring at the girl's back with a fervor that rivaled Ailwin's own, but it was not longing that marked his features. His jaw twitched, and he nodded as he locked eyes with Lovelace.

"Aye," he said.

"I can get us there by tomorrow eve," she said matter-of-factly as she rose. "We'll leave tonight."

And with that, she turned, the faded yellow of her skirt sweeping over stone the only sound of her passage as she faded into the dark of her inner cavern.

At least, Lovelace thought as he watched her disappear, *now we know what's next.*

Chapter Sixteen

They took pains to leave the cave without a trace of their occupancy. The girl had instructed as much. She told them to pack their satchels and scrub the floor of fire marks while she disappeared one last time inside the cleft in the cave wall. Moments later, she emerged; a bulky package strapped to her waist, the tangle of her dark hair pulled into a tight braid at the base of her neck.

Lovelace felt a twinge of regret as they left the shadowy confines of the cave. What treasures did the girl keep hidden in the cavern, and how did she navigate the tunnels, so that she could move like a ghost through stone?

From the moment they decided she would lead them to Alev, the girl had assumed command like a seasoned general. Her fluid stream of orders left the three men in no doubt of her capacity. It was she who decided they go when the moon was a quarter way through the sky, who instructed they not speak as they crossed through a field of exposed granite boulders, and who advised they walk in a certain stretch of stream, rather than brave its muddy banks. Her keen eye caught the flint of cobwebs festooned beneath the low-hanging branches of dogwood. The spiders' silk was poisonous, she warned, it would burn their skin with a fierce and lasting pain.

Ailwin trudged behind with heavy wrapped feet, silent and grim, his face pale in the moonlight, his torment barely concealed. They had no choice but to follow her lead. She knew the mountains and could guide them better than they could on their own. And so, they followed her like sleepwalkers, no words passing between them as they moved up, then over and finally down the mountains in a march both joyless and swift.

They had no allies to call upon, no amount of time or skill that could make them stronger than Alev. To abandon Pif to

Alev's whims or offer up the girl like some sacrificial lamb was unthinkable. They would make their stand, no matter the cost, though Lovelace was fully aware that the cost was, without doubt, their mortal end.

As they descended down the eastern portion of the pass, the sun rose a pale yellow, and the moon became a whisper in the sky. The route was cut deep into the mountains, densely populated by pine and spruce. It was colder here, and Lovelace flexed his fingers, willing sensation back into their tips. Onward, they picked their way down the steep grade until the world was bright and covered in dew, until they reached a plateau with an outcrop of boulders wearing lichen for coats.

Gunnar dismounted from the saddle and nodded to the girl, who stared at him with eyes that betrayed no feeling.

"Stay here with her," Gunnar said to Ailwin.

Ailwin straightened, nodding once.

"If we're not back by eventide, leave. You have a place you can retreat to?" Gunnar said, handing Ailwin his cloak. The girl gave a bob of her head.

"There are many hidey-holes in these mountains."

"Good," Gunnar said.

"You'll not let him die on my account," she said, her gaze far away.

"Aye, lass, we'll do our best," Lovelace said. "How much further 'til we reach the stone circle he spoke of?"

"You are acquainted with the telling of time?"

Lovelace froze.

"Aye..."

So she had lived in a place where time was kept.

Her eyes floated upwards to the low-hanging bough of a pine. "About a bell and a half, I should think."

Lovelace clapped a hand on Ailwin's shoulder. "Keep like an owl, aye?" he said. The boy pressed his lips together and nodded. His dark eyes were searching Lovelace's, searching for some sense of assurance, some guarantee that they might see one another again. It was not a surety that was Lovelace's to give.

"Give the bastard what he deserves," Ailwin said.

"We'll do our best, lad," Lovelace said as he turned to face the girl. The way she stared at him was unabashed and unnerving.

The white flare. She. A wild, fiercely strange young woman upon whom so many groundless hopes were hung. They had searched for her. They'd found her. And to what end? He didn't even know her name.

"Good luck, Lovelace," she said, her brown eyes piercing, running him straight through.

He bowed his head to her and crossed his arms to his chest without thought. She was dactyli, after all, whether she knew it or not.

"Thank you kindly, m'lady," he said, looking to the path ahead where Gunnar had already gone and disappeared from view. He turned to follow, each step a hammer on the nail of his uncertain fate.

***

They walked in silence for a long stretch.

A death march.

Yet they walked toward it with a strange willingness.

Gunnar led the way, his strides long and purposeful, navigating over fallen logs and through the tangles of clematis vines, threatening to ensnare them.

Lovelace followed. It was odd that he felt no fear, no tug in his legs to turn and run. He could no more dredge up any sense of trouble than a river could deny its course.

"Funny, that," he mumbled, sidestepping a slender pine sapling growing in defiance from the crevice of a rock.

"What's that?" Gunnar asked from ahead.

"Oh, just thinking about the end," Lovelace said. "I'm imagining everything short of Alev transforming into a dragon and swallowing me whole, and I just can't be bothered."

Gunnar snorted. "Dragons don't exist."

"It's too bad you didn't spend more time in the Tasglann," Lovelace said. "There was a dactyli – Aquimore, I believe – who posited that they did, some 3,000 years back. There are still vestiges of their worship to this day, particularly up north near Skole. Only among the most superstitious of the common folk, of course. It is difficult to extract a sgeul in those parts, not since they started mining and blasting rocks, razing trees. Aquimore was of the mind, based on his research, that dragons were not common in the Grasp, but that a small group of them would roost for winter in Mt. Ide, just south of Skole. I've seen them in Aquimore's sgeulachd on the subject."

Gunnar snorted again. "So you say. A flock of dragons roosting in the mountains like chickens in a coop. That is funny."

And he laughed, a tinny sound that jangled through the forest. Lovelace grinned. "Aquimore thinks that dragons and chickens share a common ancestor, or that chickens are descended from dragons. He wasn't too clear on that point, come to it..." He trailed off, more curious about what Gunnar might say next than about remembering Aquimore's conclusive thoughts on chicken pedigree.

If Gunnar made a sound of acknowledgment, it was lost in the rhythm of his boot-step over fallen leaves. They returned to silence and strangeness, the stretch of pass before them twisting and steep, the gradual light of day dawning all around.

They descended the mountain like that for a time until, to Lovelace's surprise, Gunnar cleared his throat.

"I'm not going to die here," he said. "And I can't think I'd leave you in the fire. We are bound to elude death, at least today," he said, not looking back. He spoke with such easy confidence,

Lovelace dug his fingers into both of his ears, freeing them of wax. There was something else in Gunnar's voice, something dreamy and elusive.

"Come again?" Lovelace said, jogging to catch him up.

Gunnar regarded him out of the corner of his eye, took a deep breath and rolled his eyes skywards, as if already regretting his next words.

"There was a seer; I was seven."

Lovelace erupted with laughter, the sound of it so great he shook with its force.

"You've got stones, Gunn, I'll give you that. Are you telling me that you believe in fate? Sons to dust, man. We could have had some interesting conversations." Lovelace wiped his eyes and saw the faint edge of a smile traced onto the corner of Gunnar's mouth. He was matching him stride for stride and they were well over halfway down the pass, edging ever closer to disaster. And here was Gunnar, claiming that today was not his day, on account of a fortune told twenty-some-odd years ago.

"I don't," Gunnar said.

"You don't what?"

"I don't believe in fate," Gunnar said, his grin so wide that Lovelace could see the back of his teeth.

Gunnar laughed. It was silver, the sound of it thunderous, hearty and sweet. "But," he said, recovering himself enough to speak, "I was taken to a seer when I was seven," he said. "She was...notable, where I come from. I was having night terrors, dreams of death. I could not eat or sleep for the fright of them. But she told me that I could not die so long as the harbinger lives, that we would be born apart but joined together, in life and then, in death."

"And you think that the girl is the harbinger?"

The air grew tighter around them, fraught with something that could not be seen or touched.

Gunnar noticed it too. His jaw tightened, and his fingers flexed by his sides. *Not long now,* Lovelace thought.

"I thought it was another, wanted it to be another, once," Gunnar said, his limbs taut, ready, "But I was wrong."

The miraculous "She," Lovelace thought. The one he'd been on the brink of sharing all those nights ago. *Before Pif and Ailwin came barging in.* Lovelace opened his mouth to ask but was cut short by a sudden dizziness. The pressure in the air had dropped, and Lovelace's ears hummed. It was almost impossible to breathe. The air was heavy, acrid, like a battlefield after the fighting has ceased. Lovelace thought of buzzards, and bones picked clean.

They stopped dead on the outskirts of the stone circle, appeared before them suddenly.

Alev was nowhere to be seen.

Lovelace's heart raced, and he turned, clapping a hand on Gunnar's shoulder.

"It has been an honor to walk beside you these fifteen years past," Lovelace said, his tone low and fast. "Much as I..."

"Save your sap, Lovelace. Today is not our day," Gunnar said, and he strode boldly into the clearing.

"Alev!" he bellowed, head thrown back, thistledown hair shining, sleek in the late morning sun. "Come out, you fiend, you base, motherless wretch!"

Leaves rustled overhead, rattling and snapping in protest as Gunnar summoned the wind, and Lovelace watched for one long moment, stretched paper-thin.

He charged headlong into the center of the standing stones, focusing his luth, sharpening it, imagining vines like manacles and cracked earth and felling blows from trees brought to menace by his will.

Combat would be better served by fire or wind, or even water, all of which could be used to attack with precision rather than brute force. Or perhaps it was just that Lovelace lacked the inventiveness to bring his earthly powers to bear for the harm of another. He shoved aside these feelings of smallness, of insubstantiality, and moved to stand near enough to Gunnar that the tips of their shoulder blades touched.

Hot, turgid air swirled around the clearing in a whorl, lifting the hair from Lovelace's sweat-laden brow and together, they waited.

A chorus of heartbeats, more than his own and Gunnar's. It was the heartbeat of the forest, the heavy, sticky thump of it loud in his ears as he focused his luth to subtler and subtler levels of scrutiny. The hair on the back of his neck prickled. Beside him, Gunnar tensed in anticipation.

Without warning, fire erupted all around them, and the hair of Lovelace's brows and lashes was singed to ash.

Amid the fiery chaos, Gunnar kneeled and pressed his fingertips into the earth at his feet.

Gradually, the towering wall of flames surrounding them faltered and drew back until it was reduced to a low-burning hedgerow.

Lovelace felt faint. Gunnar had thinned the air, just enough so that the encircling fire could not maintain its size, and he could see beyond its walls. It was enough for Lovelace to gather himself and visualize waves crashing. The ground beneath them rumbled, groaned and a torrent of earth, moldering and damp, rose and fell to smother the flames.

As the fire sputtered into steam and smoke, the clearing grew still, save for the quiet hiss of hot soil.

Then, piercing the silence, laughter, pitched high and keening, rang out, and Alev stepped forth from behind the tallest standing stone.

At last.

He looked much as Lovelace remembered him; tall, lean, handsome in a drawn, severe sort of way. But it was his dress that drew Lovelace's eye most. Draped about his body were robes of darkest red, so dark as to seem almost black, like garnets beneath the pale glow of a new moon. They shimmered with such subtle provocation they could only have been woven by magic. Of what kind, Lovelace could only guess.

Alev stood before them, unmoving, his gaze calculating, dispassionate.

"Motherless wretch," Alev echoed. He began to slowly pace before them, his eyes flickering between them with avid leisure. A talisman, pendular in shape and glowing red, rested in the center of his chest beneath his robes.

"What an unkind thing to say to a brother so long absent. Where are your manners, Gunnar?"

Quick as a lash, he flicked his wrist and sent a searing bolt of flame from the palm of his hand. It struck Gunnar square in the chest. He staggered backward but managed to catch himself so that he did not fall. Glittering traces of flame wormed their way through the fabric of his shirt. He made no attempt to smother them and straightened, eyes flashing dangerously. But Gunnar knew what Lovelace did: an outright attack would be fatal, and so he stayed his luth.

Instead, they waited, the smell of charred fabric strong. *How quickly we burn*, Lovelace thought distantly. They needed Alev to make an error, and to seize upon it. It was the only chance they had.

"I must say," Alev said, continuing his pacing appraisal. "I am surprised to find you both, out here in the world and with children in tow, no less. It is not the dactyli way. Rats live in holes, after all. They only scamper out when they believe it is safe. When they are hungry." He cocked his head in mock consideration. "Rats always run back to their holes in times of danger, but then, I suppose you've heard that you don't have much of a hole to run back to."

"Where is the boy?" Lovelace asked.

Alev adopted a look of surprise. "Why, he's here. In this very clearing. He is a maundering little thing. I had to keep him quiet. On and on, he prattled, and somehow, everything he had to say was woefully bereft of any real meaning or worth. Is he kin of yours, Lovelace?"

Lovelace ignored the jibe and scanned the surrounding area. There was no sign of Pif.

"I would be careful with your magic, Lovelace. You nearly killed your boy with your brutish hoeing. Once a dirt farmer, always a dirt farmer, I suppose."

Fresh horror bloomed within Lovelace as he looked down at the freshly turned earth beneath Alev's feet. Pif was underground.

Faint glee spread across Alev's face.

"Lucky for you, I put him deeper than six feet, though I cannot promise that your little stunt did not weaken the walls of his enclosure. I am not earth-coalesced, after all, so I cannot guarantee structural integrity, or air supply, for that matter. I'm not quite as clever as you when it comes to making mud pies and castles in the sand."

Lovelace felt a steady, somewhat frenzied pulse beneath his feet, and relief washed over him. Pif would be safer there, for now.

Alev had ceased his pacing and stood to face them, so close that Lovelace could see the curvature of his skull beneath his skin. Beside Lovelace, Gunnar tensed. "Soon," read the language of his body. Lovelace moved his weight into the balls of his feet, the subtle shift of his stance responding, "I'm with you."

"And where, pray tell, have you been these seven years? Searching for the mother that left you?" Lovelace asked.

Alev's eyes glittered. "I've been preparing," he said, as if this was the most obvious answer in the world, as if he was surprised that Lovelace was stupid enough even to ask.

"Preparing for what?" Gunnar said.

Alev gave a short laugh and then recomposed his features, the look he put on deadly serious. "To put an end to things for which I do not care," he said, beginning to count on five fingers. "The dactyli order. Men who do not take me seriously. Women who do not take me seriously, for that matter. Anyone who takes beautiful things for granted. But it is not just endings I'm after. Beginnings, boys. When I am finished with the ending of things, it will be the beginning that will be the most exhilarating."

Lovelace let out a small, dry laugh.

"And I'm to take it that you know the weight and measure of beauty?"

Alev's eyes bored into him. When he spoke, he was quiet.

"Power is beautiful, little Love. Or haven't you realized that all this time that you've been running about, churning up earth and making barley grow where it has absolutely no right. Oh," he said, adopting a tone of mock sympathy, "I'd forgotten. Your powers have always plagued you. The burden of being a dactyli. You and Gunnar with your crises of existence. No women, no children, no home save a shared slab of rock at the edge of the Grasp. It's all so dreadfully sad and lonesome."

He reared on them, and Lovelace flinched. Alev's hands fluttered idly by his sides. Small flames had sprouted from each of his fingers.

"Never mind that you can alter and organize the very matter on which we stand into whatever shape you wish, that Gunnar can transmute and control the very thing we need to breath. Never have you imagined what you could truly do. No, you are content to play at parlor tricks so that you can find more sorry boys like you. So that you can perpetuate a tradition built on bookish lies and a false hope that people can be saved by truth. Your complacency sickens me."

There was an edge to his voice that was split between reverence and mania, and he began slowly circling the perimeter of the stone circle, crowing as he went.

"There is no truth so absolute as power. Mankind has shown time and time again that they do not know what to do with it. They squander it, misplace it, give it away like pennies to a pauper. Dactyli are not special. There is a seed of power that lies within each person. I take it you've met my red knights?"

"Aye, we did," Lovelace said, keeping his eyes fixed on the foremost stone before him. "Made quick work of them, as it happens."

To their left, Alev nodded, unperturbed. "I should hope so. They are soldiers of fortune. Wastrels, outcasts. The worst sort of men. But they show what is possible. That power can be awakened; power can be grown."

Alev's speech was ripe with fervor, the skin of his exterior split, revealing a pit of madness within that chilled Lovelace to the bone despite the heat in the clearing.

"Where have you been then, all this time?" Lovelace asked. He shifted his weight again to feel for Pif's subterranean heartbeat. It was still there, the hammering vibration of it fortifying, worth fighting for.

Alev paused, as if he was unsure whether or not he had shared too much. The bright gleam in his eye dimmed as he turned his gaze down to his feet and folded his flame-tipped fingers before him. When he looked up again and met Lovelace squarely in the eye, the cold veneer of control, of calculation, was returned.

"Now, now, Lovelace," he said. "Surely you didn't think I'd afford you the privilege of such information. Besides, if I did, I would have every reason to kill you on the spot instead of offering the honorable option of a duel."

"I do have a question for *you*," Alev said, swooping in on Gunnar from their right. When he moved, his dark robes glimmered red, like the underbelly of some strange fish.

"Ask it then," Gunnar spat. "And be quick about it. We came here to parlay, not watch you prance about in your finery."

Alev rubbed the base of his thumbs in a slow, alternating rhythm, pausing overlong as he looked Gunnar up and down.

"I called this meeting," he said. "I will *prance* as I see fit. As it pleases me. Thus is the nature of power, Gunnar, or perhaps you still don't understand. Allow me to show you."

Gunnar began to choke. He clutched at his throat, scrabbling at it with desperate fingers, his mouth turned toward the sky as he gulped and gasped for air.

Lovelace watched, ensnared by indecision, as Gunnar beat at his chest like a wild beast in an effort to force air into his own lungs.

"You are not the only one who can play with air. While I am perhaps not as dab a hand as you at thinning it, I can make it hotter. Careful, Gunnar. From what I understand, if they expand too much, your lungs will likely burst."

Gunnar wheezed and heaved. With his hands on his knees, he pulled labored, rattling breath into his lungs. The few lines between his brows, around his eyes and mouth had transformed from tracery to deep grooves. His jaw was locked so tightly that the sinews of his neck jutted out like cords of taut wire. And yet, slowly, he managed to unfold his pain-stricken form until he stood tall again, his head held high.

"Ask your question," he said, his voice a hoarse whisper.

Alev regarded him curiously, then shook his head.

"Why do you insist on pretending that you are good?"

"Come again?" By the look on Gunnar's face, this was not the kind of question he'd expected.

"Don't play the village idiot. When you first came to the Meorachadh, you were too cold by half for a boy of fifteen years. You took to your lessons like a bird who has just discovered that he has wings. You were the same as me. You were formidable. You had potential."

Alev continued to circle and stopped short when he was behind Gunnar.

Gunnar continued to stare ahead, listening, waiting.

"But that was then," he leaned in with a whisper. "You have squandered your power. Squandered it by choosing to be a ranger, running around with a glorified farmer doing just as you're told. Squandered it with the dull weight of your desire for others to think you good."

Slowly, Alev came back around to face them, his eyes studying Gunnar's face with something like regret traced upon his features.

"And for what? How can you not see," he said. "How weak you've become...I will admit that your unwillingness to welcome your true nature has often plagued me. There are so few like us. So few that are unbound. Don't you see, Gunnar, it is our brokenness that makes us powerful. We are not bound by those narrow conventions of love, of desire."

Alev held both hands aloft, his palms facing skyward in supplication.

"And because I am not beholden to that which restricts, that which confines, I know only satisfaction. Power is my only ally, and I revel in the taste of it, the smell of it, the sound of it, the feel of it, the sight of it. It strikes awe or terror in the hearts of those fortunate enough to witness it."

Lovelace rolled his eyes skyward.

Enough of this.

"You want the man to answer the question," Lovelace said. "Stop your blathering and let him answer."

Gunnar let out a dry, singular hack. It sounded at first like a cough but was, miraculously, a laugh.

"Broken I might be," he croaked. "But I am nothing like you."

Alev frowned. "Perhaps not. Ah well..."

For a single, suspended moment, the clearing was quiet.

"I suppose I've had enough rekindling of old bonds," he said abruptly. "I challenge you both to a duel. If you win, I will give you the boy. I will let you walk away with your lives. If you lose, I will kill you and the worthless twit and the girl will be mine. I assume she is not far from here."

The look on Lovelace's face must have betrayed him because Alev stopped short and smiled.

"Just so. Really, Lovelace, it was ill-considered, bringing her this close. It was your idea, wasn't it? Did you really think she'd be safe?"

Lovelace put aside Alev for a moment and focused instead on a creeping sensation that he had willed to form in the pit of his stomach. It welled up, grew heavy and whorled inside of him. He summoned the smallest bit more of his luth and directed it to move the snaking sensation down into his feet, his fingertips, letting it gather there like coiled rope.

Alev continued. "The girl is powerful; one might even say uniquely so. It would be impossible to tell without testing her limits for myself. Ah," he said, watching Lovelace open his mouth to speak. "You're curious about how I do it without the orb, how I keep finding your flares before you do. So many questions. Lovelace, the perpetual tyro..."

Lovelace continued to focus on the energy he had begun to build in his belly, hands, and feet. Of duels, he knew only theory; there had not been one among dactyli for at least a hundred years. Doubtless, Gunnar and Alev were doing the same – pooling their energy. To channel with the precision and force required to kill would be massive. The fight would be a show of mastery and force. It would not last long.

"Why don't I believe you? That you'll let us and the boy walk free?" Lovelace asked, stealing a glance at the ground beneath his feet. Peeking out beneath the matted oak leaves were the yellow pinheads of mushrooms, tender green shoots – his luth, leaking from the bottom of his feet.

Alev stood there, either unaware that Lovelace was hardly listening or too power-drunk to care. "The possibility that you will win is smaller than ..." he trailed off, a sly smile curling his lips.

"The terms?" Lovelace pressed. "We fight to yield then, come what may?"

Alev shrugged. "At your pleasure," he said, sweeping both his arms down and to his sides, his palms facing forward.

Lovelace did not hesitate. He did not bother to identify what offensive approach Gunnar might take. There was no strategy, only anger, fear and a raw savagery that coursed through him.

With a fierce cry, he used his luth to raise a towering standing stone behind Alev high into the air. He brought it hammering down to earth, like a bludgeon swung by the unseen hand of an invisible god.

Alev raised a cupped hand over his head, and a blinding light erupted from his palm, meeting the striking stone in midair with a deafening crash. The stone halted abruptly with such force that it trembled in midair. For a moment, it hung suspended, Alev holding it aloft with the delicate gold chain of fire extending from his hand.

"Crude," he said. "But faster than I expected." He waved his hand, and the stone began to hiss, the color of it darkening from dusty gray to coal black.

"Mother preserve us," Lovelace said under his breath. "Could do with a bit of water right now. Gunn?" He asked hopefully, not taking his eyes off Alev.

Gunnar was rocking back and forth on his heels, his gaze elsewhere, lost in whatever channeling he was attempting to conduct. Like a shot, the stone shattered into dozens of pieces, each glowing a dull, ruddy red. The fragments broke ranks and moved about the clearing, hovering above their heads, taunting them with the grimness of their potential. They hissed and spat shards like projectiles onto the ground below, where they sizzled and sprouted small flames.

"I...can't...get...near...him..." Gunnar said through gritted teeth, apparently attempting to take the air from Alev's lungs to no avail.

"Forget it!" said Lovelace, willing limbs to snap. "Move these!" Dozens of low-hanging branches from the surrounding oaks splintered free of their trunks.

Gunnar whirled his arms like a pinwheel and sent the branches sailing through the air, aiming at both the airborne rocks and Alev. A curtain of flame, orange-white, shot up to conceal him, and three branches sailed through it. The impact was deafening; the sound of wood splintering vibrated through the clearing. Lovelace's heart leapt; had he been hit?

The remainder of the branches walloped the red-hot floating rocks, the smell of burnt wood and leaf ash heavy in the air. When the boughs and stones made contact, they exploded in a riot of color and sound, littering the clearing with burning limbs and glowing shards.

The conjured curtain of fire parted to reveal Alev, unharmed, his fingers twisting, shaping bolts from the flame at his fingertips.

He sent them sailing, one by one, at each piece of stone that had fallen. In defense, Lovelace tried to will the rocks to rise, to strike. But they would not do his bidding; they followed the orders of a new master.

One by one the bolts struck stone. Brighter and brighter, the stones glowed, throwing off more waves of heat. Each breath of air burned his lungs, and the stones melted until they were puddles of lava that crept toward each other, drawn together by the power of Alev's luth.

The puddles formed a river that snaked its way around Lovelace and Gunnar. They stood shoulder-to-shoulder, losing ground by degrees to the encircling lava. It crept over fallen branches, the heat of it withering and all-consuming.

"One...has to...wonder why he hasn't shot...us wi' one o' those things," Lovelace grunted as he sent forth saplings from the earth, to either wound or ensnare, but to no avail. Alev danced around each new tree that reached for him, extinguishing their unnatural lives before they could begin with his bolts of flame. His black robe glittered red, catching the light as he whirled and swerved. Abruptly, he reared up, a fire bolt as big as a pitchfork hovering just above his hand. He sent it sputtering through the air, straight toward Lovelace's chest.

Lovelace heard a small hiss beside him, and the bolt sputtered, flickered and faded into thin air. A storm of bolts rained down upon them, each of them accompanied by the same hissing sound, each of them dying or else becoming so weak they only smarted when they made contact with arm or shin. It was Gunnar, sharply siphoning air into his mouth, contracting the air around them each time one of Alev's bolts was fired. Lovelace realized then, with an almighty clench of his heart, that the fires surrounding them were much smaller than those throughout the clearing. *They have as little to feed on as possible,* Lovelace thought, his head swimming. Gunnar had been using all of his strength to neutralize Alev. It was the only reason why they were still alive.

In desperation, Lovelace sent a branch from the nearest oak to reach for Alev. It bent toward him, years' worth of growth extending, green tips reaching, grasping, hardening to wood at wondrous speed. Alev was so focused on the fashioning of his firebolts, he seemed not to notice as the absurdly long branch reached down to capture him in its woody embrace.

But it was too slow. Alev bent low and made as though to scoop water from a well. Molten globules of lava rose up to rain down upon the yearning branch. It sputtered, slowing in its path until it stopped dead mid-grasp, the new growth of it withered, charred patches like boils burning on its new-made surface.

Lovelace's luth was slipping, the coils of energy spilling from him now shriveled and taut. Alev, meanwhile, appeared undiminished, his focus unwavering.

Lovelace dared not pull up more earth, lest he create a cave-in and condemn Pif to death. Gunnar's repeated thinning of the air around them had made him lightheaded and dizzy, his vision blurred, his breath ragged and harsh. With a desperate spinning thought, he recalled the prophecy of Oi, the inexplicability of the sgeul, the strange vines that had choked those ancient trees. He fixed his eyes on Alev, who was preoccupied with the formation of another attack, his face a mask of concentration. The arm of a vine, thick as a forefinger, sprung from the earth at Alev's feet. It twisted and curled upwards behind him like a silent serpent. It reared, and Lovelace closed his fist. The vine struck, looping around Alev's neck like a noose. Lovelace squeezed. The vine constricted, and Alev stumbled backward, the fires around them flickering and shrinking in intensity by degrees.

Alev's eyes bulged. He groped at his neck, fear plain in his eyes. For one surreal moment, he did not look like Alev at all, but like a small boy in robes that were far too large and far too fine for one such as he.

But then, Alev remembered himself. Removing his hands from his neck, he closed his eyes, a look of calm subsuming his features. A vein in his neck bulged as he channeled his luth, and the vine burst into violet flame. Beside Lovelace, Gunnar inhaled sharply.

An angry red weal revealed itself as the vine recoiled and fell, lifeless, to the ground. The mark was livid, a fresh brand, and Alev opened his eyes.

"Your last mistake," he declared as he raised his arms overhead. "But no matter."

The moat of lava surged forth and erupted into flame, blazing and belligerent, trapping them in a perilous inferno. Alev rose his arms to the sky, beckoning the flames to rise until they became a towering wall of fire that grew first upwards then inwards, knitting itself together until the two men were sealed in a fiery tomb.

Lovelace's skin seared, his clothes reduced to cinders. He could feel the sweat evaporating off of his paper-dry skin. The flames were deafening, a relentless roar that drowned out all else.

"Well?" Lovelace shouted. "It's going to be by fire no matter how you slice it. Can you jump us out of here?"

Gunnar nodded weakly. He turned, gripped Lovelace's forearms and they were propelled upward through the ceiling of flame, falling in a heap at the edge of the standing stone circle.

And Alev was there, above them, his robes red, reflecting the fire's light so that he himself appeared ablaze. His face was white, alight with triumph. Lovelace's clothes were ash, his body prostrate, awash in unbearable heat. Somewhere in the distance, an animal screamed. *So this is how I die,* Lovelace thought. *Naked and roasted like a sow with its mate in springtime.*

Lightning struck, cracking the earth somewhere nearby, shaking the ground beneath them. The clearing erupted in a brutal orange light, vivid and merciless.

The vault of flame had grown, consuming all the other fires near it, now a swirling inferno that towered over the canopy's crooked top, blotting out the sun and the sky.

"You insult me, Gunnar," Alev sneered as he approached. "Lightning is more fire than air," he said, bringing his hands before him as though cupping an invisible sphere. Lovelace closed his eyes and crossed his arms feebly to his chest. The screaming grew louder. It was piercing, more strident and shrill than any sound Lovelace had ever heard. He felt his head might split in two and squinted in pain, Alev a blur before him.

And then, as if the Mother herself had snapped her loving fingers, the world was consumed by an embracing light, dazzling and white. The standing stones, the cyclone of flame, the ruined oaks, Alev, Gunnar. All lost to a light so white, so blinding that Lovelace could see nothing, hear nothing save the scream, mounted to such a pitch that all other sounds were buried beneath it.

The smell of char grew distant. Something sweeter, more aromatic moved in, as if on a clearing wind. Lovelace thought lavender, or possibly sage, and wondered why it smelled of herbs in the space between life and death. He could feel the bulk of Gunnar beside him, but he could not move to reach him.

And then, just as suddenly as it appeared, the light began to shrink. Inwards and inwards it recoiled, its white fingers succumbing to a darkness that was as total and profound as death itself. It was not long before the light was nothing but the prick of the thinnest of pins and then it was gone, the world swallowed whole, and Lovelace with it.

Chapter Seventeen

A bluebird darts nervously above a green pond, his sapphire wings aflutter. He keeps his distance, aloft, in a flap over the object of his enchantment below.

A solitary crane. White, peerless. She stands serene in an alpine lake, beside a meadow with a shock of wildflowers. Periwinkle, scarlet, gold winks out from the sea of tall grass, wavering in the gentle wind.

"What do you reckon?" The bluebird swoops low, alighting on a cattail, taking care to keep a respectful distance from the crane, who is focused on the hunt.

She swoops low her mighty neck and in one arcing, downward motion, scoops up a skittering crayfish. Mottled brown and glistening, its claws clack, frenzied, against her bill. She swallows once, twice, and the crayfish disappears.

"What about?" the crane asks. She takes two slow, folding steps further along the pond's edge. The hunt continues.

"Will they live?" the bluebird chirps. He ruffles his feathers, a nervous habit.

"They will live," the crane says. She sees another crayfish, this one basking on a flat rock that wears soft green algae for a coat. The afternoon light dances across the skeletal armor of the crayfish, born suited for a life of battle. She makes the necessary calculations to ensure she does not miss.

But the crane is one step too far out of range, and so she must dive. Forward she lunges, and down, her neck taut, reaching. The crayfish perceives his end is nigh and propels himself away. Safety is not far; he can see the dark underbelly of it a short swim away.

Too late. The crane takes him in her pointed beak, sends a cascade of water into the air as she raises the crayfish skyward and thrusts him down her sleek, slender throat.

She pauses a moment, looking up to consider the bluebird sitting there on the tip of a swaying cattail.

"No more poppy, bring me the holligold," she says, staring at him with dandelion eyes. The bluebird tips his beak at her, delighted in being at her service. He takes off to scour the field of wildflowers for the one his mistress seeks.

***

Lovelace woke to a world of darkness, disappointment tugging on the edges of his thoughts. He had expected something grander, more profound than the wet rock smell of water, the sound of it seeping through joints in cold stone. Death, it seemed, was nothing but a cave in which to dream.

A distant glow winked softly. A candle, flickering like a star in the corner of his vision. All around him, the world was carved from stone, worn smooth by the passage of damp, dark eons. Lovelace wondered if he had become rock, transformed by some unfathomable force into the stone he'd so often pressed into service.

Then, a voice broke through the silence, followed by a face. Her face. It hovered above him like a moon in a sea of darkness, and the curtain of her hair tickled as she peered down to examine him.

He supposed he knew that stone, like trees, were sensate. But they were considered impartial, without joy or pain, wants and needs. And the girl's hair had given rise to a fearsome itch that he longed to scratch.

"Can you hear me?" she asked gently. And to Lovelace's surprise, Ailwin appeared in his line of sight. His face was gaunt, with more edges than Lovelace remembered. He bore a fistful of flowers and peered down at Lovelace anxiously.

"I brought more poppy, just in case," he said. "I wasn't sure which one was holligold so I brought all of these."

The girl rolled her eyes, a small smile playing at the corners of her lips. Lovelace found himself wanting to smile too, though he couldn't quite understand why. If he was stone, he ought to spare no affection. Not for the girl, not for Ailwin, not for anything. And how was it that they were staring right at him?

Before he could ponder these points further, the girl leaned in and lifted one of his eyelids.

Lovelace let out a yelp. It was a queer, strangled sound that had no shape, because he could not move his tongue or lips. With an abrupt, joyless twinge, he realized that he possessed not just eyes but a tongue and lips as well.

He wasn't sure how he felt about having a body. Or about not being dead, two sudden details which, given present circumstances, didn't seem at all desirable.

"Ah! You *are* awake!" she said. She pressed two delicate fingers to the soft space at the base of his throat, and a strange sensation flooded his mouth and belly, as if she'd poured sun-warmed pine sap down his throat. He coughed and sputtered, his innards rattling uncomfortably against the still-frozen cage of his ribs.

"Where are we?" he asked, his voice hoarse and weak.

"Back where we started. The cave, in my chambers, below."

"Where's Gunn?"

The girl's face betrayed a flicker of worry, but it was gone before Lovelace could be sure it was even there.

"He's here, beside you. He hasn't woken up yet. He's..." she hesitated. "...not in a good way. But he is alive."

"What've you done to me?" he croaked.

She blushed, though it was not heightened color that bloomed in her cheeks but shadow. "I'm not sure how best to describe it. I've...frozen you. Fixed your bodies in place so that I can go about my herb work. I can lift it, I think..." she said and began to stare fixedly at Lovelace's chest in a way that made him expressly uncomfortable.

Already by her gaze he could feel the first hot trickles of blood through his veins, the slow rise of fever to his skin. His heart gave two loud, sickly thumps in his chest. It sounded like a drum and felt like a cudgel. "Ah...no, that won't be necessary," he said. If her strange freezing magic was keeping whatever unworldly pain awaited at bay, she was welcome to keep doing it.

"Mother take my dignity," he muttered as the agonizing sensations ebbed. In their place crept the memory of Alev, the terror of his boundless fire bond.

"He's dead," she said, sensing his dread. "We left him there, unconscious. We only just got you out in time. The whole eastern side of the mountain is burning, there's a great cloud of smoke settled from Raita to Lazare."

An uneasy quiet followed her words. Lovelace might've expected the news of Alev's death to buoy his spirit. But her words were a hollow chalice, and his fear remained heavy, fixed as an anchor thrown to the bottom of the sea. *It is impossible,* he thought. *Alev cannot die by fire. She has not seen what I have seen.*

Alev was once a boy who became a dactyli. And now? He was the closest thing to a godhead that Lovelace could conceive. How does one kill a god? It was a question sure to torment him for as long as he drew breath.

The border city of Lazare was miles from the foot of the pass, two or three days' ride from Raita, the small village at its foot. A fire that size was impossible, yet its source was even more so – Alev, whose powers defied comprehension.

"I think," she started. "It's...your being...bound as you are, that is, I think it's also helping to replenish your...what do you call the thing that you use to channel your power?" she blushed again, this time more deeply.

"Luth," Lovelace intoned, staring at her shadowy form in amazement. It wasn't just that she spoke directly to him or that she had performed some kind of healing that transcended any known craft.

He watched her closely, studied her gestures and sounds as she examined him with a practiced eye. There was a change in her, a shift from the wild, restive creature she had been to something steady, something strong.

She was looking at him with eyes that were familiar, like he was a friend.

Like she trusted him. There was something else, too. Lovelace studied the slight of her lips, the keenness in her eyes, the almost imperceptible noises she made deep in her throat as she moved her hands lightly over Lovelace's chest and then his shoulders. *The girl,* he thought, *is pleased.*

***

Lovelace slept in frenzied bursts, often rousing from fitful dreams of fire and light and a blackness so deep and complete it had no beginning and no end. Time lost all meaning in this void between waking and dreaming, with no sunlight to penetrate dark corners or mark the passage from day to night.

The third time he stirred from his fathomless rest, the smudged face of Pif floated above him, a grin spread from ear to ear. A feeling like warm honey spread over his chest before he succumbed once more to sleep's tangled embrace.

When he stirred for the fifth time, she was removing a herb poultice from his chest. *The boy is alive,* he thought, remembering.

The eighth time he woke, he heard the low whisper of Gunnar's voice, thin as smoke.

"Your luth," the girl said in reply, the word strange on her tongue. "Do you feel it returning to you?"

A pause, then a mumble.

"Oy, Gunn. S'at you, mate?" His words were harsh and cracked, but he was pleased to find his voice returned to him.

There was the hush of two in private conversation who have discovered another pair of ears in attendance. Lovelace heard shuffling, and Pif came into view.

"What's amiss, m'lord? Can I get you anything, anything at all?" His face was, as always, earnest as a new bud in springtime.

"Gunn!" Lovelace tried to shout. At least, he thought he was trying to shout. Given the expression on Pif's face, it must have been more of an unintelligible screech.

Pif patted his head and gave him a sympathetic look. "You wish to speak to m'lord Gunnar? That it? M'lady Cora...?"

The girl floated into view.

"Cora?" Lovelace hacked, trying and failing to find an eyebrow to raise at her bemused shadow of a face.

"It is the name Pif has given to me. We have been swapping stories, Ailwin, Pif and I. After one in particular of mine, Pif saw fit to give me this name. How do you feel?"

Lovelace tried and failed to count the dozens of ways he could answer that question. Instead, he gave himself over to bewilderment that the girl – Cora – spoke of story-time as if they had not just spent their first few days together wondering whether or not she would bite.

"Gunnar," Lovelace called hoarsely and then added, "When can I have my body back?"

"Gunnar is awake," she said in a hushed tone.

"Can I talk to him?" asked Lovelace, his question treading altogether too near a plea.

It was an injustice, that the girl – Cora – presided over him, lording over his right even to speak. His mind veered sharply toward even more basic functions, and shame overcame him.

"I can give you your body back," she said. "And you can speak with him, too. Do you feel yourself ready?"

It felt like years had passed since the standing stone clearing went up in flame, since he'd seen the sun or tasted warm bread.

How long had he been trapped in this endless void of waking and dreaming?

"Aye, I'm ready," he said, his voice barely above a whisper.

She nodded and leaned forward, pressing two fingers to the apex of his sternum and staring fixedly at something only she could see.

"It's been twelve days," she said quietly, and she began her subtle magic. Lovelace felt sweltering heat return. It welled up, congealed on his skin, like fat risen to the top of a soup pot. It would need to be skimmed.

His heart stuttered and flopped over in his chest. Then, it began to beat with a clangorous vigor, "Live life, live life, live life," it echoed with insistence.

Sensations thundered through him like a summer tempest, pelting every inch of him with wet heat that singed and sparked.

"Is it too much?" she asked, pulling back, uncertain.

"Fine," he said tightly, through teeth he could now grit. His stomach gave an almighty lurch.

He was painfully aware of his physical form after floating through that strange, bodiless place. He silently gave thanks that it was not as agonizing as the first time she'd begun to give him back his body. Still, a cold sweat had broken out on his brow. He pawed at it ineffectually, let his hand fall to rest on the stone beneath him and rolled over, gasping.

Gunnar lay paces from him, motionless as a corpse. His face was a series of sharp angles, the candle's flickering light casting impossible shadows onto his cheekbones and jaw. He looked like nothing so much as a man who recently died of starvation.

"You've taken soup in your sleep," Cora said in Lovelace's ear, startling him.

Silently, she helped him up so that he sat propped up against the stone wall like a rag doll, bent as the waist, his shoulders slumped.

"He has taken no food," she said, hushed, perhaps so that Gunnar could not hear.

"Gunn," Lovelace said hoarsely. Gunnar's throat twitched, but he made no sound.

"Gunn," Lovelace said again. "How...How are you, mate? Alright?" He struggled to keep his voice from breaking as he dragged himself over to his silent companion. Gunnar's gray eyes stared skyward, glassy and clear as smoked crystal.

"What does it feel like?" Gunnar's voice was a thread, so thin it was as if his insides had all burned away, and all that remained was smoke.

"Come again? What does what feel like?"

"Being," Gunnar swallowed. "Being back in your body."

Lovelace stared down at Gunnar, and a single tear formed in the corner of his eye. Faster than he would wipe it away, it rolled down the bridge of his nose and landed with an indelicate splash on Gunnar's forehead.

"That bad?" Gunnar paused, taking two rattling breaths. "I think...I will just...go ahead...and die then. If you'll just go... and get...the little maiden?"

Lovelace let out the husk of what would have been a roar of laughter and bent low, enveloping Gunnar in a full embrace. His body was cold marble, every inch of him angular, sharp and unyielding. Slowly, Lovelace rose and patted his friend's icy hand.

"Not today, Gunnar, not today."

***

They shared the silence for a spell, the shuddering light of Cora's candles casting their damaged bodies in shadowed relief against the walls of the underground cavern.

The stillness was broken by the entreating voice of Pif, who appeared up and out of the darkness like some netherworld march hare.

"If'n you please, m'lord," he said. "Now you're awake, we've got things to tell you, and m'lord Gunnar as well. Things to tell you and plans that need making, soon's you're well enough, o' course."

Ailwin appeared beside Pif and nodded, his smooth face showing sprouted patches of fine dark hair, the very beginnings of a beard. "Pifalion is right," he said. "Cora has told us things, monstrous things. Things you've got to know about."

Lovelace's eyes drifted down toward his motionless companion. A smothered sound escaped from Gunnar's throat. It could have meant anything, but Lovelace had to assume it was outright disbelief, the same as his own.

Lovelace raised his eyebrows, a surprisingly excruciating act. *Could be I'm still dreaming,* he thought as he turned his head slowly to stare at the two boys sitting cross-legged before him.

Cora glided out of the shadows, the dark cloud of her hair partially concealing her face. She folded her legs beneath her and settled between the two boys as if they had been friends – nay, conspirators – their entire lives. Lovelace stared at the three of them, their bright faces set alight by candle's flame and the unmistakable gleam of hope.

"They are right," she said. "And you have things to tell me, I think."

She spoke with the kind of firmness that a man such as Lovelace found hard to refuse. But the blood coursing through his veins was a vicious torment, the fabric of his mind still rent asunder. What good was he? All he wanted was a flagon of ale or three or five and a nice feather bed from which he would never be called to rise, unless he desired it for himself and himself alone.

If the resolution in her words wasn't enough, the look she wore made refusal impossible. Impossible, not because Lovelace felt cowed or because she bore the kind of beauty that made the world seem bigger, brighter. No, it was because Lovelace could see it in the set of her jaw, the unflinching inevitability in her eyes. No matter what she was prepared to tell him, or whatever madcap scheme she had cooked up with Ailwin and Pif – she was right.

The girl was the key. As to what she might unlock, Lovelace had neither the presence of mind nor the substance of body to play at guessing. So he hauled himself against the back wall, folded his hands in his lap and opened his ears and heart to what she had to say.

Chapter Eighteen

It had been six weeks.

Six weeks of work – pruning, hanging, grinding and storing leaves and stems, petals and pollen – from sun up to sun down. Her days were so long, her work so absorbing that at night, her sleep was deep and devoid of dreams.

Six weeks of feeling, for the first time in her sixteen years, like she truly belonged to a place, to a people. From the first light of dawn, she and a dozen others ventured out into the fields to harvest flowers and herbs, when their vital oils were at their peak of strength. When the sun climbed higher into the sky, she retreated to the kitchens to process the last of the summer's bounty.

She had been banished from making meals on her second day, the moment she was discovered by Hettie, the mistress of the kitchens, to have an appreciable knowledge of flora.

Evenings were spent in the company of fifty-some-odd men and women, and seventeen children. Dinner was at sundown. She knew how many because on her second day, she counted fifty-one adults at dinner, and there were always a few emissaries – like Cael – who came and went.

After dinner, she soaked in the springs. Often, she would converse with others in the pools. In this way, she came to learn bits and pieces about the people who called themselves Kapnobatai. Some were born there, in the mountains of Droch Fhortan, and knew no other way of life. Things like carriages, clocks and cobblestone streets were foreign, inventions that grew up and out of a different time, a different place.

Still more found their way to the Kapnobatai in the middle of life, oftentimes having endured some calamity or other. Eliza was among them, she'd overheard two women say. Their hushed tones made Kylene think that whatever happened to Eliza, those strange scars on her legs had something to do with it.

When she was alone in the pools, she would submerge herself up to her ears and close her eyes. Beneath the surface, all was quiet and still, as if the water had swallowed all the sound in the world. During these moments, thoughts of her mother and Petra weighed heavily on her. They must surely think her dead.

She wondered about McBane and his experiments, imagining how much he would have loved the salves and oils, vinegar, syrups and teas concocted by her new companions. Most of all, she thought of her father – where in the world he might be, what he was planning, or if perhaps he was still running, hiding like the snake Osbert had pronounced him to be. She could not bear the thought of him dead.

As the weeks passed, she came to know everyone in camp by association, if not by name. There was the spindly old man who smiled toothlessly at her and said good morning across the table, his bowl of oatmeal heaped with brown sugar crystals. The girl child with bare feet who was always perched on the roof of some structure. Nadine, with her red-headed children, and Karm, the portly fellow with a nose for decoctions.

She interacted with nearly every man, woman and child in camp, and not by consequence of her own ambition. For reasons that she didn't fully comprehend, everyone found her terribly interesting. They did not flock to or fawn over her, but they were eager to understand who she was and where she came from, as well as what she found fascinating or troubling or fulfilling.

Curiosity, it seemed, was a guildmark trait for the Kapnobatai. Only it wasn't the same kind of curiosity expressed by the women of Mossbridge, who lived for the gossip that could be fetched at market, along with their weekly pantry goods. Here, each person was intent on hearing her perspective. And when she shared – her thoughts, her feelings, her ideas, her stories –

she was met with great interest, if not sheer delight, in what she had to say.

Every third night, Hendry would arrive at the pools to collect her at the bidding of Eliza. Kylene would emerge from the water, steam rolling off her pink skin as she slipped back into her new yellow robes. She would comb her fingers through her hair and make her way by the dying light of day to the circle house. Inevitably, Eliza and Rufus would be there, deep in conversation. On cue, Rufus would cease speaking when Kylene entered the room.

Rufus, she learned, had once belonged to a brotherhood of men that Kylene had thought of as more of a religious order, bygone in prominence. She learned this from Eliza, in their second meeting. She learned that this brotherhood was not, in fact, quite as whimsical in nature as she'd previously assumed. She'd thought the dactyli were just a handful of moonstruck men, clucking about on solstices and equinoxes, claiming oracularity and living in seclusion, as her father had always led her to believe.

***

"Clucking about on solstice?!" Lovelace said, indignant. "Moonstruck? By the Mother! Is this what it's come to, out in the world? That we paint ourselves with possum guts and claim to see the future in the curling smoke of a sacrificial fire?"

Cora shrugged. "It is known that only farmers and laypeople come to you, or came to you, when A'Tabhann was held. They speak as if you have powers beyond the ken of mortal knowing. Which..." she smiled slyly, her words slow, as if she was working out a puzzle between each one, "...you do. Only you play at prophet so that the whole world doesn't come knocking. You're hardly in any history books, but...that's on purpose isn't it?"

"Aye," Lovelace said testily as he sat back against the cavern wall, chafing at the implications. His poor Mam. She had been so proud to send him off.

"May I continue?" she asked, honey-rimmed.

"Please."

***

"Rufus, would you care to share with Kylene why you rarely speak?"

The bright-eyed man fixed Kylene with a stare that made her insides squirm, but she did not flinch or break his gaze.

"When you spend enough of your life in silence, you come to appreciate that which needs saying and that which doesn't."

His words were dry as straw and had a strange, burred accent that Kylene couldn't place. She stared, unsure of what to make of the first complete sentence he'd spoken to her. It sounded to her more like an incomplete thought.

"People talk too much," he said. "Most of it doesn't matter. Words are imperfect things, anyway. Eliza does not share my sympathies and doesn't mind a mollycoddle."

Despite his point of view, his tone bore no unkindness. Still, Kylene couldn't help but feel hostility emanating from him, like she'd done something wrong. And privately, she downright disagreed with him, at least where words were concerned. She jammed her tongue into her cheek; who was she to say such a thing to a person like him?

"Well, there you have it," Eliza said, flashing Kylene a grin. "If you'll allow me the smallest bit of mollycoddling," she said the word all strung out, like it was five instead of one. "Rufus has been instrumental in helping us bridge all worlds."

Kylene stared at Rufus, daring him to do what he did that first night when his eyes had gone black, and he'd stolen her thoughts. "You mean dactyli, Kapnobatai and normal folk?"

Eliza nodded in approval. "In a sense, yes. Rufus had the privilege and burden of being a dactyli scribe for many years before coming to us. His work has given him a greater sense of history – what works and what doesn't – than most of us. You see, Kylene, the Kapnobatai, like dactyli, are record-keepers. But our records, like your records, are kept on paper and are reliant on the words and deeds of imperfect people. After all, we all have wants and desires and wills. While we've always striven to keep our histories balanced and fair, it is an impossible practice."

"Forgive me," Kylene said, her curiosity getting the better of her. She broke Rufus' gaze and met Eliza's. "But are dactyli not also men? Human. How is it that their chronicles are better than yours?"

Eliza smiled. Her teeth were small and white, her canines pointed.

"It is an excellent question. Rufus?"

Rufus harrumphed, his lips flapping indecorously.

"They're not," he grumbled.

"Why not?" Kylene asked immediately, prompting Eliza's smile to widen.

"The girl is inquisitive," she remarked to nobody in particular.

Rufus fixed her with a stare that made Kylene want to shrink down in her chair. But she didn't. She raised her chin and stared back into his bright blue eyes with as much ferocity as she could muster.

"As you've just described, dactyli are still men, and are therefore not immune to prejudice or aspiration or obligation. Inevitably, these things are a scourge to true objectivity."

"And yet..." Eliza broke in. "Dactyli have been preserving histories in an objectively more reliable way than our way of record-keeping. Might that be said, Rufus?"

Rufus made a grumbling sound, and Kylene's head spun.

Objectively more reliable?

"And how is that done?' Kylene asked, working to follow the implications of what was being said.

"Dactyli possess unique abilities," Eliza said, choosing her words with care. "They are not only able to manipulate the world around them, but also communicate with it."

Kylene's eyes narrowed as she looked from Eliza to Rufus, both of whom regarded her with expectation. Was this some sort of test or practical joke? But Kylene knew that Eliza would not play such games, and she doubted Rufus would know a joke if it flew in the open window and relieved itself wetly on his head.

"Communicate?" If this was a test, she wouldn't fail by responding too quickly. "Like you and I are right now? Speaking back and forth?"

"It's not..." Rufus began and then gave a dusty-sounding sigh.

"It's not an equal exchange," he said. "Listen, missy, and listen well. I'll only be saying it the once. The earth is alive. It lives and breathes and hears and sees, just like you and me. Dactyli go on rangings and siphon its memories – memories that do not have the same trappings of attachment and personal proclivities as our own. Once obtained, they bring them back for analysis and add them to their understanding of events – accounts from men and women, bystanders, eyewitnesses, key personnel, or what have you. Then, they reconstruct the memory anew. Reconstructed – aspects, facts – double, triple, quadruple checked. Then, they call them objective, call them the truest true."

Kylene closed her eyes. Her mind was a tangle, and the more she thought about it, the more impossible it seemed that anything could be absolutely true.

"Wouldn't those memories – those that were reconstructed, that is – still be more accurate?" she asked, her eyes shut tight.

"Yes," Eliza said while Rufus growled, "That's not the point."

Eliza waved her hand, ceding the floor to Rufus.

"They still have the stain of humanity upon them," he spat. "No matter how many times you wash a shirt that's been bloodied, it'll never be white again."

***

And so the days passed– in the fields, the kitchens, the springs – her evenings punctuated by nights like these in the roundhouse. Eliza and Rufus began, bit by bit, to unravel the plan that they had been working on with her father. How'd together they studied revolutions and warfare and forms of governance, not just from the Grasp but from other, far-away places of which Kylene had neither seen nor heard.

After each of their meetings, she left the roundhouse bone-weary, feeling like nothing so much as a sponge wrung out and left to dry beneath the hot sun. She would walk the short distance to her hammock in the dark, lessons and theories swirling through her head like leaves in a gale. The tenets of freedom. The inner workings of a successful uprising. The defining lines of oppression, of tyranny, of truth and falsehood. She felt as if she swam in a pond where neither the bottom could be touched nor shore seen, but she stayed afloat, no matter how tired her arms or heavy her head. Once wrapped inside her hammock, the warm summer air and the bed's gentle rocking motion would lull her into a dreamless sleep. And it surprised her that in some ways – not all of them, to be sure, but some – she was as happy as she'd ever been.

***

With three days left until their scheduled departure for their winter home, the Kapnobatai summer camp was abuzz. Kylene, for her part, had spent the afternoon in the dry room, a long building with a low ceiling built for the express purpose of drying the hundred-some-odd plants tended over the spring and summer months.

Kylene's domain was the holligold corner, where she sat with her back straight against the wall, separating the dried yellow-orange flowers from their brittle stems. Before her, woven baskets brimmed with plant matter. To her right, crates of empty glass jars. Light from a low-slung window cast scattered sunbeams across her hands as she worked, packing dust-dry flowers into glass jars.

The air was warm, and Kylene worked in a state of reverie, the sweet scent of dried flowers suffusing everything and everyone at work in the room.

She worked until her hands were sore. Until the light from the window grew slanted and changed from the yellow of high noon to the orange of last light. Rising from her cross-legged seat, she arced her back in one long smooth motion.

She had learned, in the last six weeks, how to stretch. To bend her body and breathe in a way that brought relief from the long mornings of laboring in the fields, sitting to work in the afternoons. She put her hands on her shoulders, twisting slowly from side to side.

It was Cael who taught her. Cael, with whom she spent most of her free time, when he was not out, greeting visitors on the mountain. Cael, whom she was meant to meet at sunset for a soak in the hot springs.

She emerged from the room pollen-dusted, her joints cracking like brittle twigs. She was eager for the springs, where her aching limbs would find relief. She nodded at Eileen and Kristof, whom she'd worked with all afternoon.

"Alright, Miss Kylene?" Kristof asked. "We're headed to supper if you'd care to join us." He stretched his arms overhead and gripped his opposing elbows with large-knuckled hands. "Honey-roasted ham today if the rumors are to be believed."

Kylene's stomach rumbled at the thought.

"I'm meeting Cael for a soak at sunset. Save me some," she smiled as they waved at her and headed toward the kitchens.

Kapnobatai were pouring into the center of camp from the day's work, most making for the kitchens. Tall, short, black-haired, white. Dark-skinned, light. Young and old. Everyone seemed in good spirits, and many waved at Kylene as she veered to the left to take the path leading to the springs. She thought of her morning in the fields yesterday, when they'd pulled up hundreds of carrots, Kylene's favorite. Orange, of course, but also purple and white and yellow and red, carrots with colors she'd never seen. Her stomach grumbled again as she began to climb the hill that led onward toward the springs; she hoped the carrots would feature alongside the ham.

The clamor of dinner-seekers fell away as she turned the bend, the din of it swallowed by the surrounding trees. She inhaled deeply. The air was thick with the warm smell of cedar resin, with the faintest trace of sulfur woven through, and she could almost feel the velvet-soft water against her skin.

She reached the top of the path and looked down upon the pools, wondering which one she would soak in that evening. A group of women were emerging from the largest, chatting as they toweled themselves dry. In her favorite – the one shaped like an egg with the perfect stone seat – a man, Juventus, and a woman, Amielle.

She picked her way down the path, deciding to wait for Cael in the last of the thirteen pools, the only one she had not yet tried. It stood further away from the rest, its surface smooth as glass, the shape of it a perfect circle no bigger than her arm's span.

Kylene tiptoed around the water's edge, returning smiles as she passed the departing women. She exchanged quiet nods with Juventus and Amielle. They, too, were preparing to emerge, Amielle showed Juventus her splayed hands, wrinkled fingers telling time, how long they'd been submerged. As Kylene passed the seventh and eighth pools – shallow, weedy things beloved by mothers with small children – she heard the not-quite-splashing sound of Juventus and Amielle, climbing out of the water.

She reached the last pool, stopping for a moment to stare at the glassy perfection of it. Its surface reflected the orange glow of the final rays of the sun while below, the water was a sumptuous teal, darker in color than any of the other springs.

Folding her robes tidily and placing them in a crack between two stones, Kylene skimmed her foot along the surface of the pool, sending a ripple across it, distorting the black shadows of trees reflected in its depths.

It was hot, this pool. Hotter than any of the other pools she had yet tried, despite its distance from the headspring. She sat on the water's edge, easing in one leg, then another. Stirring the silken water with her legs, she decided she would submerge herself and discover how deep it was, all at once.

She shoved off, sliding down and into its depths, straight-limbed as a sunbeam. The heat was overwhelming, the intensity of it sending waves of shock from head to toe, and she reached out to touch the walls of the pool. Despite the heat, Kylene pushed herself deeper, but her feet found no bottom.

A small panic rippled through her. It was so hot she feared she might burn herself, so she propelled herself up and away from the searing heat, her face breaking the water's surface to the sweet chill of dusk. With arms that trembled, she raised herself out of the pool, sputtering and gasping. Her legs dangled there in the water as she pressed her chest and arms flat along the pine needle-littered earth, her heartbeat fearsome in her breast, her cheeks abloom with false fever.

The sun had since set, and there was still no sign of Cael. Kylene lowered herself back in, her arms, head and neck remaining in the open air. Already, she was sweating freely, and when she licked her lips, she tasted salt.

She'd been so absorbed by the intensity of the pool's heat that she hadn't noticed the smell of smoke. It was not the clean-smelling scent of cedar smoke. It was something else, something acrid, something foul.

She submerged herself, the radiant heat of the pool forgotten. Clutching the edges with clawed hands, she lowered the bottom half of her face beneath the surface and was reminded, sharply, of what it felt like to share a body with a wild thing.

Her eyes darted around the springs. But the pools stood empty. Everyone had gone to dinner.

Then, above the rustling of pine needles scattered by gentle wind and the soft bubbling of the pools, she heard it.

A scream. Faint, harrowing. Shouts. The distant clash of metal on metal, metal on wood, metal on something softer still and behind it all, the indistinct roar of flame. A sickly cold sensation settled in the marrow of her bones when Kylene realized what she smelled.

Transfixed, she floated and then, she saw them. Five of them, at the top of the path. At first, she thought them peacekeepers, but no, these men wore short capes, and light armor. Instead of white, these men wore burnished orange mail over blood-red cloth.

They were unhelmed apart from one among them who wore a helmet with scarlet feathers spouting from the top. He raised his gauntleted fist, and the other men froze.

Three more men appeared, dressed all in white. Their armor, Kylene knew, was carved with scrolling vines and roses and strange birds. Peacekeepers, recognizable in a thrice.

The plumed man brought down his fist, and in unison, the men in red and in white moved forward down the path toward the pools. They were halfway down the trail when an elderly Kapnobatai man shot out of the woods behind them, his yellow robes flying, his hand clutching a rough-made spear. As he hurtled down the path, he let loose a battle cry that drove a stake through the very center of Kylene's heart.

The plumed man flicked his wrist in the air and...shot the man, though it was not an arrow loosed or a spear thrown. It was a dart made of flame.

The dart struck the man square in the chest, and he flew through the air, landing in a heap several paces back. In a panic, he beat at the flames with his hands. They licked hungrily at his robes, and as he reached for the spear that had been knocked asunder, Kylene heard hollow laughter. One of the peacekeepers raised a long bow and aimed.

She didn't see the arrow move through the air but heard the dull thump of its pointed tip find flesh. The man doubled over in agony and slow-sank to his knees, the arrow buried deep in his gut, the white-feathered shaft of it protruding like some kind of staked claim.

Kylene gasped, filling her mouth and throat with hot water that choked and burned, but she dared not sputter, would not scream. She shrank down even further, submerging all but her eyes and the bridge of her nose.

They were stopped at the first pool. A pike rested against the shoulder of one of the peacekeepers, the leaf-shaped tip rising twice as high as he was tall. At a nod from his superior, he unshouldered it and plunged it viciously into the pool. Over and over and over again, he jabbed until he was satisfied that no person hid within the pool's watery depths. He moved to the next, and the men in red headed for the largest pool, where the Kapnobatai children played, where often folks would dance along its steaming edges by the moon's silvery light.

The plumed man produced a small flask from his hip and emptied it into the pool. The way it shimmered across the water's surface could only be oil.

With a flick of his wrist, the man set the pond ablaze. Flames raced hungrily across its crystal surface, and Kylene swallowed the bile that rose in her throat.

Nine more pools. Then they would find her. There was nowhere to hide. Her only hope was to dive down. But how deep was the pool? And how hot? She could only pray that the water was deeper than the pike was long and that her breath would hold out.

She waited until the man with the pike had probed the fifth and sixth pools, until the man with the plumed helm had sent flames to skitter across the surfaces of the seventh and eighth, her heart hammering against the cage of her breast.

When they reached the ninth pool, Kylene could see their faces clear. Most of them were no older than she, boys with unbearded faces whose eyes were hard as flint.

She took a silent gulp of air, feeling for the hard rocky sides of the wall with both feet. She pushed off and dove down toward the pool's shrouded bottom, heat increasing by degrees with her every stroke. It was shocking and stark and left her so stunned that she stopped. Suspended, she hovered – immobilized – panic slithering through her insides. Slowly, surely, she floated to the surface.

Scrabbling her hands along the jagged wall, she found edges rough enough to grip and crouched vertically like a water beetle. Above her, a reflection of the burning pond nearest her flickered and danced. Her chest was unbearably tight, but she had to go further, had to go deeper.

She moved slowly, mindful of each bubble that escaped from her lips, lest they break upon the surface and betray her presence.

The darkness was total, this far down, and Kylene was burning from the inside out. Her lungs, her limbs, her fingers and toes. Her skin was on fire, from her scalp to the soft bottoms of her naked feet. She closed her eyes, a small relief that was everything and nothing.

Kylene was no longer counting how long she'd been down. Her thoughts slowed, and the distance between them grew. She found herself wondering whether she ought to pray to the Mother. *Why?* The Mother and her children were figments, fairy tales.

She let go of the wall – or it released her, she couldn't be sure – and hung suspended in that feverish dark, her limbs no longer her own. She might have been lodged in stone or falling through the air.

Without warning, she was drawn inexorably downwards, and then, she was gone. Or rather, she was no longer drowning in the starless depths of the boiling spring but found herself alone in the middle of a desert devoid of color. A fierce wind swept the land, but Kylene could not feel its lashing.

The voice of her own mother echoed overhead.

"The Mother gave birth to the first children," her voice hung, disembodied, in the air. Kylene whirled around. Andara Gemison was nowhere to be found. There was only dust and wind and rock, as far as the eye could see.

"And when the Mother looked around her and saw the earth, how lifeless, how desolate, she knew that something must be done."

Kylene heard the cry of a very small child. It pierced the wind and set her teeth on edge. She spun toward the noise and saw a woman where there had not been one before. Her hair was black as raven feathers and fell in sheets around her shoulders. In her arms, a newborn baby flailed its wrinkled limbs, wailing in misery.

"So the Mother sacrificed pieces of herself, scattering them to the earth's four corners."

Kylene watched as the woman bent low and produced a knife from the folds of her robe. She cut away her hair, great sheathes of it scattering in every direction as the wind carried it north, south, east and west. Then, she took the blade to her wrist. In one swift upwards motion, she slashed the inside from end-to-end. The woman's face remained absent of expression as she peered at the delicate cut she'd made and the red blood welling there.

Kylene saw the first drop fall. The cracked earth drank of it thirstily. More drops fell, slowly at first, then faster and faster, until they became a thin stream, a red tributary emptying into a lake bed, long gone dry. The woman fell to her knees, and the child continued to wail.

Abruptly, the wind died, shut off as if staunched at its source. In its place, a low rumbling and then a great ripping sound, like the fabric of the earth itself was being torn in two.

Trees erupted from the ground all around Kylene, from sprout to saplings to flowers to fruit. Growing, stretching, branching with impossible speed. They came so fast and thick that she soon lost sight of the woman she had last seen clutching her wrist, eyes turned toward the horizon in wonder.

A geyser shot forth from the earth in the distance, and around it, a lake began to form, from which fish jumped, silver and gleaming, and the humped backs of turtles rose like tiny islands in a sea of liquid glass. On every side of her, the desert disappeared as it yielded to the unstoppable force of a world insistent upon life.

Reverberating through it all, the steady pulse of Kylene's mother's voice.

"And the earth as we know it was born. Dark soil writhed with worms. Red foxes played in meadows, with flowers tall as trees. Hazel trees bore nuts as big as a babe's fist. And the Mother's children grew up to be healthy and hale."

"Many years passed, and in time, the Mother's children had children, and their children had children, and their children's children had children. And the Mother was glad that all of her children lived

and thrived, from the red fox to the child most wee to the brooks that babbled and the crayfish within them. For they were all her children, all born of the sacrifice of her own life's blood."

Then, the lush landscape shrunk back before Kylene's eyes, but only just.

Small structures appeared, dotted among the trees: homes, more hut than house, and children playing outside. Kylene watched as the woman knelt in the dirt with a small child, marveling at some small creature only they could see. Her raven hair again fell to trail along the earth, only now it was streaked with silver, precious metal in a bed of black coal.

"Many more years passed, and in time the Mother's children began to forget the generosity bestowed upon them by the Mother. They forgot the magic of the earth, forgot that it was just like them – a living thing, born of blood, born of sacrifice. They defaced it, starved it, drew out its every treasure. And the earth began to suffer. Food became scarce, rivers ran dry, and the Mother's children began to turn upon one other. And yet, the children did not see that they were the source of their own heartache, their own strife."

The huts transformed into houses, then castles and then, they became something else entirely. Structures that reached until they touched the sky. And as the structures grew – up and out and over and through – the vividness, the lushness of the world around them shrank and shrank and shrank still more.

"Time passed, and the earth became a desert again, dry and barren and inhospitable to those that would live. And all the Mother's children, and their children, and their children's children suffered. Many died. Those that did not lived in famine and fear. Famine of the heart, famine of the body, famine of the spirit. Some say they clung to life by eating rock tripe and the stringy meat of lizards, whose flesh was sour and tasted like nothing so much as survival."

Almost as quickly as it had taken shape, the sumptuous landscape that spread before Kylene dissolved into nothing, and she stared once more at a spiritless desert, harsh and cruel.

"And in this place of misery, the children of the Mother fashioned themselves a god whom they named Socritas. You see, Kylene, the Mother was never held as a figure for worship. She would not allow it. What need had she of worship so long as her babes were safe, well-fed and happy? Because she asked for nothing, the children forgot their Mother's sacrifice. But they did not forget that life was born in blood. So they made Socritas a god that thirsted for it. They slaughtered their own so that his thirst might be slaked. Perhaps, the children thought, that if enough blood was spilled at the right time, Socritas would once again make the earth a fertile place of joyful abundance, just like the stories they told around fires at night, in a desert with naught but lizards and dust."

With detached horror, Kylene watched as a windblown man came up behind a boy on the brink of manhood. He looked a little like Cael.

The wind's endless mourning hid the man's footsteps and so the younger man did not hear him approach. With a wild gleam in his eye mirroring conviction of certainty, the elder slit the younger's throat. Kylene gasped as the boy slid to the ground, his life's blood spilling onto the sun-baked earth.

"As she watched her children fight and kill one another, the Mother suffered. They drew lines in the sand on land they were meant to share. When she learned they had forged a god with contours of savage fear, her sadness turned to wroth. They had forgotten that they did not need a god, so long as they remembered the lessons she had taught them at her knee when they were small."

Kylene flew across a desert sea until she came again to the woman, kneeling in the dirt with a small child. Only this time, her hair was white as milk, and the child before her was still, his insides spilled scarlet.

"For twenty-eight nights, the Mother sat in conversation with the Moon. They knew that if the children continued to worship Socritas,

they would fight among themselves until they wiped themselves off the face of the earth. Socritas would be the death rattle, issuing from their waterless lips."

"Together, the Mother and the Moon decided what must be done. The Mother would usurp this false god by doing what he never could. She would save her children. All that would be required of her was a gesture so merciful it would never again be forgotten. She would return her children to life right when all was nearly lost."

Again, Kylene was swept across the earth's chalk surface to find the woman walking barefoot and naked into the middle of a dried lakebed, the same lakebed she had once filled with fresh water and fish.

The woman let loose a terrible scream. She beat her breast. She tore at her hair and skin and raged, drawing grief out of her like water from a well.

Slowly, men and women began to emerge from caves beneath the ground, their entrances dotting the once-green lake edge. They came to see who was being sacrificed in the center of the lake and whether he might be the one to appease Socritas at last.

"The Mother wailed until she was surrounded by all her children and their children and their children's children. Ragged and wicked though they were, she loved them still, with all of her heart."

"Mother!" rang the voice of one of her daughters. "Whatever is the matter?"

A man's laughter, dry as a reed, rattled across the lake.

"Can't you see, Serah?" The man said. "Mother has finally decided to join us in prayer to Socritas. See how her blood feeds the earth."

And indeed, drops of blood drawn from her grief began to fall. Where they fell, small ferns sprouted, though they pulled back in on themselves in moments, shriveling to nothing.

"Socritas has heard our prayers!" the man cried. And the people shouted with a joy that had not been heard or felt in a very long time.

The man shoved his eldest daughter toward her grandmother.

"Here!" he cried. "Socritas likes young blood best. Take Sanna!"

"Nay!" came the voice of another of the Mother's Sons. "Everyone knows it is the blood of a mother that he likes best," he said, thrusting his wife forward.

"Cut her from neck to navel. The earth will be made rich again from her innards, for they know the way of making new life."

The woman stepped forward timidly and handed her newborn child to her husband, who set him down on the brittle earth. The child screamed, his wails rising to meet those of his grandmother, her grief multiplying as she watched her children offer the ones they loved in cold blood.

"Serah and Sanna approached the Mother, weak-kneed but determined. When they reached her, the Mother ceased her lamentation. She took both of the women by their hands and raised them high above her head."

"You forget who gave you life," she bellowed. "You forget that hardship is not overcome apart but together. You forget so many things." Her voice faltered and fell, and she kissed both women's hands with her paper-dry lips. And then she let go, her eyes a furnace of rage and sorrow.

"For a moment, the Mother lost her resolve. 'Surely I should stay,' she thought. 'Convince my children of their wrongs, show them to rights, guide them back to caring for one another, for the earth that cares for them.' But then, she remembered the wisdom of the Moon — the only way forward for the earth was for the Mother to nourish it with her own life's blood. And the only way forward for the children was to worship the earth and renounce false gods like Socritas, who reflected nothing but brutality and iniquity. There was only one way for it all to last. The Mother herself would become a god, and then, become the earth, so that her children would never forsake themselves again."

"The earth was born by mine own blood, YOU," she boomed, loud as thunder, "were born by mine own blood. And with the final drops of me, born again shall you be."

From the folds of her dusty robe, the Mother produced the same blade she had used the first time. Kylene could not be sure whether it had been mere moments or eons ago that she had brought its silver tip to split the soft skin of her wrist.

Kylene watched, bewitched, as the Mother raised the blade once more. It shone like an enchanted thing, the haft of it forged from green crystal that sparkled in the scathing light of the bleak yellow sun.

"The Mother made her final sacrifice. She plunged the dagger into the heart of her womb, the very place that held the seed of all her children, the place from which all things were born."

With slow deliberation, the woman pulled the knife deeper and deeper until naught but its glimmering hilt protruded from her belly, wet with crimson blood.

The Mother sank to her knees.

Serah and Sanna moved to catch her as she swayed, their faces stunned and stricken. On the earth the Mother kneeled, her daughter and granddaughter as pillars, while her blood seeped into the ground at their feet.

"You cannot live without the blessing of earth!" Her cry pierced the expanse in every direction, and her children began to moan and weep. Some ran toward her wilted form, some clung to one another, joined together in anguish and bewilderment.

"No matter where you go," the Mother gasped, her timeworn hands grasping the blade's hilt. "No matter what you do, it is the rhythm of earth that will guide you, even..." she said, her voice harsh, ragged as an old bone. "Even if...you journey through the stars, you still need the kernel of earth."

With her children surrounding her, distraught and dismayed, the Mother wrenched the blade sideways with a vigor that belied the death looming large upon her.

The earth ran red with her blood. Turning her face skyward toward stars she could not see, the Mother pulled in one long final drink of dusty air.

With a heave, she tore the knife from her belly. It clattered beside her, sticky with vitality. Her eyes closed, and her shoulders slumped.

And to Kylene's unbroken amazement, it began again. The swift surfacing and utter insistence of living things. Only this time, it began with an oak.

From the bone-dry ground sprung a sapling, its saw-toothed leaves so brilliant a green they seemed to glow. The great oak spread its ambling limbs out and over, the dappled shade of its forearms and fingers reaching out to shade the body of the Mother from the sun's grim rays. The oak was followed by a field of large but lesser oaks, each erupting from the ground, instantaneous as lightning strike.

The land blossomed before her eyes and before she could begin to account for the emergence of each new glory, Kylene was swept away. Along the surface of the land, she flew forward, propelled by some unseen hand as if she were a seed affixed to silk, burst from an overripe milkweed pod. Over rippling forests and canyons rushing with water fresh, she hurtled. Meadows wavered, and mountainsides sprouted trees like mushroom heads. Browns and reds and yellows, blues and every shade of green brightening, diversifying and unfolding.

Then, struck by a sunset both sudden and complete, the colors, the shapes, the textures began to grow dim and fade, as if they were being slow-covered over by layer after layer of black gauze.

Then, there was only darkness, and it was Kylene speaking now, but not Kylene as she knew herself today but Kylene from a different time, a different place.

"But Daddy says that none of it's real. None of it's real, Mummy. Why do you know about the Mother and Socritas and the children if

they're not real?" Her childish voice rang out over a sea of velvet, black and twinkling.

"Just because they're not real doesn't mean their story doesn't matter. Some folks have got to remember the old ways," came her mother's dying, drifting voice. And the velvet sea faded to oblivion, where the blackness was a nothingness and nothing else at all.

Chapter Nineteen

There was a rare silence in the cave, the kind that comes when a burden is laid bare. The sound that followed was a stirring. Resonance, feather-light; the halving of that same burden, as it made its way into the hearts of those who were there to listen.

From the darkness beside Lovelace came the voice of Gunnar, faint as whisper's echo.

"How long has it been since you've left home?"

Cora looked up at the ceiling, as if she might find her answer there. The candles had burned low again, and her face was wreathed in shadow.

"I have been alone for the bloom of four springs," she said, resting her gaze in her lap. "The bloom of four springs, the heat of four summers, the mist of five autumns, the death of five winters."

Lovelace's heart clenched with a grief that surpassed all others as he envisioned the girl moving through each season alone, afraid and utterly unmoored.

It was a story that he knew well. A ruthless uprooting from family, from all that was familiar, and beloved. And then, the unrelenting onslaught of unfamiliarity – new rules, new people, new places, new terrors – an interminable tide of change that pummeled you until you were shaped into something else entirely. Cora might not bear the formal mantle of a dactyli, but she shared more with Lovelace and Gunnar than most who walked the earth.

"It's a harrowing tale, miss, and I'm that sorry to hear about the loss of your father," he said. He knew he ought to sit in silence, give the tale and its teller a moment more of respect before he gave voice to the questions that fluttered and flickered inside him like so many fireflies. But he couldn't help himself.

"It is what it is," she said.

"The pools, then," Lovelace said, treading with care. "You're quite sure that you emerged from them...different? You've never exhibited any ability before?"

Cora shook her head. "Not so far as I can remember. I suppose, in a way, I've always been different. I've always been...bookish, was what my father called me. Said I was destined to be one of the greatest scholars the University has ever seen," she trailed off, her words filled with a sense of loss.

"Suppose'n you understand now why Cora," Pif said.

"I'm afraid I don't take your meaning, lad..."

"Cora means 'seething pool' in the old language. It's the loveliest name, I think, and ne'er more suited to a person, given where she's up and come from. She says she likes it, don't you, m'lady Cora?"

Had they been in the light of day, Lovelace was certain he would see a furious blush blooming on Pif's cheeks.

So, Lovelace thought. *Ailwin isn't the only one taken with the lass.*

"I do like it," she said.

"It's a lovely name, Pif, to be sure," said Lovelace. "What's wrong with Kylene, though? An equally fine name..."

"Kylene lost her father, her family," Cora cut him off sharply. "Kylene was accosted. Kylene...killed someone. Someone who deserved it, make no mistake, but someone, nevertheless..." she paused, her voice ripe with anger. Then, she stiffened, and when she spoke again, it was with steel.

"Cora has much to learn. Cora has new friends. Cora has a purpose."

Lovelace didn't much care what she called herself so long as she stuck with them. Based on what he thought her capable of, he wouldn't want her in the hands of Alev.

"How...did you...do it?" Gunnar's voice rose up and out of the cloak of darkness. His every word came gasping, as if each had gouged him in its own good time.

"Do what?" she asked. Truly, Gunnar could have been asking after any number of things.

Lovelace felt around in the darkness for Gunnar's shoulder and found his face instead. He gave it a gentle pat, smiling to himself as he did.

"There, there, Gunn, no more words for you today. I know what you want to know, or rather, I know what you mean to ask. I'm burning with curiosity myself."

He could feel Gunnar seething, and his smile grew. This may well have been the only opportunity he'd ever have to taunt Gunnar with impunity, and he was relishing it. Gunnar would make him pay for it later, undoubtedly. It was a thought that, in the endless dark, with a wasted body, a frenzied mind, brought him feverish joy.

"What I'm sure Gunnar means to ask is, how did you save us? What element did you channel that made the white light? How did you get us back here? How did you unearth Pif? And perhaps the most mystifying of all: how in all the Mother's creations did you paralyze our bodies as you did and heal them from what could have only been lethal injury?"

Gunnar grunted in what sounded like begrudging confirmation that yes, these were the questions he wanted answered.

"I...I'm not sure I know the answers to much of what you ask..." Cora said.

He'd been afraid of that. When one has summoned their luth and put it to task with such force, there could be a peculiar sense of detachment that follows. Memory loss wasn't uncommon, particularly with the uninitiated. And if she was channeling that degree of power by accident?

"We were waiting by the road when we smelled smoke," Ailwin said, a tentative offering, his words hanging in the flickering darkness.

"Soon as she knew what it was, Ky...Cora started toward you. She was so calm; it was uncanny. I caught up with her, and she whips 'round, asking me why I was not doing the same. Going after you, that is..." he said, his words slow and thick, as if he had to unstick them from his tongue.

"I told her I'd given you both my word to watch over her, keep her safe. She just laughed. Told me safety was..." he paused, trying to wade through what was likely a deeply distressing memory for his newly minted ego.

"An illusion, safety is an illusion," she said, with what Lovelace thought was a smile in her voice.

"Right, safety being an illusion and all that. Anyhow, she told me that if I came with her, I'd keep my word just the same. So I did. Figured she was right about that."

He faltered in his speech and Lovelace could feel more than see Ailwin shiver as if chilled by the thought of what might have been had he been brave enough to make her stay.

"Couldn't have taken us more'n a quarter of a bell to get to you. The whole clearing was up in flames by then, clean-burning, mercilessly hot it was. Ky...Cora jumped off her horse and just stood there, fixed, like. Staring at it all. I yelled for her to back up. The heat was so fierce, I could smell my hair burning up. She didn't seem to hear me, though, she only stared up at the flames, like she was bewitched. To tell you the truth, I was none too sure that you were even in there; how could anyone be swept up into a fire such as that and live?" He paused, taking one big breath.

"I couldn't hear anything beyond the great roar of it, like some beast from the netherworld, up to ravage the living. And then, she just started..." he hesitated as if embarrassed by what he was about to admit.

"She started to glow, I suppose. Not like the orange glow of the fires, softer, like."

"Yeah," he said, turning it over in his mind. "Hers was a softer light, but with more substance. You could barely see through hers, so solid it was. I ran to her, yelling as loud as I could, but she couldn't seem to hear. And when I got near her, I sort of...bounced off, like. I don't even think she noticed. And me, waving my arms and yelling as I was."

They sat silently for a moment as Ailwin deliberated on how best to finish.

"Anyhow..." he swallowed. "The glow coming off her got brighter, or stronger, I suppose. It got so bright that it started to swallow the heat, soaking up the orange glow. The two glows... battled. And the white was winning, at first. At least, that's what it...felt like. What it looked like too. And then she walked right into the flames, taking the white with her. When she'd gone all the way through, she disappeared completely, and the white light with her. It was like the blaze had swallowed her whole. And then, there was a great bang, and I guess the only way I can describe it is like a wave, only not made of air or water or anything like that. Just a wave of...power, I suppose. A shot through the white." He paused again, trying to decide whether he'd done an adequate job of putting into words what exactly he had witnessed.

He inhaled mightily, bracing himself.

"That's when I really started to panic. Started running 'round the edge of it yelling for her. For you, Gunnar, Pif too. They were smaller, the flames, after she went in 'em. Then all of a sudden, the one side of the fire...opened up. Parted along the side of it as if it was made of cloth, and out you came. First Pif, and then she came through, the both of you floating on either side of her like she was some necromancer with a pair of corpses, fresh out of graves."

Lovelace had been watching Ailwin's shadow growing increasingly animated as the tale went along. He shook himself; his own memory of what transpired out there on the eastern pass would now rate as his most chilling. A prickle picked its way along his spine. He hadn't even been conscious for the most staggering bit of all.

Ailwin touched the stub of one candle to a fresh yellow taper. "She hardly looked at me, just moved like she was in some trance, holding the two of you up like puppets on invisible strings. Finally, she looked at me with this expression like, *Well, are you coming or what?* Like what she'd just done was ordinary as cracking eggs on the skillet."

"It wasn't," Cora said suddenly.

"What wasn't?" Ailwin asked.

"Easy as cracking eggs," she said, a small fire beneath her words.

"I didn't say easy," he said hastily. "I said ordinary."

"You want to know what I did?" she asked.

"Yes," rang the voices of Pif, Lovelace, and Ailwin, laced altogether by Gunnar's thin whisper.

Cora took a deep breath, cracking the knuckles of one hand and then the other.

"When I saw the flames," she said. "I just knew I needed to counteract them and get you out. Those were the two things that needed doing. One, and then the other. So. I thought about that and…did it," she said, faltering.

"What did you visualize?" Lovelace asked, pressing two fingers to his brow as he tried to work through the scene. What Ailwin described was prodigious, to say the least.

"Counteracting the flame," she said. "What feeds fire, what starves it. I've also…" she paused, embarrassed.

"I've glowed like that before, but never so fully. Only from my fingertips, mostly. Though there was the once that my whole body shone with it – the light."

Lovelace nodded. "It is not uncommon to emit a faint radiance when channeling." What he didn't say was that it was entirely unheard of to glow like a hundred moonbeams, or a piece of the sun, shattered and set free.

"Oh," she said, sounding slightly relieved. "Well, once that happened, I could feel the flames weren't nearly as dangerous as they had been. They were still monstrously tall, but their fierceness, the heat, was weakened. I could tell it wouldn't be for long, so I made my way through them and saw him standing over the two of you. That's when it happened."

"When what happened?" Lovelace prompted, his breath bridled.

"The wave that Ailwin described," she said. "I didn't know what to do. He couldn't see me, but I could see him. And seeing him made me so...angry and scared. I mean, I was already scared, but seeing him..." She shuddered, and Pif placed a hand on her shoulder.

"Go on, m'lady Cora," he said, patting her. "You'll feel better for the sharin' of it."

Cora nodded and sniffed. "There was an odd sort of separation between me and it. It was like the core of me was calm and sure...and then this anger, and fear; they were right there for me to wear. I realized I could reach out and...put them on, I guess. So I let them build themselves around me, layer upon layer, like coats of paint, and then, I screamed. I've never screamed so loud. And it hurt, the scream, like it was being torn out of me. And I guess that's what stunned Alev – the wave and my scream. I don't know if you were already senseless or if the scream did the same to you as Alev but when I came to you, you were unconscious. So I...picked you up. With my mind. It was when I did that I remembered I hadn't seen hide nor hair of Pif. The flames were starting to glow hot again, and the color returning to them. I knew I didn't have much time. It was as simple as me closing my eyes and whispering, "Where are you?" and all of a sudden, I could see him underground. I knew I needed to dig him up, so...same thing. Just thought about digging a hole and keeping Pif safe and..."

"And a great hole opened up in the sky!" Pif proclaimed. "Angled real sharp, like a giant'd come and dug a tunnel just for me with his enormous trowel, only it was m'lady Cora and she didn't use no tool – 'ceptin her mind, o' course," he added quickly. The shine in his voice was reverence, unmistakable; Lovelace didn't blame him. He felt a bit overawed himself, and he hadn't seen hardly any of what was being described.

"I suppose that's the way of it," Cora said. "The tunnel wasn't very big; he had to crawl up and through and once he did, well, you know the rest. It all happened so fast. There was no preparation, and hardly any thinking, once it'd all got underway."

Questions had blossomed in Lovelace's mind throughout her tale, like so many wildflowers after a springtime rain. But her words rang with a note of finality that curbed his brasher inclinations. She'd given her account exactly as it happened, and somehow he knew she hadn't held anything back. What more could she give him that would help him understand the perfect mystery of her power?

"Cora," Gunnar said, his voice faint and rustling. "What you have done is extraordinary. What you are, is extraordinary."

"Indeed," Lovelace murmured.

"You know what this means, don't you?!" said Pif.

"To tell you the truth, lad," said Lovelace. "I don't know what any of it means, but I'm willing to bet it's no one singular thing."

Pif let out a big sigh, evidently disappointed that Lovelace could not work out the obvious, due perhaps, to some permanent damage sustained by their encounter.

"It means…" he said, pausing for dramatic effect. "That bein' dactyli isn't exactly how you thought! Cora's gone and had her powers roused; maybe mine can be too! Maybe anyone's can!"

Lovelace pressed two fingers to his brow, pressing hard this time. It was not the first or even second conclusion he'd drawn from the experience, but Sons to dust if the boy didn't have a point.

The quiet in the cave swelled with expectation as Pif awaited his response. *What does it mean indeed?* he thought, silently cursing Gunnar for his convalescence. It was looking more and more convenient the longer this conversation went on.

"What we don't know right now is an ocean, and we're in a small canoe," he said.

"What's a canoe?" Pif asked impatiently.

"It's a longboat, better used in freshwater. Not good for seafaring except near shore," Cora said quietly.

"Ah," Pif said, thinking hard. "So...you're saying we still have a craft, then?"

Lovelace grimaced, exhausted. He let his arm fall. It dropped, leaden, to the stone beneath him. "Aye, lad, we still have a craft."

"And, if we have a craft," Ailwin put in, "Then we can...set sail. Does a canoe have sails?" he said aside to Cora.

"No."

"Well no matter," he said, "I agree with Pif that, given the evidence, it seems likely we should be able to learn."

Lovelace knew when he'd been beaten.

"It seems likely, yes," he said, unwilling, just yet, to concede. "We will do everything in our power to try and understand how it is that generations of men have been wrong for so long and what we aim to do about it." What more could he say?

"You said you had a purpose," Lovelace said to Cora, remembering her declaration and hoping to divert away from a subject that made him more uneasy than anything else ever had, combined.

"Mind sharing what that is?"

She was quiet for a moment.

"My dreams have been as far away as the moon for the longest time. To shoot for it would be foolish," she said, her voice gone soft and misty. "But now it feels as though I've been given a bow that is perhaps great enough to come within striking distance."

"Mmm," Lovelace mumbled. *And a poet to boot,* he thought, unsure of whether he and Gunnar were quite the instrument she would need to get whatever job it was she needed doing. "What is it you dream of, lass?"

"To defenestrate Osbert and the Fingers," she said, and before Lovelace could think to ask what exactly defenestrate meant, he realized – the girl was barking mad.

"I do not know what the world was like before him," she continued. "I was very young when Osbert took power."

The silence deepened, widened as if it were being prevailed upon to make space for the depth and breadth of her ambitions. "We had power before him," she went on, her voice trembling slightly. "We had freedom. Or at least the makings of it. And he took it from us. Took it away, mashed it to a pulp and fed it to us with a tiny spoon, just enough so we don't starve to death. When you've been hungry long enough, you're grateful for any meal coming your way."

"Aye, that's so," Lovelace said softly.

"So, will you help me?" she asked. She might as well have reached out, seized his heart in her fist and squeezed.

"I'd have to confer with my better half," he said weakly, his words turning to ash in his mouth. Was this not the summons he'd been dreaming of – to do the right thing, to help people?

Gunnar's voice rose, unfaltering.

"We're with you to the last, Cora," he said, as sure as he'd ever sounded about anything. And buried deep beneath his conviction was something that sounded suspiciously like emotion. "Lovelace will, too," he continued. "He just needs a bit of a shove in the right direction sometimes."

"How charitable of you," Lovelace mumbled, altogether too aware that they were all waiting for him to say yes to something that would tear him free from everything he knew. He'd done so once; could he do it again?

"Well, I don't know what we'll do with you three," Lovelace said slowly. "And we'll need allies! We can't just storm the headquarters of the Fingers and set them straight. They've got their peacekeepers and those blasted men in red patrolling amok, meting out justice and murder like they're one and the same. And half the bleeding country *likes* the fop, from what I understand."

"They're only afraid of what he will do to them and their families if they don't play along," Cora said. "They need to know they're not alone."

"Fear and loathing are funny bedfellows. Still, they lie together all the same. And there's one more thing," said Lovelace. "I can tell you for a certainty that Alev is not dead. So we'll have to add that minor detail to our list."

"I don't mean to think that we can do this by force," Cora said, her elation a bright spark in the darkness. "Even if you could teach me how to control...whatever it is I am."

"Aye," said Pif, "and don't even start to thinking you'll be leavin' me and Ailwin any which where. We've made it this far, haven't we? We'll be the first! You and Gunnar can practice teaching us the dactyli ways, so that you get real good at it 'fore you start to build your own army of earth-shapers and wind-breakers."

In the dark, inevitability settled over Lovelace. He sighed, a great heaving thing that made his bones press against his skin. And then, from deep within his belly, a strange gurgle rose. Laughter, in spite of himself. It climbed up and out of his throat, escaping his lips like a wild thing that would treat with no taming. It poured from him in an endless stream and soon deep hoots, twittering chirps, tinkling bells and faint wheezes joined the rumble of his utter surrender to the path that lay before him. *Who am I to pretend there is any other way?*

"Right," he said, gathering himself and wiping tears from his cheeks and beard. "So if not by force, I assume you mean to win by wits."

"By wits..." Cora said. "...and by magic. I mean to understand more about what I'm capable of. What we're all capable of."

"Aye well, battle magic isn't really something dactyli have done, historically. The terrain will be new for all of us," Lovelace said.

"Could've fooled me," Ailwin muttered.

"Our...curriculum at the Meorachadh did not include battle magic. Not to say that Gunnar and I haven't gotten into our fair share of scrapes over the years, but usually you don't need much to show a pickpocket or a drunk the error of his ways. This is different. Who knows how many men Alev's got in his red army. Allies, we need them. Well-connected ones, preferably with money," Lovelace said.

"Mr Pontrefait," Cora said. "He was my father and Eliza's chiefest correspondent in Omnia. He is connected to the University. And there will be others who share our sympathies, we just need to find a way to lure them out." She paused for a moment. "My father..." she stumbled on the word, a catch in her throat. "My father, and Eliza and Rufus were working to expose the underpinnings of the Fingers, reveal their lies to the people, so that they might rise up, together, and reclaim the right to a commonwealth. Their work had only just begun. The way I see it, we've got to find Mr Pontrefait. He'll introduce us to more bellringers."

"If indeed there are any bellringers left..." Lovelace muttered.

"...and if there's not," Cora said, knife-edged, "we'll see if we can't take up the mantle."

The cave was cold at Lovelace's back, rough and unyielding. The sheer enormity of what Cora was proposing had dimensions

Lovelace could not measure. And while the extent of Osbert's power was known to him only in fragments, he did know the man's grip on the land was ironclad.

A sgeul surfaced, unbidden, Lovelace's stomach turned at the recollection of an evening at the Capering Colt, not so long ago. A farmer named Tej, whom they'd known for some years, had waved him and Gunnar over to his corner booth. The man was pissed as a newt. He was crooked in his seat, eyes sliding in and out of focus. Lovelace had humored him and leaned in when he'd crooked a gnarled finger at them, urging them to come closer.

In a slurred whisper, hot breath stinking of old liquor, Tej confided in them that Osbert's spies were everywhere, that even the trees in the forest spied on his behalf. "Speak your secrets to no one," he said, lest they be found out for what they were – dactyli – and exploited for their powers or killed straight off.

Lovelace had laughed Tej down, told him that if he believed *that* twaddle, then he ought not to worry; the Mother would be coming to strike Osbert down for his maleficence just as soon as she was good and ready.

Given Cora's account of the shared attack on the Kapnobatai camp, it seemed more than probable that Alev was colluding with Osbert. To what end, Lovelace could only guess. Imagining what Alev could do in the world, propped up beside a man like Osbert, presented possibilities that made his blood run cold. Not one bad apple, but two, rotting together to create a stench that was sure to linger for centuries.

Cora's eyes were luminous in the candlelight, confusion brimming where before there was conviction.

"You *are* the ones who are supposed to know everything there is to know about the world," she said, bringing Lovelace forcibly back to the cold chill of the cave.

"Surely you know a thing or two about staging an insurrection. You know, time-honored techniques to oust a ruler," she said.

A pause followed, uncomfortable and marked by Cora's bated breath.

"You dactyli are the keepers of truth!" She burst out. Her voice was shrill and possessed notes of desperation, as if perhaps her plan had sprung a series of leaks and she was just now realizing it was not watertight.

Lovelace let out a rueful laugh. "We're naught but rangers, Cora. We set out and collect the goods we're tasked to find. I grant you, it does take training, and skill, make no mistake but that's all we rangers do. We've never put a sgeulachd together – except our capstone – much less studied them. Gunnar and I are not scribes," he said with an awkward finish. He'd never wanted to be.

"What about your library?" Cora asked.

"The Tasglann is gone," Lovelace said, and though it was never a place that held his heart, the weight of its absence bore heavily upon him. The men of their order had toiled and contributed to its vast collection for over two thousand years.

"There might still be something there, among the wreckage?" Ailwin said. "He can't have personally destroyed every sgeulachd in the place."

"Perhaps..." Lovelace said.

"And what of the borderlands? Perhaps we can find allies there," he said, sounding like a man who was well-accustomed to performing feats of epic proportions, not like the boy who had only days ago been wiping down sticky tables at the Capering Colt.

"Aye!" Pif said, "The same words were on my very own lips! Will we be going to Kythera then? Or Ulthing?"

"Could do," Lovelace said, the possibilities making him feel faint. "Any ideas, Gunn?" he asked with a flash of annoyance. Gunnar, as ever, had little to contribute. Had the man even bothered to stay awake to hear how well and truly doomed they were?

"Badi," Gunnar's whisper was ragged. He *was* awake then, the bastard.

"Badi?" Cora and Pif echoed.

Lovelace took a deep breath. Was that it, then?

It was an interesting idea, he would admit, even without an explanation.

"Badi is another rogue dactyli," Lovelace said since Gunnar didn't seem capable of uttering any more words. "Exiled for his...unscrupulous practices. Not a bad fellow. Not a good fellow, either. The sort of fellow who follows the sun, if you take my meaning."

"A levereter, mayhap," Pif said knowledgeably.

"I think you'd call someone like Osbert a levereter," Cora said, matter of fact.

"Ah, because he's eatin' liver whilst all of us' eatin' scraps fit for pigs," Pif said.

Cora nodded. "Just so."

Lovelace thought the phrase had been coined for a man who'd eat the liver from his own people just to stay in power, but he liked Pif's interpretation all the same.

"So one could say this Badi fellow knows which side of his toast has jam on it," Pif said.

"Which side of his *bread is buttered*, idiot," Ailwin muttered.

A scrape echoed through the air as Pif launched himself at Ailwin. Just as they were about to crash into one other, they were abruptly knocked back, as if an invisible wall had materialized between them.

More accurately, it was Cora who had come between them. Lovelace grinned like a fool in the dark, relieved. At the very least, he wouldn't have to play the arbiter anymore.

"Not again, you two," she said wearily. Ailwin mumbled a vague apology and settled back down to her right, so like a faithful hound, Lovelace's grin widened.

"That was clever; what do you call that?"

The ghost of a grin played on her face in the candlelight. She shrugged. "Twit screen. You were saying..."

"Badi is an interesting idea. He'll be well-connected, at the very least. He dealt in information before; I'm sure he deals in much the same now. You would undoubtedly intrigue him."

She said nothing but recoiled slightly, drawing back just enough so that the shape of her shadow shifted. Lovelace hoped it was because she was contemplating the grandiosity of her plans and realizing just how steep the uphill battle was that they would need to wage.

"We will need to lay a great many plans," she said finally, an air of reservation clouding her words that were only moments before full of vigor. "For now, we need to see you well."

Lovelace agreed. The weight of fatigue upon him was a relentless tide, dragging him deep toward murky depths. He closed his eyes, the aching in his skull a sharp reminder of the fact that by all rights he should be dead. Aberrant shadows flit like phantoms in the darkness behind his lids.

"May I?" came the soft voice of Cora, as if she sensed the pain that radiated from limb to limb, the magnitude of what it was that needed doing when their time in the cave was done. There was too much to be said, too much to ponder upon, and he could bear it no longer, not with the ache that ran bone-deep, the frayed edges of his near-spent luth. He needed time, space.

"Please," he said.

"Yes," said she, and sensation began to drain from him, like blood from a wound. It started in his chest – numbness, the gentle knitting of her healing spell – and before it could reach his fingers, he heaved his arm over his belly and to his side so that his fingers grazed the cold marble of Gunnar's. He sunk deeper into the void, his hand wrapped around his friend's, gratitude winking through him like stars as they first appear in the sky at night.

Chapter Twenty

The transit of time was peculiar in the cold quiet of the cave. With no sun to mark the passage of day to night and night again into day, Lovelace was adrift, unable to discern if seven days had slipped by or seven long years. It was as if they'd pierced a hole through the weave of time, and Lovelace was falling – or perhaps rising; he knew not which – through the omnipresent shadows that swathed the framework of its existence.

Upon his eleventh waking, he discovered his curious restraints had relinquished their hold. He curled his fingers, wiggled his toes and reveled in his freedom of movement, though a startling frailty accompanied it. The agony that had writhed through his veins, ravaged his muscle and razed his bones was gone. In its place, a fatigue that smoldered and smoked, remnants of a raging wildfire that had threatened to devour him entirely.

Once more the keeper of his own body, he found he could bear the dark no longer. He shifted his weight, pressing his palms and knees against the cold rock beneath him. Too quickly. His head spun, and his arms trembled in protest, but he held fast and reached out a beseeching hand to Cora.

Without a word, she reached for one of the stubbed candles, flickering in a chink in the wall. She planted it firmly in Lovelace's outstretched hand and nodded toward a fissure, barely visible, in the wall furthest from them. Grateful, Lovelace inclined his head and crept toward the crevice with the slow deliberation of a child who has just discovered that he can crawl.

Wasted as his body was, he passed through the narrow cleft with ease. He half pulled, half crawled through a short and twisting corridor leading up and out of the cave system's backside. Brilliant and blinding light flickered through a small opening that marked the end of the passage. Beyond this, the dense copse of blackberries concealed it from the outside world, hiding it from view. He scrabbled on hands and knees through the copse, through a tunnel better suited to a rabbit, thorns tugging at his skin and the shift he wore as he pulled himself through. He scarcely noticed. For better or worse, Lovelace was alive.

He burst headlong from the underbrush, tumbling into the woods and landing on his backside, laughter spilling from him like a man possessed by madness.

Eventide had settled, that ephemeral bell when all the color of earth slow-leeches away as it gives way to the purple-black that commands the night.

The soil beneath him was cool, and he sank gradually into its loamy embrace. Above, the canopy of cedar trees was finer than any painting, their needled green-black boughs fanning out toward one another, yearning. Snatches of sky beyond revealed a full moon rising through wisps of clouds like wraiths.

It was a feast. More nourishing, more sumptuous than any banquet ever set before him. The stifling scent of damp rock retreated as each breath of air filled him with the heady spice of cedar resin. Soon, he was dizzy – with joy, with hope, with a profound sense of belonging, a more potent draught than any ale he'd ever swallowed.

Lovelace brought himself back to his hands and knees and, bending low, pressed a tender kiss to the ground between his palms. It was long and lingering, and while he had not shared many kisses, it was among the sweetest he'd ever known.

***

Two days later, Gunnar emerged from beneath the tangle of blackberry brambles. Lovelace was sitting beneath a nearby cedar and watched as he crawled up and out of the brush.

His skin was white-washed gray, like the chill mist that skims the water's surface on a morning tide. It had an eerie, waxen quality and was stretched painfully across the bones of his skull and the bare blades of his shoulders. Lovelace grimaced, probing his own cheeks, his ribs, the bones of his wrist.

"You don't look near so bad as he does," Ailwin said quietly from behind.

The gentle chatter of birdsong filled the air above, and together, they watched in silence as Gunnar rose to stand, his movements strained as gears given over to rust.

Once upright, he spared them no glance. Instead, he moved toward the nearest cedar. His countenance, the words writ large by the lines of his body, were those of a man who had lingered upon death's threshold, only to discover he would be denied entry.

Stopping short of the tree, Gunnar pressed his spindled hands against the rough-scored surface of its trunk, bowed his head low and began, silently, to weep.

***

Three weeks had passed before they packed up what few belongings they had and ventured out of the mountains of Droch Fhortan.

Their possessions were meager: three horses, if one dared to count Ailwin's flea-bitten nag; a satchel apiece for Lovelace, Gunnar and Cora, with hers filled to the brim with a small apothecary's worth of herbs; daggers, produced with decorum by Cora for Ailwin and Pif, finely wrought and polished to a gleam, with curling vines around the hilts; a small sack of winter barley; five dense, herb-studded loaves of what Cora called coil bread, baked the night prior, in iron over the fire; two jars of orange-gold honey; a pocketful apiece of dried apricots and natus berries; one packet of dried, freshwater eel; and squirrel jerky, deemed improperly seasoned by young Master Pif, an unfortunate fact he'd made plain several times already.

All told, it was the least prepared for an operation that Lovelace had ever been.

Cold air nipped at their faces as they wound their way down the Damp Gulch Pass as a chilled westerly wind spilled down the mountain. Autumn was well underway, and it was the looming threat of winter that had ousted them from the cave. When the first storm hit, the upper portion of the mountain would become impassable, and they would be forced to overwinter in the caverns. Cora would not wait another winter for action, and neither Lovelace, Gunnar, Ailwin, or Pif could abide another moment of dwelling in the dark.

They were bound for Omnia, their reasons manifold and too compelling to deny, none of which did anything to calm the nerves that skittered and slithered through Lovelace like centipedes.

None of them had papers, those perfect square bits of vellum that the Fingers assigned to all citizens of the Grasp, with a name, physical description, district, quarter and village, meant to be carried at all times. For traveling, a piece of parchment, stamped and sealed by the local magistrate, declaring one's business. They would not get far without them.

Ailwin, the most acquainted with the current cultural norm due to his work at the Capering Colt, informed them of the casual tyranny of paper stops, now commonplace. When asked by Cora what he meant, Ailwin shrugged and replied, "Folks are saying they just ask for them when it suits, no matter how you look. Unless, of course, you've got one of those pins. The most loyal've taken to wearing these little pins with Osbert's little set of scales, issued by the Fingers, 'course. Shows that you're 'associated therewith.' That's how they call it."

Citizen and purpose papers could be forged, so long as they could ferret out the right kind of person for the job. And Omnia was a place with many kinds of people.

There was also the matter of Mr Pontrefait, the man whom Cora was so convinced would be their divining rod, an instrument of the establishment who would help them dowse out the headwaters of righteousness, and so set their cause in motion. Lovelace thought that to pin such high hopes on a person, who thus far only existed in letters and stories, was optimistic, if not entirely unrealistic.

He knew by now that within Cora ran a thread of longing, a filament that was still and would always be Kylene. This part of her, however small it might have grown, hoped that Mr Pontrefait might be the one living person in the world who would have news of her father.

And so to Omnia they would go, hoping that small signs would give way to larger fenceposts so that they might eventually stage a rebellion.

Who was he to suggest they go anywhere but? When she had just scraped together the last ragged scraps of him and Gunnar and stitched them back together. They might not be whole or even good as new, but they were alive. And for that, they owed her a pittance.

The third and final matter, then, and the one that gave Lovelace some degree of comfort, was the sheer size of Omnia. The city was a vast, sprawling jungle; five districts all unto itself. A man could hide a long while in a place of such size. Two grown men, another on the cusp of manhood, a boy who wouldn't know danger if it laid eggs in his ear and a woman who could twist not one element, but four, around her little finger? They weren't exactly inconspicuous. But they would have far better luck concealing themselves there than anywhere else in the Grasp, except perhaps the border city of Lazare, which was nowhere near so large but twice as frenzied.

Somewhere in the background of his thoughts, the muffled voice of Pif nattered on behind him, wondering aloud what sort of vermin in Omnia there might be for him to take with his sling. He had heard there were red-pelted city squirrels and that they were fat as beavers and wily as foxes.

"Nay, lad," Lovelace said. The lower down the mountain they dropped, the heavier the mist became, so now the passage was slippery as well as steep. He seemed to recall that climbing up had been much easier than this descent, with its tumbledown traces of granite shed from the mountainside and the naked roots of trees protruding from the earth, snatching at hooves and feet. But then, he'd had considerably more flesh on his bottom the last time he'd negotiated the steep grade. "None too many creatures to speak of in the city. Animals prefer best the places where man's not laid his hand, and if there was ever a place that man has touched and torn and fiddled and fixed, it's Omnia."

"Oh," Pif said, hushing in a way that suggested he was working hard to imagine such a place.

As they continued their descent, the sun's light dimmed, swallowed by the thickening mist. The only sounds were the steady drip of water from rock, the clatter of hooves and the echo of expanse, shrouded from view.

A quiet surprise took hold of Lovelace. He had expected another rendering of Pif's capture by Alev, a story which had transformed from a simple encounter to a tale of truly mythological proportions.

In the first version, a speechless Alev had merely dragged Pif down the mountainside and shoved him into a freshly dug hole with a simple, "Let's see how fond of you your friends are."

The most recent telling recanted over the dying embers of last night's fire, involved Pif scampering up the trunk of the tallest cedar in the forest, only to be plucked from the tippy top by the taloned clutches of a dragon made entirely of roaring flames. The dragon had then deposited him into the hole, Alev laughing all the while. Magically, Pif hadn't been burnt.

Lovelace did not begrudge the boy's embellishments. He understood a thing or two about the importance of rewriting certain histories. It was a thing they all seemed to understand because they had all stood by and obliged as Pif's lizard of a tale transformed into a dragon right before their very eyes. It was better this way, to let the experience build him rather than break him.

In the middle of his back, Lovelace could feel the gentle press of Pif's cheek. Somehow, someway, the lad had managed to fall asleep.

***

At long last, the Damp Gulch Pass spit them out to a night both dark and wet. A cruel wind chased them down the final series of switchbacks, the mountain like a merciless master who was openhanded with a whip.

Gunnar and his mare materialized out of the fog, shambling down the path, pale as any ghost.

"All right, Gunn?" Lovelace called, his voice echoing against the sheer face of the mountain's base.

Gunnar reared up his mount beside him and nodded stolidly as Lovelace clapped his hand to the spare shoulder of his friend.

Up ahead, Ailwin's nag stood tied to a worn wooden sign that was no longer legible.

"We've found a suitable spot for the night," Ailwin said. Lovelace looked to Cora, who was stroking the nag's cheek with a rare fondness. She gave a slight nod, a small smile playing on her lips. Given that she'd spent the last three years in hiding, Lovelace tended to think she knew a thing or two more than Ailwin about living out of doors and staying out of sight.

"Very good then, lad. Lass," he said, tipping an imaginary hat in both of their directions. "Pif! Why don't you…"

"Onto it, m'lord!" Pif's voice rang through the mist as he led their horse toward the patch of wood where Ailwin and Cora stood.

"This way, then," Ailwin said to Pif and together, they disappeared into the gloom.

"You took so long coming down," Cora said. "I was beginning to think…" she trailed off as her gaze swept over Lovelace and then Gunnar. Lovelace thought she lingered overlong on the hollows of his cheeks, the shadows like bruises pooled beneath his eyes. He straightened beneath her penetrative gaze.

"I'll not have you worried about me," Gunnar said sharply. She lowered her gaze and nodded.

Lovelace cleared his throat. "Right," he said. "Another sleep'll only do us good. It was a fine call to make. We'll sleep through the night and some of the morning. If this fog keeps up, we'll be covered enough through the afternoon tomorrow for some daytime travel."

Somewhere close, an owl shrieked, shattering the silence that the fog had laid upon them like thick-paned glass. Cora unfastened Ailwin's nag from the signpost and turned without another word, her faded yellow robes a dim lantern in the mist.

Lovelace looked down the path toward the crossroads veiled in shadow. A shaft of moonlight illuminated the start of the High Road to the furthest left – a portrait of neglect with creeper vines threatening to consume it, to return it to the wild from which it was carved.

Beside it, the Middling Road, dead in its center, with its coppiced trees and dirt stamped neat; the High Road's bright and shiny sister, made to look pretty so that its path was the one most preferred.

Lovelace crossed his arms to his chest. The crossroads might look the same, but everything else had changed – the roads that extended from it, the waypoints, the people they would chance upon along the way. There would be no going back, no matter how much he might long for the safety of the past, no matter how ruinous the road may be ahead.

He looked sidelong at Gunnar, whose eyes were fixed on the girl as she disappeared into the mist. Lovelace let out a long slow breath, the kind that clears the mind and lifts the veil of uncertainty, if only long enough so that you can catch a glimpse of what lies ahead.

Together, he and Gunnar stepped forward to follow.

Epilogue

He hurries down the winding staircase, taking care so as not to stumble. The steps are very narrow, very steep. Necessarily so.

With each step, the air grows colder, more perfumed with rock dust and the sweet smell of heliotropes. They do not grow beneath ground, of course, but he makes sure that freshly cut stems have been brought down in preparation for his visit.

At long last, he is here. It has been some time since he has been to this place, his private sanctuary. One week, at least. His job is so dreadfully time-consuming, his work so dreadfully difficult. In the semi-darkness, he reaches out for a cloak. His cloak. His fingers brush pure sable, and he sets his candle down on a mahogany chest that still manages to gleam despite the poor light in the entryway.

He wraps the deliciously soft fur around his shoulders and shivers. It is a sumptuous coat, a sumptuous coat indeed. It is too bad he can only wear it down here; it wouldn't do for his people to see him in such finery. The public eye is so important. Such are the sacrifices a ruler must make.

Taking up the candle again, he bends at the waist, touching it to another, then another, and another, and another. All over the room he hurries, touching candle tip to candle tip until the whole room is alight with a rich glow, warm as gold. He could have valarum lamps in his inner sanctum, he knows, but there is something so pleasantly old-fashioned about candles, something so delightfully quaint. What's more, gold is worth more than silver and the light that comes from valarum lamps is so suspiciously like silver in its cast. Osbert much prefers to bask in a golden light.

It will be good to finally have the fire mage on his terms, in his domain. Their meetings are always dictated by *his* whims, and he always picks the most dreadful places to meet. Last time, it was the graveyard outside of the city at midnight. And the time before that, a ruined set of standing stones in the Omnian Woods, at the new moon, no less. If Osbert didn't know any better, he might think the fire mage was just the same as any peasant who prayed to the Mother and bled themselves for the blessing of their pitiful little gardens.

But he knows the fire mage is anything but a peasant. Osbert shudders. Anything but a peasant indeed, he has seen some of what the fire mage can do. And yet, the man is in Osbert's employ, Osbert's set of long-handed pruners – or perhaps he is Osbert's shovel – he isn't entirely sure what would be considered a gardener's most useful tool, having never actually gardened himself.

The fire mage has been requesting meetings rather more frequently of late, and he has been giving Osbert increasingly less time to prepare. At least this time Osbert was able to decide the place and instruct the fire mage to meet him here, in his inner sanctum, where he is at his most comfortable, where he is most at ease. His slippered feet make a soft snick-snick-snick on the ceramic floors as he hurries toward a mirror gilt in gold, its edges scrolled with songbirds and the bursting trumpets of morning glories.

He looks at the man in the mirror, the man who is the overlord, nay, the caretaker of the Grasp, a land that is more prosperous, more prolific than any land there ever was. Osbert smiles fiendishly and brings the fingers of his left hand to grip and form a tight fist before him, just above his belly. *Might is right*, he thinks. What a powerful figure he cuts.

He pulls in breath, sucks in his stomach and brings himself up to his full height to behold his person in all his regal splendor and…

What is this? Is his hairline receding? He peers more closely but finds he cannot see as properly as he would like, candlelight being best suited for ambiance, not careful inspection. Huffing, he turns on his heel to fetch a candle so that he can more adequately assess the state of his hairline. He returns to the mirror and leans close to its reflective surface. His breath fogs the glass and he rears back, rubs the spot on the mirror with the fur of his sleeve and returns his face to peer at his forehead, breath held fast.

He is! *By the befouled, bedeviled swamps of Mt. Ide!* He leans even more closely to the glass, squinting one eye to bring his forehead into focus, the sweep of his straw-colored hair revealing that, indeed, his hairline is beginning to recede.

He retreats two steps backward and takes in a great gasp of air, hardly daring to believe his own eyes. Taking another step back, he appraises himself again from top to bottom. He balls his hands into fists at his waist and puffs up his chest, rotating his head this way and that.

Well, you can hardly be blamed for losing a little hair, he thinks, inviting logic in. *It is, after all, so dreadfully stressful being you. We will just have to have Ermo fix it into a new style, a new style for a new time.*

And a new time is coming; he and the fire mage are making absolutely certain of it. The fire mage is but an instrument in the making of it, of course, but a very valuable one. One might even argue he is the most valuable instrument that any one man had at his disposal, ever.

But in the end, it is Osbert who will bring the Grasp to the world, who will bring the world to the Grasp, as it was in the days of old. At least, this is what the fire mage has told him: that there was once a time when many provinces such as the Grasp existed. He strokes the soft sable of his cloak and admires the reflection before him. The fur shines silver because it is dyed with actual silver. He wanted gold, of course, but his alchemist – whatever his name is – told him it was impossible. Still, Osbert is luminous in the furs, shiny as a silver coin, regal as any king, as splendid as...

"Hello, Osbert."

Osbert jumps and the candle he is holding falls with a clatter to the floor. Its wrought iron holder cracks a ceramic tile neatly in two.

Curses upon curses! He bends to pick up the holder, regretting very much that the first thing the man will see is his backside. Swiftly, he sweeps up the snuffed-out stub and turns toward his guest.

"H-hello, early you are," he says, smoothing his hair and trying very hard to appear as though he has not just been startled nearly to death. His heart is pounding. How had he not heard the fire mage enter through the grate on the sanctum's other end? He touches his forehead and finds sweat beaded on his brow, despite the chill of the underground chamber.

"There is a circumstance that has arisen that will require my attention later this evening," the fire mage says. "And I was so..." he takes in a long draft of the air and surveys the room around him. "...eager. To see this inner sanctum that has brought you such a profound sense of well-being." He bows his head.

But the fire mage does not sound very eager. He doesn't look eager, either. If anything, he looks bored, perhaps a little ill, even, but then, the fire mage has always been a little peculiar. Osbert smiles generously at his visitor.

"Thank you, thank you. It was all beginning to feel a bit unbalanced, what with all the good work I've done – we've done – that I should live so frugally. I work so very hard, you know, and a man needs a space tailored to him. This," he says with a sweeping gesture of his arms, "is a room befitting of my stature, as I'm sure you've ferreted out for yourself."

When the fire mage says nothing in reply, Osbert decides to be magnanimous. After all, they are partners, of a sort.

"Nothing I can help you with, this...circumstance of which you speak?" If the fire mage requires aid, of course, Osbert can see what he can do.

The fire mage breaks into a wide smile and Osbert can't help but feel most uncomfortable for its abrupt presentation. Why does the man have to be so damnably frightening at times? It is unseemly.

"No, you needn't trouble yourself," he says at last, moving over to the fireplace with its lovely speckled marble columns. He clasps his hands behind his back and stares into the empty grate so that Osbert can no longer see his face. Dreary is the word. The mage is always so dreary. Or perhaps dour is a better fit.

"I suppose you can't have a fire down here?" he asks quietly.

Osbert is momentarily struck by the fire mage's robes. They are black but they shimmer dark red in a way that makes Osbert feel covetous, covetous indeed. If only he could ask the fire mage who his tailor is, so that Osbert might have robes of such quality, but he does not wish to appear vain. The fire mage, he is sure, holds him in the highest esteem. He can't have his character come into question by way of vanity. It can't be the first question he asks him, at the very least.

"Hmm?" Osbert replies, remembering the fire mage's question. "Fire? No, no fire down here, not even a chimney installed, simply no place to let the smoke...Where there's smoke, there's fire they say. What am I telling you that for?" Osbert gives a hearty laugh and abruptly cuts it short. He's forgotten; the fire mage has a terrible sense of humor. Dour indeed.

"In all seriousness, if there was smoke issuing from the earth of the Fingers' garden, it would be so dreadfully suspicious, and people would grow very curious, or else very religious about the whole thing. They would ask questions. Perhaps even wish to dig it up. It quite defeats the purpose of a secret inner sanctum, if smoke is seen to be issuing from it. No, the fireplace is there simply for a sense of homeyness, a sense of sophistication."

The fire mage unclasps his hands from behind his back and waves his hand over the hearth. Osbert hears a small pop and the room is instantly awash in a blue light, strong enough that it overthrows the soft orange glow of the candles completely. It is harsh, so very harsh and Osbert doesn't like it, doesn't like it one bit. He frowns and opens his mouth to ask the fire mage just what he thinks he is about, just what he intends by disrespecting Osbert in such a way.

"This flame will not smoke," the mage says quietly, staring down at the flames.

"No smoke you say?" Osbert says. Still, it is quite hot.

He pulls at the stock of his silk tunic beneath his furs. The heat is growing unbearable, stifling...He is loathe to remove his sable cloak but remove it he does, laying it neatly on a spindle-legged side table. "And how did you learn that neat little trick?" he asks the mage, striving to maintain his mien of manly authority. Let the mage see that he can take a little heat.

The fire mage does not respond but lingers in front of the fireplace, his head bowed toward the flame. Finally, he looks up and turns to face Osbert.

"It's nothing," he says with a smile. "Just a little trick for the parlor."

"How perfectly splendid," Osbert murmurs as he tries and fails to picture the fire mage attending anything that remotely resembles a social gathering. *Though he would make for a rather delicious addition to our bacchanals,* Osbert thinks as he moves to sit in his favorite wing-backed chair, with its mustard velvet upholstery, its cushions overstuffed with goose down. The mage is a bit awkward but really, with his fearsome visage and that uncanny ability to play with fire, well, he'd be positively lionized.

But now is time for business. Time enough to bring the fire mage into his inner circle. For now, his inner sanctum is enough. He motions for his guest to please sit across from him on a loveseat made from the same fabric but with not nearly so sumptuous of stuffing in its cushions.

"Tell me," the fire mage continues as he circles around the couch and comes to stand behind it. His hands grip the ornately carved back of it, and his eyes rest on Osbert. They are black as inkwells, so deeply absent of color that it would be easy to find oneself lost in their depths.

"How did our combined troops fair against my old friends?" he asks.

"Ah," Osbert wipes his brow with the back of his hand. It comes away wet, and he rubs it hastily on the side of his chair. "Just the thing I wanted to speak with you about. I sent your burned ones, the ones I have quartered here, and my peacekeepers, two hundred troops. They were set to mount a siege but upon arrival, discovered the door to be quite open, and no one within, or without, for that matter. The grounds were searched, top to bottom, nothing so much as a shrew to be found; the whole place was as empty as a bird's nest after the fox, as they say. The men returned expediently, clean as the day they took leave of their mother's wombs, morally speaking, that is," he says, concluding the report with a chuckle and a smile. It really was such a delightful outcome, such an unforeseen jewel of an acquisition.

The fire mage is staring at him. It is a blank look that makes Osbert expressly uncomfortable because he is not sure how to interpret it. Ordinarily, Osbert is so good at reading people but the fire mage always confounds him. He is as inscrutable as a cat, and twice as impersonal, an aspect Osbert sometimes finds rather intriguing but in other, more pressing moments – like this one – it is a most undesirable trait.

"Did you destroy it, then?" he asks. "The fortress. And the hall of glowing stones?"

"Destroy it?" Osbert laughs. "Why that would have been entirely unnecessary, my good man! Did you not hear me? The enemy was *without*," he chuckles again. "No, no, no. The men brought back the glowing crystal specimens for research purposes, of course, and perhaps for the further funding of the Fingers. Such curious stones! And no doubt very valuable. As to the fortress, they left the place very much in tact. Such a historic piece of architecture, so solidly built! It would have been a shame to do away with it, and for absolutely no reason whatsoever."

He doesn't tell the fire mage that he sent one of his more inexperienced captains to lead the siege, or that he raised that same captain to the rank of colonel of the peace for being so shrewd, so prescient in correctly assuming what Osbert would want, what Osbert would need; that Osbert would, of course, prefer the place remain intact, that he could make good use of such a finely constructed fortress. A garrison, perhaps, or a southerly respite for him and his top officials, when the demands of the city become too stifling, as they so often do. He already has the winter headquarters in Prasad, and the high-water flats in Lazare. A little isolation in an exotic locale will be good for rejuvenation, good for ingenuity. Acquiring this southerly fortress has, in fact, turned out to be one of Obsert's more brilliant ploys of late, and one he is quite proud of, one he's...

A great clap of thunder cracks through the room, and suddenly everything is horribly, startlingly, unavoidably dark. *But how can this be?* The earth encasing his sanctum shivers, and all of his candles and the blue flames in the hearth are extinguished.

Osbert curves his body inwards on itself, gathering his knees to his chest. The room is deathly dark, deathly still, deathly...

"I think, perhaps, that you misunderstand the nature of our relationship," comes the low voice of the fire mage from...is he directly behind him? Osbert whips his head around and upwards, toward the voice but finds he cannot see a thing. He hunches even lower, feeling as though his heart might explode from his chest.

"It is possible that I am partially at fault," comes the voice of the fire mage, now from his left. Osbert strains his eyes, but still, he cannot see a single deplorable thing. What is the man playing at, that he should frighten Osbert so, that he should play such a dirty trick? He sees a faint red glimmer but only for a moment before it too is swallowed by the darkness.

"I have been too indulgent with you," comes his voice, now from the right, and the fire mage sighs. It is a long, hollow thing. It makes Osbert's stomach go sour. "You are so self-absorbed. It is unfortunate. A necessary feature, yes, but unfortunate. And very vexing for me, Osbert, very vexing. And yet, we have come so far in such a short space of time, you and I."

"In-indeed," Osbert says, his eyes darting this way and that as he tries to get a sense of where the man has gone, what the man is doing.

"Now," the mage's voice booms, the loudest yet that it has been. Osbert hears a low hissing like that of a snake about to strike, and then a pop, and the hearth is alight again.

This time, the flames are red. This time, there is smoke. With no tunnel to guide it up and into the world, the smoke begins to billow out of the hearth and slowly coats the ceiling. It is like a funerary shroud, gray and thin and very, very, very bleak. Still, the fire mage is nowhere to be seen.

And then! The fire mage is standing directly before him, drawn up to his full height. This time, the look he gives Osbert is unmistakable. It is a look of loathing. And is that...disgust? His eyes are obsidian. They seem to capture and reflect the flames, those hungry flames that leap and climb out of the chimney like they are a living thing, like they are a living thing that will burn Osbert to nothing in moments. Those flames would have regard only for their hunger, because it is what they were born to do; they are born to devour, born to destroy, born to...

"Stop sniveling and sit up in your chair; show me the man we made the anointed leader of the Grasp."

Osbert does not like being told what to do, does not like it one bit, one jot, one tittle. But the look on the fire mage's face is expectant, so he does as he is told. He presses both of his forearms to the arms of the chair and lifts himself up so that his back is flat against it. He returns his feet to the floor but finds his legs quiver and jerk with an intensity that is alarming and, frankly, humiliating. What will the fire mage think thusly of him? He tries to stop them with his hands, and still, they will not cease their violent trembling.

"Th-there," he says, raising his chin. "If you could please tell me exactly what you mean by all of this..." he coughs and briefly wonders how he will ever rid all of his upholstery of the smell of smoke. It cost a small fortune, the wool from Selworth, the silk from Prasad...

"My dear Osbert, don't be frightened. Do not forget that I am your friend. Now. The next time I make a request of you, I need you to deliver on that request *in precisely the way that I tell you*. Do I make myself clear? I have asked for very little in exchange for my whispers all these years, have I not?"

"Well, yes, of course you've been most useful but, but..."

"And have my whispers not been supremely *useful* to you, in positioning yourself as head of state?"

The fire mage has never treated him thusly. He has always been obsequious, always been helpful, always been encouraging. Osbert balls his hands into fists. No one treats him thusly. He will show him; he will give the fire mage what-for so that he will never again come into *his* domain and make him feel a fool.

"You call yourself a friend!" Osbert shouts. "You come in here, into my inner sanctum with your pomp and your pageantry and wag your finger at me for...for...For practically nothing at all! You, you..." Osbert coughs again and grabs a handful of wilted heliotropes from the vase nearest him. "Look what you've done!" Tears sting his eyes as he thrusts the sad blooms toward the fire mage, whose face shows only mild astonishment.

The fire mage sighs. As if *he* is the one who is aggravated, as if *he*...

"*I will not say this twice,*" the fire mage's voice booms again, and then he is at Osbert's throat, his hand wrapped almost entirely around it. He smells of pine tar and his eyes are black pools.

"The time has come for me to ask a little more of you, Osbert. I do hope that the next time we meet, what I ask of you will be respected. And that you will see out my wishes with all the care and attention our unique friendship deserves. Do not forget that it was I who came to you all those years ago, when you were nothing but a second-rate rug merchant slowly pissing away your family's fortune."

His hand comes away from Osbert's throat, and the fire goes out in the grate. One by one, Osbert's candles rekindle their flames. Pop, pop, pop and the room is as it was. The only difference is that thin layer of smoke, hovering on the ceiling.

"Osbert."

"Yes, yes, I haven't forgotten."

"I need to know that you will not fail me, as I have not failed you."

"No, of course not. You have my gratitude and I am...I am at your disposal," he says, though he bites his tongue. *Whosoever decided it was charmingly cavalier to offer oneself as disposable really ought to be thrown into the pit.*

He gives Alev his best, most winning smile. So the fire mage has had a little tantrum; he supposes it is what he ought to expect with these magic types. Temperamental. Entirely unsuited to the governance of things, which is why *he* rules the Grasp, not the mage.

The fire mage rears back, his eyes squinted slightly as he sweeps them over Osbert.

"Very good," he says at last. "Sorry about the smoke, I'd forgotten that you didn't have a chimney. Although," he says with a laugh. "You really ought to have a chimney, Osbert."

Then, the mage raises his arms and a thin column of orange flame goes up around him, and then he is gone, and the flame with him.

Osbert stares at the spot where the fire mage has just been. *What a useful trick that would be*, he thinks abstractedly, *to simply disappear at will*. Osbert might've done the same, given the unpleasantness of their thoroughly heated exchange. He smiles grimly to himself. Even in such a circumstance, his cleverness is unsurpassed. Heated indeed.

He massages his neck tenderly and discovers, to his horrible embarrassment, that he has pissed himself. He lets out a heavy exhale and shakes his head, slumping back into his chair. As he watches the haze of smoke drift lazily overhead, he wonders how he will rid the place of it. And then, for the first time since he met the fire mage all those years ago, he wonders what the man could possibly want from him.

Maressa Voss lives with her husband and son in California, between the mountains and the sea. She holds a degree in Classics from UCSB with an emphasis in Language and Literature. When Shadows Grow Tall is her debut novel. She is currently working on "writing what she knows" with a dys/utopian novel set in a near-future alternative Southern California after 95% of the population has left for brighter pastures among the stars.

Maressa can be found at www.maressavoss.com

Dear Reader,

Beyond the purchase of this book, you've given me the most precious gift of all: a portion of your time. We are spoilt for choice in a world that teems with opportunities, and I am profoundly grateful that you chose to immerse yourself in these pages.

Reviews are the lifeblood of a new writer. Amidst the vast sea of books, your thoughts conveyed online are a buoy that will keep this book afloat. If any part of When Shadows Grow Tall resonated with you, I humbly request your support in helping others discover it by leaving a review on your preferred online platform, requesting that your local library/bookstore carry the title or dropping a copy in your nearest Little Free Library.

You can find me on my website, www.maressavoss.com, for forthcoming works and musings.

Happy Trails,
Maressa

***

ROUNDFIRE
BOOKS

FICTION

Put simply, we publish great stories. Whether it's literary or
popular, a gentle tale or a pulsating thriller, the connecting
theme in all Roundfire fiction titles is that once you pick them
up you won't want to put them down.
If you have enjoyed this book, why not tell other readers by
posting a review on your preferred book site.

The Cause
Roderick Vincent
The second American Revolution will be a
fire lit from an internal spark.
Paperback: 978-1-78279-763-0 ebook: 978-1-78279-762-3

Don't Drink and Fly
The Story of Bernice O'Hanlon: Part One
Cathie Devitt
Bernice is a witch living in Glasgow. She loses her way
in her life and wanders off the beaten track looking for the
garden of enlightenment.
Paperback: 978-1-78279-016-7 ebook: 978-1-78279-015-0

Gag
Melissa Unger
One rainy afternoon in a Brooklyn diner, Peter Howland
punctures an egg with his fork. Repulsed, Peter pushes
the plate away and never eats again.
Paperback: 978-1-78279-564-3 ebook: 978-1-78279-563-6

The Master Yeshua
The Undiscovered Gospel of Joseph
Joyce Luck
Jesus is not who you think he is. The year is 75 CE. Joseph
ben Jude is frail and ailing, but he has a prophecy to fulfil ...
Paperback: 978-1-78279-974-0 ebook: 978-1-78279-975-7

On the Far Side, There's a Boy
Paula Coston
Martine Haslett, a thirty-something 1980s woman, plays hard on the fringes of the London drag club scene until one night which prompts her to sign up to a charity. She writes to a young Sri Lankan boy, with consequences far and long.
Paperback: 978-1-78279-574-2 ebook: 978-1-78279-573-5

Tuareg
Alberto Vazquez-Figueroa
With over 5 million copies sold worldwide, *Tuareg* is a classic adventure story from best-selling author Alberto Vazquez-Figueroa, about honour, revenge and a clash of cultures.
Paperback: 978-1-84694-192-4

Readers of ebooks can buy or view any of these bestsellers by clicking on the live link in the title. Most titles are published in paperback and as an ebook. Paperbacks are available in traditional bookshops. Both print and ebook formats are available online.

Find more titles, and to sign up to our readers' newsletter, visit: www.collectiveinkbooks.com/fiction